THE EDEN RUSE

AMADIOHA'S REBELLION

DEZ UDEZUE

Copyright © 2024 by Rango LLC

All rights reserved.

No part of this book may be reproduced in any form or by any electronic or mechanical means, including information storage and retrieval systems, without written permission from the author, except for the use of brief quotations in a book review.

To Lina, my invaluable primary beta reader: Your unwavering commitment through countless iterations has shaped this work profoundly. Your insights were a compass guiding this book to its final form.

To my family and friends: Your patience, honesty, and encouragement kept me going, even in moments of doubt. This book exists because of your steadfast support.

INTRODUCTION

For years, when asked about The Eden Ruse, I struggled to encapsulate its essence. "It's a story of many things," I'd say, before hastily changing the subject. But that hardly does justice to the 7+ year journey that brought this book to life.

At its core, Eden Ruse is a fusion of experiences—lived, observed, and imagined—spanning continents and cultures. My upbringing in Nigeria and subsequent life in the United States exposed me to many diverse narratives that demanded to be woven together.

This novel draws inspiration from different mythologies and histories: the Igbo and Yoruba mythologies of Nigeria, the historical kingdoms of Senegal and Ethiopia and various biblical stories. However, it is crucial to note that the Eden Ruse is not a historical account but a work of fiction that merely draws inspiration from these rich stories.

Beyond its plot, Eden Ruse explores the complexity of human nature. It is not a tale of good versus evil, but an examination of how our unique experiences, needs, and desires shape our perceptions of each other and the world around us.

I guess Eden Ruse is indeed a story of many things—a reflection of our interconnected world and the myriad ways we navigate it.

PART I
REBELLION

Realm of Kirina

Kingdom of Kush

Orisha
Niri

Sin

Abisina

Aksum

Ikora

…odun

Baol

…oum

1

THE RAID
REALM OF KIRINA

"Attacking the Vodunese during Rara will incur the wrath of their gods," Damballa Weddo cautioned, his voice low as he and **Amadioha Kamanu** walked under cover of the dense undergrowth surrounding the Vodun outpost. Damballa, Amadioha Kamanu's second-in-command, had a striking mohawk that melded into the intricate tattoos adorning the sides of his head. He was lanky but agile, a trait that usually benefitted him during combat. As they made their way through the dense foliage, he moved with the grace of a panther, his footsteps barely disturbing the leaf litter beneath his feet.

Despite the scorching midday sun beating through the forest canopy, a chill ran up Amadioha's spine. "Is it wisdom that guides your words or the insidious whisper of fear that breeds doubt in your heart?" he asked.

"You are my Eze, my leader, and my brother in arms." Damballa rested his palm over his heart. "My voice is for Niri, above all."

"Niri above all," Amadioha repeated, the words feeling heavy and uncertain on his tongue. "What about our God? Chineke does not rest easy while his people suffer under the oppression of the Vodunese."

Damballa placed a hand on Amadioha's shoulder. "I also have anger in my heart. But if we take this step... if we do this... there can be no turning back."

Amadioha stared into the distance. "My father spent countless years plotting and scheming to expunge the Vodunese from our lands, learning lessons from the Wollof secession. But now he is old, and the Vodunese mines still carve scars into our lands, their soldiers still trample our fields, and their lords still grow fat on the sweat and blood of our people."

"Your father was a wise man," Damballa said.

"Still wise." Amadioha inhaled the humid air into his lungs. "He has taught me so much and molded me into the Eze I am today. But urgency, the burning need to act decisively, is a lesson I must learn on my own."

While the thrill of revenge was exhilarating, Damballa was right; they stood on the brink of an irreversible choice.

I cannot be afraid. Any warrior with fear in his heart deserves to die.

Ahead, Reebell Kanu, their chief scout, lay prone on the damp forest floor. His eyes, narrowed in concentration, scanned the outpost. Leaves clung to his red pants and the double axe strapped to his back.

Damballa paused for a moment as they neared within earshot. "It has only been a few months since you became Eze of Canis. Revenge may mend old wounds, but is this how we start your rule?"

He could be annoyingly persistent.

Reebell rose, his bald head reflecting the harsh sunlight. Beads of sweat trickled down his neck, leaving trails in the fine layer of dirt that coated his skin. As chief scout, many knew him for his stern demeanor and eagerness for combat. "If you fear battle so much, retreat to Niri and join the Anwasi council," Reebell said, turning to Damballa.

"Someone has to be the voice of caution around here." Damballa narrowed his eyes.

"Your Vodunese blood makes you weak. Who is your loyalty to?"

"I am more Niri than you'll ever be," Damballa hissed, his nostrils flaring.

Amadioha stepped between them and shoved them away from each other. "This is not why we are here," he growled, his eyes flicking from one to the other.

My men have a burning anger, a passion that needs to be let loose. I must make sure that they are facing the true enemy and not each other when it emerges.

"Tell me what the scouts have seen," he told Reebell.

Reebell relaxed his frown as he crouched down, his hand grasping a nearby stick. He traced a crude map onto the forest floor. "The outpost lies here," he muttered, jabbing the stick into the soil. "Watchtowers at these points." He traced four spots around the central mark. "The scouts report fifty soldiers, but the miners number in the hundreds." Reebell made another circle just next to the outpost. "They would overwhelm us if we attacked now. But the outpost will be more vulnerable during Rara when the miners return home to celebrate."

Amadioha nodded. "Damballa, breathe in the scent of those flowers," he said, gesturing at the delicate blooms dotting the undergrowth. "Those are Niri flowers, not Vodunese. They grow from our soil, nourished by our rivers and streams. This is our land."

Damballa would not relent. "The border is disputed."

Reebell scoffed, the sound grating, his disdain for Damballa's caution clear in the twist of his lips.

"Not disputed by Niri," Amadioha said.

"You still need blessings from the Anwasi council. Without their support, we risk dividing our people."

"The men of Canis will follow their Eze with or without the council's blessing." Reebell's eyes flashed with anger.

"They may follow with their feet, but not with their hearts."

"Enough of this," Amadioha said through gritted teeth. His breathing sped up as he felt a heaviness in his gut. "Reebell, how do we attack?"

Reebell leaned in, lowering his voice. "There are four watchtowers here and another outpost a half hour's ride away. If the alarm horns sound, reinforcements will come quickly," he explained. "We must kill the men in the towers first to silence them before they can raise the alarm."

"If they raise the alarm, we should be as worried about the soldiers in those tents," Damballa said.

"Then we make sure they do not raise it." Amadioha nodded with a grunt. "Anything else?"

Reebell bit his lower lip. "A lord is stationed here."

The presence of a Vodunese lord at the outpost was a precious opportunity they could not squander. A lord would have valuable information on supply lines, other outposts, and troop deployments. "We need that one alive." He turned to Damballa; the question in his eyes needed no voice.

Damballa stood upright. He plucked a leaf from a nearby branch and ripped it in two before letting it fall to the ground. "I opposed this course of action. But the plan is sound."

Amadioha motioned to Reebell and then toward the deep of the forest. Reebell nodded and melted away into the bushes.

"Make sure every warrior understands the consequences if the Vodunese learn this raid came from Niri," Amadioha said.

"If they trace this act back to us, the other Ezes will be just as much a threat," Damballa said.

"Let the chickens squabble while the leopard prowls," Amadioha dismissed the concern with a wave.

"Maybe our foolishness will unite them," Damballa smirked. "A direct attack on a Vodunese outpost is bold."

We will unite the Ezes one day, but it will not be because of foolishness.

"My brother, once close, is now estranged," Amadioha said. "Our wives, our daughters, and our *nwanne* will all live and die, never knowing true freedom. This attack is not bold; it is necessary. If you have any more doubts in your mind, say them now."

Damballa's eyes met his, a storm of emotions swirling within them. "Even though half of my blood is Vodunese, I will correct their wrongs. If in your heart you believe this is what we should do, then we will do it."

"We will start here, and one day, we will unleash a strike so powerful that everyone throughout Vodun will feel it. But today, the bear who cannot reach the top of the tree will settle with the fruit on the ground."

"I am not a bear," Damballa smirked.

"Then you should eat more to fill out that skinny frame."

Damballa laughed. "You think you look good now, don't you? With your diet, your belly will drop when you get to my age."

"You are barely above twenty, and I am older than you."

The banter momentarily took Amadioha's mind away from the seriousness of their situation. He grabbed the hilt of his double-sided axe from behind him and unfastened it. The blade was a third of the weapon's length, its sharp edges glistening in the sun. The leather wrapping of the handle was faded red, its color gone from years of use. Amadioha gripped it firmly, feeling its familiar weight as he turned it sideways and extended his hand toward Damballa. "For Niri... for Canis."

Damballa pulled a dagger from his waist belt and placed it on his chest. "For our brothers and sisters." His eyes finally glinted with the same determination burning in Amadioha's heart.

THE TORCHES' flickering lights cast dancing shadows on the Anwasi council room's weathered walls, revealing its humble nature. A faint aroma of herbs and burning wood hung in the air. The room was devoid of grandiose ornaments, its bare essence reflecting the uncomplicated wisdom of those gathered within its confines.

Chief Amobi Umoren, the head of the Anwasi council, sat at the far end of the room, commanding the attention of the seven council members seated in a circle around Amadioha. His once-dark hair had long since turned white, creating a striking contrast against his ebony skin. Despite the slight tremor in his right hand and the stoop in his shoulders, his eyes remained sharp, glinting with an intelligence honed over many decades.

The soft glow of torches illuminated the other council members' faces as their eyes fixed on the young Eze. They all wore striking red caps crafted from rich velvet that stood out against their off-yellow robes. Around their necks were chains of white stone linked by threads sitting just atop their chests. Dark chalk lines encircled their eyes. Chief Amobi Umoren, while chief and leader of the council, dressed like everyone else.

"In three weeks, Canis plans to attack the Vodun outpost next to Jeaune mine," Amadioha declared. He wore red pants with a red cloth wrapped around his arms. The flickering light bounced off his bare torso.

A ripple of discontent met Amadioha's words. The council members exchanged glances and whispered. There was one empty seat where Ikenga Umoren, the chief's son, would sit. He was often missing whenever Amadioha addressed the council.

"Are these warriors fighting under the banner of Canis or Niri?" Dozie Kena, a recent addition to the council, asked, his voice cutting through the murmurs. Dozie could not have been much older than Amadioha, but his balding head and the deep bags under his eyes added years to his face. His lean frame filled out the council robes poorly. When he spoke, his words carried a sharpness that betrayed his eagerness to prove himself among the elders.

Amadioha met his gaze. "I have not involved the other Ezes in this matter. I come before this council seeking your blessing and support."

"The council cannot give you its blessing to attack inside Vodun unprovoked," Chief Umoren interjected.

"The Jeaune mine lies within the Niri borders," Amadioha countered. "It is our land and resources the Vodunese seek to exploit."

Dozie stood and stepped forward, his robes rustling as he pointed at the map of Niri hanging on the wall. "Not according to our map," he said, his finger tracing the contested border, his eyes challenging Amadioha to refute the evidence before them.

"A map drawn by the same people who exploit us," Amadioha said, raising his hand in protest.

The council room erupted in a fresh wave of murmurs, the voices of dissent growing louder with each passing moment. Amadioha's heart sank as doubt and hesitation spread across the faces of the men whose support he had come to seek.

"Step outside while the council considers your words," Chief Umoren commanded.

Amadioha bowed and stepped out, the heavy wooden door closing behind him with a resounding thud. The cool evening air did little to calm his racing thoughts as he paced, his mind churning with the possibilities of what he would do if the council refused to support his cause. Minutes crawled by, each one an eternity, until the creak of the door shattered the silence. Amadioha's heart leaped into his throat as Dozie's eyes peered through the narrow opening. "Come in," he said.

Amadioha's jaw clenched as he re-entered the council room. *They rarely move this quickly when the answer is yes.* His fingernails dug crescents into his palms as he fought to maintain his composure.

"The council has denied your request." Chief Umoren said with cold eyes.

Amadioha's heart pounded against his ribcage, a furious drumbeat echoing the rising tide of his anger. The bitterness of injustice filled his mouth as he stared back at the council members, their faces a sea of indifference. *I am fighting to liberate our people. Why would these men, who sit in judgment, stand in the way of our freedom?*

"*Koca ci!*" he cursed. "I will attack the outpost, with or without your blessing," he said as he swiped his hand.

"What is this?" Dozie demanded. "Who are you to defy us?"

"I am Amadioha Kamanu, War Eze of Niri!"

Gasps rippled through the council room.

Dozie's eyes widened, his mouth agape. He glanced at the other council members before finding his voice. "War Eze? Who has declared war?"

"Any warrior who goes to battle without the blessing of this council dances with death," another council member warned.

"No Canis warrior fears death," Amadioha retorted.

"If you go, you will go alone," another council member interjected, his voice sharp. "Have you considered the consequences of your standing in Niri?"

"Have you considered the consequence of your standing if we succeed without your blessing?" Amadioha looked him square in the eyes.

"You skirt tradition and spit on our customs!" Dozie jabbed his finger at Amadioha as he spoke.

"Customs that have allowed Vodun to invade our lands and divide us," Amadioha countered, his voice rising with each word, his arm sweeping across the room, pointing at each council member. "We cannot cling to the past if we hope to forge a better future for our people."

"Think about the lives of the men you rule," another council member said.

"Do you care about my warrior's lives or your position of power?"

"No Eze has ever defied the will of this council in matters of war." Chief Umoren finally spoke, his voice carrying through the room like a gust of wind, forcing everyone to quiet. "Amadioha Kamanu, will you be the first?"

Amadioha parted his lips, the words of defiance poised on the tip of his tongue, but the weight of Chief Umoren's gaze bore down on him, stealing the breath from his lungs. At that moment, he knew he had lost the battle, that pressing on would invite ruin upon himself and his people. A searing pain lanced through his side like a warrior's blade had found its mark, but he swallowed the bitter words, forcing them back down his throat.

"I will not," Amadioha said.

Chief Umoren nodded. "Will you renege on your title of War Eze?"

"Yes," Amadioha said, the words dragged from his lips like a heavy stone.

"This matter is now concluded," Chief Umoren declared, his voice ringing with finality. "Amadioha Kamanu, the council thanks you for your presence and understanding. May Chineke guide you in your future endeavors." With a sweeping gesture of his hand, he motioned for Amadioha to take his leave.

This is why Vodun sits in our nation and takes us for fools. Amadioha did everything to calm his breathing as he stormed out.

AMADIOHA STOOD down the hall from the council room, his gaze fixed on the window. The Luminary, an imposing structure housing the Anwasi council, was close to the water's edge. The constant rhythm of the waves against the shore filled the air, threatening to dull Amadioha's senses and draw him into a trance-like state. The cool, salty breeze from the sea blew against his skin, carrying the faint scent of fish and seaweed.

Damballa, ever-present at his side, had attempted to engage him in conversation, but Amadioha found himself at a loss for words, his mind still reeling from the events that had transpired in the council room.

"Amadioha Kamanu." Chief Umoren's voice pierced through his trance. Amadioha looked up to see the old chief standing next to him.

Damballa took the cue and walked away, leaving them together.

"How is he?" Chief Umoren asked, his gaze flickering toward the retreating Damballa.

Amadioha's brow furrowed, his eyes narrowing as he tried to discern the purpose behind Chief Umoren's question. He shifted his weight, the unease in his stance betraying his confusion. "Damballa has been by my side through every trial and tribulation," Amadioha said. "His counsel and unwavering loyalty have proven invaluable."

"And what of his mixed blood? Has his Vodunese heritage caused any rifts in your court?"

Amadioha paused to think. Damballa had been his most trusted confidant. Yet, the shadow of his Vodunese father always lurked in his mind, a nagging whisper of doubt he had never silenced. "To defeat our enemy, we must first understand them," Amadioha said. "Damballa's grants us valuable insight into their ways and weaknesses. It is a strength, not a liability, in our fight against their oppression."

Chief Amobi Umoren smiled. "The council will support your attack. You have our blessing."

Amadioha's jaw dropped, and his eyes widened with disbelief. "You will support us? Why did you not say it during the meeting?"

"The other council members were not yet agreeable."

"What is the point of leadership if you cannot impose your will?" Amadioha asked, his voice tight with frustration. His brows drew together, a deep furrow forming between them as he struggled to understand the council's hesitation.

"The point of leadership is not to impose your will, but to understand the will of those following you."

"So you baited me," Amadioha said. He raised an eyebrow, a faint smile forming at the corners of his mouth. "Baited me so I could show them how serious I was about this attack, about the future of our people?"

Chief Umoren ignored his statement and continued, "If you are caught, the repercussions will be great—repercussions that all of Niri will feel. You could lose everything."

"I cannot lose what I do not have." Amadioha clenched his fists at his sides. "And as long as the Vodunese remain on our lands, as long as they oppress and exploit our people, I have nothing. No true power, real freedom, or future to call my own."

"Big words for a young Eze," Chief Umoren said. He clasped his hands behind his back, his posture straight as he looked out over the sea. "Even if we must go against our customs to achieve our goals, we must first understand them, know the reasons behind our actions, and the consequences of our choices."

"I understand our customs. I have studied them all my life—the history of our people, the traditions that shaped us, and the sacrifices made in the name of our freedom."

"Yes, you have," Chief Umoren agreed. "But those who follow you, the warriors who look to you for guidance and inspiration, may not have the same level of understanding. Rules, laws, and customs exist for a reason: to maintain order and stability and to ensure the needs of the many outweigh the desires of the few."

Amadioha scratched his chin, his gaze fixed on Chief Amobi Umoren's face. "Chief Umoren, as always, your counsel is wise," he said, bowing his head. "Please accept my apology for my behavior in the council room. I allowed my passions to control me. Your guidance and support mean more to me than any personal glory or satisfaction."

"You are like your father in so many ways," Chief Umoren said, a warm smile spreading across his face. "Amadioha Kamanu, War Eze of Canis, may Chineke guide your hand and grant you victory in the coming battles."

THE OUTPOST HAD four towers with a horn in the middle of each. If a soldier sounded the alarm, its piercing blast would travel for miles, alerting the entire region to their presence. The success of their mission and the fate of their people hinged on their ability to silence their warning system before it shattered the stillness of the night.

When the sun dipped below the horizon, Amadioha and Damballa crept toward the first watchtower, their forms melding with the lengthening tree shadows. The Niri warriors wore red pants with exposed torsos. Armor would be too heavy, slowing them down when agility was necessary.

Two ladders, one on each side, led to the top of the tower, where vigilant watchmen stood guard. Amadioha gripped his double-headed axe in his calloused hands, squeezing until his palms tingled with numbness. Beside him, Damballa strung an arrow to his bowstring, his keen eyes narrowing as he took aim.

Amadioha emerged from the bushes with a light step, the soft rustle of leaves barely audible above the whispering wind. Another Niri soldier followed, mirroring Amadioha's every move. The watchtower loomed above them with a weathered wooden frame and thatched roof. The ladders, their rungs worn smooth by countless feet, clung to the sides. Amadioha strapped his axe to his back and gripped the ladder. Rung by rung, he ascended, his pulse quickening as he neared the top. There, he paused, awaiting the signal to strike.

A flash of light pierced the darkness, followed by another, the signal Amadioha was waiting for. In the distance, the sharp cry of a bird split the air. "Coo-coo, coo-coo," it trilled, a code that sent a surge of adrenaline through Amadioha's veins. Above him, a curious eye peered over the tower's edge, the watchman drawn by the unexpected noise. Amadioha saw the man's eyes widen in horror as he spotted them in the moonlight.

Before the watchman could draw a breath to cry out, an arrow whistled through the air, finding its mark on the soft flesh of his neck. The warning scream that bubbled in his throat died stillborn, trapped by the shaft piercing his windpipe. He toppled over the edge and fell to the ground with a loud thud.

Amadioha burst onto the top of the tower, his axe already in his hands. At the center of the platform stood the alarm horn, a behemoth of brass and copper that dominated the space. Its bell, wide enough for a man to crawl inside, gleamed in the moonlight. The horn's curved body stretched half the length of the platform, its mouthpiece hovering at chest height, ready for a guard's urgent breath. Thick leather straps secured it to a frame of sturdy oak beams. The air here hung thick with the mingled scents of unwashed bodies, lamp oil, and the acrid tang of nervous sweat.

Two Vodunese guards flanked the horn, their positions just out of reach of its mouthpiece. Amadioha launched himself at the nearest, his feet thundering across the wooden platform. In perfect sync, the other Niri fighter lunged at the second guard, their coordinated assault preventing any chance of alarm.

The soldier's hand flew to his sword, but before he could draw his blade from its sheath, Amadioha was upon him. He brought his axe down in a vicious arc, the razor-sharp edge cleaving through flesh and bone as it buried itself deep in the man's chest. The soldier's eyes bulged, his mouth opening in a silent scream, and he crumpled to the ground, his lifeblood staining the wood beneath him. But even as

Amadioha savored his victory, a cry of pain and the sickening crunch of metal on bone snapped his attention to his comrade. The Niri soldier, his footing lost on the slick planks, had fallen before he reached his target. The Vodunese man, his face a mask of rage, drove his sword into the fallen warrior's chest, the blade sinking to the hilt as he stilled the beating of the Niri man's heart.

A wave of anger surged through Amadioha. The pain of loss was a twisting knife in his gut that threatened to double him over. But he pushed it down, forced it into the depths of his being, knowing he could not afford to succumb to grief, not with so much at stake.

The Vodunese soldier's gaze darted to the horn, its polished surface gleaming in the moonlight, then back to Amadioha, his eyes narrowing as he weighed his options. Fight or raise the alarm? The decision hung in the balance. The soldier's sword, still dripping with the blood of Amadioha's fallen comrade, his nwanne, caught the light. He picked the fight and charged at Amadioha.

The soldier's blade sliced through the air, a whisper of death Amadioha barely dodged. He tumbled forward, the rough planks scraping him as he rolled, the metallic tang of blood and sweat filling his nostrils. The man was fast, his movements a blur of speed and power that kept Amadioha on his toes, his heart pounding in his ears as he fought to stay alive. The soldier struck again. Amadioha was a fraction too slow. Pain exploded across his chest as the blade found its mark, tracing a line of fire from his collarbone to his hip. Blood gushed from the wound, dripping to the floor as he staggered. His axe fell from nerveless fingers, clattering against the wood. The Vodunese man pressed his advantage, his sword stabbing down, seeking to end the fight once and for all. Amadioha, his breath coming in ragged gasps, threw himself to the side, the blade missing him by a hair's breadth as it sank deep into the wooden surface, the impact sending splinters flying.

Amadioha lunged for his fallen axe, his fingers closing around the haft just when the Vodunese soldier wrenched his sword free, the blade grating against the wood with a sickening scrape. He surged to his feet, his axe held high, the metal gleaming in the moonlight. The

Vodunese man raised his blade as he prepared to meet the blow. But Amadioha's axe, forged from rare and precious Canis steel, was no ordinary blade. It crashed down upon the soldier's sword, and the force of the impact shattered the inferior metal, sending shards flying like deadly rain. The axe head, unimpeded, continued its lethal arc, cleaving through the man's chest in a spray of blood and bone, burying itself deep within his body. The soldier crumpled to the ground, his life extinguished like a candle in the wind.

Amadioha sank to his knees, his lungs burning as he gulped down air, the coppery taste of blood and the acrid tang of sweat coating his tongue. For a moment, he allowed himself to close his eyes and center himself, drawing strength from the knowledge that he had survived and struck a blow against the enemy. Slowly, he pushed himself to his feet, his gaze falling upon the still form of his fallen comrade. He reached out and closed the man's eyes with a gentle hand. The man had given his life for a cause greater than himself and had sacrificed everything for the dream of a free and united Niri. The afterlife would welcome him with open arms and grant him the peace and rest he deserved.

The night air was still, the silence broken only by the distant jungle sounds and the pounding of Amadioha's heart. No alarms meant the other towers had been taken care of. With a grunt of pain, Amadioha climbed down from the tower, his wounds throbbing with each movement, the wood biting into his palms as he descended. At the base, Damballa waited, his face a mask of concentration as he scanned the surrounding area for any sign of trouble. When Amadioha's feet touched the ground, Damballa raised his hands and splayed his fingers wide in a silent signal.

Five minutes.

It was the longest wait of Amadioha's life, each second stretching into eternity as he fought to control his breathing, to still the trembling in his limbs and the pounding of his heart.

Another flash of light erupted from the depths of the forest—the signal, the moment they had waited for, the point of no return. From the shadows, Niri warriors emerged, their forms melting out of the darkness, their weapons glinting in the moonlight as they surrounded the camp. They charged with a roar that shook the ground, descending upon the blue and purple fabric tents in a wave of fury and steel.

Amadioha and Damballa raced into the outpost, their feet pounding against the grassy floor. The battle raged around them, the cries of the wounded and clashing steel a deafening cacophony threatening to overwhelm their senses. But they pushed on, their eyes fixed on their target, their minds focused on capturing the Vodunese lord.

As they sprinted through the camp, a sound cut through the battle, a sound that made Amadioha's blood run cold. The blare of a horn echoed through the night, making his head snap up in panic. Where did it come from? Who had sounded the alarm? They raced through the tents as the horn blared, its piercing cry a clarion call that would carry for miles, alerting every Vodunese soldier within earshot to their presence. The sound was so loud and pervasive that Amadioha knew those deep within the heart of Niri herself would hear it.

Amadioha's gaze darted around the camp, searching for the source of the sound that shattered their carefully laid plans. Then he saw him, a man, his naked body glistening with sweat and blood, crouched in the shadows, blowing into a smaller version of the horns adorning the watchtowers. The sight made Amadioha's stomach clench, his mind reeling at their mistake. How could they have missed him? How could their scouts have overlooked a crucial detail?

"*Koca ci!*" The curse tore from his lips. His fists clenched at his side, and the muscles in his jaw tightened as he fought to control the rage boiling within him.

The twang of a bowstring, the whisper of an arrow, then a sickening thud as the shaft found its mark, burying itself deep in the soldier's neck, silenced the alarm. The man's eyes bulged as he collapsed to the ground, the horn falling from his lifeless fingers. But even as the noise faded, replaced by the gurgle of the man's dying breaths, Amadioha knew the damage had been done. The clock was ticking, each precious second slipping away, bringing them closer to when the full might of the Vodunese army would descend upon them.

"We need to call off the attack now!" Damballa's eyes were wide with fear as he grabbed Amadioha's arm, his fingers digging into the flesh.

"No!" Amadioha's voice was steely. "We came here for the lord. We will not leave without them." He squared his shoulders. "We finish what we started."

With renewed determination, they continued toward the main tent.

A man dressed in finer attire than the others stood before it, his sword dangling at his side: the Vodunese lord. A tight-fitting shirt adorned with embroidered gems hugged his frame, the precious stones catching the moonlight and casting a dazzling array of reflections across the ground. Amadioha raised his hand, signaling Damballa to stay back as he attacked.

The lord stood his ground and sliced his blade toward Amadioha. Amadioha ducked, the air rushing above him as the weapon passed mere inches above his head, ruffling his hair and sending a chill down his spine. He dropped his axe and tumbled forward, his body moving on instinct, fueled by the adrenaline coursing through his veins. He came up behind the lord, his fists clenched, his muscles coiled and ready to strike. With a grunt of effort, he slammed his fist into the lord's kidney, the crunch of bone and tissue sickening beneath his knuckles.

The lord cried out in pain, his body jerking forward, his sword arm dropping to his side. Amadioha stepped closer, his heart pounding in his chest, his breath coming in ragged gasps. He opened his palm behind the man's neck, focused his mind, and channeled the power thrumming through his veins. Electricity crackled at his fingertips, the energy building, gathering. Amadioha released it, a surge of lightning erupting from his palm and into the lord's spine, targeting the spot where nerves and bone met. The bolt seared through the man's body, frying every synapse and nerve ending. The lord's body went rigid, his muscles seizing, his limbs jerking in a dance as he crumpled to the ground. His eyes, wide with terror, stared at Amadioha, the realization of his body's betrayal, of the utter helplessness consuming him, sinking in with a sickening finality.

"My legs!" the lord gasped, his voice high, edged with a raw, primal panic. "I can't feel them. I can't move them!" His face was a mask of horror, his eyes bulging as he struggled to comprehend his predicament.

Amadioha retrieved his axe and brought the blunt end down on the lord's temple, rendering him unconscious.

"Stop him!" a shout came from behind them. Amadioha turned to see a Vodunese soldier leaping onto a horse at the outpost's far end.

Chaos. This attack was chaos.

The animal reared, its nostrils flaring, its hooves churning the blood-soaked ground as the soldier dug his heels into its flanks, spurring it into a desperate gallop. The horns had alerted Vodunese soldiers far and wide of the ongoing attack, but a lone survivor would reveal their identity. If this man carried word of the assault to the Loas, all Niri would suffer the consequences.

Amadioha steadied his breath, channeling his energy into a crackling electricity that danced at his fingertips. It yearned to arc through the air and incinerate the fleeing soldier. But before he could unleash it, Damballa clamped down on his arm.

"No!" he hissed, his eyes urgent. "How many men in our realm can call forth lightning? The burn marks it will leave on the ground... the Loas will know beyond any doubt this was our doing."

For a moment, Amadioha teetered on the brink, but he wrenched himself back from the precipice with a monumental effort, the muscles in his jaw clenching with the strain.

Damballa unslung his bow and aimed. The distance was great, the Vodunese man moving fast, and the angle challenging. He loosed the arrow, and it arced through the night. For a heartbeat, Amadioha feared Damballa had missed, and the soldier would escape to bring doom to them all. Then, with a dull thud, the arrow found its mark. It punched through the soldier's back, piercing his heart, and sent him tumbling from his mount, his limp body hitting the ground in a cloud of dust.

∼

Inside the main tent, the air was thick with incense and sweat. Flickering oil lamps cast dancing shadows on the colored fabrics that lined the walls. Plush carpets in intricate patterns adorned the floor, their fibers worn in places from frequent use. A large, ornate desk stood in one corner, its surface cluttered with maps, scrolls, and other documents.

Amadioha loomed over the paralyzed lord, his eyes smoldering with intensity, the flickering light casting ominous shadows across his face. "Supply routes, soldier deployments. You will give them all to us if you want to live," Amadioha said, his voice a low, menacing growl.

"I will! I will even show you the way to the Mysters! Just fix my legs, please!" the lord pleaded, his words tumbling out in a desperate rush. "I will do anything you want."

"He is not a lord." Damballa's thoughts invaded Amadioha's mind. Damballa was the only person Amadioha knew who could project his thoughts, a skill that proved invaluable in such moments.

"What do you mean?" Amadioha thought back, his brow furrowing in confusion.

"He speaks more like a common soldier. And Vodunese lords do not beg."

"Everyone begs. They just need the right motivation."

"Vodunese lords do not beg." Damballa stepped forward. Amadioha grumbled but stepped back, yielding the floor to his second-in-command.

Damballa crouched low, getting eye level with the man, and spoke in fluent Vodunese. "We know you are not a lord. If you want to live to see the morning, you will tell us where your lord is."

The man's eyes widened in shock, confirming Damballa's words. "You betray your people?" he responded in Vodunese.

Most people living close to the border were usually fluent in Niri and Vodunese, a necessity born of proximity.

"Why are you pretending to be a lord?" Damballa asked, ignoring the man's question, his gaze unwavering.

The man struggled to move again, fresh sobs welling up as he confronted the reality of his paralysis. "I was afraid," the man said between cries.

Damballa got up with an annoying smile. A silent "I told you so" hung between them.

"Where is your Lord?" Amadioha said, his patience wearing thin.

"I don't know!" the man pleaded. His face contorted as he shook his head, hoping movement would return to his limbs. "He disappeared a day ago and has not returned."

The man was prepared to give them bogus information. And Amadioha would have been none the wiser. He seethed.

These men are nothing more than cowards, abusing their authority when it suits them but crumbling like sand when faced with formidable opposition. The sudden realization calmed his nerves and gave him the belief that his dream was possible.

"He is telling the truth." Damballa's thoughts invaded Amadioha's mind again.

"I don't believe him."

"The warning horn was sounded. We cannot be here when reinforcements come," Damballa thought.

"Don't you think I know that?" Amadioha frowned.

"Then why do we keep wasting time here?"

Amadioha grumbled as he swiped his hand through the air.

"Please, help me," the man begged, his head futilely turning from side to side in an attempt to move his paralyzed body. Spittle dribbled from the corner of his mouth.

A Niri man burst into the tent, his chest heaving and eyes wild, sweat glistening on his dark skin. The sudden intrusion sent the incense-laden air swirling, making the lamplight flicker. "My Eze," he gasped, "a scout reports someone ... something ... watching us from the forest."

Amadioha's brow furrowed, his hand tightening on his axe. "Vodunese reinforcements already?"

The warrior shook his head, his braids swaying with the motion. "No, my Eze. It was... a feathered man."

"Feathered man?" Amadioha's voice was sharp with disbelief. "What do you mean?"

"A man with wings, my Eze," the warrior replied.

Amadioha exchanged a glance with Damballa, whose face remained impassive. "Wings? A demon?"

"I do not know, my Eze," the warrior admitted. "We have surrounded the area but have found no one."

"How could they tell it was a demon and not a man from afar?" Damballa thought to Amadioha.

"Its wings were extended outwards? Is that not what the man said?" Amadioha thought back.

"Why would its wings be extended outwards?"

"I don't know. Maybe we can ask nicely." Amadioha frowned before striding out of the tent, with Damballa and the messenger following close behind. The cool night air was a welcome reprieve from the stuffy interior. They walked through the camp, stepping over bodies and debris, the soft grass muffling their footsteps. As they neared the tree-line, the Niri warrior pointed to the scout who had made the report. Four other men stood around him while many others searched the forest.

"What did you see?" he asked the man.

The warrior shifted, dead leaves crunching under his feet. "My Eze, I... I may have been mistaken. The adrenaline from war, the excitement... maybe it was just a bird."

Amadioha's gaze swept the dark forest again, the hairs on the back of his neck standing on end. A chill breeze whispered on his face, carrying with it the faint metallic scent of blood from the Vodunese men who lay dead at the outpost. "Search again," he said.

Damballa's hand on his shoulder made him turn. "We have no time," his second-in-command urged. "Our window is closing."

Amadioha hesitated, curious to confirm what, if anything, this man had seen. Finally, he nodded.

"Burn everything," Amadioha commanded. "Take the bodies of

our fallen and any gold or valuables, but leave the rest. Make it look like the work of common thieves."

While the outpost burned and the flames cast an eerie orange glow against the night sky, Amadioha and his men melted into the forest, their forms swallowed by the shadows.

∾

Amadioha's journal: Inner turmoil between father and son

The meeting with my father today has left me more conflicted than ever. As always, his presence filled the room, his wisdom apparent in every measured word. Yet, for the first time, I found myself questioning that wisdom, seeing hesitation where once I saw only strength.

We spoke of Niri's future, of Canis' future and the growing Vodun threat. Father counseled patience and diplomacy, the same tired rhetoric he's clung to for years. "We must bide our time," he said. "Wait for the right moment." But when is that moment, Father? When Vodun's boot is on our throat? When there is nothing left of Niri to save?

I love him. By Chineke, I love him more than I can express. But today, I saw not a bright star but a guttering candle, afraid of its flame.

He spoke of the plans we made years ago, the whispers of rebellion that never came to fruition. "It wasn't the right time," he said. But I saw the regret in his eyes, the weight of chances not taken. How many opportunities have slipped through our fingers while we waited for the "right time"?

And then there's the matter of my brother. Father didn't speak his name, but his presence hung between us like a shroud. Would he still be alive if we had acted sooner? If we had struck against Vodun when we had the chance? Father's caution, his endless deliberation... did it cost me my brother?

I cannot make the same mistakes. I cannot let fear of action become inaction. Niri needs more than careful words and diplomatic niceties. It requires a leader willing to seize the moment and forge our destiny with fire and steel if necessary.

Chineke guide me. For I fear that the path I must walk may take me far from the man that my father raised me to be. But if that is the cost of a free Niri, then it is a price I must pay.

2

A BREWING INSURRECTION

*L*ord **Legba Samedi** awoke with a gasp, his heart hammering against his ribs. The dank dungeon's chill seeped into his bones, his skin slick with cold sweat. His tongue rasped over cracked lips, yearning for a drop of water to ease his parched throat.

"It happened again, didn't it?" came a ragged voice.

He turned to the emaciated form in the corner of the cell. Ogou's sunken eyes peered out from a face rendered skeletal by starvation. His shirt hung in tatters, exposing jutting ribs and protruding hip bones. Sassier prison was one of the most heavily guarded in Vodun, the last place a lord like him would have expected to find himself. He shivered as if a breeze had just blown through the square box that had been his home for the last two months. "The dream was so vivid this time," he whispered.

Ogou's gaze sharpened. "The same as before?"

Legba's mind returned to the dream.

"He has not returned, Ma. I will bring notice as soon as we find him," Marie's handmaiden said.

"Liar!" Marie's chest heaved, her breaths uneven as another contraction gripped her stomach, causing her to cry in agony. Her hand instinctively sought comfort in the rhythm of her unborn child's heartbeat. Unlike her

previous child, who had arrived too early, this one was determined to make a delayed entrance into the world.

The door to her left burst open, revealing two women with wrappers tied around their waists. One carried a jug of water and a glass, while the other held a transparent blue container filled with fluid. The first woman hurried to bring the water to Marie's lips, but Marie swiped it away, sending the glass clattering to the floor, where it shattered into countless pieces.

"I want my husband, not water!" Marie screamed. "Get him in here now!"

Another contraction seized her body, the pain even more intense than before.

"I could feel what my mother felt and hear her thoughts... even the strands of hair on her handmaiden's head were clear to me." Exhausted, Legba pulled himself up against the wall.

Ogou shifted, drawn in by the gravity of the story.

Legba refrained from overanalyzing his cellmate's unusual interest, finding joy in the simple pleasure of sharing his thoughts with another person instead. "I still feel her pain. Deep inside, my mother knew her baby was killing her. I was killing her." Legba's next breath caught in his lungs. He rubbed his hand on his stomach, expecting to find a baby bump.

Ogou peered at Legba, urging him to go on with his eyes.

"Her feelings were mine. The pain she felt when she learned about my father's death... it was too much."

"That is where the dream ended last time?" Ogou asked.

"It continued. It was like the baby had also heard the news. It... I mean I, wanted to come out. Born with blood in my eyes and mouth, I struggled for life while the handmaidens scrambled to revive me. I could sense my mother ebbing away as they tried to save me." He paused and readjusted himself. His back cracked as he straightened more. "The memory ended when she took her last breath."

Ogou leaned into his corner. "You speak as if you truly lived this, as if these people were real."

"*Fout Tonne!*" Legba cursed. "I am certain it was my mother."

"With how things are going, madness might claim us before hunger does. Gods of Vodun help us," Ogou said.

Legba's stomach growled as if taking a cue from Ogou's words.

"You never heard the story of your birth or saw your mother. For all we know, a milking cow birthed you!" Ogou laughed.

Before the dreams had started, Legba had longed for any connection to his family—a memory, a drawing, anything that would remind him of them. The dreams had to be real; it would be too cruel for them to be nothing more than a tease. Loss had already marked his life, his family taken from him one by one until he stood alone, adrift in a world becoming increasingly empty. He met Ogou's laughter with a frown.

Ogou raised his hands in defense. "You grew up an orphan. That is all you know."

Before Legba could respond, the rattle of armored boots echoed down the corridor. A man strode into view, wearing a steel breastplate etched with arcane runes. Deep shadows ringed his eyes, the skin sagging like the weight of unspoken worries.

"Fout Tonne! What madness is this?" the man snarled.

Legba flinched, but the fury in the man's gaze fixed on Ogou. A ripple of foreboding prickled Legba's skin. The man's armor gleamed too brightly, and the hilt of his sword appeared too new for a mere guardsman.

Ogou sighed. "I was desperate. I had no choice," he said.

The man flexed his hands on the bars. "I waited over a week like a fool!"

"Plans changed," Ogou said, pointing to Legba. "He has the dreams. I observed them for many nights."

Legba's breath caught. *The dreams?*

The man scoffed. "So you said of the last five!"

"This time, I'm right. I swear it!" Ogou insisted.

The man's lip curled. "Did you know this man is a deserter? He ran away, abandoning his outpost during an attack. Radha Rhamirez Loa will not tolerate us bringing someone like him to her court. If you are wrong—"

"We must stop the brewing insurrection in our lands," Ogou interrupted. "By the Gods of Vodun!"

Legba's voice quivered. "Who are you people?"

Both men turned on him. "Silence!" they hissed in unison.

Legba cringed as their voices echoed off the stone. When he dared meet their gaze again, Ogou's gaunt form had vanished. Outside the cell bars stood a tall figure in swirling white robes, his once sunken face restored to vigor, framed by vibrant silver hair.

A magician! Magic was rare in Vodun, and those who could wield its power were royalty, dangerous, or sometimes both.

"Ofeli, we tread a knife's edge," Ogou said. "But we are close to ending this."

Ofeli grimaced. "I will not be made a fool again. If this fails—"

"The Sacred Master will handle the Loa," Ogou interrupted. "There is no time for your bruised ego."

"It's our necks on the block if she disapproves," Ofeli growled.

"We both knew the risks."

Ofeli shrugged in defeat, then kicked the cell door. "Guards!"

Heavy footsteps approached at a run. A guard skidded to a halt, staring bewildered at the cell with only one person inside. "Where did—"

Ogou twirled his hand. "Unlock this cell. Now!"

The guard paused mid-sentence, his face a mask of confusion. In a trance-like state, he pulled out the keys and moved to unlock the cell.

Legba watched the guard and wondered if Ogou had used those powers to control him at any point. *The dreams.* They had started before Ogou's arrival but had become more frequent and intense since then.

"Stop!" Ofeli commanded. The man stopped, glancing at him with an empty expression.

"How many times must I tell you? No magic." Ofeli narrowed his stern eye at Ogou.

Ogou shrugged before twirling his hands again, releasing the guard from his trance. The guard shook his head, confused by his momentary lapse. Ofeli retrieved a document from inside his armor, stamped with an official blue seal. "Radha Rhamirez Loa has sanctioned our investigation. This man is vital to it. Release him at once."

Still dazed, the guard took the paper Ofeli offered, scanning its contents with trembling hands. "I should speak to the warden first."

Ofeli pressed his lips into a thin line. "Best not to keep the Loa waiting."

"Yes, Mesye!" The guard saluted before hurrying away, keen to avoid further confrontation.

Dread congealed into terror in Legba's heart. What fresh nightmare was this?

~

THE CARRIAGE JERKED TO A STOP, and the door swung open to reveal a frail older man, the driver, gazing inside.

Ofeli was intimidating, yet Legba had found Ogou's newly revitalized form even more uncomfortable. He was relieved when Ofeli recommended that his old cellmate travel ahead of them to the Mysters.

"Out of the carriage, both of you," the driver commanded, snapping his fingers. "Before someone spots us," he added, motioning for them to leave.

"We are not yet at the Mysters," Ofeli stated, his eyes narrowing as he studied the driver's face.

"Near enough for me. Get out! Come on. And hand me the rest of my money."

"The gate was the deal," Ofeli retorted.

"Look, the last time I ventured closer, they detained me for hours," the driver confessed, his voice desperate, his hands flailing as he spoke. "Searched me over and over, accusing me of smuggling."

Ofeli looked at Legba and motioned with his head for him to exit. He extracted a pouch of coins from his pocket and flung it at the coachman. The man scrutinized the payment, his grip firm yet dissatisfied. "The money is not complete," he protested.

"Fair exchange is never robbery." Ofeli's voice was icy as he leaned forward, his fingers grazing the hilt of his sword with quiet menace.

The man spat on the ground in disgust. Out of fear or annoyance, he vaulted onto the carriage and set off, heading back up the road they had come down.

Emerald-green grass stretched out on both sides of the winding path, punctuated by magenta and fiery orange exotic flowers. Sunbeams pierced the overhead foliage, casting dappled light and shadows everywhere.

An odd sense of tranquility settled on Legba as they trudged toward the castle. The irony was that he was approaching Vodun's third most formidable seat of power. The atmosphere was more akin to a secluded haven, reminiscent of a peaceful stream tucked behind a lively waterfall where one could bathe in warmth and relaxation. Frequently, the deceptive calmness led to the Loa's enemies underestimating the might of Limbe.

As they reached the crest of the path, the majestic Mysters loomed ahead. Two massive statues, clad in bronze armor and adorned with strands of blue metal reminiscent of Ofeli's garb, stood guarding the entrance. Each statue grasped a lit torch in the hand furthest from the door. Despite the midday sun, the flames that danced atop them emitted an eerie blue glow, casting peculiar shadows across the landscape. As the fire crackled and whistled, the once prevalent citrus aroma from the surrounding trees gave way to the smoldering incense's sharp scent. In their opposing hand, the statues gripped a spear, its length matching the stature of the behemoths. They weren't ordinary stone creations; their spear tips gleamed with the same bronze sheen as their armor, hinting at a purpose beyond mere decoration.

Legba stopped, his eyes widening in wonderment at them.

Ofeli nudged him. "Keep moving!"

Legba had heard a legend that the statues were once human warriors, champions renowned for their bravery but undone by their arrogance. Wary of their growing power and influence, the Loa had petrified them as a punishment and a warning against such hubris.

Whispered rumors claimed the statues could discern the intent of any visitor; they would strike down anyone entering the castle with malice in their heart.

The stories' truth was questionable, but the Loa's reputation was undisputed. Despite ruling over lesser land and commanding a smaller army than her peers, she had never faced defeat within or beyond her kingdom's borders.

They passed the statues without incident, approaching another door guarded by two more statues, similar yet smaller than the first pair. The doors opened to reveal an expansive room with an oval ceiling that soared high above, creating the illusion of touching the heavens. Legba felt both insignificant and in awe. Majestic pillars, intricately carved to resemble armored warriors in mid-stride, held the towering roof aloft. The grandeur of the decorations and ornaments was staggering, reflecting the whispers that it was the most lavish structure in all of Vodun. Its opulence surpassed Kal Mysters, home to the Bondye, Voduns' revered spiritual and military leader. The grandiose display of wealth had made the Loa more enemies than friends, especially among those who felt she was beneath them.

Two men stood on guard at the entrance they had just walked through. "What is your business here?" the first asked. His armor, similar to Ofeli's, shared its gleaming bronze glamor.

"I am Lord Ofeli of the Mysters Guard," Ofeli said. "This is Lord Legba. We are here to see the Sacred Master."

Why would one of the most powerful magicians in Limbe want to see me?

The guards exchanged glances. "The Sacred Master?" the first asked as he sized up Ofeli and Legba.

"Yes," Ofeli responded.

The guard tilted his head upward. His body froze as an inky blackness swallowed his eyes. After a few seconds, they returned to normal. "You are ordered to the Sanctum." His face was flustered.

Doubt gnawed at Legba's insides. As they advanced, he wondered about the guard's reaction and what it meant for him.

∼

IN THE MYSTERS, Legba's prison attire stood out starkly: torn baggy pants, worn-out black boots, and an unfastened leather shirt. While navigating the halls, the guards became fewer and fewer, replaced by hundreds of people clad in tunics that were fastened with ropes adorned with silver knobs. The people briskly went about their chores, largely ignoring their presence. The hallway boasted a flawless marble floor, smooth and uninterrupted, with no crevices or distinct blocks. Torches illuminated the walls, their flames casting an endless blue glow reminiscent of the statues outside.

"What will the Sacred Master do with me?" The silence after twisted a knot in Legba's stomach as sweat covered his palms. "What does the Sacred Master want with me?" he asked again.

Ofeli stepped forward, seizing Legba's arm and yanking him. Legba winced as his shoulder scraped against the sharp edge of Ofeli's armor.

"Does everyone else in Naes talk as much as you do?" Ofeli asked.

"I didn't—"

"All this magic makes my stomach queasy. The sooner I get you where you need to be, the quicker this is over," Ofeli said, clearing his throat.

"I—"

"Listen. Not talk," Ofeli insisted, irritation growing on his face.

Legba wanted to scream at the man who had taken him from his cell. He wanted to scream and refuse to walk further until he learned more. Instead, he straightened his back and kept silent.

Two guards who had noticed their tense exchange approached.

"Is there a problem here?" one asked.

"Not anymore," Ofeli said. "I was just telling him to get moving."

The men roved their eyes over Legba, their faces contorting with disgust. One wrinkled his nose as if assaulted by a foul stench, while the other's lip curled into a sneer. Ofeli shoved Legba forward again, and the guards continued past them. The rest of the path to the

Sanctum was a labyrinth of turns and doors, leaving Legba astounded at Ofeli's unerring sense of direction.

∼

THREE VASES HOVERED above the entrance of the Sanctum, releasing a blue liquid. As the door's crest neared, the fluid morphed into mist before vanishing. Two guards, covered from head to toe in armor, flanked the door. In their hands, oversized axes tilted toward each other, blocking anyone from passing.

Legba's heart raced as the longing for his simpler life grew. Even his prison cell seemed like an escape.

The guards kept their gaze straight ahead. They were protecting royalty, so they would never turn their heads, only their eyes. It was something even a lord knew.

"State your business," they said in unison. Their voices rumbled like an echo in a deep cavern.

Legba tried to shift backward, but Ofeli's arm on his back stopped his retreat.

Ofeli drew a deep breath. "The Sacred Master has called for us."

An oppressive silence hung between them, each second stretching longer than the last. Legba glanced back at Ofeli but received only a blank stare. Finally, the guards pulled their weapons back, clearing the way in.

Legba's breathing grew shallow. *Is this some kind of test?* One step forward, and they might cleave him in two. His uneasiness escalated as his doubt rose. The Sacred Master wanted to punish him. But what punishment involved him coming all the way here? He thought about running again. This time, a surge of energy entered his legs and encouraged him to act against all reasoning.

"Do you think I have all day?" Ofeli shoved Legba from behind harder than before, sending him tumbling into the door. Legba tripped over his leg, bracing for impact. Surprisingly, he passed right through and found himself sprawled on the chamber floor beyond.

Moving through the false door was like traveling from the Mysters to the inside of a mountain. The walls and ceiling were rough, brownish-gray rock, reminiscent of a cave's interior. There was an icy chill from a gust of wind, even though the room was windowless. A man loomed over a rustic wooden table at the room's far end. He wore a hooded cloak like his old cellmate, who stood next to him. The man's hair was silky white, as was his beard.

"This is the deserter?" the white-haired man boomed, his voice echoing as if amplified.

"Yes, Sacred Master," Ofeli said from behind Legba.

A shiver traveled down Legba's spine.

"So, you are the one they call Lord Legba," the Sacred Master said. "The deserter."

"Yes, Mesye," Legba said in a trembling voice. "I never had the chance to explain."

"You will address me as Sacred Master." The man's eyes widened, as if sucking Legba's very essence from within.

"Yes, Sacred Master," Legba corrected himself.

"The morning before the attack, you were nowhere to be found," the Sacred Master said sternly. "Later, your unit was massacred and the outpost burned."

"I... I was distraught." Legba's voice broke, memories flooding back. "Three days prior, someone brutally soiled and murdered my sister. While I was searching for her assailant, forces who I now believe to be the Niri, Amadioha's men, ambushed my unit. The grief clouded my judgment and led me astray."

The Sacred Master's staff glowed a subtle blue, drawing Legba's attention. "You dare use personal misfortune as an excuse for your failure?"

Tears welled in Legba's eyes. "She was the last of my family. The surprise attack, my unit's slaughter... it all compounded. I deserve to have perished with them. I might be a broken leader, but it was not cowardice."

A moment of silence filled the room. The Sacred Master turned to Ogou, murmuring in hushed tones. Legba, sensing the immense weight of the situation, edged back, only to be halted again by Ofeli's presence.

"Don't even think about it," Ofeli whispered in a voice low enough that only Legba could hear.

"Bring him in!" The Sacred Master's voice boomed.

Legba turned around to see five guards entering through the now-open door. Two of them dragged a sixth man across the floor whose face shifted between various stages of anguish. A stump was present where his right arm should have been.

Three guards approached Legba with deliberate, threatening strides. They grabbed him and threw him down on his back, pressing his head against the cold floor. A shocked cry escaped him as his breath was forced from his lungs. Pain flared at the back of his skull, only to be dulled by the adrenaline coursing through him.

"I'm not a deserter!" Legba's voice cracked as he pleaded.

The Sacred Master pressed a blade across the front of his neck. "Stay still or lose your head," he ordered.

Legba's fears of coming there had morphed from mere paranoia into stark, biting reality. He ceased his struggle but continued to plead his innocence.

"How the next few moments unfold will shape your fate. For the last two weeks, someone has been stealing from us. This man here is a suspect. Do you know what the punishment for stealing in Vodun is?"

Why would he ask me that? "You lose the arm you committed the crime with," Legba said. "Sacred Master! I did not steal. My story is true!"

"And what is the penalty for murder?"

Murder? The accusation jolted him. *Did they think I could be working with the Niri?*

The Sacred Master waved his hand dismissively. "I assure you, this is not the most important thing I have to do today."

"A life taken, a life given, Mesye," Legba whispered.

"If you address me as Mesye again, I will cut your tongue!" he snarled, reaching for the dagger at his belt.

Swallowing hard, Legba managed a shaky response. "Sacred Master."

"Tell me if this man stole from our Loa."

The man's eyes were like a lost animal, oblivious to what was happening. "I have never met this man before," Legba asserted, spittle flying from his mouth as he wrestled with his restraints. In retaliation, the guard holding him delivered a punishing blow to his stomach.

"I was counting on it," the Sacred Master said with gleaming eyes.

The two burly guards hoisted the captive from the cold stone floor, suspending his body over Legba. With a dispassionate slice, the Sacred Master carved a harsh line of red across the man's exposed chest. A stream of blood gushed forth from the wound, filling Legba's nose, eyes, and mouth.

The metallic taste overloaded his tongue as the guards maintained their gruesome tableau. Finally, they let the man crumple to the floor. Once the guards released their hold, Legba wiped the thick, iron-tinged blood from his eyes. The blade used to slice the man's chest lay next to him, and the Sacred Master had moved to the other side of the injured man.

After an eternity, Legba straightened up, the room falling into a weighted silence as all eyes focused on him. His gaze fell to the man on the floor, squirming and crying out as he tried to stop the bleeding. Legba glanced at the blade as a fury built inside him. It urged him to do evil and gave him the energy to execute its desire.

When the man's blood invaded Legba's senses, a vision took hold of him; it was a flash of the stranger's life, impossibly vivid, like the dreams of his mother during his birth. He did not have enough time to ponder this because another merciless truth unfolded before him: this man was the one who had stolen his sister's life.

She was a complete nobody to him. On that night, the man had seen her by chance, followed her to her tent, and took advantage of her. When she fought back, he bashed her head in a moment of rage. Then he went about his day like she was nothing.

The memory of her had stopped there. The man, called Josue,

had not thought about her more than twice again since that day. With that revelation, a surge of raw emotion rushed through Legba, set ablaze by a primal rage that had lain dormant, awaiting that moment.

"Why did you do it?" Legba roared, his voice echoing in the charged silence. He was sure the man was responsible, although he did not know how. He glanced at the Sacred Master, who offered a subtle nod. It was a test, a cruel game they had lured him into, but he did not care.

He grabbed the blade and rushed at the man on the floor. The man opened his eyes in surprise and confusion as Legba planted the knife in his heart. Legba pulled the dagger out and stabbed him again. And again. And again. He stabbed him until the man's torso ripped so much it became skin dangling on bone. And even then, he didn't stop. His hands trembled. His heart beat against his chest. "Why did you do it!" he screamed at the heap of flesh and bone on the floor.

And then, when he moved to stab again, his body froze. It was as if the air around him had solidified, an invisible vice gripping his limbs. He strained against the spectral restraint, muscles tensing, veins bulging in futile resistance. His arm, mid-swing, hung suspended, frozen. A bewildering sensation overtook him as his body, defying gravity, levitated. He twisted and turned, a marionette in the air, slowly rotating to face the Sacred Master. With a mere flick of the Sacred Master's wrist, the blade slipped from Legba's grasp. It sliced through the air before embedding itself with a thud into the stone wall.

"I have seen enough," the Sacred Master declared, a glint of excitement dancing in his eyes.

"This is what I promised," Ogou said.

"You have proven me wrong." The Sacred Master's voice was a distant blur. "Begin preparations at once."

The invisible force relinquished its hold as quickly as it ensnared him. Legba plummeted to the ground, his body crumpling under its weight. He gazed aimlessly at the ceiling, lost in a daze.

∼

THE BEAST'S breath engulfed Legba's face before he saw it. Hot and humid, it reeked of decomposing flesh. It filled his nostrils and stung his insides long before the snarly growl, low but deep, reverberated throughout the room. Legba opened his eyes to see an animal that looked as if it had just crawled out of the bowels of pain and torture. The creature's eyes glowed blue, and its hunched back made it appear bigger from the front. Its teeth were too big to fit in its mouth, and its claws gleamed stark white.

Startled, he recoiled, pressing himself against the wall.

"He is awake," said the Sacred Master. He wore a red scarf around his head, a loose garment draping his chest, and had a toothed necklace gracing his neck.

The Loa stood beside him, her presence commanding and ethereal. Her skin bore a rich, dark brown hue, and her intricate, braided hair cascaded down her left shoulder. Every strand was painstakingly arranged, just as detailed as the ornate decorations adorning the hallways of the Mysters. A golden band with an emblem of a beast's open mouth encircled her neck. As Legba gazed at her, a profound sense of awe enveloped him, surpassing anything he had seen through paintings and statues.

"My Loa." While bowing his head in deference, Legba stayed alert; ears pricked for any sudden movements from the beast. With a gesture from the Loa, the Sacred Master produced a vial from his pocket, holding it up.

"So this is the one," the Loa said, "who sees the past inside blood."

"Yes, my Loa, we found him in a prison in Anane. Ogou was—"

The Loa raised her palm to silence him. Her presence was even more commanding than the magician next to her.

The Sacred Master looked at Legba, his eyes narrowing. "Baron Ayizan and some of her knights were attacked near one of our camps in the north," he said.

Legba felt the worry form lines on his face. Ayizan was his baron. "What became of them?" he asked.

"She lives," the Sacred Master said. "For now. But the long sleep has plagued her."

"I should have been there to protect her," Legba said, putting his hand to his chest.

"You could not save your men at the outpost, but you think you could protect your baron?" the Loa asked as she fixed him with a doubtful gaze.

Legba bowed his head, stuttering out an apology. "I—"

"Tell me who is behind this," she demanded as she leaned forward.

He wanted to approach the Sacred Master, but the beast stood between them. He took a step, then hesitated as it bared its teeth.

"*A nana bari*," the Loa said.

The beast purred before retreating next to the Loa. "Delphine only bites when threatened, which is not a problem here."

Her condescending tone did not faze him. He was happy his Loa would embrace him with her presence. All Legba had done since coming to the Mysters was practice his ability again and again. It took only a few drops of blood in his eyes from the vial he took from the Sacred Master and a few seconds for him to zero in on the right memories of Ayizan. He dreamed.

Ayizan was walking with several Vodunese soldiers to meet a fellow baron. Seeing what his baron saw... being her, was strange. The day was overcast. Dusk was approaching. Masked men appeared from the trees. Ayizan's fear rose within Legba as the men advanced, their weapons drawn and their eyes burning with a rage that consumed them. The attackers' attire resembled Ayizan's command, yet subtle differences caught Legba's discerning eye.

The fabric of their clothing appeared rougher, its texture distinct and unfamiliar. Legba's mind raced as he studied the intruders' movements, their gait, and how they wielded their swords. His photographic memory, honed through countless travels both within and beyond the borders of Vodun and Niri, proved invaluable. As he analyzed every detail, the pieces fell into place, and he discerned the origins of the mysterious assailants. A whisper of caution urged him to halt, but insatiable curiosity silenced it, compelling him to go deeper.

He opened his eyes and poured a couple more drops into them while the Loa regarded him with growing interest. He searched for more of Ayizan's memories and went places he should not have. His singular focus was to please his Loa, to atone for the ghosts of his past mistakes.

"Nine men and two women," Legba said. "From Freshwater Naes."

"A long way from the incident," the Loa said. "Are you sure?"

"I have full confidence, my Loa." He stole a glance at the Sacred Master, who remained stoic. "I know all their faces. If you would like, I can draw them."

"Excellent," she commented, rising to her feet.

He audibly cleared his throat.

"Is there more you have not told us?" she asked.

"Please, my Loa, I beg your forgiveness. I dared look where I should not and found something troubling."

"Do not waste my time."

"It's beyond my comprehension, but I bore witness to Ayizan's memories—memories of a plot to dethrone you, entwined with other Loas."

"Name them," she demanded.

"Ghede Ghadou Loa and Anaise Pye Loa."

"Ghede has always been duplicitous, jealous of my growing influence in Niri. But Anaise... Who else is involved?"

"My Loa, most of Ayizan's Knights." Legba was uncomfortable exposing his baron, but his loyalty was to the Loa. He gave her all the names.

"Validate the deserter's account," the Loa commanded. "Should his words bear truth, we must act without haste. The treachery appears to run far deeper than we expected."

"Yes, my Loa!" the Sacred Master said.

"Act discreetly. Maintain silence," she instructed. "It's imperative the origin of our findings remains concealed."

The Eden Ruse

With a hesitant voice, Legba asked, "How did you know I wasn't involved?"

She looked at him and laughed. "Because you are a coward. And no coward would try to overthrow me."

The words stung more profoundly than he would have expected. He couldn't comprehend what entered him, but what he said next brought forth an unknown confidence. "Wait!" he shouted.

The Loa opened her eyes wider, surprised by his outburst. Delphine growled excitedly, hoping for her master to unleash her.

"I have betrayed my vows. I left my unit to die. Allow me to serve under the mages. Let me learn. Let me atone for my failings."

The Loa and Sacred Master had given him the chance to avenge his sister. He owed them a lot more than he had given.

Her surprise lingered for a moment, then morphed into a smile. "You have already served me well."

"And I can continue," Legba said. "You call me a deserter, yet I may have saved your kingdom."

"Do not think yourself bigger than you are," she snapped.

Legba bowed his head. "Allow me to repay you, to repay Limbe, to repay Vodun for my transgressions. I yearn to be seen as more."

An eternity of silence passed before she spoke. "Lord Legba is absolved of his title. He will bear the title Papa henceforth and serve under your guidance. Teach him your ways, train him like yours, and show me what more use we can have of him."

Legba rose, holding back a triumphant smile. Conscious of the eyes upon him, he fought to keep his composure.

Although looking displeased, the Sacred Master refrained from voicing his discontent. "Of course, my Loa." His frown promised Legba there would be consequences.

With a grand gesture, the Sacred Master's eyes darkened to obsidian. In a blink, she and the Sacred Master shimmered into transparency before vanishing. Legba stood alone in silence, an icy knot of trepidation unfurling within him.

Papa Legba's journal: Anointment as Lord and future aspirations

Today, I stand taller than I ever have before. The weight of my new title, "Lord," rests upon my shoulders, not as a burden, but as a badge of honor. Baron Ayizan's words still ring in my ears, the ceremony imprinted into my memory with the permanence of a tattoo.

The hall was resplendent, adorned with the visage of our great Loa, Radha Rhamirez. Her portraits and statues seemed to watch over the proceedings, lending an air of divine approval to my anointment. For a moment, I allowed myself to imagine her there in person, her piercing gaze upon me as I swore my fealty. But I quickly dismissed the thought. I am but one small man in the great nation of Vodun; it would be presumptuous to expect the Loa herself to attend.

Still, as I knelt before Baron Ayizan, I felt a connection to something greater than myself. The pride that swelled in my chest was unlike anything I had ever experienced. This is what it means to be part of something monumental, to have a purpose that extends beyond one's own desires.

I swore my oath with every fiber of my being. To serve Vodun, to uphold its laws and values, to be a beacon of its power and benevolence. I vowed to be worthy of this title, to make Baron Ayizan proud, to bring honor to the name of Radha Rhamirez Loa.

And yet, even as I embrace this new role, my

thoughts turn to family. To my dear sister, the only blood relation I have left in this world. As soon as the ceremony concluded, I requested a posting at Jeaune mine. My heart soared when Baron Ayizan granted my wish without hesitation.

The prospect of being near my sister again fills me with a warmth I had almost forgotten. Family and duty, intertwined at last. I can serve Vodun while also protecting and supporting my sister. It feels like the pieces of my life are finally falling into place.

3

A FATHER IS LOST

*A*bstract paintings adorned the Luminary's corridors, their vibrant colors muted by the flickering light of wall-mounted lanterns. Burning oil mingled with the musty air, creating an oppressive atmosphere. **Ikenga Umoren** trudged through the winding passages, each heavy footstep echoing in the gloom. He was so lost in thought that he didn't notice the figure approaching until they collided. Startled, he looked up to see Amadioha steadying himself.

"I didn't expect to see you here," Ikenga said, his brows furrowed in confusion.

Amadioha's deep red robe, embroidered with intricate white threading, swayed when he placed a comforting hand on Ikenga's shoulder. His eyes, usually sharp and calculating, softened with sympathy. "Your father was a great man. It was an honor to work alongside him when he led the Anwasi council," he said. "I would not miss the chance to pay my respects, no matter what. The council will be in good hands if you take his place."

If? Why would he say "if"?

"The honor was his," Ikenga said. "It was just two years ago we stood next to each other, with you ready to put your younger brother in the ground."

"The Vodunese have committed a great crime against us both. No man should have to go through what we have," Amadioha said.

"The Vodunese?" Ikenga asked as his eyes narrowed. "They did not kill my father."

"Sudden heart failure, wasn't it?" Amadioha raised an eyebrow.

"He had been sick for a while," Ikenga replied, his mind reeling from the questions. Burning incense wafted through the air, mingling with the musty air of the ancient building and the lanterns' burning oil. The combination made his stomach churn as a bead of sweat trickled down his back.

"Indeed," Amadioha said.

The faintest idea of any truth to Amadioha's words was unsettling.

"Walk with me." Amadioha gestured down the hall.

"The sinking feeling in your gut... how do you get over it?" Ikenga asked as they walked.

"My younger brother's death took a toll on my relationship with my brother. We had always had our differences, but after the funeral, our arguments escalated, each more bitter than the last. When our mother passed not long after, it was the final straw. He left for Sine, leaving me to pick up the pieces of our broken family." Amadioha paused, a flicker of warmth softening his features. "If it hadn't been for Ijele, I don't know how I would have survived. She was my rock, my anchor in the storm of grief threatening to consume me."

They entered a large, circular room, its high ceiling supported by carved stone pillars. Murals depicting scenes from Niri history, colors muted by time, adorned the walls. A tall statue of Chief Amobi Umoren, Ikenga's father, dominated the room's center. The dark, polished stone captured his likeness in detail. The statue's eyes held a depth of wisdom and compassion that transcended the material.

Surrounding it was a shallow pool of crystal-clear water, its surface shimmering in the flickering light of countless candles. The candles, each nestled in a small, lotus-shaped holder, floated on the water, their soft glow casting dancing shadows on the walls and illuminating the statue with an ethereal light.

They approached the pool, their footsteps echoing in the room's stillness. A small table stood nearby, its surface lined with rows of unlit candles, each one a deep gray. They each took a candle from the table, holding it reverently.

"Our ancestors are watching. Let us honor your father's memory, ensuring the light in the afterlife guides his spirit," Amadioha said.

Ikenga nodded, his eyes fixed on the candle in his hand. He took a deep breath, then lit it using a flame from a floating candle in the pool. Amadioha followed suit. Together, they placed their candles into lotus holders, setting them adrift.

Two Vodunese soldiers marched in, covered to their necks in armor. They looked around for a few seconds before leaving as quickly as they came. Soldiers were usually present at big gatherings, coming and going as they pleased. Their presence irked Ikenga like a dirty spot on a white cloth.

"If you truly believe Vodun caused your brother's death, how did you move forward, seeing them so deeply entrenched in our daily lives?" Ikenga's voice was above a whisper.

Amadioha's eyes glinted, and for a moment, Ikenga thought he saw raw, unfiltered pain in their depths, a glimpse into the unhealed wound still festering in his heart. "Who said anything about getting over it?" Amadioha asked. "Every morning, I wake to the same haunting reality, the knowledge that my brother's killers walk free, as Vodun thrives from our work and labor. Some days, I can push it to the back of my mind and focus on the present. But others... the anger burns in my heart. I have tried to bury it, but the seeds have sprouted, becoming an overgrown forest."

Amadioha's story, true or not, was too heavy to bear. Ikenga felt a weight pressing on his chest until he struggled to breathe. The walls of the Luminary closed in around him, the once spacious room suffocating and claustrophobic. Ikenga mumbled an excuse, his words tumbling out in a rushed, incoherent jumble. He turned on his heel and hurried outside.

Chief Amobi Umoren's funeral was the most significant event Niri had seen that year, drawing high-profile guests from all corners of the nation and neighboring Orisha. Over three hundred mourners, a sea of shadowed faces and muted tones, filled the vast space behind the Luminary. Some stood in solitary contemplation, their eyes distant and thoughtful, while others engaged in hushed, reverent conversations.

The lush field of vibrant green grass beneath Ikenga's feet gradually gave way to fine, soft sand on his right, each grain shimmering under the sun's touch. The gentle gradient melted into the boundless, rhythmic embrace of the ocean, its waves singing a mournful lullaby. As he gazed across the meeting of grass, sand, and sea, he breathed, taking in the scents of wet sand and seaweed intermingling with burning incense.

Near the entrance of the Luminary, a group of women dressed in traditional black-and-red attire performed a slow, rhythmic dance. Their movements embodied the sorrow and grief permeating the atmosphere. Painted intricate white patterns, symbolizing the transition between life and death, covered their faces. Their mournful chant rose and fell, carried by the gentle breeze.

Further away, Utaka, his cousin, presented a formidable figure, arms crossed over his barrel-like chest, his face a stoic mask, betraying no emotion. However, the minute movements of his eyes revealed a depth of unspoken thoughts as he engaged in conversation with Moremi Nago.

Moremi pushed a stray lock of her dark hair away from her face, her skin glowing under the sun's glare. Though not tall, her presence was commanding, the defined lines of her shoulders conveying a quiet strength.

She turned to Ikenga, her features softening into a gentle smile. "How are you holding up, my love? I can't imagine how this feels for you."

"I have not had the chance to feel anything... not yet. It is like a bad dream." Ikenga's voice floated on the edge of numbness.

"Perhaps better that way," Utaka said, uncrossing his arms.

Moremi narrowed her eyes at Utaka. A flash of scorn crossed her face before she softened her gaze back toward Ikenga. "I am here for you." She wrapped her arms around his neck as she kissed him. "We will get through this together."

Together.

Her last word lingered in Ikenga's mind. A tingle surged from his belly, overwhelming him with unprocessed emotions. *If it hadn't been for Ijele, I don't know how I would have survived.* Amadioha's words repeated in his mind.

"Now that I have my late father's *Esi*, maybe your parents will see us differently," Ikenga said.

"Your father passed his Esi to you?" Moremi's brows arched in surprise.

"Yes, just a few weeks ago. I wanted to share the news in person, but I didn't realize it would be under these circumstances."

A broad smile spread across her face. Her fingers traced the lines of worry on his forehead.

"Ikenga Umoren!" The call from the harried funeral organizer interrupted their conversation. "Your mother needs you inside."

I hope Amadioha is not still there. "In a moment," Ikenga replied, sharper than intended.

"Go ahead." Moremi's tone still carried a hint of joy. "I will tell my father the news."

"Not today." Ikenga lowered his gaze. "Not here."

"Of course. That was insensitive of me. Whenever you are ready." Moremi kissed Ikenga again before leaving with a gleeful skip in her step.

Not far away, Nago Sango, an imposing figure noticeably larger than Utaka, stood with Moremi's three brothers. For a brief second, they locked eyes, although Ikenga quickly averted his gaze.

"A lie can take care of the present, but it has no future," Utaka said, interrupting Ikenga's thoughts.

How can he know? "Today is not a day for riddles," Ikenga said, faking confusion in his expression.

"Do not treat me like a fool, cousin," Utaka said, his tone firm but restrained.

"At my father's funeral? What are you accusing me of?"

"A sin of which any doubt is gone."

Ikenga grabbed Utaka's shoulder and pulled him close. "Lower your voice before someone hears us."

"You cannot avoid telling her the truth."

"Do you want to know the truth? Nago Sango would never allow me to marry his daughter without the Esi."

"You will bear that cross now or later when it weighs heavier." Utaka's tone was flat, almost nonchalant.

"My mother and sister are broken. I am broken." Ikenga's voice cracked. "I am fatherless." Releasing Utaka, he turned his gaze to Moremi, who was conversing with her father.

If it hadn't been for Ijele, I don't know how I would have survived. Amadioha's words rang again in his head. "You would let me lose the last thing I have left."

"You cannot lose what you do not have."

"Once I take my place at the head of the Anwasi council, nothing will stop my marriage to Moremi."

"Today is a day of sorrow and grief. If you tell her you lied now, she can understand you are not in your right mind."

But I will lose her if I tell her! I can't lose her! "No. I have no choice," Ikenga insisted, his jaw tightening as he glanced at Moremi again. He balled his fists at his sides, shaking his head. "I have no choice," he repeated, his voice barely a whisper.

Utaka shook his head. "Even the sun has a choice of whether to rise in the early morning. Chief Amobi Umoren was a great man. Do not tarnish his memory."

But the sun has no choice in the matter! I have never seen it do anything different!

Fresh grass and blooming wildflowers filled the air. Ikenga and Moremi lay side by side in the vast field, the night sky a canvas of glittering stars. Ikenga sought Moremi's hands, their fingers intertwining, the warmth of her touch sending a pleasant shiver down his spine.

She's my everything.

"Do you remember the first time we met?" His eyes fixed on the celestial display above.

"You were so nervous, stumbling over your words," Moremi said.

He grinned, turning his head to gaze at her. "Southside berry, love you very," he whispered, reciting the lines of the first poem they wrote together. "Melting on tongue, flowing down, tasting like cherry."

"Just like our first kiss," she murmured, her fingertips grazing his cheek. "I remember the sweetness lingering on my lips."

"What I remember is me wanting to court you and you refusing. You said your father would not be happy about you marrying someone from Niri."

"Eastside chocolate, this love I feel belate," she continued. "This slowness, un-acting, waiting, what you may think is hate."

"That was one of the few things I was hoping you would be mistaken about," Ikenga said.

"My father has come round."

Ikenga sighed. "He fought against Niri during the Niri-Orisha war."

"That was many years ago. Before even our time."

But the scars of the past run deep. "It is well known he was against the peace agreement. It was only signed because your grandfather was king of Orisha."

Moremi snuggled closer to him. The scent of her hair, a delicate blend of jasmine and lavender, filled Ikenga's nostrils. "Let's focus on the beauty of our words," she whispered. "I like the next part best."

They continued their poem together. "Northside scent, on this love, our heart is bent. Oh, God, give us this sin. We promise we shall not repent. From the clouds, our hearts descent to the ground, the floor, the meadows. This union, our will intent."

Moremi's eyes sparkled with a memory as the gentle breeze carried the distant sound of music. "Remember our first dance?"

"How could I forget the disapproval on your father's face as he watched us, his eyes cold and unforgiving?" A wistful smile tugged at the corners of Ikenga's mouth. "He despises me because my lineage needs an Esi to wield powerful magic."

"Your lineage has ruled the Anwasi council for many decades."

But for how much longer? "And our numbers dwindle with each failed transfer from father to son."

"But you have your father's. That is all that matters," she said and kissed his cheek. "I want to hear more of this poem."

You cannot lose what you do not have. Utaka's words rang in Ikenga's ears. But he couldn't tell her the truth. *Not now.* "Westside river, glistening in the sunlight. When I don't see you, I can feel the shiver. And then, with your touch, a quiver. This queen, this angel, this diva, forever by my side."

"The way you held me, the way our bodies moved in perfect harmony... it was like the world disappeared, and it was just you and me, lost in the music and each other's embrace."

Ikenga's fingers lingered on Moremi's smooth skin. "At the north, we put this forth. On to the south, without a doubt. In the east, for a lifetime at least. And the west... good, better, best."

"Our love has taken us in every direction," Moremi whispered, her breath warm against his cheek. "And through it all, we've grown stronger, our bond unbreakable."

This is where I belong: in her arms, forever. Ikenga cupped her face, his lips meeting hers in a tender kiss. The sweet and intoxicating taste of her filled his senses. As they parted, he rested his forehead against hers, their breathing mingling with the gentle rustling of the grass beneath them.

∽

IKENGA'S FOOTSTEPS echoed through the hallowed halls of the Luminary as he headed to his father's old office.

The Luminary went beyond being a place of magic; it was the beating heart of Niri's mystical world. The council members, chosen from among the most powerful and skilled magicians in the land, served as advisers to the many Ezes, offering guidance on economic and military matters. Because the ruling Eze's usually did not agree in most matters, the council's wisdom and foresight were critical in steering Niri through countless challenges over the years.

The Luminary's influence, however, reached far beyond simple counsel. Very few people had an affinity for magic; even fewer wielded it well enough to do anything useful. The Luminary was a place of learning where those with a natural ability for magic could hone their skills under the guidance of the most experienced practitioners.

As Ikenga approached his father's office, his mind filled with dreams of the future. He imagined being sworn in as the leader. Among the esteemed guests, Moremi's father would bear witness. Regardless of how he felt about Niri, he would not say no when Ikenga asked for his daughter's hand in marriage.

But when Ikenga opened the door and found someone else seated in his father's chair, he was shocked. Dozie Kena, another council member, looked at him with a neutral expression, his hands folded on the desk before him. He had a striking presence. He wore a deep blue kaftan embroidered with intricate gold patterns, cinched at the waist by a matching sash, over his tall, lean frame.

"What are you doing in my father's seat?" Ikenga demanded.

Dozie stood, greeting Ikenga with a respectful bow. "You don't know?"

"Know what?" Ikenga asked, his brow furrowing in confusion.

"Your ascension to the head of the council is being challenged," a voice said behind him.

Ikenga spun to see the Keeper of the Luminary standing in the doorway, his ancient eyes fixed on Ikenga with a piercing gaze.

"Challenged? By whom?" Ikenga asked, his heart pounding in his chest.

"By the council," the Keeper said. "Dozie will serve as a placeholder until we resolve the matter."

Ikenga's world spun out of control. *This can't be happening. Not now.* "This is an insult to my father's memory. How dare you tarnish his legacy like this?"

Dozie glanced at the Keeper, who nodded. Then he reached behind the desk and pulled out a piece of paper.

"It was your father's wish," he said, holding out the paper.

Ikenga snatched it and scanned the words written in his father's hand. The authenticity was undeniable, but the letter's contents left Ikenga in shock.

It called for a challenge to Ikenga's ascension to ensure someone genuinely dedicated to serving Niri would lead the council. *Genuinely dedicated? What does that mean?*

Ikenga's mind raced as he considered the implications of his father's words. He had no Esi, and he would never win a challenge. *You will bear that cross now or later when it weighs heavier.* Utaka's words rang in his head. "You can't do this. It's my birthright, my destiny."

The Keeper narrowed his eyes. "Birthright?" he asked. "The council exists to serve Niri, not you. Your father had the clear understanding that you lack."

Ikenga opened his mouth to protest, but the Keeper cut him off with a wave.

"How many council meetings have you missed in recent years?" the Keeper asked. "How active have you been in the Luminary's affairs? When was the last time you set foot in this building before your father's funeral?"

Ikenga's cheeks burned with shame. He couldn't answer the Keeper's questions because the truth was damning.

"You spend more time with that Orisha girl than you do with your people," the Keeper continued. "Is that the leader we need? Someone who puts his desires above the needs of his nation?"

The words stung like a slap across the face, and Ikenga found himself unable to respond. The Keeper was right, as much as he hated to admit it.

"The challenge will take place in two weeks," the Keeper said, his tone softening slightly. "Prove your worth, and you may yet lead us. But we will do what is best for Niri, even if that means having someone else at our helm."

~

"Fourth Purgatory," Ikenga said to the back of Utaka's motionless body. "Take me there. Please." His voice carried a weight of determination that made the silence after echo with unspoken urgency.

Utaka's compound showcased his grit and craft. It wasn't merely the house's size that awed Ikenga, but the understanding that his cousin's hands had shaped and placed every stone block. Two doors, double the height of the tallest man in Omoron, hung open at the back of the compound, allowing a peek inside the magnanimous property. Utaka had stained the doors yellow and made the material with a unique mix of elements he had created in fire. It was so rugged and durable that the Omoron military had replicated it in their army's weapons and shields. Massive panes of glass on the second floor exposed the indoor plants, blending seamlessly with the external foliage. A Forest bordered the back of the house, giving him maximum privacy.

"No," Utaka said. He sat cross-legged in the grass. Patterned tattoos covered his torso. His hand moved slowly, cutting through the air in circular motions. A mesmerizing ball of pure white flame swelled and shrank, dancing in harmony with the rhythm of his gestures. A dull, red glow emanated from the tattoos on his back, pulsing in synchrony with the ebb and flow of his muscles. Though his arms conducted the fiery ballet, his rejection echoed with a hushed intensity that seemed meant for Ikenga's ears alone.

"I need to go," Ikenga pleaded.

"I heard you the first time," Utaka said. "And I think you—"

"The council is challenging my ascension." It was the painful truth Ikenga had just come to accept.

Utaka turned to him, causing the white flame to flicker and morph into a fleeting yellow hue before fading away. Untangling his legs, he rose to his feet. "Why would they do that and go against your father's name?" he said as he edged toward Ikenga.

Ikenga held his hand out, motioning for him to stop. "We have little time."

Utaka stopped and gazed at Ikenga. "Cousin, I—"

"It was my father's wish. He did not think I was fit to take his place." Ikenga shook as he spoke. He had built up anger against his father since he had learned it from the other council members. But voicing the words, giving them form and life, multiplied the plain and brought it into the landscape of his reality.

Utaka took a deep breath, and his chest expanded. Despite their lifelong familiarity, his cousin's imposing presence unnerved Ikenga. With a step forward, Utaka gently lowered Ikenga's pointed finger and replaced it with a comforting hand on his shoulder. An immediate sense of relief washed over Ikenga as if the touch had unlocked a hidden valve, allowing his pent-up distress to flow freely.

"Nwanne, I am sorry." Utaka's gaze lowered. "But now is the time to grieve."

"My mother brought me into this world." Bitterness laced Ikenga's voice. "My father did not carry me. In his last moments, I wonder if he regretted his failure of a son... one without the drive he expected. I have no need to grieve."

"What does that have to do with Fourth Purgatory?" Utaka asked.

"My father always said our ability to absorb an Esi made our family powerful."

"No. No." Utaka furrowed his brow as realization dawned over him. "He must have also told you why those before us didn't conjure new spirits?"

Ikenga sighed. "I know it has risks."

"Risks? It's outright dangerous!" Utaka exclaimed. "You have barely mastered the basics of your limited magic, and now you want to summon a new Esi?"

Ikenga fell silent, the gravity of his choice weighing on him. Then, with a resolute nod, he reached into his pouch and withdrew a collection of weathered papers. "I must," he insisted, pushing them closer to Utaka.

Utaka's brow furrowed. "What is this?"

"The summoning ritual."

Utaka's eyes widened in disbelief. "Where did you get this?"

"At the Luminary," Ikenga said, his gaze shifting to the horizon. "An Observer said my father asked him to give it to me."

Utaka let out a mocking laugh. "An Observer? Why would your father trust anything to a Vodunese?"

Ikenga shrugged, a hint of uncertainty in his eyes. "He wouldn't," he admitted. "The man was probably lying, but his intentions seemed genuine."

"Never trust a man from Vodun. If there is one lesson Chief Amobi Umoren taught you and me, it is that."

"Look at it," Ikenga urged, gesturing to the papers. "I had them dated. They are authentic."

Reluctantly, Utaka took the papers and examined them. As he read, his expression shifted from skepticism to grudging acknowledgment. "Hmm," he mused, his brow furrowed in concentration. "They are consistent with my limited understanding."

"We have to try."

"In Fourth Purgatory, though?"

Ikenga nodded. "I know it's dangerous, but it's also far away from prying eyes. What would it mean for many others in our line if we pulled this off? The magic we would yield... the influence our families have would grow again."

"Since when did you care about bloodlines and influence? You only care about Moremi."

Ikenga shook his head, his expression hardening. "I don't. I admit it. But you do."

"I have never seen you demand something like this," Utaka said, "and your newfound fervor worries me."

"Nago Sango's ill will toward Niri is deep. Even if I somehow win the challenge to the council, once he knows I did not get my father's Esi, he will have enough reason to stop me from... stop me from..." Ikenga threw his hands in the air. "I need this because of Moremi."

"Nago Sango cares about status, not magic," Utaka declared. "If the council accepts you, it would be illogical for him to block the marriage."

"Usually, we would be at opposite ends of this conversation."

"Perhaps I have gotten wiser, and you have gone in a different direction," Utaka smirked.

"No one knows what is in Fourth Purgatory. The historical texts disagree with the official records."

"Precisely the reason we should not go," Utaka shot back.

"It is the only solution I have. I have to try something."

"We could die, or worse, get caught. It would not just be us who would suffer the consequences. Our loved ones..." Utaka's voice faltered.

"She is my heart," Ikenga whispered. "If I lose her, I lose everything."

A rare expression of hurt crossed Utaka's face.

"I did not mean it like that," Ikenga said. "You know you are my family, too." Ikenga's eyes were heavy. "Fourth Purgatory is the only place I can do this. I could be the most powerful council member if we find the right spirit. I would go from a big inconvenience for Nago Sango to a desired suitor for his daughter."

"What are the classes of fire?" Utaka asked.

Ikenga bristled at the question. "I am not a child."

"Then tell me. What are they?" Utaka insisted as he narrowed his eyes.

"Yellow, red, blue, white, black," Ikenga said. He hated it when Utaka treated him like a child.

"There is a reason the fire from your hands blows red and mine blows white, isn't there? You are not ready for something like this. A transfer takes a tamed spirit from one vessel to another. Comparing that to a summoning is like comparing riding a horse to Navigation."

"Yet the first time I asked you what it was like to Navigate, you said it was like taking a journey on a swift animal." Ikenga surveyed Utaka's body language. He was warming up to the idea, but it was a fine line to walk with this man. You could lose the conversation forever if you pushed too much. "You would be the first Navigator alive to go there," he said, using Utaka's pride to convince him.

"And I would have a secret that no one would know!" Utaka said.

"We would know!"

The tattoos on Utaka's torso pulsed between dull and bright red. That happened when he was excited.

"Moremi cannot know." Ikenga mustered laughable confidence in his voice.

Utaka raised his brow. "You are going to do this and not tell the person you are risking both of our lives for?"

"If she knows, she will not let me go."

"And around here, people think I am the one who is mad." Utaka sat in his original spot and crossed his legs again. He moved his hands in fluid motions as a white fireball emerged in the space before him.

It was Utaka's way of saying yes. Ikenga turned and hiked through the open grass field before his cousin changed his mind. The walls of Utaka's house appeared to bend toward him as he walked away—as if to probe him and ask why he had unsettled their master.

~

Chief Amobi Umoren's journal: Reflections on my son

The weight of the day's events sits heavy on my shoulders as I pen these words. Amadioha Kamanu stood before the council today, seeking guidance on his quest for vengeance against Vodun. The meeting was tense, yet I found myself marveling at the young man before us.

The fire in his eyes, the conviction in his voice, the strategic mind behind his words - all of it spoke of a leader born, not made. As I watched him articulate his position and consider our counsel, a familiar ache bloomed in my chest. An ache born of pride in this remarkable young man, and of deep, gnawing regret for what my own son is not.

I remember as if it were yesterday when Amadioha and Ikenga were born. Amadioha's father and I had such hopes and dreams for our boys. Where did I go wrong with Ikenga?

My son. My flesh and blood. The heir to my legacy. And yet, he seems content to fritter away his days, showing no interest in the responsibilities that should be his birthright. The seat I have held for him on the council remains empty. I knew, in my heart of hearts, that he wasn't ready for such a position. But I hoped... oh, how I hoped that the weight of the role would awaken something in him; that he would rise to the challenge and grow into the leader Niri needs.

Instead, he chooses to spend his time with that Orisha girl, Moremi. I have nothing against love. But there is a time and place for everything, and Ikenga seems blind to the needs of his people.

Why can't he be more like Amadioha? The question haunts me, keeping me awake in the dark hours of the night. Where Amadioha shows drive, Ikenga shows apathy. Where Amadioha seeks to serve, Ikenga seeks to avoid.

I find myself wondering what I could have done differently. Did I push too hard? Not hard enough? Was I too stern, too unyielding? Or perhaps too lenient, allowing him to shirk his duties without consequence? The questions plague me, each one a thorn in my side.

4
ESHM

*I*kenga grappled with the emotions warring within him. The raw ache of his father's death loomed over him like a dark cloud. Then there was the helplessness and sadness. A piece of him was being ripped apart by the chance of losing Moremi. Mixed with the fear and guilt was a strange sense of relief—perhaps, deep down, he believed he did not deserve her. He could forgive himself when she was gone as long as he kept trying, even if he failed. Yet, another feeling lingered on the periphery of his mind, one that started after they had Navigated to Fourth Purgatory. It toyed with him, elusive and faint, never strong enough for him to fully grasp it.

"What are you doing?" Utaka's voice woke him from his thoughts.

It was night, or it was day. There had been a constant feeling of dusk since they had arrived. Ikenga's gaze locked on the distant whiteness. The whipping wind, combined with the monotonous view, entranced him. The atmosphere refracted the light off the snowflakes, giving the forest a surreal, blue glow. And the snow blanketed everything—rocks, stems, and the forest floor. It blurred the paths, making every direction indistinguishable. As Ikenga returned to reality, so did his other senses. The cold made the hairs on his back stand straight. His triple-layered jacket was woefully inadequate against the bitter weather they had underestimated. He had to conserve his magic; otherwise, he would not last long.

"Someone is following us." Ikenga finally translated his feelings into words.

Utaka looked at him in confusion.

"I think someone else is here."

"You think?" Utaka's voice carried, slicing through the wind's muffled roar.

"We should make sure we are—"

"Don't tell me you are getting cold feet, son of Umoren. The place for that was when you came to my home to disturb my peace."

"Yes, my feet are cold. I do not have magic tattoos keeping me warm."

"Koca ci!" Utaka cursed as his eyes flashed white for a brief second. "I swear on Chineke's name, if you—"

"If I am right. You know what that means." Ikenga shivered.

Utaka's gaze swept over their surroundings. The snow was falling so fast that it already covered their footsteps. With a sky devoid of stars or moons, it was a miracle Utaka knew where they were going. He swore under his breath again and took a couple of steps backward.

A branch, snapped by the wind's force, fell near Utaka. He ignored it as he kneeled and buried his hand in the snow. Within seconds, the snow melted into a pool of water before sizzling and evaporating. As the gas escaped, it crystallized back into ice, falling around the edges and creating a miniature canyon encircling his kneeling form. He closed his eyes and remained still.

A drop of sweat traveled down Ikenga's back, followed by a shiver.

"They are moving fast." Utaka's face stayed down.

A wave of relief washed over Ikenga, brief but profound. He'd been right—Utaka would spare him his scorn. But nervousness soon clouded his triumph. "Who is it?"

"They are hiding from me." Utaka raised his hand from the ground and stepped back into the snow. The melted water quickly froze into ice.

"Niri or Orisha could have sent them. We cannot kill them." Ikenga's breathing intensified.

A glimmer of fear flashed in Utaka's eyes, and his tattoos ignited with a fierce, red glow. "No Navigator in Kirina could have followed us here. Not through the path I took."

"Unless…" Ikenga started.

"It's something that was already here," they said together.

"One of us is going to die. We decide now if it will be it or us," Utaka said.

A sinking guilt gnawed at Ikenga. "We can capture it. Find out more information. Then decide what to do later."

Utaka let out an astonished laugh. "I have known you for most of my life. And never have I once thought you a fool. But now I sway in a different direction." He grabbed his twin daggers from the back of his belt and refastened them in front of him. When the snow touched their tips, it sizzled and evaporated before turning to ice crystals again and falling to the ground.

Ikenga met Utaka's gaze, his eyes betraying his defeat.

"Over there." Utaka pointed ahead, where the rocks were high enough that their peaks stood above the snow. "I will create a trail past them and around those trees. You will stay hidden behind it. When it passes, you will make one straight swipe through its neck." Utaka paused. "If you miss, our fate is in the hands of Chineke."

Ikenga reached over his shoulder and gripped the sheath of his sword, Formless. As he pulled out the weapon, his fingers brushed the words etched into its base. *For our ancestors, those alive today, and those not yet born.* He had not been born when the words were written. He internalized them, recreating his bond with his weapon. Its blade reflected the blue diffused light, refracting off the snow. He welcomed the handle's warmness.

"I am sorry I brought you here," he said.

Utaka scowled and turned from him. "You are a dark cloud that blocks the sun. But the sun is a yellow dagger." Utaka cracked his knuckles as he spoke. "On your seventh birthday, that voodoo witch, the one from whatever city it was in Vodun, she read my palm and told me this." He turned back to face Ikenga. "I understand her words better now than I did then." He grabbed Ikenga's forearm and pulled him close.

The heat from Utaka's body and the smell of roasted charcoal from his breath made Ikenga shiver in fear. Ikenga was not a daredevil when he was young, but he had always thought he was not afraid to die. The trepidation that traveled deep inside his bones now made him doubt that. *I curse you, Father, Chief Umoren. I curse you for allowing me to be what I am today. You should have pushed me and made me a better man.*

~

IKENGA SPOTTED his reflection in the ice on the ground. He had been in the world for over two-and-a-half decades, but only saw a scared little boy looking back. He re-sheathed Formless and kicked away the snow next to him, exposing the forest floor. Fingers numb with cold, he retrieved a jagged rock and clenched it. *What if the thing coming for us is not our enemy?* It was a stupid thought, but he had never killed before and did not want to start.

He closed his eyes and focused on the oncoming danger. It was close enough that he sensed each step it took toward them. It resonated in his ears, stretching seconds into agonizing minutes. When it drew nearer, just ten steps away, he plotted a surprise attack, aiming to knock it out with the rock before Utaka returned. With a tighter grip on the rock, he opened his eyes.

Eight steps.

Shifting toward the path, he half-crouched and brought his right leg on its tiptoe.

Six steps.

His muscles coiled like a spring. He drew his arm back, poised to strike. As if sensing the imminent conflict, the snow swirled fiercely around him. Beads of sweat, indistinguishable from the melting snowflakes, traced paths down his face. His heart slowed as he awaited the next step, but it never came. He strained his ears harder but heard nothing.

"Koca ci!"

Releasing the taut strings of his mind, Ikenga allowed the natural chorus of snow and wind to filter back in. A rustle from behind spiked his adrenaline. Rapid footsteps encircled him from left to rear, a predator's dance. He swung his hand and threw the rock without looking as he rotated his torso. Their pursuer was sizably shorter than him, wearing a long cape with the hood up. It moved quickly, dodging the projectile with ease.

With determined strides, Ikenga advanced. He drew Formless from his back, the blade whispering through the air when he lunged forward. But his adversary, a shadow in motion, twisted elegantly, evading the weapon's deadly kiss. Within a fraction of a moment, it was right next to him. A quick elbow to his neck and torso disoriented him. Through the haze of pain, Ikenga glimpsed the silhouette leaping skyward. It spun with a blur of movement, extending a leg in a graceful arc that culminated in a thunderous kick to his forehead. The impact of its foot felt like an iron rod. He flew backward, his grip on Formless failing as it fell and disappeared into the snow.

A shiver of cold laced with searing pain radiated through Ikenga as he crashed into the snow's embrace. Gritting his teeth, he shook his head, banishing the blur from his eyes, only to see his attacker's looming figure descending upon him with relentless fury. It straddled him as its fist flew at his head. Bracing for the hit, he threw his arms up in defense. A blistering pain shot through him as the blow splintered his wrist. He grabbed its hand and wrenched it closer to him. With his half-broken hand, he planted the root of his palm just below its neck. It shrieked as it tumbled off him.

That sounded like a woman. He squeezed his wrist and scanned the ground for Formless. *No time to find it.* He returned his gaze to his attacker.

The battle had stripped off its hood, revealing a face of smooth, youthful skin surreal in its innocence. Her eyes, deep pools of brown encased in starkly defined lines, sent a ripple of shock through Ikenga's heart. Her hair was thick and long, pulled back into a bun.

"Moremi?" His eyes darted around, but they were alone. "What are you doing here?"

She tried to talk, but only a cough and a wheeze escaped her mouth. He raised both hands and hurried to her side to help her.

Utaka erupted from the forest, a living inferno. Flames wreathed his torso, dancing wildly as if alive, casting a fierce, primal glow on the snow-covered surroundings. He landed in a fighting stance with both daggers drawn. The ice below him melted quickly as the water on the ground boiled. The same shocked expression that covered Ikenga's face traveled to Utaka. Moremi was on the ground, still struggling to breathe.

~

THE FLAMES DANCED near Ikenga's face, their warmth grazing his skin before retreating to the fire's heart. They reached up, nearly touching the ice-clad ceiling. Water droplets hissed and evaporated into steam, twirling into the cold air as shimmering ice crystals encircled the fire. Utaka, who had kindled it, stared intently, his presence as unpredictable as the flames. The fire's glow cast deep shadows under Moremi's eyes, tracing fatigue lines across her face. She sat next to him, avoiding his gaze.

Ikenga reached out and squeezed her shoulder. She recoiled like his touch burned, scooting away and casting a shadow of rejection over him. "You can't avoid this conversation forever. Look around; we are miles from everything familiar." He swept his hands across the dimly lit cave, emphasizing their isolation. "Is this really how you choose to handle things now?"

She shifted again and turned her gaze to the other side of the cave. They had taken cover inside because the snow had become sleet, and the temperatures had dropped even more.

"I am the one who should be upset here." Ikenga raised his hands and kicked a rock into the fire. The flames became excited as the ice on the rock evaporated. He stole a look at Utaka. The dull red of his tattoos had faded slightly, and they were primarily black. But he kept a stoic expression.

"You promised... you swore you'd never lie to me," Moremi said.

She spoke! Ikenga glanced at her. For the first time that day, their eyes connected. "I didn't."

"Make sure the next words that leave your mouth are the truth."

"I never meant to deceive you," Ikenga murmured, his words weighed down by regret and helplessness. It was a dance they often did—her leading, him stumbling. "It wasn't my intention."

"For nearly three years, I shared my heart with a man I thought I knew." Moremi's voice cracked. "Now, when I look at him, it is like staring at a stranger."

Ikenga flung his hand in the air, exasperated. "If you did not know the man you shared your heart with, how did you find your way here?"

"I want the truth. Tell me now!"

He took a silent gulp of air and tried to buy himself time, fishing for words. The lies he'd recently told her whirled in his head, but he wasn't sure which truth she sought.

"Your father." More tears fell from her eyes. "He did not pass his Esi to you. You looked into my face and told me differently."

A dose of relief traveled through him, and then a tight knot formed in his stomach. *She was brilliant. She was smart. But how could she have figured it out?* He thought she had just followed them blindly. However, he was not sure how she had done that either. "How did you find out?"

"You lied to me," Moremi said between sobs. She turned her eyes back to the fire.

Ikenga stood and moved toward her, but she raised her hand, stopping him. His chest ached like she had just stabbed him with a sword.

"If Nago Sango found out my father did not pass his Esi, he would never let me marry you."

"I am not Nago Sango!"

"It is more his decision than yours!"

"You would want to marry me. Yet you cannot trust me."

"I feared... I was afraid you'd see me as a lesser man," he admitted, averting his gaze.

"You are a lesser man for lying to me! We could have found another way."

"Always so idealistic!"

"We could go to Aksum, Abisina, anywhere." Lines of tension creased her forehead as she gazed down.

He was talking to a rock. "He would pursue us to Kirina's furthest reaches and hunt me with relentless fury." Ikenga steadied his trembling hands, striving for calmness. "Imagine that life, Moremi. Imagine the shadow we would cast over our future, our children's lives."

"You could have told me the truth."

"You must know why we came here."

"After three years. This? How can I trust you anymore?"

"I didn't tell you because you would follow us if I did. I would never put the woman I love at risk. I would never do that to you."

"And what are the third, fourth, and fifth reasons you will give me? What if you came here and never returned? What if you died? I would never have known what happened to you."

"What if I had stayed? What would the point of being alive be if we could not be together?" His eyes fell to the ground as his body slumped.

Utaka shot up from his seat. He had the stoic, blank expression he usually had when suppressing his feelings. The flames danced more as he stepped into it and approached them. They flickered off him and dissipated as he stepped out of it.

"Do you grasp the gravity of where we stand?" He pointed at Moremi. "Do you think you are in your father's castle in Orisha? All you have done since you came here has caused us problems."

"That's enough," Ikenga said, taking a small step toward Moremi.

"I wasn't talking to you!" Utaka's voice elevated. "Your boyfriend here was supposed to slice off the head of our pursuer, not attack it with a rock. What do you think the retribution from the most vengeful man in Orisha would have been? His incompetence is the only reason you can fill his ears with complaints."

"Her head is still attached to her body," Ikenga said. He tried to maintain his posture, but he shifted. "If you are mad, direct it at me."

"Mad?" Utaka said. "We would be done by now if she hadn't shown up. I would be mapping the path through the Abyss home. Instead, I am listening to you two babbling about 'trust me, trust you.' By Chineke! Mad is an understatement." His voice reverberated through the cave. Chunks of snow dropped from the surrounding ceiling.

Moremi chuckled under her breath, then belted out a full laugh. Utaka and Ikenga both turned to her in shock.

"Did I say something amusing?" Utaka asked, bewilderment flashing in his eyes.

"I'm sorry." She laughed again. She was good at goading Utaka, but her timing made Ikenga nervous.

"You said you would have been done by now. I couldn't help but see how you have been traveling in the wrong direction since you got here."

"Nonsense," Utaka said. "You have no idea where we are going."

"Our shadows are supposed to follow the wind," she said.

Utaka's eyes darkened, and he took an intimidating step. His heat was overwhelming. Ikenga hastily shed his sheepskin jacket, letting it fall onto a nearby log, sweat dripping from his brow.

"How did you get here, anyway?" Utaka sneered. "From what I understand, you are a novice Navigator. Even local jumps would be difficult for you."

"By following your Noise," she said. "I suspected you both were planning to come here. I just had to know when you left."

"You followed my Noise through the Abyss? Impossible!" Utaka said.

"Navigating through the Abyss is also impossible! Yet here you are," Moremi countered.

"Even I could not follow a Navigator's Noise through that path."

"And because you cannot do something? It means I cannot?! You're—"

"Enough!" Ikenga said. "Both of you! All we have is ourselves. We must stick together."

Utaka hissed. "I will not manifest an Esi with the daughter of Nago Sango anywhere nearby. He will not stop with us in his quest for retribution if anything goes wrong. She could have died coming here without us knowing. Even that would not have mattered to him. Our lives are at stake just by her presence."

Ikenga glanced away for a second as he digested Utaka's words. "Is she right?"

"Did you listen to anything I just said?" Utaka barked.

"Is she right? About the shadows?"

"No! I mean, maybe. I don't know. I am the first Navigator to travel here in recent times, and I am sure I can figure it out."

"We have been traveling for two hours. It would take us two more to reach where we started," Ikenga said as Moremi smirked. "We bolster our defenses and reinforce every binding. I will bear the brunt of the risk. At the first sign of danger, we retreat, no arguments."

"Absolutely not," Utaka said. "Not with the daughter of Nago Sango."

"I can take care of myself!"

Utaka raised his brow, and a subtle smirk played upon his lips. "Your naivete surpasses your looks. And trust me... that is a high bar to cross."

"Your incompetence outweighs your ugliness. That bar is very low!"

Ikenga did everything in his power to hold back a laugh. But a smile still materialized on his lips.

Utaka growled as fire flared in his eyes. "What did you say, woman?" A flame danced at the tip of his pointed finger.

Moremi clenched her fists, and they turned a metallic gray.

Ikenga raised his hands and stepped between them. "She has

nowhere to go. We can find the Esi together or return to Kirina empty-handed. Together."

Utaka's lips curled into a grimace. "For the sake of all of us..." He focused on Ikenga as he grabbed his hand and pulled him close. "She had better be worth it. Whatever you feel, whatever you think you will feel in the future, none of that is worth the price we will pay if this fails." He flicked Ikenga away and gathered his things as he exited the cave.

What if he is right?

The thought of losing Moremi dwarfed the possibility and buried it deep in his mind.

∼

HOURS of meticulous retracing led them to the enigmatic Cave of Souls. As the cave's shadowy mouth greeted them, they realized she had been right all along—they had been venturing off course. The cave, like the other one yet uniquely different, was a panorama of dull, red walls densely covered in markings. Desperate scratches, suggestive of trapped beings' futile attempts to escape, marred the walls. The air reeked of an odd mix of sulfur and citrus, each inhalation an intense assault on Ikenga's senses. The tourniquet wrapped around his bicep made his veins bulge and his arm swell. A small needle drained his blood into a leather flask.

"It's so much." Moremi's gaze dropped.

"Manifesting an Esi is no small feat." *As if this is not my first time doing this.* Ikenga paused as their gaze connected briefly, and she glanced away. "That is why I did not want you to be here. This is why I did not open up to you. We need Utaka's blood for a beacon to draw the Esi to our realm. Once it arrives, mine acts as a magnet, ensuring it comes to me. Without enough blood, the Esi will not anchor." He squeezed her shoulder with his other hand. "The most important thing to me is that both of you stay safe. At the first sign of something going wrong, Utaka will immediately reverse the process, and we will leave. And if anything happens to me, you can say I ran away from my home because of my grief."

"Don't say that." She focused on the bucket. "Nothing is going to happen to you."

Near them, Utaka used a cloth soaked with his blood to mark intricate inscriptions on the cave's floor. His movements were fluid and purposeful, deceptively looking like someone well-versed in the ritual. He painted with an unmistakable air of confidence. It contrasted with the heavy shroud of doubt clouding Ikenga's mind, eroding his resolve.

"We don't have to do this." New tears formed in her eyes. "We must try another way. We can be together with or without this Esi."

Ikenga sighed. "You understand your father's stubbornness more than anyone. He turns a deaf ear to all—be it his council, me, or even you. Without this ritual, my family's standing would crumble. Our future together would be over."

"We can wait." Her voice shook. "We can buy some time until we figure out a way that won't put you at risk. Let's go back. If we cannot find another way, we will come here again."

Ikenga pulled the needle out and dropped it on the floor. "You and Utaka, you both are the ones who matter to me the most in the world." He stepped around the container. "This is the one thing I have been most sure of in my life."

More tears formed in her eyes.

"We have gone through this a thousand times and practiced every situation. We will be safe," he said.

"A thousand times, yet you were both going in the wrong direction when I found you."

"It was a minor mistake."

"The ritual could have a mistake."

"It won't."

"What if it does?"

"There won't be a mistake! There won't be because there can't be!"

"I can't accept it," she cried, growing louder. She rested her head on his shoulder, her hand softly beating against his chest.

Utaka had approached them without either of them noticing. "We have always had our differences," Utaka said softly. "But right now, your words only distract him. To survive this, he needs unwavering focus—nothing else matters." He put a hand on her shoulder. Her head was still on Ikenga, but she softened. It was a rare moment and, for a second, the most peace he had in a while.

She stepped back, her eyes downcast—familiar lines of defeat Ikenga had seen too many times before.

An excitement danced in Utaka's eyes, anticipation he struggled to mask. But Ikenga, as always, saw through the façade. Utaka was as complicit as he was in their current predicament. *If only Utaka had said no to me, we would be in Niri.* Ikenga would have lost everything, but at least they would be safe.

~

A CONTAINER BRIMMING with a mixture of their blood sat ominously in the cave's center. They had painted a red circle around it—a fail-safe to confine the Esi within a defined boundary. Utaka danced around it, his movements seemingly random, his torso twisting and turning in a ritualistic dance. His shoulders rose and fell in rhythm with his undulations. He moved his hands with wild, frenzied movements, as if swatting away a swarm of stinging bees.

Ikenga, striving to mirror Utaka, constantly lagged two frustrating steps behind.

"Listen to my movement," Utaka said as he swayed. "Feel it."

Ikenga focused and tried to shut out everything else. Instead, his balance betrayed him, sending him sprawling face-first onto the ground.

"Koca ci!"

Utaka stopped. He approached Ikenga and extended his hand to help him up. "Remember what we practiced. Follow me with your mind. Not your eyes."

"With my mind." Ikenga nodded.

"Get it together," Utaka said. He glanced at Moremi, who peered hypnotically at them. "Get her out of your mind." Utaka moved away and returned to a more intense rhythm.

Ikenga closed his eyes and focused again. He replayed the patterns in his mind, feeling each one despite Utaka's silent grace. He sensed Utaka's breath, then every motion of his body. The rhythm permeated his senses—a beat and tempo his mind recognized. It engulfed him. Then, it guided him. It willed his knees to move, then his hands and waist. He yielded to it and acquiesced his body to every request. When he finally opened his eyes again, he and Utaka moved in unison. Beneath the chaotic surface of their dance, a strategic method simmered.

"It begins," Utaka declared.

He moved to a new pattern. Ikenga did too. The music was different. He felt it and followed.

Utaka pulled out the daggers fastened at his waist and pointed them outward, invoking a burst of fire that formed a pulsating sphere above the bloody container. With their bodies rooted, they moved their hands as if sculpting an unseen sphere. Under their hypnotic manipulation, the fire twisted, enlarged, and contorted.

Utaka chanted, "All things that have been before will be again. All things dead can rise. Esi, ghost of the past, ghost of the present, I call you to manifest."

The fire glowed slightly brighter. Utaka chanted again, and Ikenga followed along. As the duo continued their spellbound dance, the fire danced along, expanding with every passing moment. The smell of sulfur grew stronger.

"I feel it now," Utaka voiced with excitement. "It's coming." His eyes ignited, a bright white fire blazing within their depths. "Remember everything we practiced for our sake."

His head jolted upward, eyes fixed on the cave's ceiling. It was not part of their dance. There was no rhythm to follow. The intricate tattoos adorning his skin pulsed with a mesmerizing dull-white luminescence. Utaka's body shook. "Esi, ghost of the past, ghost of the present, I call you to manifest," Utaka said. "Manifest yourself!" With each powerful utterance, the ice blanketing the cave floor surrendered to the heat, melting into glistening puddles. A trickle of sweat dripped from his head.

The fire that danced between them blazed brighter, morphing into a dazzling, near-transparent white. The temperature in the room rose.

Utaka shuddered violently. A convulsion ripped through him, forcing him to one knee. "Esi, ghost of the past, ghost of the present, I call you to manifest." His voice echoed across the cave.

The white flame got bigger and burned hotter. Ikenga removed his shirt and retreated.

Utaka, with both hands on the ground, struggled to hold his head up. "Esi, ghost of the past, ghost of the present, I summon you," they both shouted.

A fierce gale tore through the cave, stirring the accumulated puddles and dislodging sharp icicles from the ceiling, which plummeted like hailstones. The brilliant flame slowly coalesced into the shape of a man. Ikenga released a gasp he had been holding in. While the body was almost formless, the face was defined enough to see its expression. A confused look crossed its face as it stared around the cave. Its hollow eyes traveled from Utaka to Ikenga and then to Moremi.

Utaka rose from his crouched position. The cave cooled slightly. "Now!"

Ikenga shut his eyes and reached inward, striving to draw in the Esi. He called it from his head, sensing it in the same way he perceived the tune of their dance and willed it to come to him.

The Esi cast a menacing leer at Ikenga, its form hovering over the cave's floor. It had formed the beginning of legs. The intense stare burned an imaginary hole through Ikenga's chest. It floated closer again, and Ikenga's heart raced. He kept his eyes on it and called to it again. If his heart beat any faster, it would burst from his chest. "Come to me."

"Where am I?" the Esi asked. Its voice reverberated across the entire cave. The wind emanated from where it stood and blew on Ikenga as it spoke.

It wasn't supposed to do that! Ikenga glanced at Utaka. "It talks?"

Utaka shrugged. "It wasn't supposed to."

"Should I respond?" A knot formed in his stomach.

Utaka nodded once.

Ikenga mustered the courage to address the entity. "The Cave of Souls."

The Esi's body transformed from a white flame to a more solid, humanlike figure. "The Cave of Souls," it said. It turned its head to Moremi and then back to Ikenga. "Who has brought me here?"

Ikenga looked at Utaka again.

"Keep engaging," Utaka said, slowly circling the Esi, gripping his daggers tightly.

"Esi of the past. It is I who have brought you here," Ikenga declared.

"For what purpose?"

"I will consume you and combine your energy with my body."

The Esi's laugh was sick and loud. The sound lingered on Ikenga's skin even after it stopped. "I combine with no one!" It turned back to Moremi and moved but stopped short of the circle.

"Venture beyond the circle, and you will be destroyed." Utaka pointed his knife at it as he delivered the stern warning.

It turned toward Utaka. "Who are you?"

"I am Utaka. Son of Ozioma Zika."

"That one lies. Does he not?" the Esi said. "You are the one who brought me here."

Utaka's jaw dropped.

The container of blood emptied, and the Esi took full physical form. Its head and entire body returned to semi-transparent white. The blood vessels under its skin were visible, but not its organs. Its black eyes sunk into its skull.

"You are right, Esi of the night," Utaka said. "I am the one who brought you here. But you will combine with him before this ends."

"Why do you call me Esi?" It swiveled, its semi-transparent form lurching toward Moremi. To their surprise, it moved out of the circle.

What? "What did it just do?" Ikenga asked.

The Eden Ruse

"Call to it! Stronger!" Utaka panicked.

"Esi of the past! Come to me." Ikenga tried to focus and will it closer, but his heart was beating too fast. Every step the Esi took was slow and deliberate, resounding with an eerie calm.

"This is over!" Ikenga said. "Moremi, get out now!" His eyes flared as he chanted the words to reverse the summoning. Utaka followed, and both men shouted at it. The Esi's form manifested further; its ethereal skin solidified into stark white.

"It's not working!" Ikenga said. The cave's temperature had risen so much all the ice had melted.

"Tell me something I don't know!"

In their panicked states, they had not noticed Moremi had not moved from her spot since the Esi had appeared. She was standing straight up with wide-open eyes and a motionless body.

"Do something!" Ikenga shouted.

Utaka pointed his daggers at the Esi. A white flame appeared on the tip and formed a ball in front of him before launching straight at it. The flame went right through it and hit the side of the cave, creating a crater so deep Ikenga could not see the end. The entire cave shook and creaked as if it would collapse. Pieces of rock fell from the ceiling.

It stopped and turned toward Utaka. "You who brought me here? Why do you try to kill me?" It cocked its head to one side.

The edges of Utaka's blades lit again. The Esi's eyes glowed as it shot a burst of black fire out. In one heart-stopping moment, Utaka was engulfed, his figure consumed and reduced to nothingness.

"Nooo!" Ikenga rushed to where Utaka had been standing. He was in a dream he had to wake from. He slapped his head hard, but the gruesome reality continued. "No, no, no, no!" He dropped to his knees. His voice was a raw, jagged edge of confusion and anguish. "What did I do!?" he screamed as tears rolled from his eyes. He glanced at Moremi, who had not even remotely registered what had happened.

"What are you?" Ikenga slumped into the space where his cousin once stood. It stopped advancing toward Moremi and turned to him.

"What am I?" Another sickening laugh followed. "I was born in the beginning and known to the first man and angels. I am Eshm," it said. "I was at peace until you brought me back here. I will make you rue the day you dared to summon me."

A crushing weight settled on Ikenga, his heavy bones pulling him down into despair. He wanted to run toward Moremi, but his legs rooted to the spot.

Eshm issued another laugh, a sound so vile and discordant it curdled the surrounding air. Then it turned back to Moremi and ran toward her, its body turning back into an amorphous blob.

"Moremi!" Ikenga screamed. But she was too far gone. He watched in horror as the thing called Eshm absorbed itself into her.

~

Ikenga's journal: Painful encounter with Moremi's family

The sun had barely set when my world collapsed around me. Moremi and I were walking near the outskirts of Orisha, lost in our own little haven of whispered dreams and stolen glances. Then, like a thunderclap on a clear day, we stumbled upon her father, Nago Sango, and her oldest brother.

The disdain in their eyes... by Chineke, it was a weight so heavy it nearly drove me to my knees. Nago Sango's lip curled in poorly disguised contempt, while her brother's gaze cut through me like a blade. And then, as if the silent judgment wasn't enough, I heard it. A whisper, meant for each other but carried to my ears by a traitorous breeze... I cannot bear to write the words they said here.

Two words. Just two words, and yet they've burrowed into my heart, festering like an open wound. The anger burns hot in my chest, threatening to consume me. How dare they? How dare they look down on me, judge me, when they don't even know me?

I want to leave. To run far away from the judgment, the sneers, the whispered insults. To protect what's left of my battered pride. But the thought of life without Moremi... it is like imagining a world without air. How can I breathe, how can I exist, in a reality where she's not by my side?

Why can't they just like me? The question echoes in my mind. I like them. I respect them. I want nothing more than to be part of their family, to prove my worth to them. I've tried so hard to be polite, to be respectful, to show them the best of who I am. But it's never enough. Never.

Do they not see how their rejection wounds not just me, but Moremi too? I'm lost. Torn between my love for Moremi and the crushing weight of her family's disapproval. Part of me wants to stand tall, to fight for our love, to prove them all wrong. But another part, the part that whispers doubts in the dark of night, wonders if they're right. Am I truly worthy of her?

I don't have the answers. All I know is that I love her. And right now, in this moment of pain and doubt, that has to be enough.

It has to be.

5

RADA MYSTERS

"**Y**ou look like you have not slept since last I saw you." Ofeli slammed his cup onto the table with such force that wine sloshed onto the worn tabletop.

"I haven't." **Papa Legba** mustered a tired smirk that didn't reach his eyes.

Since Legba joined the Mysters, he and Ofeli had grown close. They sat in a secluded corner of a drinking inn near it. Ofeli preferred spending more time far away from the castle with his growing distaste for magic. Legba's face was hollowed out with sunken, deep eyes. He had lost almost all the weight he had gained in his first year here. Ofeli, however, looked like he had gained double the weight Legba had lost. His bald head gleamed, mirroring the shine of his polished armor. The Loa had handsomely rewarded him and Ogou for quelling Ayizan's insurrection.

"Amadioha Kamanu will be here soon. Inviting the enemy onto our doorstep worries me," Legba said.

"Amadioha?" Ofeli let out a weary sigh and drummed his fingers on the table. "Questioning the Loa's strategy is a good way to throw away all the goodwill you have built with her."

"When I first came here, she told me she valued subjects who challenged her."

Ofeli laughed. "Do you know one of the best lessons my father taught me? Beware the boy who cries wolf, for his false alarms erode trust until the day when danger is real and no one believes him."

"Last time, you told me your mother said that."

"My mother, my father, what's the difference?" Ofeli raised his hands in surrender. "Fine. Tell me what your issue is." A cheesy smile crossed his face. "Pretend my face is just as smooth and sexy as the Loa's." He licked his lips comically.

Legba ignored Ofeli's jest and continued, "Amadioha has a lot of respect in Niri—more than I have ever seen. Some say as much as Ojukwu." He wiped his forehead. "Someone with that much influence can be dangerous. His soldiers love and follow him, not us. He is loyal to Niri only, and his men are loyal to him."

"You base this on the one year you spent there before being arrested for deserting?" Ofeli remarked in a sarcastic tone. "You have not been to Niri in over three years."

"A year is enough to know a man," Legba said. "Three years does not change. I was not there when my unit was attacked, but I suspect it was him."

"They are of a lesser lineage," Ofeli remarked. "After our efforts for their betterment—gratitude, not resistance—should be their response. Orisha, Aksum, Marine Naes. Do you think those families do not aspire to be in a position such as ours? Yet they all accept their place, do they not? We do not need their love. We need their fear and respect."

"They might bend to our rule now," Legba said. "But the spirit of Niri's people is unique, their pride untamed and deep-rooted, unlike any I've encountered."

"Amadioha swearing public fealty will help our Loa counter Ghede Ghadou's influence in Niri," Ofeli said. "You saw his duplicitous plots firsthand. He is still reeling from his father's losses in Sine during their rebellion. This will be good for her, for Dan, and for the

Mysters. Therefore, good for us." He crossed his arms and frowned. "You think about Amadioha more than you think about your wife."

"I don't have a wife."

"That's the problem. We need to get you a woman to take all this nonsense off your mind."

Legba put his hand over his cup, and when he opened it, the cup disappeared.

Ofeli gasped in astonishment. "I've never seen you do that trick before."

Legba opened the palm of the other hand. The cup appeared there.

"How did you do that?"

"There is an endless hole in Nowhere. I send it there, and it falls forever. If I know when I sent it there, I know how far it has fallen. Then I can bring it back."

"Nowhere?" Ofeli asked with curious eyes.

Legba nodded, his eyes gleaming with pride. "Since my training with blood memories has progressed, I can now access nearly all my mother's memories. Each day brings a new dream, a new chapter of her life. It's like having a family again." A smile played on his lips. "Through her memories, I've learned about things and places that were once lost to time. I have mastered skills of Navigation even the Sacred Master cannot do."

"Hmmm. Perhaps you could use that trick to conjure up a wife."

Ofeli's jest made Legba ruminate in his thoughts. "I abandoned my unit," he confessed. "Instead of punishment, the Loa allowed me to learn these gifts. Now, with my mother's memories, it feels like I have a family again. I only wish to serve our Loa and repay Vodun for all it has done for me. Why won't she let me?"

Ofeli rubbed his forehead and sat back in his seat. "Shall I tell you a story? I used to be a farmer. Then I became a trader. Eventually, I started working at the Mysters."

Legba leaned back, a hint of impatience in his eyes. "You've shared this tale with me many times."

"I have not told you I have five brothers and sisters, all spread

The Eden Ruse

across Vodun. They are working in many different jobs. I may not have the most glamorous work, but when I go home every night, my bed is softer than theirs. And all it took was for me to mind my own business all these years." Ofeli took another drink. "Did you ever think no one takes it seriously because it's not something we should take seriously?"

"The Niri would never—"

"Submit to Radha Rhamirez Loa. Yes, I know," Ofeli cut in, running a hand over his face in exasperation. "I heard it from you the first time."

"When you pulled me from that jail cell, do you call that minding your own business?"

Without warning, a splash of wine drenched Legba, abruptly silencing their conversation. He swiveled, coming face-to-face with a looming figure. The man, heavyset and imposing, stood over him like a dark cloud. His shirt, coarse and stained, strained against his broad frame. White bandages, grimy at the edges, encircled his wrists like shackles. "My apologies," the man sneered. "The stench of the Loa here is nauseating."

Legba tensed, his hands clenching into fists beneath the table.

The man laughed. More voices followed. Five men lined up behind him as the bar quieted.

Legba shot a quick, questioning glance at Ofeli, who responded with a subtle warning shake of his head.

"You need permission from your little outside-town bitch to do anything?" The man laughed again.

Legba knew there had always been brewing resentment toward the Loa in Limbe, but some critics had gotten bolder. He stood, maintaining eye contact with the man as he rose.

"Don't," Ofeli murmured under his breath. "It's not worth it."

Legba turned to face the man. "We will be on our way," he said. He picked up his bag from the table and attempted to walk away, but the man blocked him.

"If you leave, the stench remains. How will you compensate me for that?"

How can these men benefit so much from the Loa's grace yet be so disrespectful? "I don't want any trouble," he said.

"Trouble? Trouble starts when outsiders like you come around here too often." All the men laughed.

Legba tried maneuvering around him, but the man shoved him in the chest. "What will you do now that your protector is far away and can't help you?"

These men need to pay.

"Let it go, Legba!" Ofeli's voice wavered.

Legba shoved him back. The push wasn't forceful, but caught off guard, the man stumbled and fell, his body hitting the floor with a resounding thud. A snicker erupted from one of the five men standing behind him, only to die when met with their leader's furious glare.

The man's eyes gleamed with malice. "Make them beg!" he bellowed to his comrades.

The first man, emboldened yet unsteady on his feet, lunged at Legba with a wild swing at his face. His lack of coordination made him sloppy, but less predictable. Legba swung his head to the right and planted his arm into the man's mid-torso. The man groaned and bent over. Legba connected his knee to the man's forehead, sending him sprawling on the floor. The other men assessed the situation before rushing them simultaneously.

The biggest man went for Legba first, and the three others went for Ofeli. He tried the same jab to Legba's head. Legba moved his head to the right, but the man extended his leg and floored Legba. A surge of irritation bubbled within him for not foreseeing the move. As Legba scrambled to his feet, the man pulled out a blade and stabbed it toward him. Legba's body shimmered, becoming translucent as he Navigated through the thin veil between physical spaces. The blade passed harmlessly through his ethereal form, leaving the attacker bewildered and grasping at empty air.

Legba, seizing the moment of confusion, re-materialized in the room. Before his assailant could react, he drew a dagger from behind his back and plunged it into the assailant's leg. A piercing scream filled the air, and the man stumbled and fell, clutching his wounded limb. Shortly after, a loud bang startled all of them.

"Enough!" a voice came from behind the bar, the owner scrunching his face in fury.

"You and you!" he shouted at Legba and Ofeli. "Get out and do not come back!"

Legba's gaze shifted to Ofeli, sprawled on the floor, grappling with two of the assailants. Despite a few bruises painting his face, Ofeli appeared relatively unharmed. Legba extended a hand and helped him to his feet.

"This is not over!" the leader said when they walked past them.

As they hurried out, Ofeli's features twisted into a mask of disgust and annoyance. "Out here, friends are rare," he said. "Continue like this, and you'll alienate those few you have in the Mysters."

"They insulted our Loa. They deserve retribution."

Ofeli sighed. "Radha Loa has enemies everywhere, both inside and out. Picking fights with every inconsequential dirt whisper is a waste of time."

～

TORCHES CAST A BLUE, eerie glow across the armory walls, their flames burning relentlessly day and night. In his three years at Rada Mysters, Legba had learned that magic touched everything there. The armory's extreme dryness, always leaving his lips cracked, ensured the weapons didn't rust. It kept their edges lethal.

Amadioha Kamanu, Eze of Canis, would reach the Mysters in two days. He easily secured a victory for the Loa in a skirmish against the Empire of Kush. She had gotten the rising star of Niri to draw his sword for her. Amadioha had won. She had won. She was always multiple steps ahead of everyone. Legba remembered how she had squashed Ayizan's insurrection before it even started. She had known about his blood magic. She had known who killed the sister of a lowly lord. So why did he not trust she knew what was right with the Niri?

Amadioha stood on the verge of becoming a full Vodun Baron, a rank many coveted. Soon, he would pledge his loyalty, swearing his allegiance directly under the Loa's command. This was a stepping stone for her in moving her house from the middle to the upper class. But as far as Legba was concerned, an army of Niri warriors, regardless of who they swore to, was coming to their doorstep.

He'd visited the armory daily for the past two weeks, inspecting the weapons before leaving. He wasn't sure what he was expecting to find each time. But he did it all the same.

The expansive hallway branched into twenty rooms, each filled with weaponry. Further down the hallway, a woman stood alone. He rarely saw anyone else there, especially not at such a late hour of night.

"Who are you?" He moved his hand to grip the handle of his dagger on his hip.

Her eyes, bright with curiosity, lingered on his blade before tracing the rest of his form. "You're not from here. What is your name?" she inquired.

"I am Papa Legba. Born of the beasts of Nana Buruku. Servant to the Loa."

"If you descended from beasts, why aren't you on all fours licking my feet?"

He took a step toward her. "What wrong have I done for you to insult me?"

She shrugged. "I only say what I see."

"Who are you?"

"Around here, some call me Ayidda, but my birth mother called me Weddo."

Pausing, Legba studied her. Despite her disheveled hair and ragged clothes, her face was stunning, and her skin was smooth. Of medium height with a shapely body, her arms hinted at strength, reminiscent of manual labor. As she took a few steps toward him, his grip on his dagger tightened. Her movement was like a dance, entrancing him, his head swaying with each step.

"Day after day, you come in here. What do you think you seek?" she asked.

His eyes darted around the hall, as if expecting to find places where someone could hide and watch. "I need to make sure we are ready with the right weapons if the enemy decides to—" He broke off, realizing he was offering explanations to a stranger.

"Who is the enemy? And how would they strike?"

He gritted his teeth. "I don't know."

"How can you know the right weapons if you don't know how they will strike?"

He was getting irritated by her line of questions. "Speak plainly, woman. I do not have time for this."

"Are you a slave?"

"Slave? What? No. I mean… of course not." His coat bore the official mark of the Mysters guard. He was confused why she would ask that question.

"You are the Mysters' guard, are you not?"

"Yes," he said, squaring his shoulders.

"You are not from here."

"I am here at the request of the Loa."

"So, you are not here of your own free will."

"No… I mean, yes. I will return home one day."

She paused, eyes narrowing. "So, you are a slave."

"I am not a slave, woman. I am here because I choose to be."

She let out a brief laugh. "You're here at your Loa's demand, not by choice. That makes you a slave."

"Enough of this," Legba scoffed. "I am taking you upstairs now."

She took a single step back and undid her garment. It dropped to the floor, revealing her naked body. Unlike the dirty and ragged cloth that covered her, her body was as flawless as he had ever seen. Her skin glowed a dark amber, even in the blue light. As the light flickered across, it seemed her hips were moving and gyrating.

"So tell me, slave, what choice do you want to make now?"

Legba felt like he did not have control of his feet. They took two steps toward her like a magnet was pulling him in. He had no desire to resist. She grabbed his face and kissed him.

He pulled away. "What do you think you are doing?"

"The slave is not used to making his own choices."

He grabbed her and pulled her lips to his. Her breath tasted like tart citrus. The scent of her disheveled hair filled his nostrils as she kissed his neck.

Why is that smell so familiar?

"Papa Legba?" A man's voice came from around the corner in the hall.

She pushed him away, and a look of panic crossed her eyes. Legba turned around just in time to see a guard entering.

"Papa Legba, the Loa is looking for you." The man bowed his head.

"Of course," Legba said. "By the way…"—he turned around to find Ayidda Weddo, but she was gone—"Did you just see…" He pointed at the back.

"See what, Mesye?" The man raised an eyebrow in confusion.

Legba looked around the room again. "I was just talking to someone," he stammered, still disoriented.

"Is there someone else here?" The guard looked around.

"Her name was…" Legba stopped, the words dying on his lips. He took a breath. "Let's go."

"Mesye? Are you sure?"

"I've been spending too much time here." A laugh escaped his lips.

The guard gave a reserved chuckle, and a bashful look crossed his face.

∼

THE LOA UNLEASHED a swing at the golem's stony neck. It ducked, causing her blade to cut through the air. The golem, resembling a crude assembly of gray rocks, had undefined features except for its distinct hands and feet.

Like the guards, full armor adorned her body, while her head, strikingly exposed, betrayed a confidence against her foe.

Inside one of the myriad chambers of the Mysters, she practiced her routines, a ritual she undertook daily. A circle of her courtiers surrounded her, with Legba standing close to Zaka, the Sacred Master.

As the golem lunged forward to stab her with its sword, she parried, the metallic clang reverberating throughout the chamber. She knocked the golem across the room with a forceful knee to its head. It landed with a loud crash, its blade clattering on the floor a few feet away.

Intense pressure in his skull disoriented Legba, a pressure that had been building since he left the weapons storage facility. With blurred vision and a weighty head from sleep deprivation, he struggled to discern reality from his tired imagination. He closed his eyes, and the fleeting memory of the citrus kiss lingered on his tongue.

The golem regained its footing and charged toward the Loa with renewed vigor. Anticipating its move, she deflected its blow and, with a fluid rotation, aimed for its neck. It tried to shield itself, but her blade cut through one arm. Before it could react, she seized its other arm, broke it off, and flung it aside. The golem leaped in desperation, only to be caught midair and hurled into a wall, shattering on impact.

The Loa approached Legba and the Sacred Master. "These exercises are getting easier." The sweat dripping from her face seemed to tell a different story.

"Your swordsmanship is improving," the Sacred Master said, his smile tight and eyes flickering with apprehension.

"Or your magic is getting weaker," she countered with a sly smirk.

The Sacred Master shot her a wary glance, his brows furrowing with concern.

As the Loa began removing her armor, the metal plates clanking softly, Legba hurried to assist. His fingers brushed against her intricate braids, adorned with rich brown, black, and dark red hues. The scent of her hair, a mix of oils and sweat from the sparring session, filled his nostrils.

She let down the topknot, and her hair cascaded down her back like a waterfall of twisted ropes. Legba gathered his courage, his heart pounding against his ribcage. "My Loa, might I have a moment?" he murmured. "I must speak with you." He fought to keep his focus, blinking rapidly against the encroaching blurriness that threatened to consume his vision.

She frowned. "If this is about the Niri Eze again, I don't want to hear it."

Legba had gone against Ofeli's wise counsel, frequently bringing his concerns about Amadioha to the Loa. Each time, the annoyance and frustration grew in her eyes, the tension between them thickening like a suffocating fog. Ofeli had warned him, but Legba had been too stubborn to listen. And, as he stood before her, he could feel the strain in their relationship, a chasm widening with every passing moment.

"My Loa, I fear we are making a grave mistake."

The frown on her face deepened, her eyes flashing with anger and disappointment. Legba regretted his words, watching as deep creases formed in her once smooth skin, her beautiful features contorting into a mask of disgust and frustration.

"Everyone. Out. Now!" she bellowed. Her eyes swept the room, daring anyone to disobey.

Those gathered hurried toward the door as if there would be a grave punishment for the last to leave.

She stared at the Sacred Master. "You too."

The Sacred Master nodded. He turned and left the room, the heavy wooden door creaking shut behind him, leaving Legba alone with the seething Loa.

"Do you know the name of the last Loa of Dan before me?" she asked, her fingers working to remove her armor piece by piece.

"Yes, my Loa," Legba said, his posture upright. "Jose Loa"

With a last tug, she removed the last piece of her undergarment, letting it fall to the floor. Legba's eyes widened as he took in her naked form, her dark skin glistening with a sheen of sweat. Many scars covered her torso and her legs. Heat rose to his cheeks, and he averted his gaze, focusing on a spot on the wall behind her. The rustling of fabric filled the room as she dressed in her everyday garments.

"When Jose Loa was on his deathbed, he had no heirs to succeed him," she said, her voice full of bitterness. "He chose me as his successor, a decision many questioned. Some called me lucky, claiming I didn't deserve my position."

"We should put down anyone who utters such words," Legba said.

A mirthless chuckle escaped her lips, the sound harsh and grating in the room's stillness. "Even before I ascended to the rank of baron, I noticed my Loa was childless, despite the countless women he bedded," she said. "No heirs, no bastards. For nearly a decade before his death, I observed he could not have children." She paused, a sly smile playing on her lips. "I worked tirelessly to become his closest confidant, his most trusted baron. I knew that when the time came, I would assume his throne."

She put on her crown and turned around to face him.

"Every other Loa in Vodun inherited their title and had their power handed to them on a silver platter. But me? I earned my position through sweat, blood, and tears. They despise me, not because they doubt my worthiness, but because my existence is proof of their inadequacy."

Legba looked at her in awe. The best way to die would be in her service.

"I tell you this story instead of casting you out of my Mysters because as much as you have been a pain, you have also been useful," the Loa said. "Never bring doubt to my tactical acumen again. Never be more a pain than you are useful."

"I—"

She raised her hand to silence him. "Go back to your quarters. I do not need subjects in my court who are not fully here." The Loa leveled a gaze at Legba, a faint glint of contempt in her eyes. If the Loa trusted the Niri Eze, then he should, too. He buried his doubt and hurried away with a nod.

Stumbling into the sprawling halls of the Mysters, the fog in

Legba's head thickened, intensifying his disorientation. Seeking clarity, he rode into the forest. With the sun casting elongated shadows that danced among the trees, Legba traveled deeper in. The oppressive air weighed him down, though he couldn't tell if it was the environment or his faltering state. Time warped, and within an hour, his symptoms grew more malevolent. Dizziness washed over him, and the familiar forest transformed into a kaleidoscope of distorted shapes and colors.

Consumed by desperation, Legba mustered his remaining strength to guide his horse back to the Mysters. But a forceful tug on the reins halted the horse, sending him hurtling into the underbrush. He braced himself, his body careening through the trees. As pain exploded across his senses, darkness rushed in, swallowing his consciousness whole.

～

THE RESOUNDING HORN blare reverberated across the forest, stirring the air. Legba's eyes fluttered open, and a sharp, metallic tang invaded his mouth. His vision was a chaotic tangle of branches and leaves, remnants of a shattered tree. Memories flooded back in flashes—the violent jerk from his horse throwing him, the ground rushing up to meet him. Groaning, he pushed himself into a seated position, head throbbing with a persistent, muffled ringing.

How long was I out for? The ringing intensified, morphing into a clear, distant sound. It was the emergency horn of Rada Mysters, its ominous echo a signal of imminent danger, only used in times of attack.

Amadioha! A surge of panic rippled through Legba. His horse stood over him, watching from the moment he'd fallen. Time was slipping like sand through fingers—returning to the Mysters on horseback would cost him dearly. Duty echoed in his heart; the Loa had chosen him as her protector. Failing was not an option. He reached out, his hand trembling as he stroked the horse's mane. It nickered a soft, understanding sound, as if sensing his storm of emotions.

"I'm so sorry," he whispered. Sorrow veiled his eyes when he shut them, gathering a moment's peace. He clasped the horse's head. "If there is an afterlife for creatures like you, they will honor your sacrifice."

The horse's face withered, its flesh receding as if being drained. Panic sparked in its eyes, its body convulsing in a futile struggle against the inevitable. It thrashed, trying to break free from Legba's unyielding grasp. But it was in vain. Within heartbeats, all that remained was a sculpture of bones and hollowed skin.

Fifteen stone watchtowers encircled the Mysters. Their vantage points would provide an unobstructed view of what was unfolding. He closed his eyes and focused on one of them. The moment's urgency pressed against him, yet a rash move could be fatal. The scent of the forest dimmed as his form blurred, edges melting into transparency, and the rustling of leaves dwindled to silence, his sight plunging into an abyss of darkness.

A sudden weightlessness enveloped him, and he soared over the forest. In a mere heartbeat, his eyes snapped open to the grim reality of the watchtower. Nausea clawed at his throat, and despite his best efforts, a torrent of half-digested food splattered against the stone floor. The intense mix of vomit, iron, and decaying flesh assaulted his nostrils. His gaze fell to the four Mysters guards sprawled, gruesome axe wounds marring their chests.

"Amadioha!" His breathing increased, the wrath boiling within him. He strode to the tower's edge, overlooking the courtyard. Five Mysters guards kneeled in defeat, their hands bound. Legba's eyes widened in horror as the Niri soldiers swung their axes, dismembering the defenseless men in a relentless, bloody spectacle.

My Loa! The thought jolted him. If she were still alive, she would be in her receiving room. Closing his eyes, he envisioned the chamber in detail. The vile stench of death faded, replaced by the airy transition. The opulent aroma of incense and polished wood enveloped him, heralding his arrival in the chamber.

Delphine stood by the unyielding door, her snarl echoing through the room. His Loa stood with her sword drawn, missing the usual confidence he had seen in her. The ominous pounding on the door signaled relentless foes. Sensing Legba, Delphine whirled, baring its fangs. The Loa's gaze met his, ablaze with betrayal.

"Deserter!" The accusation dripped from her lips like venom as she shifted into a defensive stance. Delphine's growls deepened, claws scraping the floor in warning. "I knew you would run at the slightest sense of danger."

Run? Why would she think that when I was the one that warned her? "My Loa! I came as soon as I could." Legba placed his hand across his chest and fixed his gaze on Delphine as he dropped to one knee.

The Loa's eyes pierced into Legba, searching, questioning. Beside her, Delphine bared her teeth in a menacing display, her muscles tense in anticipation of a command. The mistrust in the Loa's eyes was clear, yet the constant banging on the door tilted her decision. With a reluctant nod, she signaled a temporary truce.

"Rise!" she ordered. "We must send for reinforcements."

Legba shook his head. "There is no time. The Niri have breached the castle. If anyone was able, they have already sought help."

He doubled over, a harsh cough racking his body. Droplets of blood flecked the floor, side effects of his rapid Navigations. Dizziness clouded his vision, each breath a battle against the encroaching weakness.

The Loa's expression faltered, her resolve momentarily wavering. With a resigned motion, she slid her sword back into its sheath. "We surrender then. The Bondye will barter for my freedom," she said, though her voice lacked conviction.

"I witnessed their brutality—unarmed soldiers butchered upon surrender. The Niri are not here for prisoners. We must flee!"

The Loa's face contorted into disgust and disdain. "Flee my Mysters? Vodun does not flee! I will never flee!"

The ominous scrape of the doors cracking open resonated through the chamber.

The Loa's eyes ignited with a fierce blue glow. "Hold them off; buy me time," she commanded. Striding to the nearest pillar, she placed her hands on the statue. A vibrant blue aura radiated from her palms, the air crackling with energy.

Five soldiers burst through the doorway in a tangle of limbs before regaining composure and lining up in a formidable line. Clad in vivid red trousers, their bare chests glistened with sweat. Dual axes glinted in their grasp. Legba raised both hands. In his mind, he reached into the abyss of Nowhere, recalling two broadswords. With a shiver of air, the blades solidified in his hands.

Battling his weakness, Legba squared his shoulders. He knew standing against the men was a near-impossible feat, but even seconds of delay could mean salvation for his Loa.

"How many souls shall I escort to the afterlife?" he bellowed in Niri, defiance burning in his eyes.

The soldiers charged, axes raised. Legba crouched, bracing for impact, set on felling at least two. As they converged, a guttural stone grinding filled the room. The soldiers paused, shock crossing their faces. The Loa's magic had awakened the pillar—a towering golem, clad in stone armor, burst forth, barreling past Legba toward the attackers. Their weapons bounced off its armor as its rocky arms crushed their heads and bodies. Delphine's sharp fangs helped finish the ones who survived the initial onslaught.

Legba whirled around and caught sight of the Loa—a fallen figure of exhaustion crumpled on the floor. Her skin was pallid, her chest heaving; the immense exertion of her magic had drained her of strength.

Barely audible, the Loa's voice was a raspy whisper. "I am... so weak." She attempted to rise, her arms trembling under her weight, but her strength betrayed her, and she fell back to the ground. "Poisoned," she gasped.

The woman in the armory! Of course, it had been her.

The water source for all the Mysters passed through the dungeons connected to the armory. That is what the woman had been doing there.

How can you know the right weapons if you don't even know how they will strike? Her words haunted Legba. It had been right in his face, and he had missed it. That kiss had knocked him out in the forest, and now, everyone at the Mysters was seeing its effects. They never had a chance.

A new figure emerged through the doorway, markedly different from the rest. He wore a white shirt and billowing red pants. His striking blue eyes scanned the room with a calm, calculating gaze. He had to be Omoro, Amadioha's top magician. Legba knew about him from his time spent on the border of Niri.

The golem's hulking stone form lunged at the newcomer. Unfazed, Omoro raised his palm, an aura of control emanating from his stance. In mere moments, the golem crumbled mid-assault, disintegrating into a cloud of dust and leaving a hollow shell of armor clattering to the ground.

"We must leave now!" A newfound surge of adrenaline ignited Legba's senses. More Niri soldiers burst in as he spoke, encircling the enigmatic man.

Legba rushed to the Loa's side and slid his arm under her shoulders to hoist her up. Together, they dashed toward the room's far end, their movements a desperate struggle for survival. Seeking refuge, they huddled behind the Loa's towering throne.

He stole a glance back and saw Delphine launching herself at the soldiers. Her fangs glistened, poised to rend flesh, but the soldiers were quicker, sidestepping with practiced agility. Delphine's assault met only air as their axes came down on her as she hit the ground. She slid across the floor to the door, her claws scraping against stone as she struggled to her feet. With a defiant snarl, she rose once more—only to crumple a heartbeat later, her strength finally giving out as blood pooled beneath her.

"Delphine!" the Loa's cry shattered the air, a raw explosion of fear. Driven by instinct, she whirled around, ready to dash back into the fray for her loyal companion.

Legba latched onto her arm, yanking her back from imminent danger. With her usual strength diminished, she yielded more quickly than expected. They hurried to the hall's end, Legba's heart racing with fear and determination. "We are trapped!" he shouted.

Rage twisted the Loa's features as she snapped, her fury manifesting in a burst of power. The wall before them quivered and split, conjuring a narrow escape passage through her sheer will.

The attackers bore down on them, their presence so near Legba could detect the acrid tang of their sweat. He and the Loa jumped through the opening, their pursuers a hair's breadth behind. As they cleared the threshold, the opening snapped shut with merciless finality. One soldier made it through; the other one was caught mid-lunge and cleaved by the closing wall—his head and hands trapped outside while the rest of his body was sealed within. The isolated soldier, confronted by his grim situation, spun on his heels. He chose survival over valor, sprinting away from his failed pursuit.

The Loa's eyes ignited an intense blue. Raising her hand, she wove her magic through the air. The fleeing soldier's body jerked to a halt as if trapped by invisible strings, then levitated off the ground, suspended in midair. "Get back here!" the Loa commanded.

A helpless puppet in her grasp, the soldier floated in the air, drawn back toward her by her commanding magic. She pulled out her sword and sliced him in half. With another coordinated motion, she dismembered the other one trapped in the wall before resheathing her blade. "Every one of them will pay."

∼

LEGBA'S LUNGS BURNED, his breaths ragged from their relentless flight since escaping her receiving room. The once grand castle was a macabre tableau of death. Niri corpses littered the ground, but five of their own surrounded each one. Their soldiers, weakened from the poison, never stood a chance. The fallen they passed were like physical blows to the Loa. Even in silence, Legba felt the weight of every loss pressing down on her, none more so than Delphine's.

"We need to get out of here," Legba panted, his breath clouded in the frigid air.

"We will not yield my castle," the Loa shot back.

"The poison afflicting you is the same they've used on everyone else. If we are to seek vengeance, we must first survive."

The Loa did not want to lose. *Vodun does not retreat.* Everyone who ever gave their life in service of their nation learned that. But if they did not survive, then all would be lost forever. "If we go to the Bondye, his actions will be swift," Legba said.

"And risk being mocked by them? Never!" She scrunched her face like she just tasted the bitterness of the idea. "We will go to my other barons, raise all the forces in Dan, and retake this castle with my army."

Legba frowned, her words heavy in his mind. He understood her pride, but the practicality of their situation demanded a different path. "With the utmost respect, my Loa, though we can muster a formidable force with the barons, the cost in lives will be grievous."

"When you first came here, I told you I brought you here for your magic, not your strategic counsel," the Loa snapped as her eyes turned blue.

"Had you heeded my counsel, we might not be in this predicament! I warned you about Amadioha and the Niri!" He hurled his sword, which lodged in the stone wall with a thunderous clatter.

The Loa hovered her hand over her sword hilt.

He kneeled and cast his gaze downward. "Forgive my impertinence, my Loa. I spoke in haste, not disrespect."

"You arrived a timid man, fueled by the rage of the injustice done to your sister. But do not mistake our current situation for weakness; I will strike you down."

I am calm. I am not a man controlled by rashness or impulse. I am calm. He repeated those words in his mind. "My life is for you to do as you please."

When he looked her in the eyes, he noticed the transformation in her expression—a journey from solemn resolve to surprise, then to unmistakable pain. After that, the front of her garment turned red with blood, and her body fell to the floor, revealing three men further down the hall.

The man at the center commanded attention, his eyes alight with an intense glow. Electric sparks danced from his fingertips as he moved with purposeful strides toward the Loa's fallen form, casting eerie shadows against the walls. He stood just over six feet tall, his physique solidly built yet agile. Adorning his waist was a striking red sash. He wielded an oversized double-sided axe in his hand; the blade gleaming in the dim light. His bare chest was a canvas of intricate tattoos, all inked in white. He had deep blue eyes and a crown of gold with red gems embedded around it on his head.

"Amadioha," Legba muttered.

He had grown a lot in height and size since the last time Legba had seen him as a little boy, but his face still looked the same. Legba ached with fatigue, each muscle screaming in protest from the relentless fighting and the strain of Navigating. He needed another animal to draw power from, but there was none. Amadioha was not taking any prisoners. The sword implanted in the Loa's back stuck out from her front. It had barely missed her heart.

"My Loa."

Blood spattered out of her mouth. "Save us."

She has called on me. I have to answer.

He closed his eyes and opened them again, but the loud ringing returned. Before he even started Navigating, a sharp pain seared through his body, igniting every nerve.

Legba pressed his hand against the Loa's chest, focusing his dwindling strength on their escape. Their forms dematerialized, only to solidify once more. He coughed up blood, his strength further diminishing.

She has called on me. I have to answer.

Realizing the situation, Amadioha shifted from a walk to a jog, then broke into a run. He drew back his axe and hurled it at them. Papa Legba watched the blade sail through the air. His and the Loa's bodies faded again—quicker. The blade's edge connected with his face just as their bodies turned translucent and disappeared. It would have embedded itself in the wall where they once stood, its edges slick with droplets of Legba's blood.

Amadioha's journal: The cost of Vodun's influence

The stench of rot and decay clings to my nostrils even now, hours after leaving the village. Damballa and I traveled to the outskirts of Canis today, to a small farming community that sits on the border with Kwale. What we found there makes my blood boil and my heart ache.

The villagers' faces were gaunt, their eyes hollow with hunger and despair. Their crops, once lush and bountiful, now wither in the fields. The earth itself seems poisoned, refusing to yield the nourishment our people so desperately need.

And the cause? A Vodunese manufacturing operation that squats on our land like a festering wound. The stench of chemicals taints the air, and the once-clear streams run murky with waste. When confronted, the Vodunese overseers had the audacity to deny any wrongdoing. They claim their operation brings "prosperity" to Niri. Prosperity! As if coins in a few pockets could offset the destruction of our very land!

What enrages me most is not just the presence of this blight on our soil, but the complacency of my fellow Ezes. How can they not see the poison seeping into the heart of Niri? How can they allow foreign interests to ravage our resources, to starve our people? Instead of uniting, we continue to squabble with each other about inconsequential things.

I raised the issue at the last council meeting, expecting outrage, a call to action. Instead, I was met with tepid concern and outright dismissal. Eze Namudi of Kwale, whose own people suffer alongside mine, spoke of "diplomatic solutions" and "maintaining good relations." Good relations? While our people starve?

Even Damballa urges caution. "We must gather more evidence," he says, "build a case that cannot be ignored." But how much more evidence do we need? The proof is in the withered crops, the sickened livestock, the haunted eyes of our people.

I feel as if I'm shouting into a void, my words lost in a sea of complacency and fear. Do the other Ezes not understand that every concession, every blind eye turned, erodes our sovereignty? That each Vodunese operation allowed on our soil is another crack in the foundation of our freedom?

Something must be done. Perhaps it falls to me alone to take a stand. For I cannot... I will not stand idly by while Vodun slowly chokes the life from Niri.

Chineke, give me strength. For I fear the path ahead may lead to conflict not just with Vodun, but with those who should be my allies. But if that is the price of true freedom for Niri, then so be it.

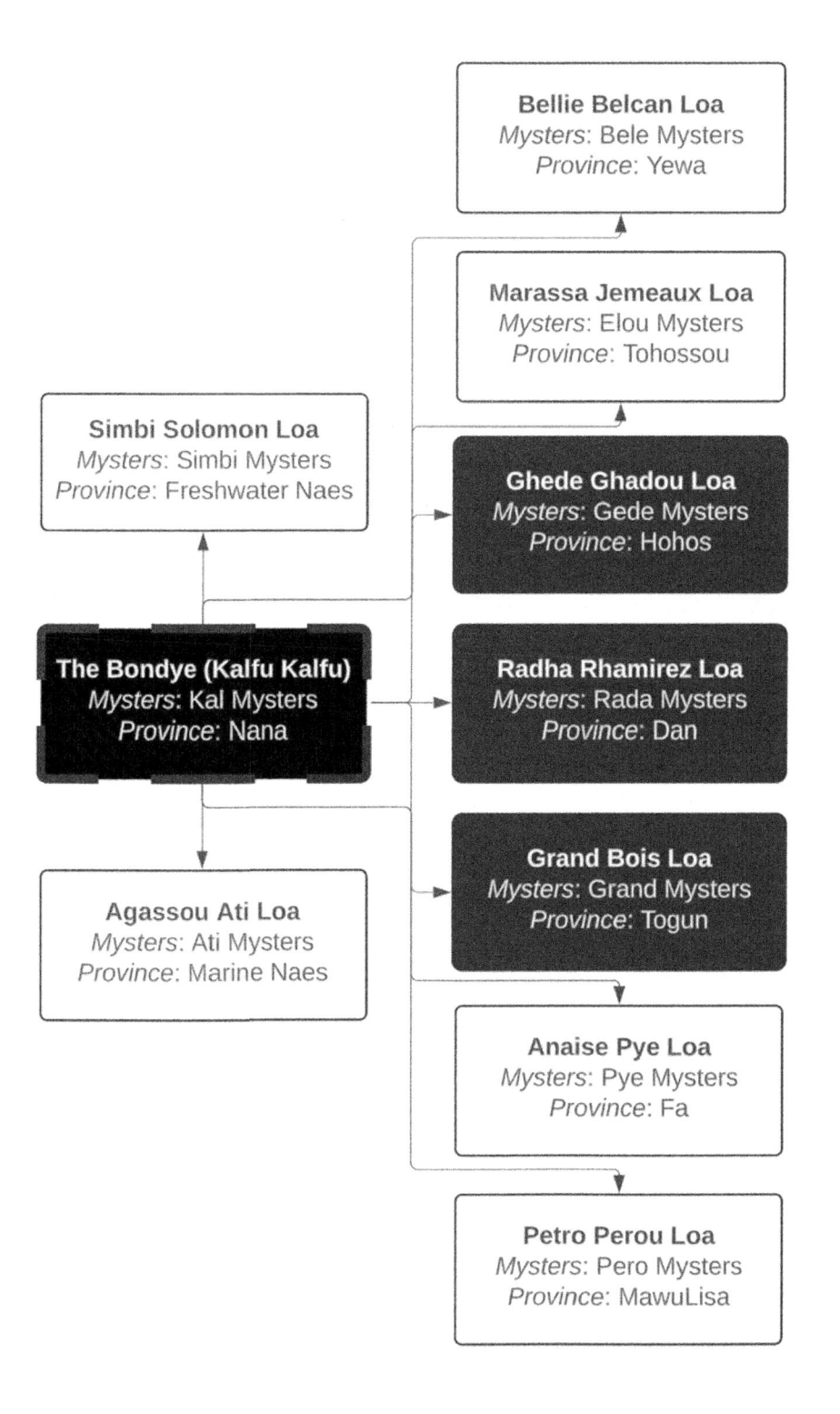

```
                    ┌─────────────────────────┐
                    │    Bellie Belcan Loa    │
                    │  Mysters: Bele Mysters  │
                    │    Province: Yewa       │
                    └─────────────────────────┘
                                ▲
                    ┌─────────────────────────┐
                    │  Marassa Jemeaux Loa    │
                    │  Mysters: Elou Mysters  │
                    │   Province: Tohossou    │
                    └─────────────────────────┘
                                ▲
┌─────────────────────────┐   ┌─────────────────────────┐
│   Simbi Solomon Loa     │   │    Ghede Ghadou Loa     │
│  Mysters: Simbi Mysters │   │  Mysters: Gede Mysters  │
│ Province: Freshwater Naes│   │    Province: Hohos      │
└─────────────────────────┘   └─────────────────────────┘
            ▲
┌─────────────────────────┐   ┌─────────────────────────┐
│  The Bondye (Kalfu Kalfu)│──▶│   Radha Rhamirez Loa    │
│   Mysters: Kal Mysters  │   │  Mysters: Rada Mysters  │
│    Province: Nana       │   │     Province: Dan       │
└─────────────────────────┘   └─────────────────────────┘

                              ┌─────────────────────────┐
                              │     Grand Bois Loa      │
                              │ Mysters: Grand Mysters  │
                              │    Province: Togun      │
                              └─────────────────────────┘
┌─────────────────────────┐
│    Agassou Ati Loa      │   ┌─────────────────────────┐
│  Mysters: Ati Mysters   │   │     Anaise Pye Loa      │
│  Province: Marine Naes  │   │  Mysters: Pye Mysters   │
└─────────────────────────┘   │     Province: Fa        │
                              └─────────────────────────┘

                              ┌─────────────────────────┐
                              │    Petro Perou Loa      │
                              │  Mysters: Pero Mysters  │
                              │   Province: MawuLisa    │
                              └─────────────────────────┘
```

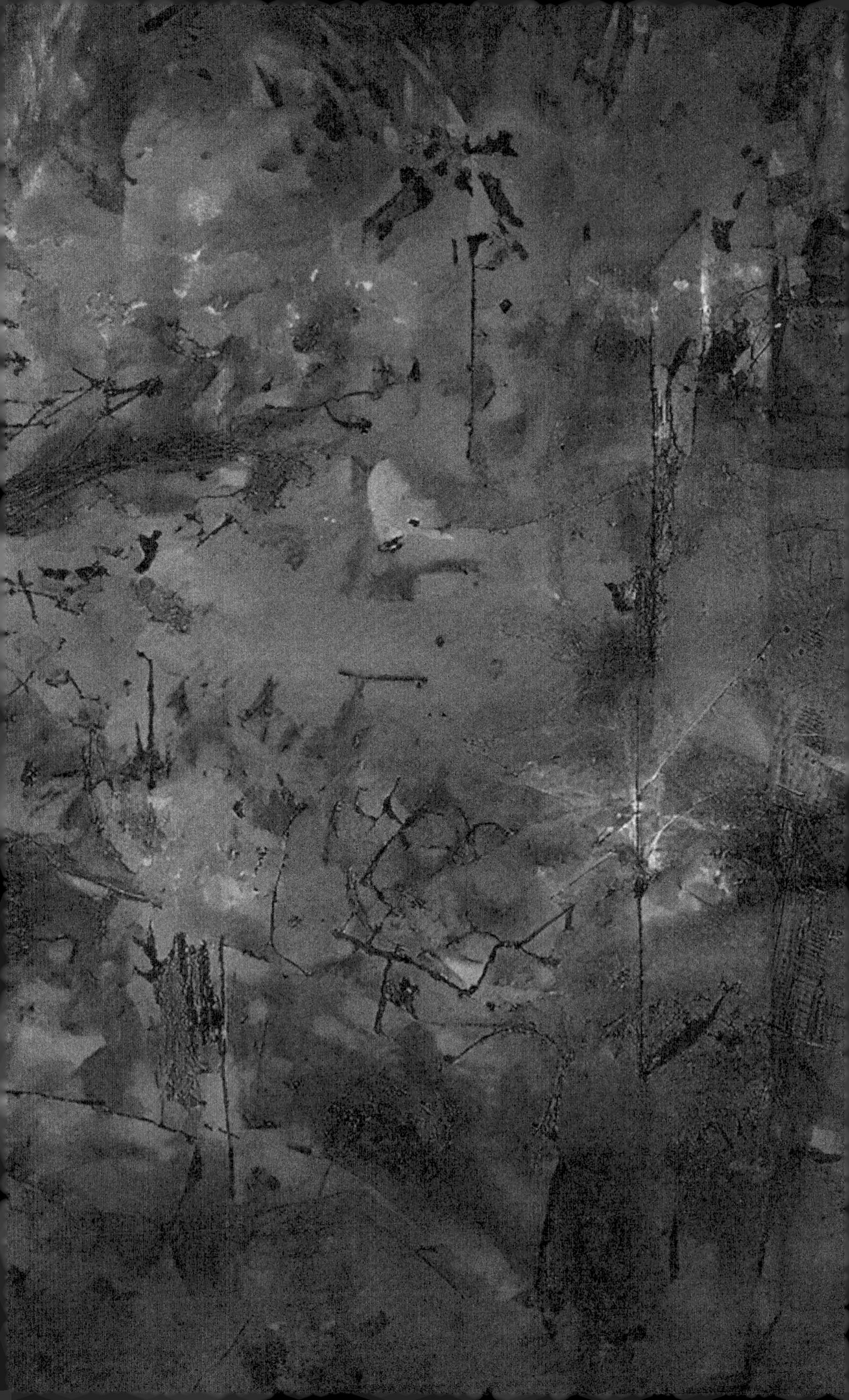

PART II
A DYING WORLD

Realm of Hell

Aamaris

Federation of Heres

Kingdom
of Isha

Qataban

's Land

Masina

Ebos

Kingdom
of Sasobek

Galanis

Island of the Dead

6

THE BLIGHT
REALM OF HELL

*I*nside the cramped confines of the aircraft, the forty-four soldiers of Kakuten 47 and 48 sat in a tense, suffocating silence, their bodies strapped into the unyielding embrace of the metal seats. The only illumination came from the faint, ghostly light of Hell's night sky filtering through the small porthole windows, casting an eerie glow over the plane's interior.

A violent shudder ripped through the aircraft as turbulent winds seized control. **Major Lilith Saeon** gritted her teeth, the seat straps biting into her flesh—the only thing keeping her from becoming a demon projectile. Amid the chaos, her watch flashed insistently, the name "Abbadon" illuminating its face. For the past half-hour, his calls had grown more frequent, more urgent. Dread seeped into her veins.

Could he have discovered my actions so soon?

She silenced the watch before the call could connect. A message followed, its words glaring up at her from the screen.

Answer immediately. Do not make me do this, the text read.

She knew Abbadon too well and understood the implications of his threat. She unbuckled her restraints, nearly losing her balance as another violent wave of turbulence rocked the jet.

Curious eyes from the seated Kakuten darted in her direction as she stumbled toward the cockpit, fighting to maintain her footing amid the relentless shaking of the aircraft. She burst into the cockpit, her voice cutting through the sound of the plane. "Kill the comms now!" she shouted at the pilot.

The pilot swiveled in his seat. "Excuse me, Major?" he asked, his eyes searching her face for an explanation.

"Now!" Lilith repeated, her words barely audible over the sound of the turbulence.

A moment of static crackled through the plane's communication system, followed by the unmistakable beginnings of Abbadon's voice. The pilot reacted swiftly, cutting off the transmission before the first word fully formed.

"Was that... Major Abbadon?" the pilot questioned, his brow furrowed in bewilderment.

"No," Lilith replied.

The pilot hesitated, then ventured, "Permission to speak freely?" Another violent bout of turbulence chose that moment to strike, catching Lilith off guard and sending her stumbling to the floor.

"Denied!" she snapped, frustration and pain mingling in her voice. "*Kalla!*" she cursed, struggling to regain her footing. "Do your job and get us to our destination."

The plane descended, its powerful engines whirring as they fought against the harsh winds and driving rain. The technology that allowed the aircraft to maintain its stealth came at the cost of reduced speed and maneuverability, making landing a tense and precarious affair.

As Lilith and her team offloaded their equipment, another message flashed across her watch, Abbadon's name once again demanding her attention.

I will take this up the chain if you do not answer me, the text warned.

Lilith's heart plummeted, dread settling in the pit of her stomach. She knew her ability to keep Abbadon at bay was rapidly diminishing. When he was in this state, there was no predicting what he might do or how far he would go to get what he wanted.

She distanced herself from the bustling team, ensuring she was well out of both earshot and eyesight before tapping her watch to return Abbadon's call.

A holographic image of him materialized above the device, his face contorted with barely contained rage.

"Kalla!" Abbadon cursed. Sweat glistened on his brow and his long hair hung in disarray around his face. "What are you doing with two of my Kakuten units? How dare you forge my authorization?" he demanded, his eyes boring into her through the holographic projection.

Lilith struggled to maintain an air of innocence, plastering a look of bewilderment on her face. "I thought you received a notification about it?" she said, her voice carefully crafted to convey genuine confusion.

Abbadon's hands slashed in the holographic projection. "Kalla! I am looking at the authorization right now. You forged my signature and General Gadreel's!"

Lilith's façade crumbled. "I had no choice," she confessed in desperation. "Bringing you in would have brought in Central Command. It would have gotten bogged down in red tape. The lead would have gone cold."

"Terminate the mission immediately," he demanded.

The Sons of Lamech were a threat to Masina, even if no one else believed it yet. The thought of abandoning her mission and letting the lead slip through her fingers was unthinkable.

"I can't do that."

"Terminate the mission, or I go straight to the Upper Council."

"They will not have all the details. They could take action that would put the mission and the lives of the team at risk."

"If you do not terminate, that will be on your conscience," he snapped.

"That may be your opinion," she said. "But the mission is a go."

Abbadon's arm swiped across the hologram. Lilith imagined him flailing and seething into a holographic image of her on the other side and was grateful distance separated them.

"I am coming there right now!"

That is the last thing I need.

If Abbadon came in a single unipod transport, he could be there within a few hours. She had to think fast.

"The Flares will hit soon. Our transport cannot take you back," she lied. Temperatures usually went up to 150 degrees from the usual 100 to 115 range during the Flares. It made being outside for more than a few minutes lethal for almost anyone.

He scoffed. "The Flares are not for another eight hours. You must really think I am incompetent."

Her attempt at deception had fallen flat. Time was of the essence. She had to complete the mission before he arrived.

~

Masina had tried to wash the memories of the Forgotten Forest from her history, but a cloth stained with blood always remains red. Her armies had done what was necessary; they had ripped out the spine from the Ebos people who had used these areas as the centerpiece of their war—figuratively, of course. Some people called the Ebos terrorists; others called them freedom fighters. But as far as **Kapten Eliakim Seres** was concerned, there was only one word for anyone that did not fight with Masina—enemy. They had crushed the Ebos quickly and brutally. The chancellor, the unelected head of the Masina Military, had told them this was needed to prevent future conflict. "Brutality now will save lives later," he had said. Eliakim was unsure if he believed it, but he was a kapten in the Kakuten Special Forces. His only option was obedience.

Today was the first time he had returned to Sharik Hora since the war. The trees in this part of the forest reached high to the skies, their red leaves intertwining to create a ceiling over the ground. They blocked most of the sun, creating an endless night for all who walked here. As the rain fell, it funneled together through the leaves like multiple faucets pouring onto the forest floor.

He took a deep breath, filling his lungs with the musty air, then released it with a sigh as the tension in his shoulders loosened. He chewed his lip, staring at the life-size hologram of the forest. Their low-flying drones were updating the maps in real-time. A cluster of blue dots close behind him, Kakuten 47, was awaiting command. Kakuten 48 was stationed south where their transport had landed. About a half mile north, a single blue dot signified his chief scout, Private Senet Marbas.

Something about their mission had felt strange from the start. Since Masina had annexed Sharik Hora from Ebos after the war, the military freely entered and exited the region. Yet, their orders were to arrive by stealth plane, and Major Lilith, not Major Abbadon, was leading them. They were here to investigate and take down the Sons of Lamech, a notorious hate group that operated in the eastern part of Hell. This level of secrecy was unusual for an operation like this.

Yet, something else bothered him more: that single blue dot on his hologram.

"Reset," his voice was low and deep.

The hologram disappeared as the hovering disk floated higher off the ground. It attached itself to the watch on his hand as he headed toward her.

∽

THE GROUND WAS ELEVATED, and the trees sparser. Senet prostrated on a mound of rocks, observing something Eliakim could not see. She glanced back and hurried down before he got close. Even with the rain and wind, she knew he was coming.

"Kapten!" she shouted, and saluted.

She was tall and slim, with straight, long hair and a youngish-looking face, which made people underestimate her skills and intellect.

"The scout with eyes behind her head." He let a stoic expression linger on his face. "They say you see and hear everything... everywhere."

Her gaze dropped, and she bit her lower lip, struggling to contain a smile. "Proximity sensors," she gestured to the device strapped to her wrist.

"At ease," he commanded, his eyes lingering on her for a moment longer. It was the fourth time she had halted his team's movement through the forest. She claimed there were inconsistencies she needed to investigate, but the stops were too frequent. She was up to something, and he was going to find out what.

"Remember Ozeth? The Basin of Greed?" he began. "You were a rookie, yet you tracked and located a rogue soldier for hundreds of miles. Basic gear, no air support... that was impressive."

Her cheeks flushed with pride, and she shuffled her feet. "I am sworn to fulfill my oath. I did what was required of me."

"Do you understand what is required of me in this mission?" He narrowed his gaze.

"You are the mission leader," she responded.

"Yes, and as the mission leader, I shoulder many responsibilities." His voice turned stern, and the pleasant tone evaporated. "What is the role of the mission leader?"

She hesitated, lending some support to his earlier theories.

"Answer my question, Private," he demanded.

"We are here to locate and neutralize the group tagged as the Sons of Lamech," she said. "We must capture their leader alive. As the mission leader, you are to ensure that the operation is successful."

Without missing a beat, almost too confidently.

"As our forward scout, how often have you stopped us to investigate inconsistencies?"

"Kapten, I—"

" 'Kapten, I' is not a number," Eliakim pressed.

"Four," she admitted.

He unsheathed his pistol from its holster, his finger hovering over the trigger. He aimed it at her, his brow furrowed in accusation. "How does an Ebos spy survive so long in the Masina military? You are working with the Sons of Lamech, aren't you?"

Senet's eyes widened in surprise, her hands raised in defense.

"Spy?" she stammered. "Kapten, I... I am loyal to Masina. I have always been loyal. From birth, through life, and till death."

A Flare, a period when the outside temperature would get too high for demons to survive, was coming. But it wasn't for another eight hours. She had to have another angle with her delays.

"You are a spy. Or you are incompetent and stupid. And we have just established you are not incompetent."

"Kapten I—"

"Kalla!" Eliakim cursed. "If the next words out of your mouth are not a confession, they will be your last." Triumph coursed through his veins. He had thought on his feet and caught something many other kaptens would not have. If he could get a confession from Senet right there, his superiors would hold him in high regard. She was well-known; exposing her treachery could be as rewarding as completing the mission.

She cleared her throat and dropped her shoulders. "I have been slowing us down. But I promise you, I am not a spy."

An uncanny level of confidence returned to her.

He kept his finger on the trigger as his eyes darted around. "I am going to need more than that."

"We needed to rest," she said as she looked away from him at the path ahead.

"Kakuten 47 have traveled distances far beyond without rest."

"The stops are for you. Not them."

The words hit him like a bullet. A tightness gripped Eliakim's chest. Panic set in as he realized he had stopped breathing. He coughed and gulped in a lungful of air, his heart pounding. "The one thing I despise more than a disobedient subordinate is a disrespectful one." He tried to project confidence, but he could not hide the tremble in his voice. His fingers quivered as he forced them to loosen their vice-like grip on the trigger.

She knows, but how? He dismissed the thought. *There is no way she can.*

Senet shook her head, her eyes fixed on the ground. "Your limp," she said. "After several miles, it becomes obvious. No one else may have noticed it yet, definitely not Major Lilith. She would have pulled you otherwise." Her voice trailed off into a mumble as Eliakim's mind raced. He had known about his limp for a long time, but never thought it would be a problem on the mission. As Senet's words sunk in, he realized the gravity of the situation.

He let out an uncomfortable laugh. "Not only are you a terrible spy, but you are also a bad liar."

"With all due respect," Senet paused, her gaze never leaving Eliakim. "My job is to see things before everyone else does—the nervousness in your posture. The confidence in your voice you used to first engage is gone. I stand by my assessment."

Eliakim looked at her with a dumbfounded expression.

"I can think of reasons you think keeping this hidden would be beneficial," she continued. "I assure you, people with less discretion than me will soon notice." The bashfulness he had seen and heard from her had disappeared. "I am on your side."

Eliakim approached her. She tilted her body back slightly but did not move. He re-holstered his pistol when they were close enough to hear each other breathe. He dropped the charade and clouded his nervousness with newfound anger. "Being too smart for your own good did no one any favors," he said. "Kalla! The only side you are on is doing what your commanding officer says. Keep this knowledge to yourself. Consider that an order."

Senet steadied her gaze on him. Rain poured down her face. Another succession of lightning strikes lit up the sky, accentuating the red in her eyes.

"Private Senet," Eliakim's jaw set into a grim line. "I am going to need an audible acknowledgment."

"The Blight," she said.

He blinked at her in confusion.

"Your condition. It's what they call it back in Masina—the Blight," she said. "Nagging injuries that don't heal. Rumors of demons infected by it are spreading in some circles."

During a training exercise some weeks prior, Eliakim sustained injuries. Most of them had healed, but his hip had gotten worse. He had feared what was happening to his body, but was even more frightened to seek help. Her words comforted and panicked him simultaneously. Others were going through what he had.

"How can you know this?"

She opened her mouth to speak, then hesitated, wiping her face. "Kapten, it would be wise to move soon. Taking this long may arouse suspicion."

"Answer me!"

"The victims... they vanish. Rumor has it they are moving them to clandestine medical facilities in Axos for experimentation."

Eliakim shuddered again. Sweat from his face mixed with the pouring rain. A nauseating knot twisted in his stomach, a portentous sign he recognized all too well.

"Who is moving them? Clandestine medical facilities?" his voice trembled as he asked.

"Kapten." She looked to the forest, then back at him.

He imagined himself walking around the rest of his unit with everyone watching him, studying his walk, and laughing at him. Major Lilith would arrest him and haul him back to Masina City. A secure, unmarked truck would transport him in chains, sending him off to some underground facility where they would run tubes and experiments on him for the rest of his miserable life.

He couldn't draw any suspicion to them. She was right. A hint of resignation passed over his face. He tapped his earpiece three times, turning it into full broadcast mode.

"We are clear to move out!" he shouted.

He disabled his earpiece and looked her in the eye. "This is not over,"

Mud squelched under his boots, the rainwater pooling deeper in the sandy depressions. A slight twinge in his right thigh made him flinch as he headed back toward his unit. Each stop barely eased the throbbing ache gnawing at his hip. He could not wait for this mission to be over.

∽

"Kapten!" Senet's voice came to life in his earpiece. "We have possible path contamination." Little time had passed since their last encounter.

Eliakim raised his hand and clenched it into a fist. "Eureun!" he shouted. All the soldiers stopped in unison. Their light grumbles didn't surprise him. It was too soon between stops.

Can I trust her to have the right level of discretion?

As he broke from the rest of his team, he noticed he had unconsciously rubbed his thighs together every couple of steps.

"If your aim is to avoid attention from—"

"Cluster munitions fragments buried in the ground." Senet interrupted him. She spread her hands inside the hologram to zoom in.

"Kalla!" he cursed.

He rotated the hologram and zoomed in some more. The halos were half a mile ahead of them. "How bad?"

"Critical," she said. "None of our scans picked this up. This is one of ours." She zoomed in on the first unexploded missile. At the end were red flaps with a shield and the upside-down sword of Masina. She swiped her hand, and an aerial map of the region came up.

"There was not supposed to have ever been any military activity in this area," she said.

"Officially," Eliakim frowned. "How long do you need to find a solution?"

"You don't understand," she said. "There is no acceptable margin of safety we can proceed with. Eagle Eyes needs to deep-scan the entire forest."

His eyes opened wide. "Deep scan would take days!"

"It would have to fly close to the ground." She shifted her weight. "Depending on how thick the rest of the forest is, 'days' could be optimistic. Our mission is no longer viable."

His face reddened. "This better not be another game."

"The cluster munition fragments have proximity sensors. One step in either direction, and we lose everyone. The war with Ebos was a decade ago. Enough time for the ground to shift. Our low-flying drones could easily miss them."

The Eden Ruse

Eliakim looked at the forest floor before taking a step back. "It's a good thing we have the best scout in Masina with us."

He turned to her as his face became stern again. Terminating the mission would mean he would need to wait even longer for a successful promotion to major. He needed it now. His body was failing him.

"With all due respect, I am responsible for our unit's safety as the head scout. My recommendation is to abort," Senet said.

"Acknowledged," Eliakim said, "I order you to find an alternate solution."

Senet looked up from the ground and faced him again. She made a salute and straightened her posture. "My oath prevents me from knowingly subjecting my team to this risk."

Eliakim lost his patience. His commanding officers would never take such insubordination. As he closed the distance between them, the pain traveling up his hip was the worst it had been so far. His hand wrapped around her neck. He squeezed it enough for his grip to dig into her bones. "Kalla! You will follow my orders, or I will relieve you of duty. Then, if we all end up dead because the next in line cannot fix this, it'll be on you."

Her spine went rigid. "If I tell Lilith—"

"You will do no such thing!" Eliakim shouted. Drops of saliva splashed her face before being washed off by rain.

He removed his hand from her neck and stepped back as he deliberated his next move. He was the mission leader, but Lilith was in the control center a couple of miles south. If she caught wind of Senet's recommendation, his authority would crumble.

"All the east region Kakutens are under the command of Major Abbadon, yet Major Lilith is the commanding officer," he whispered. "We came here in a stealth plane, notifying none of the local police. Open your eyes. You are foolish if you think telling Lilith her special mission is not viable will save you."

The silence stretched between them, each waiting for the other to blink first. She had feigned bashfulness but was a slippery, petulant scout.

She put both hands inside the hologram and swiped until a 3D topography map of the forest appeared, the added details from the drones painting a more intricate picture. "I am sure Eagle Eyes will have a solution soon, and we can move forward," she said, avoiding eye contact.

"I trust you will."

∽

EVERY PASSING MINUTE without a word from Senet intensified Eliakim's unease. The relentless downpour had subsided to a gentle rain, but it did little to ease his growing agitation. He remained vigilant, monitoring all private comms within his unit, hoping to catch any sign of Senet's betrayal. A sudden buzzing in his ear startled him, causing him to tense his back. With a swipe of his right hand, he attempted to ward off the pesky bug, but it eluded his grasp. Suppressing a groan, he ignored the discomfort as the pain in his hip flared again. The knowledge of his condition's secret name had only intensified his suffering.

Another bug, its eyes disproportionately large compared to its body, invaded his personal space. Frustrated, he tried again to swat it away, but his efforts resulted in nothing more than hitting himself. Muffled laughter reached his ears, prompting him to turn and face the culprits—Biba and another sniper in Kakuten 47.

Biba, despite his remarkable skills, was small, making Eliakim wonder how he handled the massive sniper rifles slung across his back.

"Private Biba, is there something funny?" Eliakim's irritation seeped into his words as he suspected he were aware of his condition, much like Senet.

"No, Kapten!" Biba snapped back and went into a salute.

"At ease," Eliakim grumbled, his stern eyes still fixed on Biba.

"Kapten, may I?" Biba took a step toward Eliakim.

Eliakim's brows furrowed in mild annoyance, and he waved his hand dismissively. "Go on,"

Biba shot his arm out with impressive speed. He clasped his palm to the right of Eliakim's ear, then opened it to show the crushed remains of the bug. Eliakim wore an unimpressed look. "Get back into formation!" he barked.

Biba's shoulders slumped as he stepped back and fell in line. His gaze dropped, and the faintest hint of disappointment shadowed his eyes.

Good. Someone other than me should have a bad day today.

"Kapten, I have a solution," Senet's calm voice cut through the group broadcast.

Eliakim's heart lifted. He tapped his earpiece twice. "Copy. How do we proceed?"

"Four degrees on coordinate forty-five, three hundred yards right. We confirmed the contamination is isolated to a small area."

Eliakim couldn't help but break into a grin. "Let's move it!" Audible cheers came from the rest of his team.

∼

BARELY TWENTY MINUTES into their march through the forest, a sharp, piercing noise sounded. Like a bee on overdrive, the frantic buzzing struck a nerve deep within Eliakim. In Masina City, where he'd executed countless drills as a private, robots often aided in disarming proximity mines. When a mine's sensor activated, a centrifuge within it would whirl, generating an ominous hum as explosive liquids mixed. It was a unique, harsh sound. Once the deadly hum began, a mere two and a half seconds separated them from a fiery explosion. If someone stepped on the unexploded part of a cluster munition, that would be the exact sound it would make.

He recalled Senet's warning: *We risk losing the entire unit.* He had started the day trying to secure a promotion to major, but now he was evading the shadow of death.

His eyes snapped shut, breath hitching in his throat. He reached behind him, fingers curling around a small, circular disk on his belt. He brought his hand before him and traced a triangular pattern across the disk's surface with his thumb. Half a second spent, two more remained—if he was lucky.

He twisted his torso as his hand swung up and around him. Pain traveled through his hip. He had to roughly triangulate the source of the sound. The rain and thunder made it difficult, but his best guess was right above where Biba stood. He pulled a time dilator from his belt, an experimental device they had received on this mission that slowed time down about a hundred times for a short range. By the time he had turned around to face Biba, another half-second had passed. Bracing himself, he dug his toes into the ground, steadied his head, and hurled the dilator with all his strength. It cut through the air in a slow-motion arc through the falling rain. His aim was his lifeline, the last barrier against impending doom. The device landed beside Biba as the ground ruptured in an explosive roar. Around Biba, a small, translucent sphere materialized, the rising smoke from the blast seeming to move in a surreal, slow motion.

"Bomb Protocol! Evasive cover, now!" Eliakim's voice cut through the air.

While the rest of Kakuten 47 scattered like leaves in the wind, he surged forward, cutting a path straight toward Biba. As he closed their distance, his heart pounded against his ribcage, threatening to shatter the bones. He collided with his sniper's upper torso just as the fire from the explosion engulfed part of his leg. They careened to the ground, landing just beyond the perimeter of the time dilation sphere. They rolled through the mud until, finally, Eliakim pinned Biba beneath him. Eliakim's wings tore through his shirt, erupting from his back with a surge of power. Their dull-white feathers scattered the falling rain droplets into a misty haze. He plunged his wings into the ground, forming a protective canopy around them. He could only hope the others had found cover as the effect of the time dilator faded.

His wings buffered the initial wave of the detonation. Multiple pieces of shrapnel pierced them, wedging between his feathers. Each puncture sent jolts of agony through his body. A secondary blast catapulted them hundreds of yards through the air. Clutching Biba close,

Eliakim encased them within his wings just as they slammed into a tree. He landed on the ground face first, followed by Biba, who crashed onto his back, expelling the remaining breath from his lungs. A groan or scream lay trapped inside him, silenced by the brutal impact.

Half of his face was submerged in a cold puddle—smoke, gunpowder, and burnt flesh filled his nostrils. A desperate attempt to move proved futile, his body unresponsive. As the ringing in his ears intensified, the world around him flickered, fading in and out of focus. Then, as though a dark veil had been drawn, everything went black.

∼

ELIAKIM AWOKE to the pungent smells of burnt metal and soil invading his nose. As he forced his leaden eyelids open, the blurred image of his chief medic hovered over him. Her face came into focus, anxiety etched into her furrowed brow. Her skin was pale, almost chalky, contrasting with the deep green of her eyes.

"This might hurt." Her slender fingers trembled as they gripped the shrapnel jutting from his side. She paused, meeting his gaze before wrenching the serrated fragment free in one smooth motion.

A lance of pain shot through him, eliciting a guttural groan.

"Your wounds are healing remarkably fast. You always were resilient," she said.

His fingers brushed over the healing gashes on his torso. She was right. But as he shifted, a sharp agony erupted from his hip, threatening to draw a scream from him.

The Blight was localized to a small part of his body.

The medic's brows furrowed together as her bright green eyes clouded with unease. "That explosion did a number on you."

"Don't just stand there stating the obvious," Eliakim snapped, gritting his teeth against the pain. He needed her to leave before she examined him more closely.

She rifled through her pack and produced a syringe as long as his hand. "Inject this stimulant into your arm. It should help counter the fatigue until you can properly recover," she said.

"Will this give me the boost I need to finish the mission?"

She studied him with a critical eye. "Let's assess how you respond to the first dose."

"Double the dose," Eliakim rasped out.

"I wouldn't recommend that," a voice said. Eliakim turned to find Senet, who seemed to have materialized from the shadows.

Before Eliakim could object, Senet stepped forward and plucked the syringe from the medic's hand. "I'll take it from here," Senet asserted.

The medic objected, but Senet silenced her with a sharp glance. "That one is probably in greater need of medical attention," she said, pointing to Biba.

The medic raised her hands in surrender. She picked up her bag and hurried in his direction. Though his entire right foot was missing, his body had already sealed the wound. He was alive.

Senet retrieved a vial from her pocket, emptied its contents into the syringe, and handed it to Eliakim.

Suspicion clouded his eyes. "You did this, didn't you? Trying to finish the job?" A nervous laugh punctuated his words.

"If I wanted to get rid of you, I would have phoned in your empty threats to Major Lilith."

With shaking hands, Eliakim grabbed the syringe and plunged it into his thigh, releasing the mysterious serum into his body.

"This will numb the pain in your hip, allowing you to complete the mission," Senet said.

"You had a way all this time?"

"If you are too loud, someone might hear us."

Eliakim grumbled. "I went against your recommendation. If we had turned around, this would not have happened. Why would you help me?"

Before Senet could reply, a new presence cast a shadow over them: Major Lilith. She did not have the friendly camaraderie Senet did. As she approached, her piercing red eyes bore into him.

Snapping to attention, Senet saluted. "Major!"

"As you were," Lilith said.

With a grimace betraying the searing pain, Eliakim's trembling hands found the ground. Each push was agony as he tried to hoist himself up.

"You can stay right there if you need to," Lilith said.

He knew it was a command, not a request.

With an imperious flick of her hand, Lilith gestured for Senet to distance herself from their conversation.

"Kapten." Lilith's voice was as cold as ice.

Mustering strength, Eliakim proudly said, "Major, we avoided any casualties."

"A Kakuten does not get praise for cleaning up his mess."

"Sorry, Major, I thought—"

"I was assured you were the best." She interrupted him. "But it looks like the best isn't good enough."

Her words burned him deeper than her eyes. He had taken too much disrespect from his team, and now his commanding officer was adding to it. How dare she?

"Major, I—"

She waved her arm again for him to keep silent. The gesture infuriated and embarrassed him even more. "Clean yourself up. I need a complete damage assessment.."

"Consider it done," he said.

She turned and departed, leaving Eliakim seething. Gathering saliva in his mouth, he spat where she had stood.

7

SONS OF LAMECH

A few hundred feet from the explosion's aftermath, Abbadon stood motionless. His skin, usually off-white, had a darker hue. His face always wore a permanent frown, making him look nothing short of gruesome and intimidating when he was angry.

"You have crossed the line," he said. A flicker of irritation narrowing his gaze. Abbadon always made **Lilith** feel small, his broad shoulders eclipsing her petite frame.

"You were not supposed to know," she replied. "We would have been back in Masina City by now with Lamech in our custody."

The Kakuten 47 soldiers were scattered around, tending to their wounds and salvaging what they could from the ruins of their equipment. Amid the chaos, it was miraculous that they all had survived.

"Have you lost your mind? You forged a general's signature. Do you think capturing Lamech would make that go away?"

"The general won't notice unless he has a reason to look."

"You can't hide the damage to our equipment. There will be questions about what you are doing here, and now I am implicated, too." Abbadon said.

"You would have had the perfect cover if you had not come."

"We must terminate this immediately."

Again. By the book. What a square. "Neutralize the Sons of Lamech and capture their leader. My mission remains the same," she said.

"I don't think you get it." Abbadon turned to face her, his agitation visible. "My soldiers could have died, and your only concern is the mission?"

"Their oath was to the badge, not you," Lilith retorted.

"Don't get smart with me. Not now." Abbadon's frustration bubbled over. "Kalla! Their badge compels them to follow the chain of command, not a rogue major!"

"These are your soldiers, are they not?" she said with a tinge of sarcasm. "So then, why am I responsible for their incompetence?"

Abbadon had always been risk averse. He would never have even made it to major had it not been for her dragging him along. But the moment he took that step, he forgot how he got there.

"The destroyer," she said. "That was your call sign when we were kaptens. Every mission we completed wasn't because we quit when things went south. We would give our all in this life and the next for Masina. That was what we swore."

Abbadon spat on the ground. "We did this for a long time. Side missions, unorthodox strategies, enormous risks... We both made major. Wasn't that the point of everything? To rise higher than anyone thought possible. Two demons, one born to a thief and another a prostitute." He paused, as if rearranging the words he was about to say. "Now, I'm not sure what drives you. This mission... I know it is personal for you with the Sons of Lamech. They despise seraphim just for existing. But perhaps that makes you too invested."

"Made major?" Lilith scoffed. *My promotion was one of the most miserable days of my career.* "They sidelined me behind a desk, then gave you Kakuten East."

"You always had a way of looking at things," he said. "You have been very effective at internal intelligence. Too effective."

"I am not a hound that wags its tail when put on a leash!"

"Very far from it," he said. "General Gadreel keeps telling me you are my blind spot. I believe him."

"His name would not be on your tongue if not for me," she

snapped. "Do not pretend you did not get as much out of me as you gave."

Abbadon's eyes widened as a look of astonishment traveled across his face. He ran his hand down his shirt and straightened imaginary creases. He turned away from her and took a single step. "You think I risked it all so many times just because of what was in it for me?"

"The resilience we show in the face of adversity. That is strength," she said. "Are you an asset or a liability?"

His hands clenched into fists. "I won't be reckless. I am not some naïve recruit anymore. People depend on me—that is leadership. My end will not be from a bullet I did not need to take."

Lilith shook her head in disappointment. "Do you think our founding leaders relied on protocol to defend Masina? Our nation was built on the blood of people who took risks and stepped out of their comfort zone. The blood of many soldiers before us who did not back down at the first fear of failure."

"I need no lecture on our history," he said. "We won the war and many others after. What is the point if we keep on fighting? Today, the Sons of Lamech. Tomorrow, who? Are you here for Masina? Or here for Lilith?" He sighed. "Sometimes passion is a double-edged sword."

Lilith's face reddened. She told herself she would never be in this position again. But using Abbadon was the only way she could have done this. "The moment an officer is unable to complete their duty, they must resign immediately."

"You have lost your mind if you think you can stage an Article Three intervention," he said.

"The only court of law to answer to is both of us. I am asking you, Major Abbadon. If you are not able to fulfill your mission, then you are duty-bound to step aside."

The disgust on his face made her wince. She wanted to back down and agree with him but she couldn't stop. That was her weakness and her strength.

He took a few steps toward the mobile control room, where she had monitored the mission before the explosion. "If your unorthodoxy and scrappiness are beneficial to Masina, ask yourself why your superiors put you behind a desk and gave me Kakuten East." When he turned his head, he had a pained expression. "After this mission, we are done. The next time, I will go straight to the Upper Council. I do not care if the mission is already in progress."

As she watched him move away, his figure shrinking in the distance, the wind picked up, whipping dust against her face. His words stung, their hurt magnified by the kernel of truth in them. Yet she was rooted to the spot, unable to bring herself to go after him and resolve their differences. She had to continue the mission.

∽

LILITH'S INFORMATION placed their target right where she stood. Yet beneath her feet, the ground was mud and jagged rocks. Kapten Eliakim's team scoured the area, finding nothing but sparse trees and imposing mountains.

"Enlarge," her voice was a whisper. A spinning disc emerged from the watch and hovered above the ground before her. A holographic display materialized, presenting a detailed terrain map. Tiny blue dots illuminated it, each representing the position of Kakuten 47. She zeroed in on the one person who would be the most useful.

∽

AS LILITH APPROACHED, Senet turned to face her. In her grip was a device similar to Lilith's watch, but larger and more intricate, its rectangular screen glowing in her hands.

"Major!" Senet stamped her foot and gave her a salute.

"I need anything you've got,"

Senet shook her head, a disappointed look crossing her face. She tossed the screen into the air. It went into a spin and hovered over the muddy terrain. An imposing hologram, nearly their height, flickered to life above it. "Our drones have scoured the vicinity," Senet reported, her tone flat. "Nothing but endless rocks."

Lilith's gaze locked onto the map, analyzing every contour and symbol. She maneuvered the holographic terrain, sliding it left and right, her hands orchestrating a silent search for answers.

"Do you see something, Major?"

"Negative." Lilith shook her head. She was getting nervous. The mission had already cost too much. They couldn't leave empty-handed. They watched intently for another minute.

"Hold on!" Senet's voice ran out.

Lilith glanced at her, startled.

"South, twenty. West, thirty."

Lilith obliged.

Senet's eyes widened in realization. "That's how they did it,"

"Translation?" Lilith frowned as she raced to find what Senet saw before she revealed it.

"Look closer, Major." Senet zoomed in on the hologram.

Lilith strained, but she saw nothing of significance.

"Examine the rocks in the center. Compare their patterns to the surroundings."

Lilith gasped in astonishment.

"It's made from the same material as the surrounding rocks. Some of it could even be buried underground," Senet said.

"If it was thick enough…" Lilith pondered aloud.

"Our scans would never detect it," Senet completed her sentence.

An unsettling sensation gnawed at Lilith's gut. "Building structures embedded in Krinote rocks? Ebos isn't this advanced." She tore her gaze from the holograph. "The Sons of Lamech were merely a loose collection of hate groups, rebels, and insurrectionists spanning across the eastern part of Hell. How did they develop the expertise for stealth buildings?" Lilith paced, her mind racing. They had evaded detection for so long, and she had always thought it was because the government was not taking them seriously.

Senet shrugged in response.

Lilith tapped her earpiece and called Eliakim to join them.

"Deploy our deep scanners," she said when he arrived. "I want to know how big this structure is, every bend, every room, everything inside. Double-check our Navigation disruption systems. No one goes in or out of this area," Lilith said.

Eliakim nervously cleared his throat. Around them, every eye was fixed on the hovering hologram.

"Major, the blast obliterated our deep scanners. If we involve Central Command, with precise coordinates, their long-range satellites might penetrate the building."

There is no way we are ready to deal with Central Command now.

"Central Command will interfere," she said. "We will do this the old-school way."

"Are you sure?" he asked.

Lilith shot him a glare that said everything without her needing to open her mouth.

"Of course, Major!" Eliakim stuttered as a flash of red washed over his face. "There are two possible entrances. We can split the team across both and work our way up. Or we could do it one at a time and have a small force covering the back. Another alternative is to—"

"Are you asking me for directions on how to do your job?" she mocked. "What about a three-way call with the chancellor so he can give his input?"

"Of course not, Major!" he stammered before hastily turning away, avoiding her gaze.

∽

"CLEAR!" Eliakim's voice echoed through the hollow corridor. He and his four-person squad had just charged into another room down the hall. Operating in a tight group of five, their rear guard inched backward, eyes vigilantly scanning behind them as the squad advanced. Lilith trailed them a couple of feet behind.

The entire structure mirrored the exterior, adorned with intricate patterns and designs carved into the rock. The interior was an uncanny blend of a natural cave and an artificially produced structure, echoing with hollow, subterranean sounds yet marked by the deliberate straight lines and corners. From the sheer scale and precision, it appeared someone had excavated the entire formation in situ or shaped the native rock into a concrete-like structure. As she entered the room nearest her, she grazed her fingertips against the cold, rough texture of the entrance's edge, the mineral scent of the rock filling her nostrils.

The Sons of Lamech posed a significant threat, justifying the extreme measures she had taken to find them. But a nagging uncertainty gnawed at her as she surveyed the sophisticated structure. The technology required to create such a thing was rare, even in Masina. It was as if she were staring at a puzzle with its central piece missing, and the implications unsettled her deeply.

This room had been turned into an office with scattered desks and chairs. All the drawers were disappointingly empty. She ran her hand over the surface, finding no trace of dust. Someone had been here recently. The bare walls had light fixtures at the top.

A building made of rock in a remote forest in Ebos has working electricity.

At the end of the room, translucent material covered the windows. She swung them open, inviting a wash of light into the room. Despite its translucency, the window felt rigid, almost as unyielding as stone. It could easily be mistaken as part of the walls from the outside.

"Clear!" Eliakim's voice echoed from the floor above her. With a heavy sigh, she closed her eyes, hoping they would find something or someone.

∼

KAKUTEN 47 huddled near the building's entrance, the untamed grass stretching out in a semicircle from the frontage, bordered by imposing monoliths. Lilith sighed, rubbing her temples. "We must have missed something," she said to Eliakim.

Eliakim's shoulders slumped, and he dropped his gaze. "Major, we've combed every corner of the building. If there were something to find, we would have found it."

"Do it again," she commanded.

"Yes, Major." Eliakim signaled his unit. They abruptly ceased unpacking and re-shouldered their gear.

"Why are we wasting more time here?" Abbadon glanced at the watch on his wrist.

"We could have missed something." She avoided eye contact with him and stared back at the building.

"We need to think about damage control, which is what we should have been doing hours ago. We need to get ahead of the news and think about what we will tell the council. They will—"

"I don't care about the council!" she retorted. She covered her defeat and disappointment with anger.

"You may have thought little about the future of your career, but I can assure you, I have many more years to spend as a major."

"Kalla!" She took a defiant step back and pivoted away from him.

"I helped you against my better judgment. It's over," he said.

Lilith turned around and took two steps toward him. Abbadon rocked back on his heels, a flash of surprise flicking across his features. She raised her hand in surrender. Their height difference was more pronounced as she met his gaze.

Abbadon's rigid posture melted, relief washing over his features. "We will continue to learn from mistakes."

"Kapten," she shouted to Eliakim, "order your men to pack up. Let's go home."

"Yes, Major," Eliakim replied, his hesitant smile failing to reach his wary eyes.

"We have more unresolved business," Abbadon said. "But we will discuss it at a more appropriate time." He moved toward the boulders surrounding the building.

"Major Lilith." Senet's voice called out. Lilith turned to face her. "Forty-five minutes," Senet exclaimed.

Lilith furrowed her brows. "What?"

"It took us forty-five minutes to cover the building." Senet glanced up at the structure as she spoke. A level of excitement filled her voice. "We spent about five minutes on each floor. Five minutes on each floor, nine floors. That's forty-five minutes."

"And there is some point you are getting to?"

"There are thirteen rows of windows in this building," she said, pointing to the top.

Lilith assessed the building and counted. Her face dropped. "There was no—" she started.

The whizzing reached her ears before she spotted the flash in her peripheral vision originating from one of the top windows. *Snipers.*

The bullet struck Eliakim squarely in the head. The way it shattered his skull suggested the use of diamond rounds. As the rest of his torso flew through the air, blood and flesh splattered her face, painting it the same red as Senet's eyes. His dismembered body landed with a loud, sickening sound. As another flash emanated from a different window, Lilith's wings exploded from her back, encircling her in a protective shield. The feathers, darker than most, glistened with a deep, ethereal shade of charcoal, their magnificent wingspan stretching twice the length of her body. A bullet tore through them with a resounding blast, its deadly trajectory burying itself in the top of her shoulder. Her wings absorbed most of the impact and prevented her arm from being torn off. A primal scream escaped her lips, echoing her agony as searing pain rippled through every fiber of her being. She tumbled backward as more gunshots sounded.

One by one, Kakuten 47 fell, struck by unseen snipers. The precise, deadly shots targeted their heads and hearts. Screams, gunfire, cracking bones, and the squelch of feet running on mud filled the air. She ran in a zigzag path toward the boulders surrounding the building. The last time she felt that vulnerable was during the Masina-Ebos war. As she neared, she saw Abbadon on the ground, blood gushing from his neck like a relentless torrent. His wings had protracted, and a gaping hole in the left one was the only thing that kept his head attached to his body.

"No, no!" she cried, her heart pounding as she surged toward him.

Bullets continued to whiz through the air, the agonizing screams cutting deep into her. Each cry was like a physical blow, and her body trembled with fear.

With a powerful flap of her wings, she managed to drag Abbadon to safety, propelling them both behind cover.

Kalla! Why do you weigh so much?

As she dragged him behind a massive boulder, a stray bullet nicked his leg, a close call in the relentless hail of gunfire. She pressed her hand against his chest, feeling the flutter of his heart—weak, yet stubbornly rhythmic beneath her trembling fingers. In a desperate bid, she drew her pistol, firing two rounds into the dirt to generate heat. She then pressed the hot barrel against the gash on his neck, singed flesh mingled with the metallic tang of blood as it cauterized the wound.

"Stay with me, you stubborn fool!" she shouted as his body convulsed. Blood sputtered from his mouth. "Today is not your day to die. Not on my watch."

His pallid skin and shallow breathing spoke of a wound too deep for self-healing. She rotated her wrist, but the holographic device on her hand had suffered irreparable damage. A viscous black fluid pooled beneath a jagged crack in the glass. She tossed the broken device aside, only to have it obliterated by a barrage of bullets.

"Kalla!" she shouted. She slammed her hand on the ground. She tapped her earpiece and tuned it to the local broadcast frequency.

"Kapten Orgun, do you copy?" Lilith asked.

"Major," he responded. Kapten Orgun of Kakuten 48 was still stationed at the makeshift command center a few miles south.

"Mass casualties. Abbadon is critically injured. I need an immediate bypass to Central Command."

Lilith's mind flickered to the inevitable uproar once they discovered the unsanctioned nature of the mission.

"Major! Do you need reinforcements?" Orgun said.

"Negative. We're pinned down by multiple enemy snipers in elevated positions."

"Copy that, Major," Orgun said. "Setting up the relay now." He barked commands in the background. It took almost thirty seconds before she heard him again. "Major, you are live with Central Command."

"Central Command, do you read me?"

"This is Central Command. Loud and clear."

"We are pinned down at coordinates zero, delta, 45.54 54.55 67.22. I repeat zero, delta, 45.54 54.55 67.22. Mass casualties. Major Abbadon is in critical condition. Requesting air support immediately."

"I have no record of any mission at this location," the operator said.

"I don't have time to explain," she shouted. "Verify my identity by voice."

The line was silent for about five seconds. "Confirm coordinates zero, delta, 45.54 54.55 67.22," the operator said.

"Coordinates confirmed."

"Air support en route. Forty-five minutes ETA," the operator said.

"Major, you are going to want to hear this," Orgun interrupted.

What else could I want to hear? "What?" she asked.

"We double-checked our readings to confirm. The next Flare is happening in less than thirty minutes."

"That's impossible," Lilith said. "Our mission parameters don't have it for another few hours."

"Major, we checked it three times."

"Central Command, can you verify?" Lilith asked.

There was a long silence filled with the barrage of bullets before the comms came to life again. "There appears to be significant atmospheric shifts in your location. Kapten Orgun's assessment is correct. We must recall our air support."

Lilith's breath caught in her throat. Bullets rained in a relentless spree, hammering against the barrier to Lilith's left, mere feet from the boulder serving as Senet's makeshift shield. The air was thick with the acrid stench of shells and the sharp tang of fear. Each bullet strike was a brutal percussion, chipping away at the rocks and sending shards flying. Time was a merciless enemy; All the snipers had to do was keep them pinned for another thirty minutes, and they would all be dead from the heat of the Flares.

"Level the building with Sentinel. Do it now!" Lilith shouted into her comms.

"Major, you are in the blast radius. Your probability of survival is too low to take that course of action."

Not much better than being burned by the heat.

"Kalla! What is your name, operator?"

"Faro," the operator said. "Private Faro."

"Listen to me Private Faro. I do not intend to lose any more soldiers today. Find me another solution." Exhausted and desperate, Lilith slumped behind the rock as bullet sounds continued to fill the air.

"Five snipers," Senet's voice crackled over the broadcast channel. "Three on the top floor, two beneath. I have locked on their precise positions, except for one: elusive, more patient than the rest. He could be in either of two locations."

"What are you suggesting?" Lilith asked.

"Snipers one to three are on the top floor," she said, "the first at the far-right window. The second, two windows to the left. The third, three windows further. They're prone, nestled at the left bottom of the window. The others, positioned dead center, are ten inches off the midpoint, likely elevated on some makeshift perch."

Lilith glanced at Senet, who sat with her legs crossed and her hands on her knees like she was meditating. She could have sworn Senet's body became blurry for a few seconds. She blinked, attributing the anomaly to her strained nerves.

"Three seconds to shoot," Senet continued. Her eyes were still closed. "One to steady, one to aim, and one to fire. There is a rifle next to the bottom half of Kapten Eliakim's body. If we can reach it, we can eliminate the threat."

"You can triangulate sniper positions based on just the sounds of the bullets?" Lilith asked, doubt heavy in her tone.

"Yes, Major," Senet confirmed.

The confidence in Senet's voice did little to calm Lilith's skepticism. "The snipers will kill you long before you get near it," Lilith said.

"They would take *me* out," Senet said. "But *you* have a higher chance of success." She opened her eyes and moved into a crouch to stare at Lilith.

She was serious.

Lilith looked down at Abbadon. His chest expanded and contracted in slow movements. Senet's plan was suicide. But Abbadon had said it. *If it is not old age that kills me, it will not be a bullet that I didn't have to take.* It was her mess. She pulled him into it. It was her responsibility to pull him out.

"Central Command, copy," Lilith's voice was tense as she spoke into her earpiece.

"Major. I know you didn't ask for our recommendation, but we strongly advise against Private Senet's plan," Faro said.

"You are right," Lilith said. "I didn't ask. In ninety seconds, I need you to target a location exactly one click north of here."

"What is your objective?" Faro said.

"Eighty-nine seconds," Lilith said. "It is important the timing is exact."

"What is—"

"Eighty-six seconds," she cut him off.

"Copy that, Major," Faro said.

The blast would give her a few seconds head start. It was not much, but she would take whatever she could. She looked down at Abbadon, and a deep sadness filled her. She put her hand on his shoulder.

"Till our last breath," she said to him. "Till my last breath."

His body struggled to heal itself. A single tear traveled down her eye. "Live or die, our fate today will be the same," she said. "If we do not speak again here, I hope you find what you expect to see in the next life."

Fifteen seconds left.

She closed her eyes and took a deep inhale, calming herself.

Ten seconds.

The urge to retreat clawed at her, but the thought of leaving Abbadon's fate to chance was unbearable. If he perished because of her hesitation, regret would haunt her for eternity. She remembered an old saying her father used to repeat.

Nothing comes from nothing.

BOOM!

The explosions rocked the ground. Lilith took off from the safety of the only thing that had kept her alive and rushed into the open field toward the dismembered part of Eliakim's body. One second to aim at her heart or her head. Another to steady their hands, and then a third to pull the trigger.

Boom.

Before the crack of the rifle reached her, she was already sinking to her knees, sending her body into a controlled slide across the ground, her torso arching backward. Four bullets whizzed over her, making circular vortexes through the air. She sprang back up and took two more steps toward the gun. One more second to re-aim. Another to steady the weapons. She dug her heel into the ground and twirled in the opposite direction, away from the gun. Three more bullets whizzed past, going through where her next expected step would have been. They had aimed lower.

As she had guessed, after missing twice, they fired more quickly. She sprinted in a zigzag, her movements like a dance of survival across the battlefield. One bullet missed her thigh, but the vortex grazed it, drawing blood—no time for pain. The rifle lay just a few steps away—almost within reach.

Senet's words triggered a sudden realization: the last sniper had been holding their fire, making it difficult to pinpoint their location. An idea sparked in Lilith's mind as she dashed toward the gun. At the last moment, she unfurled her wings to their fullest span and hammered them into the ground, forcing herself to an abrupt halt. She arched her body backward and lifted off her feet into a backflip. The bullet from the last sniper buried itself in the ground just in front of her.

"Kalla!"

Tumbling forward, she retracted her wings as her back hit the ground. She grabbed the rifle mid-motion, disengaging the safety. Before landing on her feet, she squeezed six shots into the building.

Less than fifteen seconds had passed. Her heart beat heavily with excitement. She had succeeded. Senet's plan had worked. It worked because she was still standing.

"Move on the eleventh and twelfth floor now!" Lilith's voice boomed with urgency.

"Affirmative, Major!" The resolute voices of what remained of the Kakuten echoed in her ears. Her jog transformed into a sprint as she closed in on the building.

She leaped, and her wings unfurled, powerful flaps propelling her skyward. They wrapped around her as she dove. Lilith smashed through the window on the top floor, glass particles embedding into her. She hit the floor in a roll, rising into a defensive lunge with one palm planted firmly on the ground. Four demons occupied the space amid scattered papers and walls shrouded in computer screens. The setup resembled a sprawling data mining operation rather than a ragtag conspiracy. Her wings extended, launching shards of glass across the room. Three of the four demons screamed in agony as the shards lodged in their heads and torsos. They crumpled to the floor in pain-ridden heaps.

The remaining demon charged at her with a diamond-plated dagger gleaming ominously in his hand.

These demons are more funded than the Masina government itself. How did they stay under the radar for so long?

Lilith retracted her wings as the demon swiped at her with his weapon. She lashed out with her foot, striking the side of his knee. The sickening crunch of bone reverberated, and he let out a strangled scream, the dagger slipping from his hand. Hobbled and desperate, he lunged at her, aiming a punch at her face. With a calculated move, she trapped his incoming fist in her right hand, using her left to hook under his armpit. With a brutal twist, his elbow snapped with an unforgiving crunch. A piercing scream tore from his throat. She yanked him toward her and snatched a blade from her belt, pressing the cold, sharp edge against his trembling throat.

"Lamech the Grotesque," Lilith said into his ear. "Tell me where he is. Tell me now." Her heart pounded in her chest as she spoke.

"Outside this room. The second door on the left!" he said. "I don't want to die! Please don't kill me."

"You don't want to die?" Lilith hissed as she sliced his neck open. "Then you should never have been born." She stabbed him three times, then buried her knife into his head from the top. His limp body fell from her hands to the floor.

∽

THE WALLS WERE HIDDEN behind stacks of cardboard boxes, reaching from floor to ceiling. Papers stapled to them covered the visible spaces between the stacks. As Lilith moved further down the room, she noticed a board with photos and papers stapled to it. Her index finger brushed her pistol's trigger, which she kept pointed downward as she crept on. The board displayed pictures of the entire Masina Upper Council, with arrows showing the chain of command. Below, most of the Lower Council members' pictures were neatly stapled together.

In Masina, the military ranks and council members were a matter of public record, a fact that seldom raised an eyebrow. However, what arrested her attention was the bold, ominous inscription to the left: *COVERT*. Beneath this declaration, the photos of three demons stared back at her. The Upper Council's shadow members were known only to an elite circle, including the chancellor, president, and a few others. The revelation that the Sons of Lamech might be privy to the clandestine knowledge sent a chill down her spine. It was inconceivable that the chancellor would betray such secrets. Yet, the alternative was a more harrowing prospect.

She would have to verify if the information was accurate. She captured a mental snapshot of their faces before igniting them with a lighter, tossing it aside as she pressed on.

"You and your filth infiltrate my lands, my place, my home," the voice whispered behind her, its spiteful tone crawling under her skin, "and now the rotten stench of a Seraphim fills my lungs."

Keeping her pistol aimed at the ground, she turned slowly, her finger hovering half-pressed against the trigger. "Lamech." The hairs on the back of her neck stood up.

In circles, they called him "Lamech the Grotesque," a name that was not lost on him. His upper body, a twisted caricature of normality, sat atop spindly, underdeveloped legs. The right side of his form loomed over his left, a monstrous asymmetry burned into his flesh. Acid burns marred half his face, while scaly skin encased his larger arm. An oversized chain, its end burdened with a spiked metal boulder, hung heavily around his neck.

Lilith took two steps back. "Under the jurisdiction of Section 1554c, decreed by the Military Code of the esteemed Military Region of Masina, you stand accused of heinous crimes against the nation."

"Masina rejects your kind, yet you come here and spew her venom." An unimpressed look crossed his face. "You wield no power here. Masina—a nation stripped of all legitimacy, a crumbling edifice of authority. It is a diseased entity, its very essence riddled with decay, a rot gnawing relentlessly at its core. Like a plague, it spreads, an insidious infection that seeps into its neighbors, engulfing everything in its path with a creeping, destructive flame." He glanced downwards and spat. "My followers, restless in their pursuit, shall find no peace until we deliver the cure—a salvation that extends beyond this blighted land."

"Put down your weapon! On your knees! Hands behind your head!" she commanded.

Lamech and people like him were the reason she sometimes felt like she was not good enough, even as she rose through the military ranks. Every one of them had their own misguided story of what motivated them. She steadied her grip on her pistol. Her gaze locked onto the man whose followers had tried as much as possible to make the lives of people like her miserable. "On your knees and hands behind your head!" Her words were for Masina, but the fire in her eyes was personal.

"I will purge eastern Hell of your kind, returning our people to their rightful grandeur."

Each word he spoke stirred a nest of hornets in her chest. Her fingers itched to pull the trigger, but she knew he was more valuable alive. "Do you think you are the first Malakh purist we have killed or captured?"

"You cannot stop what is already in motion."

"Just as I found you, we will find the one who takes your place, and the one after that, and the one after—"

She stopped mid-sentence as he swung his bigger hand over his body. The chain whirled around him, sweeping up the boulder in its momentum. With a powerful heave, he launched it directly at her.

She dodged, sliding into a perfect middle split. Leaning back, she tracked the boulder's trajectory overhead. Squinting with one eye, she aimed her pistol skyward and fired twice. Her shots severed the chains, detaching the boulder that smashed through the room's rear wall, leaving a massive hole. She swiveled back to face Lamech. He was already in motion, the chain discarded, a knife glinting in his clenched fist as he barreled toward her.

He lunged, his gleaming blade aiming for her head. She planted her palms on the cold, hard floor, sliding her body backward with a swift push. The blade's edge hissed through the air, mere inches from her face, severing a solitary strand of her hair which fluttered to the ground. Before he could recalibrate, she was a blur of movement, springing up and closing the distance with two rapid steps.

He swung again, the blade whistling menacingly. Anticipating his move, she executed a deft tumble forward. The blade sliced through the air where she'd just been as she landed behind him. Without a backward glance, she drew her weapon and fired two calculated shots, each bullet finding a home in his legs. His scream echoed in the confined space as he crumpled to his shins. She leaped, her knees becoming twin hammers, striking either side of his head. As she descended, her elbows drove down on his head with as much force as possible. There was a loud crack from his skull.

With a wild scream, he spun in a whirlwind of desperate fury. He sent her flying across the room like a weightless projectile. She collided with the opposite wall in a thunderous crash. She crumpled to the ground, the sickening pop in her knee heralding a sharp, searing pain that radiated up her leg. Fighting through the agony, she pushed herself up and limped toward him. He crawled toward the door that exited into the hallway. She fired two shots, the bullets striking the floor just inches from his reaching hands.

"It's over." Her voice was steel, even as her arm trembled with the weight of the gun she kept trained on him.

"It is just the beginning." He punctuated his words by spitting a glob of blood onto the floor.

Her face mixed with confusion and disgust. "Do you think you are special? No force in Hell can hurt us. Why do you think you can?" She took two more painful steps toward him. "Soon, no one will speak or remember your name. We will find all your followers and destroy them."

Lamech's body arched as he broke into a laugh.

Lilith pointed her gun at his foot and fired off a shot. The bullet pierced his flesh, followed by a scream from him. More blood pooled around his leg.

"Why do you do what you do? Do you hate yourself so much that you can exist only in chaos?" she asked.

"Freedom and prosperity, the lies your people tell while they continue to oppress us in occupation and control," he said.

"Since Masina has controlled Sharik Hora, it has prospered more than any other part of Ebos. Can you not see the good we bring?"

"You have done nothing but stop peace."

Lilith looked at him with disdain. He had been reduced to a desperate demon in turmoil. "Why do you have the identities of the hidden members of the Upper Council?" She finally put the other thing that had been bothering her into words.

"If only you knew the events you set in motion, you would wish you had never come," he proclaimed.

She wanted to snap his neck. It would make her feel better. "It will be much more pleasurable talking to me than the interrogators back in Masina City."

A smile returned to his face as he started laughing. "Foolish child." He pulled out a knife, previously hidden in his pants.

She huffed in bewilderment as she aimed at his head. "Why can you not see that this is over?" It was too late before she realized the intended target was not her. He put the sharp blade to his chest, where his heart was, and stabbed himself.

"No!" she screamed as his body slumped.

She dropped her gun to the floor as she hobbled across the room. She placed her finger on his wrist and crouched beside him. His pulse was almost nonexistent. Her gaze swept the room in a cautious arc to ensure no one else was near. No one could see what she was about to do. As her mouth opened wider, her incisors extended, doubling in length. She bent Lamech's head to the side and buried them into his neck. Her eyes rolled back in their socket as the blood, a stream carrying Lamech's memories, flowed into her.

What secrets were you willing to die for?

His body, on the brink of life, was in a state of distress. The rush of images nearly overwhelmed her: *rallies, violence, rousing speeches, a charismatic demon leading his followers against Masina. But most of all, the man's unyielding conviction.* She scanned some more and landed on a memory of interest. *There was a woman. Her face was blurry. There was another demon who she could not see at all.*

"The shipment will leave at port four five nine as planned," *the woman said.* "The Eden Protocol will—" The images faded before coming back into focus. "Make sure it is done right this time, Daeva. Or you know what the consequences will be." It wasn't Lamech's voice, but that of another demon.

Everything went black as Lamech's body went limp. He was dead.

The Masina Government Headquarters, also known as the "Dome," was a sprawling labyrinth of architectural might comprising seven towering structures. An average demon could stroll from one end to another in an hour. Building three stood out—a magnificent, sixty-story, half-oval structure with subterranean depths shrouded in secrecy. Its glass façade glittered under the sun, casting prismatic reflections. Rumors hinted at celestial materials woven into its inner walls, but truth and myth were inseparably entwined there.

In the stuffy confines of a windowless room inside the building, **Lilith** and four other intelligence operatives convened for their monthly debrief. They sat around a central table, a holographic display at its center casting an eerie glow across their faces. Three hours of mind-numbing briefings had already passed, each second grating against Lilith's nerves like sandpaper. She suppressed a sigh, her fingers twitching with the urge to do anything other than endure another moment of this.

The analyst stood, his tall, lanky frame unfolding from the chair. His bushy gray hair was neatly combed over, and wire-rimmed glasses perched on his nose. He manipulated the holograph with long, bony fingers until a rendering of Hell appeared. Red circles covered the map, with the biggest being in neighboring Ebos.

"We know the Flares have always been a nuisance," he said. "But their intensity and duration have increased at an alarming rate, culminating in a record 155 degrees during the last incident in eastern Hell."

Lilith leaned back in her chair. The Flare incident had happened four hours earlier than expected during the mission in Sharik Hora. Between that, and the discoveries about the Sons of Lamech, something was off.

"The relentless heat is damaging our equipment faster and faster, driving costs to the sky. What was once a minor hassle has escalated into a crisis threatening our national security," the analyst continued.

"National security?" Lilith scoffed, raising her eyebrows. "Last I checked, we were not the only nation in Hell."

"Our equipment is more advanced," he said. "But with that comes a higher sensitivity to extreme conditions."

"That doesn't sound more advanced to me," she said dismissively.

A few chuckles broke out around the table.

The private shot the laughing analysts a stern look. "Major, this is serious," he pleaded.

Lilith held up her hands in mock surrender. "Can we recommend altering our production methods?"

He shook his head. "Our resources are already thin as it is. We are spending more and more on the development of advanced long-range weaponry to counter the Aamaris threat."

This was the real punishment intended when I was moved from Kakuten East to internal intelligence: having to sit through these briefings. "Then we take this to the Lower Council," she suggested, "and request additional funding."

"In an election year?" he asked. "The Lower Council will be far more concerned with issues that directly impact voters. Infrastructure, job creation... defense spending will be a tough sell."

The irony that national security was not an issue that swayed voters was not lost on her.

Peace is hard to appreciate in the absence of war.

She sighed, massaging her temples. "Draft the request. Our job is to make recommendations. They can sort out their priorities. Anything else to report?" Her internal voice begged the analyst to say no.

A tense silence fell over the room as he manipulated the holographic display again, bringing up a dizzying array of graphs and data points. "Kakuten 47 and 48 left behind a sensor array after the explosion. It was badly damaged, but still functional."

Lilith's thoughts drifted to Abbadon, lying unconscious in intensive care. A pang of guilt struck her—she hadn't visited him yet. But the whirlwind of recent events had consumed her every moment. The mission's primacy was absolute. Surely he would understand that. Wouldn't he?

"The abandoned equipment captured unprecedented readings during the Flares. We seized the opportunity to run simulations. Our goal was to predict the Flares more accurately and improve our asset shielding. But we uncovered something... alarming."

"Get on with it," she snapped. The trickle of information was testing her patience.

He paused instead. The silence stretched as Lilith waited for him to continue. "We believe we may have seven years left based on our estimates."

"Seven years left... for what, exactly?"

"In seven years, the Flares will be so frequent and intense they will render eastern Hell uninhabitable. Masina, Ebos, parts of Sasobek and Qataban... lost. And Aamaris may fall even sooner."

Lilith paled. "Uninhabitable," she repeated, her voice barely above a whisper. Her mind raced, a million questions colliding at once. Why hadn't they led with that critical information?

"What do you mean by uninhabitable?" she pressed.

"Life outdoors would become impossible for any meaningful length of time," he clarified. "Our support systems would degrade with limited means of repair until, eventually, we'd all be trapped."

"Who else knows about this?" If this information leaked, the chaos that would ensue would be unprecedented.

"No one outside this room."

"Confidence level?"

"We are still running more simulations," he said. "Getting the data was a fluke, but we can replicate the measurements during the next Flare."

Her buzzing watch distracted her from the news. Multiple messages from General Gadreel's assistant flooded the screen, the last demanding her presence in his office.

She tapped out a hasty reply to the message. *In classified briefing.*

The response was instantaneous. *His office. NOW.*

Her next breath caught in her chest. She had an inkling of what was about to happen and knew her day would continue on a downward spiral.

LILITH'S FOOTSTEPS echoed as she traversed the pristine, almost sterile floors of the forty-ninth level. Each step resonated, mirroring the thudding of her anxious heart. General Gadreel had summoned her, bypassing two levels of their chain of command—a move that rarely heralded good news.

As the leader of Homeland Security, he was one of the permanent members of the Upper Council. In the shadow of his vast influence, Lilith had risen through the ranks of the military, a fact she was always acutely aware of in his presence. She knocked on his door only once, hoping he would not answer so she could retreat to the safety of her routine.

"Enter!" General Gadreel's voice boomed, much to her dismay.

The room's grandeur always resonated with Lilith every time she entered. He sat behind a broad mahogany desk to her right, its presence as commanding as his own. The surface gleamed under the soft, diffused lighting, reflecting the sternness in his eyes. The wall behind him, adorned various medals and commendations, showcased his illustrious career. In front of her stood a towering steel bookcase overflowing with books on military strategy, history, and governance. The general's reputation was not just that of a decorated officer but of a scholar whose wisdom was as renowned as his tactical acumen.

He tossed a hefty folder of papers to her, the bundle landing with an ominous thud. "What is this about one of *my* intelligence officers leading a raid in Sharik Hora?".

Her heart sank further as she realized the news had reached him far too quickly. "General, I can explain."

"Sit down!" he commanded. His eyes moved to the seat across the table from him. She followed like a trance.

"Imagine my surprise when General Adramalech briefed me on this mission. Half of Kakuten 47 dead, a major on life support and another critically injured." He pulled another folder from under his desk and opened it. "Authorized by me." A curious look crossed his face. He pulled a file from the folder and slid it across the table. "I have been here long enough to know what looks like your doing."

Her words caught in her throat as she looked at it. "General, they were terrorists. Delaying the mission was an unacceptable risk." Even as she spoke, her words felt flat, unconvincing.

He pulled another paper out of the dossier and stared at it. "Terrorists?" He raised an eyebrow. "Our intelligence labeled them as a hate group." He slid it to her.

Lilith's eyes flicked to the paper. "Diamond bullets, stealth buildings..." She hesitated, the knowledge that Lamech had the identities of the Upper Council's clandestine members burning on her tongue.

He scratched his chin. "I have read the briefing already. You did not know any of these details when you forged my authorization."

"General, we have uncovered a web of planned attacks in Masina. And that is just from the little we have decrypted so far. This could be a breakthrough, a chance to strike at our enemies preemptively."

"Your closeness to this work has made you a liability."

"Sir, the life of every soldier is a continuous gamble." The words escaped before she could stop them. Lilith stiffened, immediately regretting her boldness.

His movements were calculated as he reached under the desk. An SR-17 handgun emerged, its presence sending an icy shiver down her spine. "I have ten thousand under me. Yet you occupy more space in my head than half of them combined. If we are all expendable, maybe I should put a bullet in you right now."

Her breath caught in her chest as his gaze hovered over the gun.

"Every year, since Masina annexed Sharik Hora from Ebos, they hold a local election to determine if they want to re-integrate with the Ebos government or stay under Masina rule. And every year since then, the results bend more unfavorable for us."

Politics! The military was becoming more political than the government these days.

"The governor of Sharik Hora was here today lodging a formal complaint," he continued. "When he decides he is no longer happy with the current arrangement, what influence do you think he will have on the next election?"

"Sharik Hora benefits more from us than they would ever have under Ebos's rule," Lilith said in frustration.

He slammed his fist on the table as he stood. "People vote based on fear, sometimes hope… not economic statistics. I would expect a major of the Masinian army to have a basic understanding of this."

Lilith sank into her chair and glanced at the pistol on the table, which bounced from the vibration.

"I put up with your methods, cutting corners. You were a pain in my spine. But you have lost the big picture. And now I see it is my fault." He sat and leaned back in his chair. An eerie calmness came over his face. "Moving you behind a desk was not clear enough of a message."

Lilith's words tumbled over each other. "General, with all due respect, we did not form our nation by following the rules. The Sharik Hora government is as leaky as a faulty faucet; they would have given them a heads up."

"This nation formed many decades ago," his voice remained steady. "Unless you plan to form a new one, you will adhere to our rules or face the full force of the law."

"I—"

"You have lived your life without consequences. I have recommended your case to the military tribunal. For your sake, I hope your past service influences them positively."

Without consequence? Wasn't putting me behind a desk consequence? The words were like a blow to her face. *"It is just the beginning."* Lamech had said. *How am I supposed to perform my duty if I am being hauled in front of a military tribunal?*

"General, they could dishonorably discharge me."

"In the meantime," he said, ignoring her. "You are to cease all field military activities effective immediately. Every piece of intelligence you gather in Data Warehousing goes through Central Command without exception. Do you understand? Any deviation, any failure to comply, will cause an expedited tribunal review with a much less favorable result. This is a nation, not a zoo."

Lilith jumped up from her seat and gave a salute. "Yes, General!"

"Now get out of my office," he said.

Lilith walked toward the door as briskly as she could without breaking into a run.

9

ASSASSINATIONS

A majestic king-sized bed stood at the heart of the semicircular chamber, elevated gracefully atop a platform. Every inch of the room, from the minimalist furniture to the barren walls, was born of **Lilith's** desire to disconnect from the world. The pristine white sheets, matching the bed frame, contrasted the obsidian floors. Floor-to-ceiling windows filled most of the walls. From the vantage of her building's 130th floor, Lilith gazed upon a sweeping panorama of Masina City, a mosaic of lights, sounds, and heartbeats. In these parts of town, the battle for the skylines was fought fiercely between the trees and the skyscrapers. There was an urban legend that they grew so high because they were trying to get back into heaven. Lilith did not believe in heaven. If paradise was not in Masina, then it could not exist.

A golden cascade of light streamed through her bedroom window, silhouetting her naked body and bathing her raven-black hair in a hue that shimmered almost blond, like a transient secret. It was late afternoon and the sun was setting fast.

"You are doing it again," Abezethibou said.

She smirked. "No, I am not."

"Not what?"

"Not doing it."

"What is it?"

"I don't know." She turned to face him. "But whatever you said I am doing, I am not."

Bez smiled. "You look so beautiful when you are frustrated. It should be illegal."

"*Jelema Bodo!*" she exclaimed, a playful admonition in her voice. "Stop with the corny lines." Her gaze danced mischievously over his form on her bed. His flowing hair cascaded like dark waves. She longed to lose herself in his deep-blue eyes.

"I don't know. They have worked pretty well on you."

She let out a light laugh. "Your luck may run out one of these days." He was the calming anchor she always yearned for.

He patted the sheets next to him. "Your side is getting cold."

She took a seat at the edge of the bed. He crawled across and massaged her shoulders.

"Right there." A soft moan escaped her lips as he obliged.

He bent her neck to the left as he kissed her from behind. "The soldier who brought down the Sons of Lamech. The talk of your mission is spreading like wildfire. Even in Sasobek."

"Your intel was good," she said.

"You are being modest."

She smiled.

"Something else…" he said, "on your mind?"

"I never said thank you."

"You did at least three times." His hands stopped moving but stayed on her shoulder. "You are doing the thing again where you shut me out of your thoughts,"

"I'm not shutting you out," she said as she rose from the bed and paced toward the windows. Her gaze dropped to the floor, seeking solace in its intricate patterns, as if answers might emerge from its mazes. "Half the team is gone. Abbadon nearly died. Medical says he may never wake. Forgive me if I choose not to bask in glory right now." She wanted to tell him about her conversation with General Gadreel, but decided against it. In his eyes was an indiscernible blend of desire and concern; whether he yearned for the comfort of a hug or the intimate closeness of being inside her, she couldn't tell.

Tossing the covers aside, Bez rose, kneeling in anticipation. "You have lost soldiers many times before. They swore the oath, and they died in service of their nation. How many more would have died if your mission had been unsuccessful? They have gone to the afterlife, back to heaven with God."

"There is no God. If God existed and we lived in paradise, he would never have sent us here in the first place," Lilith scoffed. "You talk about dying for an oath, yet you're nestled safely within the marble halls of the Sasobek Senate."

"Not too far removed from what you do," Bez shot back. A shadow of hurt crossed his face, revealing the sting of her words. "You have many ways of avoiding things you don't want to say. You think I will get upset and leave? But I won't."

She strolled back to the bed, exaggerating the sway in her hips. As she crawled across the sheets toward him, he tried to protest, but her lips locked on his. Before he knew what was happening, she was on top of him. He opened his mouth to talk, but she used a single finger to stop him, trapping the words in his throat. She grabbed his manhood and slid it inside her. As he thrust in and out, she felt every atom in her body, and from his moans and expressions, she knew he felt the same. They were forceful, but intentional. Patient, yet urgent. It was over quickly, but didn't feel rushed. She felt the intensity of her heartbeat as her limp body lay next to his.

"So, are you going to talk to me now?" Bez asked as he struggled to catch his breath.

Lilith turned her head from her ceiling to him. "My plan to distract you didn't work."

"It almost did."

She hesitated. There was no reason for her to hold back. Yet, unease crept up on her, a gut feeling she couldn't ignore. "This thing we have violates every rule we swore to. If someone ever found out—"

He gave her a solemn look. "Is that what's on your mind? This thing we have here?"

"No. But the moment we discuss this, it becomes something else. Everything changes."

"I thought things changed when I tipped you off about Lamech with classified Sasobek intel."

She dropped her eyes and cleared her throat. "Sometimes, in all this chaos, I forget to acknowledge the risks you take for me." She flipped her body over as she put her hand on his face and kissed him on the lips.

"Before I met Lamech, I saw something." *But maybe the secret I really should tell him is that our world may end in seven years.*

His expression portrayed more engagement. "Saw something?"

Her phone, thankfully far from them on the windowsill, rang. She motioned to move off the bed, but Bez's hand grabbed hers. More forcefully than she had ever remembered.

"Ignore it," he said.

She scowled as she glanced at his hand around her wrist. She forcefully pulled away and shot him a disgusted look.

"I'm sorry," he stammered. He raised both hands in a defensive stance.

The phone rang again.

Lilith dragged her eyes over him slowly. "Don't do that again. Ever." She got out of bed and picked up her phone from the window. "Major Lilith," she said.

"About time you answered," the Chief of Staff to the Chancellor barked.

"My phone just started ringing," she said.

"I don't want to hear excuses!"

"Of course, General. It won't happen again." She rolled her eyes. He had not liked her since the first day they met. She had heard through the grapevine that he had tried to get her dishonorably discharged more than once.

"The Upper Council is convening. Your presence is required. Immediately."

"Upper Council?"

"I am pretty sure that's what I said."

"Yes, sir!" It was strange for them to call her in for a meeting, especially after her last bust-up with General Gadreel.

"I need you at nothing less than 100%. We are in condition zero."

He should have led with that! "Since when?"

"Kalla! Just get over here."

"Yes, sir! Consider me on my way."

"I'll consider you on your way when you are on your way." The line went dead before she could respond.

The declaration of condition zero brought back haunting memories of the Masina-Ebos War, a conflict that claimed over five hundred thousand lives. Most of the casualties were Ebosian, yet it was still a tragedy. Now, as history threatened to repeat itself, she felt a conflicting mix of nerves and a guilty spark of anticipation.

∽

"Holy burning fire of Hell," Lilith muttered as an oppressive blast of heat assaulted her. The underground garage, a mammoth cavern dwarfing the building above, felt even hotter than the scorching outdoors. Beads of sweat formed on her face as she surveyed the rows of vehicles stretching into the distance. Plain walls with reinforced beams every twenty feet enclosed this exclusive domain of military personnel and their families.

"Major!" The gravelly voice of the parking attendant cracked through the stifling air as he hastily rose from his chair to salute her. Wisps of gray hair crowned his head, but the pronounced hunch at the top of his back truly betrayed his age. He had to be at least two hundred years old, but he could be closer to four hundred, for all she knew. "The Flares are coming," he said. He looked at her sweaty forehead. "This one seems worse than all the others. Unprecedented. Our system keeps getting overloaded." A bashful look crossed his face as his eyes turned to the floor. "The blasted management board," he grumbled, "Still dragging their feet on the funding to upgrade the system."

I work for internal intelligence. Does he think I do not know?

She gave him an unconcerned shrug and tapped on her watch. One hundred forty degrees outside, and it had to be at least ten to twenty degrees higher inside. The air had a faint smell of mold and dust. The air conditioning was not the only thing that needed fixing. "What is the board spending all their time and money on, then?" she asked, masking her indifference as best as she could.

He shrugged.

The oversight board had been stonewalling repairs and upgrades for months. Were they lining their own pockets? Or funneling funds into some shadowy operation? She hadn't had time to dig deeper. She activated her watch, summoning her car.

"Off to save the world again, Major?" the attendant's voice hinted at playful mockery.

"You ask me that question every time, and I give you the same answer each time," she said.

"Going from somewhere to somewhere," they said together.

"Maybe one day, the answer will be different." He let out a laugh from a throat full of phlegm.

"Unlikely."

The sounds of wheels on concrete brought a relief that their conversation would soon end. The entire unibody of her car was coated in a blend of military-grade metal and volcanic rock, giving the surface chameleon-like properties. In darkness, it absorbed light, allowing the vehicle to meld with the shadows. Under bright illumination, it transformed, giving the illusion of a boulder in motion. Like her living space, this vehicle was courtesy of the Masina military. She could never have afforded either by herself.

As it inched closer, her heart sank at a crudely drawn circle marring its side. The words scrawled within read *"SERAPHIM RAT. Go back Home."* It hit her like a gut punch. Her frustration turned to disgust, but anger came soon after. Her face flushed as her breathing became inconsistent.

"Oh my dear," the attendant said as he knocked over his chair in his haste to reach her. "Oh my dear, Oh my dear." He pulled off his shirt and ran toward the car. He wiped at the side frantically. "Oh dear. Oh dear,"

"How many times has this happened?" Lilith said. "What kind of security do we have here?"

He fumbled with his shirt and did more to smudge the ink on the windows instead of wiping it off. He looked back, but kept his eyes on the floor. "I will call security immediately. I will make sure this doesn't happen again."

"Kalla!" her fists clenched at her sides. She pulled her phone from her pocket, her fingers hovering over the screen to dial the head of security. Midway through, she paused. Realizing she was already late, she sighed, acknowledging the graffiti on her car was a calculated move to provoke her. She slid her phone back into her pocket, feeling the attendant's watchful gaze as she strode past, still seething with restrained anger. The car door swung open as she approached. She paused at the threshold, turning to face him with a commanding presence. "I expect a thorough security audit on this breach by the time I return," she ordered.

He nodded. "Of course."

She stepped inside and sat back in the chair. The windshield glowed with a soft azure hue, casting a serene light across the plush leather interior.

"Good evening, Major Lilith," the car's female digital voice chimed.

"Set destination for Masina City coffee shop," she said.

"Destination accepted," the voice said.

Unlike the garage, her car's cooling system worked. She closed her eyes as the car drove itself out of the building. An invitation to the Upper Council was not given lightly. The weight of the summons demanded her full attention.

Her thoughts drifted to one of the escalating crises. The Flares, once a rare occurrence, had intensified alarmingly. From sporadic events every few years, they had progressed to annual occurrences, and now multiple incidents within a year. If her analysts' data held, they had a mere seven years to act before... what? Catastrophe? Extinction? The uncertainty gnawed at her.

"Activating shades," the computerized voice said as Lilith's car pulled out of the driveway. A thin, semi-translucent film covered the windows. Lilith glanced outside at the red road, blending in with the tree roots. This part of Masina City was filled with tall skyscrapers after tall skyscrapers. Video cameras covered virtually every inch of every building. Some people called it the concrete jungle. Some called it the surveillance city. Lilith called it home. A home she was duty-bound to protect, no matter the cost.

∼

WITH THE CAR ENGINE HUMMING, she called Eligos, a data broker with an uncanny knack for being in the know. In tumultuous times, she often sought whispers from the underground, preferring to avoid the official channels. She had helped him climb the underground ranks when she was still a private. The investment had paid off since she was put behind a desk.

"I wish I could say it surprised me to hear from you." His voice was deep and calm, like a father soothing a child. It made it easier to listen to his information, which, by the nature of their arrangement, was usually not the most pleasant.

"You were expecting my call?" A sense of nervousness gripped her.

"I wouldn't be the person you are calling now if I didn't know ahead of time that you would call," he quipped.

"That is too many words for me to process right now," she joked.

"Words were never your strong suit, were they?"

"You always had a way of saying a lot without saying much that I always admired."

"In my defense, you haven't asked me a question."

"Do you think you would be the one I call in situations like this if I always had to ask you a direct question?"

He laughed again. "I see I am rubbing off of you in all the right ways."

"Talk to me," she said.

"Grumblings. Rumors. Lots of dark chatter," he said. There was a brief pause. "Some kind of military mobilization is happening in Sasobek. Inconsistent stories. Conflicting. But something is cooking. I have not seen it like this in a very long time."

Sasobek? Lilith's mind raced to Bez. The military could not mobilize without the Senate's approval. But Bez was completely calm when she left. He had no idea what was happening.

"What about Aamaris, Ebos, and Qataban?"

"Aamaris is up to the same old shit they always are. Figuring out a way to take over Hell," he said with a laugh. "I have nothing new on them. But when I know, you will."

The nervousness inside her amplified. If Sasobek had indeed been mobilizing their military, she should not have heard that through Eligos. Unfamiliar surroundings outside her window made her break concentration from the conversation. She was on a long, straight road. The trees lining the road were a rich, russet red, their shade darker and more intense than the usual urban foliage. The beginnings of their roots towered over the car in some places, and their branches and leaves stretched over the path, blocking most of the sun. She felt like she had been transported back to the Miln mountains.

"Hold on one second." She placed Eligos on hold. "Computer, explain route," she said to the dashboard.

"Command not understood. Please try again," the digitized computer voice responded.

Lilith frowned. A slight nervousness crept in as she looked out the window again. From how the shadows fell from the trees, the car was going east instead of west. "Display Map," she demanded. Instead of a map, random letters and numbers filled the windscreen.

"Data corrupted," the car's computer announced, Lilith's dread steadily increasing.

She adjusted her posture and sat upright. There was a panel on the side of the car. She dug her nails into it and ripped it off, exposing a keypad. The right combination would disable the automated system and move the car into manual mode.

"Computer, explain route." She enunciated each word perfectly.

The car picked up speed at an alarming pace. Up ahead, the road made a sharp right. But just before that, a big sign said 'Warning: Sharp Turn' preceding the cliff's edge. Jumping out of the car in the middle of the Flares was not necessarily a better outcome.

"Computer, unlock doors!" she shouted.

"Command not understood," the electronic voice repeated.

"Kalla! Computer! Disable engines!"

"Command not understood!" the voice chirped back.

She had maybe ten seconds before she bashed through the sign and off the cliff. She might survive the fall, but not what came after.

She pried open the dashboard and retrieved a circular disc—identical to the one Eliakim used in Ebos. It was overdue for a lab analysis, but duty had kept her from returning it. She traced a triangular pattern over its surface followed by a triple tap in the middle to reverse the effect. It pulsed a brief, ominous red as she planted it on her chest. Time now moved about ten times faster inside the car than outside.

Her fingers danced over her watch, conjuring a holographic display of the car's intricate schematics. Scanning, she located the necessary information and flicked the hologram aside. The real work began as she delved into the panel, stripping and reconnecting wires in a desperate bid for control. Five real-time seconds remained. She punched in the manual override codes in the panel. Once she finished, it beeped twice, then flashed red. The manual said it should beep twice and flash green.

"Kalla!" she shouted. She pulled up the schematic again. Green wire to blue and yellow to red. She had attached the yellow to the blue and the green to the red.

With only three seconds left in the real world, she corrected the wire connections and re-entered the code. The panel obliged with three beeps and a reassuring green light. "Manual override accepted," the computer announced in a neutral tone. Immediately, a steering wheel emerged from the car's front, accompanied by two pedals for acceleration and braking from beneath. Breathing a sigh of relief mixed with lingering adrenaline, she grasped the steering wheel, veering with determination while simultaneously pressing hard on the brake pedal.

Two seconds remained in the real world.

Time crawled as the car began its perilous turn, the back wheels teetering over the cliff's edge while the front tires screeched in desperation against the concrete. With most of the vehicle dangling precariously, she let her foot off the brakes and floored the accelerator. The engine roared. The front tires gave a desperate cry as they struggled to anchor the car to safety. With a harrowing scrape, the car's side ground against the railing, the back tires finally regaining traction on solid ground. Her breathing, ragged and uneven, took minutes to settle into a steady rhythm.

Re-engaging the call, Lilith's voice trembled as she questioned Eligos. "How many reports have you seen of automated driving systems malfunctioning?"

"Hmmmm," Eligos paused for a couple of seconds. "It happens 1.3% of the time."

Lilith raised her eyebrows. "Are you certain about that?"

He chuckled. "I'm a broker of secrets, not a walking database. How would I have such precise data at hand?"

Lilith wanted to curse him out. "I forgot you are only useful sometimes," she said instead.

"Some of the time? This morning, I woke up with a hard-on, but you were not useful in helping me get rid of it." He laughed too loudly and for too long.

"I am sure you have a point somewhere in the gross output of words." She laid back against the seat and closed her eyes. The adrenaline from her close call with death still coursed through her blood.

"Are you still there?" he asked.

"I will be radio silent for a while. If you hear of something, don't leave me a message. I will call back when I can."

"You don't sound well. Did something happen?"

She hung up and kept the car in manual mode for the rest of her trip.

∼

As LILITH DROVE toward the Dome, thoughts of Bez swirled in her mind, each one a hesitant step back from the impulse to call him. Uncertainty loomed—were Masina and Sasobek allies or foes in this unfolding drama? The imposing silhouette of Building two loomed into view. She went a couple more miles west before stopping at a nondescript building. A rundown sign said, *"Masina City Coffee Shop."* Below it, a placard hung from it saying "closed." The curtains inside were drawn completely, blocking all visibility.

"Computer, return to residence, then run diagnostics," she said, a nagging feeling telling her she wouldn't be leaving anytime soon. As she exited the car, a blast of heat enveloped her like a suffocating blanket. The vehicle's door slid shut with a soft hum, and it pulled away, leaving her exposed to the punishing temperature. It was only a few feet to the building's entrance, but sweat had already drenched her clothes by the time she reached it.

She grabbed the door of the coffee shop and pulled it open. The room was eerily quiet, save for the soft tapping of keys. Chairs were stacked upside down on tables pushed against the walls, leaving the center of the room empty. At the far end stood a long, ornate counter stretching across the width of the shop. The demon behind it didn't bother to look up. "Closed," she said.

"Major Lilith," Lilith said. "Data warehousing."

The demon gave her a stern look. Her hand drifted under the counter, probably to a weapon. Lilith knew many hidden cameras and sensors were scanning her body and vitals as she walked to the end of the room, checking her gait, heart rhythm, and many other things. If the vitals determined she was not the same person she claimed she was, the demon would shoot her, and many other officers would arrive within seconds.

"Place your hand here," she instructed, sliding a white square toward Lilith.

Three needles pricked her hand and drew blood.

The demon waited a couple of seconds before speaking. "Welcome, Major Lilith," she said with an uninterested frown. She stepped aside and opened a divider. "Right this way." The demon pointed to the door behind her. "51-768," she said before ignoring Lilith and refocusing her attention on the screen behind the counter.

Lilith entered the code into a concealed panel next to the door and entered a confined room. With a jolt, the room descended vertically before abruptly accelerating, shifting its trajectory horizontally. Unlike the others, building zero was entirely underground. Officially, it did not exist.

Lilith had been to the Upper Council room before, but each time had the same effect as the first. Solid gold statues lined the walls, each depicting a president from Masina's two-century reign. Between the gleaming figures, life-sized photos of distinguished generals and political icons watched her from the walls, rendered in exquisite detail and rich color.

At the end of the room, a secured door led to a crisis communication hub, a nerve center from where the Chancellor could orchestrate military maneuvers and initiate a missile strike against any target across Hell.

On paper, President Khandoz Ramadi was the head of the council and head of state. However, decades of lazy government officials delegating their responsibilities to the military during times of war meant that Chancellor Moloch Infernis, head of the military, was the de facto ruler. Despite his shorter stature, Chancellor Moloch possessed a formidable presence, with broad, imposing shoulders that contrasted his lack of height.

General Ko'ron Bestis was head of the army. His mother birthed him on the battlefield during the sixth civil war of Hell sixty years ago. That was all he had known and lived since the first day he entered the world. He had found it increasingly difficult to thrive in the trying times of peace. His shoulders were just as broad as Moloch's, but he was also tall.

General Gadreel Malatis, more a doer than a talker, listened much more than he spoke. Although he spoke rarely, his words commanded attention when he did. Their last encounter flashed into her memory as she saw him.

General Yigit Molotiv, head of the navy, was the polar opposite; she possessed a tireless capacity for debate, persisting until her opponents succumbed to her arguments. Lilith always thought she would fare better as a politician. She was one of the longest-serving generals on the council. When you looked at her, one could tell she had been behind a desk for a long time.

"We must assemble the Lower Council and call for a vote on a full referendum to decide our next actions," Chancellor Moloch said.

"We are on the brink of war. This is not the time for politics," General Yigit said.

The chancellor seemed dismayed by her response. Lilith noticed President Khandoz was missing.

"Agreed. We must be decisive," General Ko'ron said. "This has Sasobek's influence all over it. Now more than ever, we must show strength. Seize their assets, close the borders, and take over their embassies!"

Lilith stiffened at his words. The weight of her secret relationship with Bez, a Sasobek senator, suddenly felt unbearable. As tension filled the room, she silently reaffirmed her commitment to keeping their affair hidden. The potential consequences of discovery loomed larger than ever, threatening her career and the delicate political balance.

General Ko'ron's words stoked a special tension in the room. Everyone talked over each other for the next ten minutes as Lilith watched. Chancellor Moloch raised his hands, demanding a silence

The Eden Ruse

the entire room yielded to. "Only scared animals lash out! We will not do what many would see as a declaration of war and start an unnecessary conflict. We need more details about who was behind this before taking any retaliatory actions."

"More details?" Ko'ron shouted. "As we gather details, our enemies get bolder."

Despite her late arrival, Lilith found herself thrust into a heated debate. She bit her tongue, resisting the urge to interrupt and ask for context. Instead, she observed intently, piecing together fragments of information while her mind raced to catch up with the gravity of the situation unfolding before her.

"I will have order in this room!" Chancellor Moloch said as he banged the table.

"What is the point of having a military if we don't use it?" General Ko'ron demanded.

"I said order!" Chancellor Moloch shouted even louder. His wings extended from his back and spread nearly across the room. Their white feathers blocked the light behind him and cast shadows on the table.

Ko'ron grumbled and took a seat.

"There will be no border closings," Chancellor Moloch declared. "Our military will be ready for all attacks, internal and external. But they will stand by until we have more credible information."

Just like we were ready for the Sons of Lamech. The memory of their recent mission's near-disaster gnawed at her. She clenched her fists, wondering how many more threats lurked beneath the surface, waiting to catch them unprepared. The council's confidence was dangerously misplaced.

Lilith tapped General Gadreel's shoulder against her better judgment. "General," she whispered, "what is going on?"

He turned, his gaze heavy with solemnity. Chancellor Moloch's last words had started another shouting match between all the council members. General Gadreel looked back at the table. "Lucifer Morningstar and President Khandoz were both assassinated." Lilith's entire chest constricted. Her breathing momentarily stopped as her mind raced to digest the words. Lucifer had been the key driver in bringing peace to Hell after the last civil war. And President Khandoz... Masina had not had an Upper Council member killed in at least a century. No one had ever been that bold.

```
                    ┌─────────────────┐
                    │ Khandoz         │
                    │ Ramadi          │
                    │ President       │
                    └─────────────────┘
                            │
        ┌───────────────┬───────────────┬───────────────┐
┌───────────────┐ ┌───────────────┐ ┌───────────────┐ ┌───────────────┐
│ Mallekith Yodi│ │ Hekate Abete  │ │ Baphomet      │ │ Ko'o…         │
│ Executive     │ │ Executive     │ │ Tademus       │ │ Besti…        │
│ Governor      │ │ Governor      │ │ General       │ │ Gene…         │
│ Governorship  │ │ Governorship  │ │ Federal Police│ │ Army          │
└───────────────┘ └───────────────┘ └───────────────┘ └───────────────┘
        │
   ┌────┴────┐
┌──────────┐ ┌──────────┐
│ Cystenn  │ │Seraphelis│
│ Vyreth   │ │ Rezus    │
│ Regional │ │ Regional │
│ Governor │ │ Governor │
│Sharik Hora│ │Masina City│
└──────────┘ └──────────┘
```

```
- Moloch Infernis — Chancellor, Military
  - Yigit Molotiv — General, Navy
  - Gadreel Malatis — General, Homeland Security
    - Zephyrus Hammadan — Commander, Cerdasan [Intelligence]
      - Azaroth Zaidi — Colonel, Foreign Intelligence
        - Lilith Saeon — Major, Data Warehousing
  - Adramalech Nolog — General, Marines
    - Belial Hari — Commander, Tactical Deployments
      - Malachi Amani — Colonel, Kakuten
        - Abbadon Vexxar — Major, Kakuten East (46-80)
          - Eliakim Seres — Kapten, Kakuten 47
            - Biba Eziz — Private, Sniper
            - Senet Marbas — Private, Scout
          - Orgun Elos — Kapten, Kakuten 48
        - Baelgor Viril — Major, Kakuten West (1-20)
```

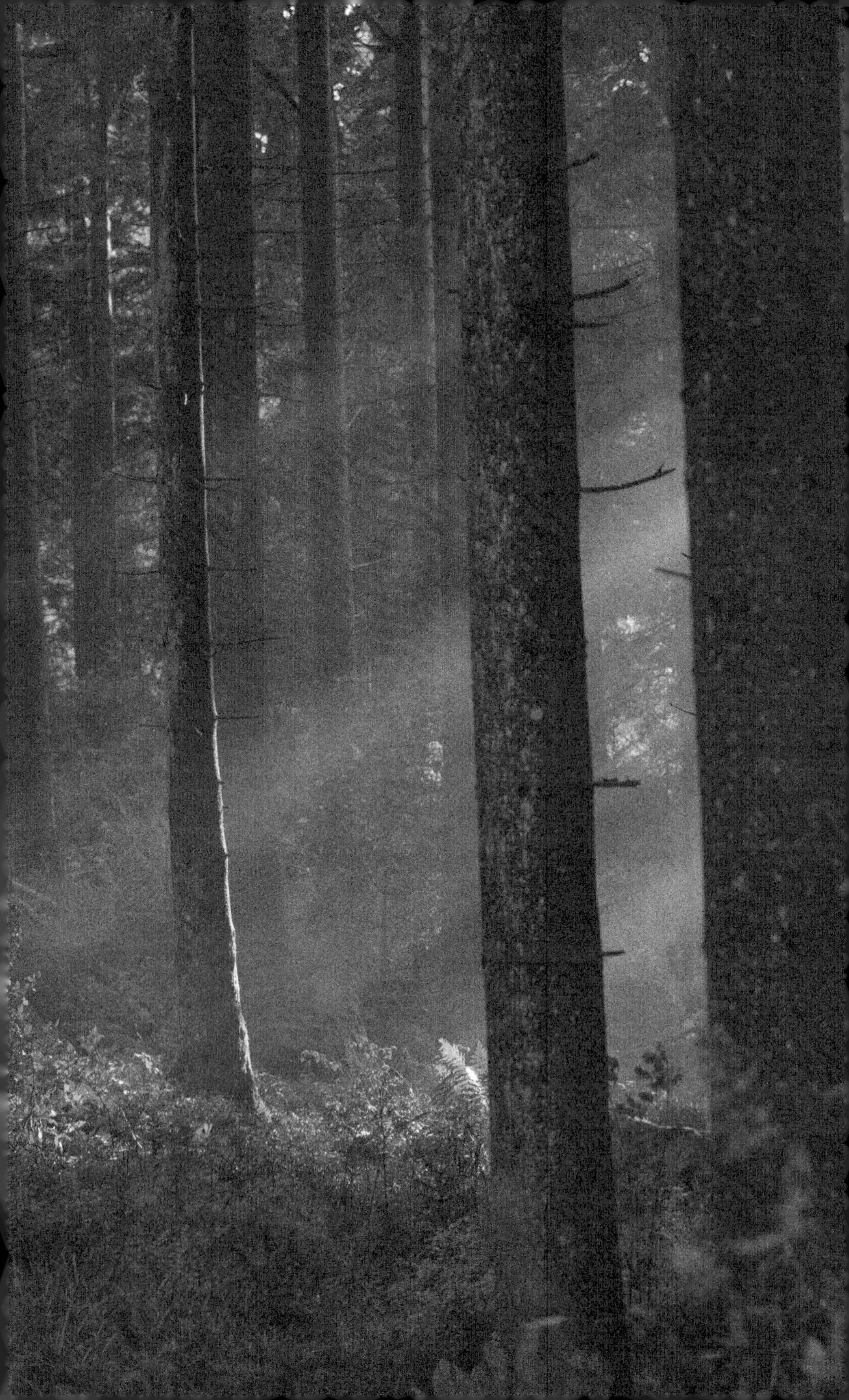

PART III
A BATTLE

10

UNLIKELY ALLIANCES
REALM OF KIRINA

*T*he pungent odor of spoiling meat and fish hung in the air of Abisina's Ertale Market, mingling with the sweat of countless bodies pressed together in the sweltering heat. It was the week's busiest day, and the crowd created a humid, living maze. Yet **Ikenga** welcomed the chaos—it provided the perfect cover. Weaving between stalls overflowing with goods, he kept his head down and shoulders hunched, blending in as just another faceless shopper. The vendors' shouts and customers' laughter melted around him while he hunted for something, his mission known only to himself.

"Come back here!" a woman shouted to her child. The little girl ran after a stray dog that was chasing something of its own. She giggled, lost in her world. Meanwhile, burdened by unseen stresses, her mother negotiated with a vegetable vendor.

Ikenga glanced up to take in the situation, but quickly lowered his head. Though as far away from Niri and Orisha as he could be, his paranoia—which had kept him safe for two years—still loomed large. He had gotten better at only focusing on things he could control.

Vendors barked prices, haggling with tight-fisted buyers as currency exchanged hands amid laughter and arguments. The first time he had visited, he had to do everything in his power to stop from gagging. But it got better. Things always did. He raised his head because of a shadow he saw on the ground. Too late. He bumped into a man about twice his size, bouncing off the man's belly as he took two steps back.

"Watch where you are going, foolish man!" the man shouted.

Ikenga raised his hands, backpedaling into a meat stall covered in blood-spattered carcasses. The seller, wearing a torn brown shirt and trousers, flashed him a nasty look, warning him to stop interrupting his customer. He hacked viciously at a slab of meat, brutal blows thudding as his blade met wood. Ikenga winced with every chop, the strikes sparking queasiness deep in his gut.

He staggered back, one hand flying to Formless's handle beneath his robes. The blade warmed beneath his palm, pleased by its master's touch. Ikenga clenched his fist around the hilt, steeling himself. Today, he had willed it to be a small dagger so that he could obscure it from view. Parading a sword in Ertale market would do the opposite of what he needed. He hurried away and moved further into the crowd.

This area was sparser; the makeshift tables the merchants had set up in the other parts were replaced with huts and wooden cabins. He scanned the crooked line, locating the one he sought. Slipping through the door, he entered a narrow passage smelling of strange spices. Shadows played over the books cramming the shelves on either side of the wall. At the passage's end was a curtained doorway, but when Ikenga approached, an immense palm shot out and slammed into his chest.

"Where do you think you go?" The vibration of the man's voice traveled through the hand on his chest. The man the hand was attached to was so large that Ikenga could see every muscle on his body through his shirt creases.

"I'm here to see Barrio," Ikenga attempted to sidestep him, but the man moved to block his path.

"No Barrio," he growled.

"I—"

The Eden Ruse

"You step back there, or I will send you out in two pieces." The man looked like he was breathing burning air. Even in the enclosed hut, an altercation could draw unneeded attention.

I need to see Barrio. Now. Ikenga's hand glided underneath his shirt and brushed up against a pulsing Formless. One slice of his weapon, and it would be over. But Barrio would not appreciate his guard's dismembered body in the entryway of his shop. He stepped back. "Barrio knows me. You can tell him—"

The man closed the distance. Ikenga paused mid-sentence as the man buried one fist into the palm of the other hand. The burly man had made his own assessment of the situation. Diplomacy was not the option he had selected.

"I don't know who you are. But you do not want to cross me," Ikenga warned. He pulled out Formless and gripped the handle. At his touch, the weapon transformed, growing from a concealed dagger into a full-length sword. Despite his bravado, his hands betrayed him, trembling as they gripped the hilt.

The man's eyes widened, then reverted to normal, an unimpressed look covering his face. "You put that toy away now. No Barrio. Now get somewhere else." With a dismissive jerk of his head, he pointed at the door.

From further inside the hut, Barrio's voice cut in, "Let him through."

The man's posture stayed stiff, his fingers curled in a fist. He stepped back, then moved to the side. Ikenga gave him a gloating look as he slipped past him.

"Next time, I crush your head into pulp," the man said.

Ikenga hurried past him, keeping close to the other side of the wall to maximize the distance between them. He shrunk Formless back into a dagger that he fastened under his shirt.

Barrio's office was a mess of scattered things. On one side of the wall, various books that looked like they were written before the first day of the world sat in stacks. Behind him, hundreds of unlabeled jars and canisters filled the shelves. It was amazing that the man knew which was which. On the right wall lay other random items—

feathers, statues, more potions. It looked like a pawnshop and was just that to most people. Standing behind a tall counter, Barrio looked gaunt. He had always been skinny, but now, he was more bone than anything else. The light reflected off his hollowed cheeks, creating dark patches. Partially healed bruising covered the left side of his head.

"I hope my guard didn't give you too much trouble," Barrio said. "We have had more... should I say, unfriendly customers show up here recently. We are all on edge."

"A lot less trouble than you have had, it seems," Ikenga said.

Barrio waved his hands dismissively. "It's barely anything. What do you want?"

Ikenga tensed as he studied Barrio's face. Barrio was a man you wanted to shut up. Being elusive was not in his usual nature. "The herbs you gave me... I need more."

"More?" Barrio raised his eyebrows. "I gave you a supply for almost five months, just a few weeks ago."

"And now, I need more."

"Are you trying to kill yourself?"

"No, I am trying to acquire more herbs."

Barrio lunged across the table, seizing Ikenga's hand and turning it palm up. Try as he might, Ikenga couldn't stop the tremors running through his fingers.

"You can barely hold a pen, let alone a sword. And you think you could have taken out my man with that?"

"I didn't come here for a—"

"A dead customer cannot pay me."

Ikenga snatched his hand back. "Are you selling me the herbs or not?"

"If you finished what I gave you so quickly, it is a miracle you are still alive." He reached across the table again and grabbed Ikenga's hand again, then pricked him with a needle from behind the counter.

"*Koca ci!*" Ikenga winced in pain and recoiled.

Barrio let the blood drop into a bowl he'd pulled from under the table. He mixed in some herbs, set the concoction ablaze, and inhaled deeply. His head lolled back before snapping forward, eyes locking onto Ikenga. "The good news is that you are not dead... for now. Are you still having the dreams of that girl? What's her name again?"

"They are getting stronger and more frequent. I need to make it stop."

Barrio dipped a finger into the bowl, touching a drop of the mixture to his tongue. His eyes narrowed as he assessed the taste. "It's killing you," he said. "Slowly. Your life force is ebbing away. This treatment... it can only work for so much longer."

"Then what am I supposed to do?"

Barrio's gaze softened, a flicker of pity crossing his face. Without a word, he disappeared behind the curtain. The rustling of fabric and clink of glass filled the tense silence. Minutes later, he emerged, pressing a plastic bag into Ikenga's trembling hands. "You should stop treating the symptoms and focus on the disease."

Ikenga snatched the bag and dropped five coins on the table. He pushed past the curtain on his way out, hoping not to run into the hulking man again.

∼

IKENGA FELT IT BEHIND HIM—A breeze that stayed for a few minutes, then disappeared. He had already covered half the distance between the market and his home, deciding to take the longer, less busy route through the alleys. He was grateful most of the windows looking into the corridor were closed. The narrow alley seemed to compress with every step, the walls closing in, squeezing the air from his lungs like he was high above sea level.

Again, the sensation swept over him. He spun around, heart pounding. But there was no one but a cluster of dust-bitten trash cans. A gust of wind whispered past him, ruffling his clothes before it vanished. A voice, soft and insidious as smoke, said, "Someone follows us."

Turning, Ikenga faced a naked man whose skin held the pallor of wet parchment. Not a single hair adorned his body. His semi-translucent flesh stretched over a face that haunted Ikenga's darkest nightmares.

"This isn't possible," Ikenga echoed through the deserted alleyway. Hand cradling his head to keep his sanity intact, he clenched his eyes shut, his body rocking violently to shake off the hallucination. But when his eyes opened, Eshm was still there, more corporeal, his hands and toes defined. Visions of Moremi had come before, but never Eshm.

"You are not real," Ikenga said.

"I am here. You are here. If you are real, I must be real," Eshm replied.

Ripping Formless from its hiding place under his shirt, Ikenga's knuckles stretched as he gripped the handle, his hand shaking as the weapon pulsed with energy. The weapon gleamed blood-red, stretching and morphing into a curved sword. He lunged, the blade slashing through the air with deadly precision. *Die!*

Eshm vanished, leaving his blade to whistle through space.

"Someone follows us," Eshm said behind him.

Spinning, Ikenga found Eshm standing erect, hands rigid by his sides, his blank face a mask of apathy. Ikenga lunged and sliced his blade again. Just as the edge was about to find its mark, Eshm vanished, leaving Ikenga's momentum unchecked. He stumbled, his balance faltering, and the blade cleaved through one of the nearby trash cans lining the alley wall. The impact sent Ikenga tumbling, landing face-first in the garbage strewn across the pavement.

Shutters slamming shut echoed through the alley as curious residents, no doubt drawn by the commotion, caught glimpses of what appeared to be a madman flailing at invisible foes. The stench of rotting food and decay assaulted Ikenga's nostrils, causing him to gag and cough as he struggled to regain his footing amid the putrid debris.

Ikenga spat out the foul taste from his mouth and clambered to his feet, his eyes falling on a figure standing near the opposite wall. Eshm had transformed, taking on Moremi's appearance, clad in the same black outfit she had worn in Fourth Purgatory. She was barefoot, with burned feet and charred skin replacing her toenails.

"My—my medicine," Ikenga stuttered, fingers trembling as he retrieved the plastic bag.

"Don't be scared," Moremi said as she floated toward him.

Ikenga struggled to stop shaking and fumbled with the powder bag. He put some herbs in his hand but spilled it on the ground.

"Someone follows us," she echoed Eshm's warning.

Moremi had crumbled under the immense power of Eshm's possession, her body unable to withstand his overwhelming presence. Ever since that fateful day, haunting visions of her plagued Ikenga's every waking moment, a torment he believed to be his own mind's cruel punishment for failing her. However, a far more sinister possibility crept into his thoughts. Could it be that Eshm had transferred from Moremi's body to his own? The visions that had been tormenting him all this time, were they not manifestations of his guilt-ridden psyche but the malevolent workings of the spirit?

Ikenga inhaled the herbs, the sharp scent piercing his nostrils as he squeezed his eyes shut. He covered his face with his hands as he looked away. Minutes crawled. Then he dared to look. Moremi had vanished. His heartbeat had slowed, hands steady again. He retrieved Formless, scanning the alley before shrinking it into a dagger and returning it under his shirt. The bag of herbs was already half-empty.

"*Koca Ci!*" he said under his breath.

～

IKENGA JOLTED awake to a shadowy figure looming over him. He had passed out on the street after his harrowing encounter with Eshm, the medicine's potent side effects hitting him suddenly. As his vision cleared, he saw a gaunt man standing above him with a sword gripped in one hand. The stranger wore an unbuttoned jacket hanging off his skeletal frame, and a necklace of teeth adorned his neck. A cruel scar bisected his face, and loose pants draped his legs.

Before Ikenga could process the scene or question the man's presence, the man swung the sword into motion. The blade crashed toward Ikenga's head, the danger now immediate and clear. Instinct kicked in. He tightened his core and rolled. The weapon missed him and shattered the stone where his head had rested just a heartbeat before.

Ikenga lunged and drilled his fist into the soft space under the man's uplifted arm. His hope that the man would drop his sword was short-lived. The man groaned and stumbled back, his arm firmly on the hilt of his weapon.

As the stranger raised his sword again, Ikenga yanked Formless from its sheath under his shirt. At his touch, the blade elongated into a straight, glowing sword. He rubbed the markings on its hilt as his mind raced, thoughts jumbling together. It wasn't yet dusk—he couldn't have been unconscious long enough for Nago Sango to dispatch an assassin so quickly. So, who was the scarred man with feral eyes?

"Who sent you?" Ikenga demanded, crouching low and taking an aggressive stance. Eyes narrowed, he stared down at his attacker, buying precious seconds to make sense of the sudden assault from an unknown enemy. The empty street around them waited, hushed, holding its breath.

The man surged toward Ikenga again. Each of Ikenga's dodges and parries were futile, like his adversary peered into his very thoughts. The intense exchange continued for agonizing minutes until the man committed his first error.

In the heat of combat, the man rotated his left leg—the one firmly planted on the ground. The misstep offered Ikenga a glimmer of hope. He lunged, but as he did, his opponent executed an unexpected maneuver. With astonishing agility, the man sprang up, his body momentarily airborne. His foot, once grounded, hurtled toward Ikenga in a fearsome arc. It connected with Ikenga's head with a resounding crack, sending shockwaves of pain through his skull.

The blow's force sent Ikenga flying backward, his body slamming against the alley wall with a thud. He crumpled to the ground in a

The Eden Ruse

dazed heap as Formless clattered a few feet away. He groaned as the pain from the impact radiated through his head.

He clenched his fists, eyes snapping shut for a mere heartbeat. When he reopened them, his palms blazed with swirling orbs of white fire. He aimed them at the man and released the energy. The skinny man, quick on his feet, held his sword in front of him. However, the intense flames overcame the metal, shattering it like brittle glass struck by a hammer. The explosive force hurled the man against the wall on the opposite side of the alley with a bone-jarring impact.

Ikenga sprang to his feet, his eyes locked on Formless. He stamped on the blade's tip, catapulting the hilt into the air and catching it without breaking his stride. Harnessing the remnants of his power, he surged at his dazed opponent with astounding velocity. He was panting, almost to exhaustion, but he mustered every bit of energy left inside him. Raising Formless high, Ikenga prepared to deliver a decisive blow and slice his attacker in half.

The man raised his hands and shouted, "Wait! You will want to hear what I have to say."

Ikenga paused, his hand hovering in the air for a second. He squeezed his left fist as a white flame engulfed it. His instinct told him to kill the man. But his curiosity made him pause.

"Why should I let you live?" Ikenga asked. Despite the ragged breaths heaving his chest, he kept his voice steady.

"I am Papa Legba Samedi," the man said, "of Rada Mysters, right hand to Radha Rhamirez Loa. And you are Ikenga of Umoren, Son of Amobi, and current exile of Vodun, Orisha, and Niri."

"Vodun? Rada Mysters?" Ikenga asked. "Why would I want to hear what comes from your mouth?"

"A dark cloud is forming over the entire realm," Papa Legba said. "I need your help to stop it."

The words sent a chill down Ikenga's spine, but he kept a blank expression. "People who want my help rarely try to take my life first."

"I had to defend myself," Papa Legba said, raising his hands in protest.

"You tried to chop off my head!" Ikenga shouted.

"Perhaps I did not try hard enough," Legba said with an annoying smirk.

They locked gazes, neither blinking nor turning away. Gradually, Ikenga lowered his arm and eased his grip on Formless. "Leave that way and hope I never see you again."

"I am not leaving." The man's eyes flashed black.

"I would be delighted to see Vodun burn," Ikenga scowled, "do not take my mercy as weakness." Ikenga squeezed Formless and willed it into a dagger. Returning it to his belt, he turned to walk away, only to find Legba miraculously standing in his path. He put his hand on Ikenga's chest and shoved him back.

"I will not be as merciful this time. I promise you." Ikenga scowled.

"Utaka told me you would be more agreeable when you felt in control," Legba said. "Do not think you bested me because of superior skills."

Ikenga raised a brow in confusion. "What did you say?"

"How do you think I found you?"

"Do not speak of the dead," Ikenga said, anger flaring.

"Utaka is not dead," Legba's words were a chilling whisper.

Impossible! "Utaka is dead!" Ikenga's shout echoed. Enraged, he lunged at Legba.

Legba shimmered translucent, then vanished. "Utaka is in a cell in Orisha. Under Nago Sango's castle." His voice came from behind Ikenga.

No! Ikenga swirled around. "It's a lie!" Each attempt to attack Legba was met with a frustrating void, the man evading every strike.

"You are a dark cloud that blocks the sun. But the sun is a yellow dagger." Legba said.

Chills went down Ikenga's spine. Those were the exact words Utaka had said in Fourth Purgatory.

"He is barely alive," Legba said. "Not very different from you. Lack of purpose leads to the rot of the soul, then the mind, and finally the body."

"I was there when he died."

"Then surely he has risen from the dead."

Fury danced in Ikenga's eyes. "Do not mock me."

"Is that what you saw? You saw him die?"

"A ball of fire engulfed him. There was nothing left but ash." Ikenga's gaze fell to the ground.

"He Navigated away, but not before being hurt," Legba said. "How do you think Moremi's family found you? Found her?"

Ikenga slumped to the ground and put his hand over his face. "Two years! And I didn't know." A pang of guilt traveled through him. *Who is this man? And why should I trust him?* He thrust his dagger toward Legba. "I am no hero."

"My Loa once told me that only what is earned can define a person. Not what is given. To be a hero is not a state of being," Legba said. "I do not ask you to do anything. Only listen and make your own decisions. I found you. Others will. Nago Sango's attention has been on other matters. But how much time do you really have?"

"I will do what I need to do."

"What you need is absolution. Those herbs you are taking will kill you before Nago Sango finds you."

Ikenga stayed silent, unable to speak.

"You have nowhere else to go."

"My father taught me to never trust a man from Vodun. I will not forget that lesson this time. Get out of my way. I never want to see you again."

"I hoped it wouldn't come to this," Legba declared, his expression hardening as his eyes darkened again.

A new sword materialized in his outstretched hand, and he advanced toward Ikenga with deliberate, calculated steps. Ikenga conjured a white fire in his palm and hurled it at the advancing man. However, before the flame hit its target, Legba vanished and reappeared to Ikenga's left. Ikenga unleashed burst after burst of white fire, but Legba dodged each one with infuriating ease, leaving the surrounding walls and ground scarred with craters as if rocks had plummeted from the sky.

Ikenga's strength faltered, and he collapsed to his knees, gasping for breath. "I'll kill you," he vowed, blood trickling from his mouth.

Out of the corner of his eye, Ikenga noticed Legba advancing but turning required every ounce of his remaining strength. He raised his hand, but only a weak flicker of flame emerged from his fingertips.

"Sometimes the hard path is the only one," Legba said, swatting Ikenga's hand away. Legba placed his hand on Ikenga's shoulder, and the alleyway faded away. They plummeted for a few seconds before the surroundings snapped back into focus, revealing a desert landscape with fine, black sand. Two chairs materialized where they stood. Legba lifted Ikenga from his knees and sat him in one of them.

"Where are we?" Ikenga muttered with the little energy he had.

Before Legba could respond, Ikenga's head fell back, and he lost consciousness.

~

IKENGA'S EYES fluttered open to find Legba seated cross-legged on the barren ground. His gaze locked on him. "Where am I?"

"Beyond the bounds of your known world," Legba replied. "A place I call Nowhere."

The air bore an icy touch, and light winds slipped through Ikenga's clothes, eliciting an involuntary shiver. He scanned the vast expanse around them, but his gaze met nothing except endless dunes of sand. Ikenga looked at the ground and found Formless next to his legs. He grabbed it and pointed it at his abductor.

"Amadioha and Ojukwu are leading a rebellion against Vodun," Legba declared, ignoring the sword. "I can spend hours describing it all, or I can share my memories."

"You kidnapped me and brought me here," Ikenga said, standing on wobbly legs.

"I don't have time to waste," Legba said. With a flick of his wrist, a vial of dark blood materialized in his hand, its red liquid catching the light. "This will tell you all you need to know." He tossed it to Ikenga. "Three drops in each eye. No more."

Ikenga watched the vial fly through the air but did not catch it. It landed in the sand next to his feet. "Do you think I am stupid enough to fall for this?"

"If I wanted to kill you, I would have done it when you were asleep. Or maybe I could leave you here to die a long, slow death," Legba said. "The blood is tainted with magic, giving anyone who ingests it access to the memories inside them."

"Blood memories are not real." Ikenga stared at the vial in distrust.

"You are a man lacking imagination," Legba said. "That is part of why you ended up here."

Legba's words irked him, making him feel small and inadequate. But his options were dwindling. He grunted before grabbing the vial and putting the drops of blood into each eye. Within seconds, he sunk into an endless loop of dreams, more immersive than he imagined they would be.

The memories felt like his. They felt like he was living them. He visualized the day Legba first arrived in Rada Mysters, feeling his trials and tribulations and simmering apprehension toward Amadioha. He experienced the warning given to the Loa and their narrow escape from the castle. The allure of the memories clung to him, seductive as an unfinished dream. He yearned for more, trapped in the intoxicating allure of a past that wasn't his own.

"A day after the last memory, Ojukwu declared the Niri region the Independent Kingdom of Niri," Legba said. "All the active Niri spread across Vodun absconded. It was all so sudden. Many escaped. Some made it back home, but many more did not. They are either prisoners or dead."

Ikenga rose, his feet silent against the sand, joining Legba to stare at the endless nothingness. "The independent Kingdom of Niri." He had been completely removed over the last two years. "Growing up as a child, independence from Vodun was always discussed. My father made me swear never to talk about it publicly." He paused as he took two steps away. "So Amadioha was the one to do it."

"Did you listen to what I just said? Did you learn nothing from my memories? The entire kingdom is in disarray, yet you reminisce of your childhood?"

"The Vodun Kingdom only benefited the upper families. Why should I lament the crumbling of it?"

"Hmmm," Legba said as he nodded. "Some Loas in the Vodun upper house have been corrupted by a fear of losing a grip on a power they have never known life without."

"It is a power they did not deserve," Ikenga said. "A power they never deserved."

"After the Wollof secession movement, we spent years crushing rebellions, even within our ranks. Now, our trading partners are becoming more demanding. And our other enemies are becoming bolder."

"All empires rise and fall. That is the natural order of things. This one, better now than later."

"Do not patronize me, son of Umoren. Do you think I am here to recruit soldiers for Vodun?"

"I thought you were here to kill me with your sword, but maybe you will use your words instead," Ikenga smirked.

Legba scoffed. He clenched his fists, showing the most emotion Ikenga had seen from him in their brief interaction.

"Radha Rhamirez and Ghede Ghadou have been in a silent conflict for years, using Niri as a proxy many times, something you should be well aware of. Amadioha's rebellion hurt us, but the damage to Ghede Ghadou is more severe." Legba paused. "In his desperation to hold on to power, he has crossed a line so dark the entire realm is in danger." Legba looked away and stared into the distance. "He has made a dangerous pact with Asmodeus so he can take back Niri, all of it. A grave miscalculation with consequences no person has seen before."

"Asmodeus?" Ikenga felt his heart beat faster. "That sounds like—"

"A demon," Legba finished. "Asmodeus is the military king of one of the regions in Hell."

Ikenga's eyes opened wide.

"Ghede Ghadou made a deal with him to ally in the fight against Niri and any Vodun family that goes against his will," Legba said. "Asmodeus promised to help crush the uprising, and in exchange, he will be granted an area within Vodun to do as he pleases."

Ikenga shuddered. "No Navigator can bring enough demons to Kirina to make a difference. And the Brokers, they would never agree to let them through the sacred path."

With a flick of his wrist, Legba conjured a sheaf of papers and handed them to Ikenga. They looked like paintings, but as realistic as if he was there. The first was of a man who looked like a Loa in a military command center filled with contraptions Ikenga was unfamiliar with. They looked like weapons, metallic in nature. Trees and obstacles obstructed the second painting, but what he could make out was still as clear as the sun. It was the biggest military camp he had ever seen.

"Ghede Ghadou thinks Asmodeus is bringing thirty thousand here. My scout estimates a number ten times as much."

"Chineke!"

"Chineke has nothing to do with this," Legba said. "Asmodeus plans to do a lot more than shepherd a few satellite territories. We believe he is planning a full-scale invasion."

Ikenga's heart hammered in his chest. "Why are you telling me this? Take this to the Bondye and all the other families. Expose it."

"Amadioha destroyed more than Radha's military," Legba said. "He destroyed her reputation. Ghede Ghadou and Anaise will deny it and call her bitter. Her feud with them is well known. This information would be too dangerous to too many powerful people. Our family would be at risk of retribution. Her military might have grown since Amadioha attacked, but it is still a fraction of what it was." Legba took a deep breath. "We need proof. Incontrovertible proof. Then, I can go to Bondye and expose this publicly. Ghede and whoever else he conspires with can be stopped. You must help me."

Legba's words were strong. He was telling the truth or an excellent manipulator. And the allure of not having to keep hiding was appealing. "First, help me free Utaka, then we can talk more about this Vodun problem."

"It's too dangerous."

"I need to see him, or you can take me back to where you found me. I will take my chances with Nago Sango."

"Ghede's influence is dangerously large. His spies lurk in places you would not expect. Even in the heart of Niri and Orisha, there are those who whisper their allegiance to Vodun, yearning for its rule."

"Take me to his cell," Ikenga said. "You brought us here. I know you can do that."

Legba looked like he was contemplating his words. "The only reason Utaka is in jail is because you ran. If you had returned, it would be you in a cell or executed. If he sees you, the first thing he will do with the last bit of energy tethering him to this world is to kill you. Listen to me, son of Umoren, do this for me, and I will get a pardon from the Bondye for both of you. I will ensure you can both roam as free men in your home. And maybe then he will forgive you."

Ikenga chewed his lip. "A pardon from the Bondye does nothing for me. It is Nago Sango who needs to let this go."

"Unless Nago Sango is also planning to rebel against Vodun, it won't matter. He would have to comply."

Ikenga's gaze remained locked on the distant, vacant horizon. This man's argument was feeble, yet desperation forced him to cling to it. "What do you need me to do?"

Legba passed another photo, materialized with a flick of his wrist. There was a name written on it. *'Daeva Isrut'*

I need to ask him how he does that.

"Her last known location was in Sasobek."

"What am I supposed to do with this?"

"From what I understand, she has been a key player. It was personal for her, but she wants out. We can use her to get enough evidence and expose the vile alliance before it's too late. There is a small chance Asmodeus is doing this in secret and may not have broad support in Hell." Legba stepped toward Ikenga. "Amadioha's rebellion has grown. They have taken full control over most of Niri. I know this may sound pleasing to you, but it makes our timeline shorter. Ghede Ghadou will keep getting more desperate."

Ikenga laughed. "You want me to go to Hell and find this Daeva Isrut? A place I know only from books and tales?"

"That fire in your hands. You must know why it burns white instead of red. You are the most powerful manipulator of fire in Kirina with that thing you have inside you."

"Most powerful, and you still bested me."

"I said most powerful, not smartest." A smirk crossed Legba's face. "You are the one man who can survive the climate. And with the memories of the demon we captured, you will have all the information you need."

Ikenga's eyes widened. "You captured a demon?"

"That is what I just said."

"Even with the memories, I cannot speak the language."

"An immersion is a complete transfer of all the demon's memories to you. You will learn everything it knows from its birth until today. Your body will feel everything the demon has ever felt. Most people could not survive this. But if anyone can, it's you."

"If I can survive it, then others can."

Legba took a few steps away from Ikenga, then turned around abruptly. "From the moment Eshm possessed Moremi, she was already dead. The spirit would have consumed her from the inside right away. Maybe that will remove a burden from your heart. No other human walking could contain that power. But you did."

"It was my fault she was there."

"Perhaps," Legba's curtness surprised Ikenga.

Ikenga shook his head as he paced. He already knew his answer, but delaying it made him feel better. He chewed on his lip. "So I go to Hell, meet my contact, and say, 'Hey, where is Daeva Isrut?' He tells us, and we find her. We meet her with big smiles, and I tell her I am a runaway fugitive from Niri, and you serve a Loa in Vodun. She smiles more and hands us incontrovertible evidence about this inter-realm plot about demons invading our realm. We come back here and stop the rogue Loas together with the Bondye. Then, we restore order to the realm. After that, the Bondye gracefully pardons me and Utaka before we go on our way."

"Exactly!" Papa Legba said. "Except I cannot be seen with you. There are many spies there. I can take you, but you must do most of it alone. Once you have what we need, I will retrieve you."

Ikenga could not tell if Legba was serious or joking when he said that. "So I am the one who will take all the risks? Why should I trust you? Or her?"

"I don't trust anyone. Not even you. You would do well to follow suit," Papa Legba said. "A dark cloud is forming over our realm, and you would do well to help me stop it."

11

KRIMINEL'S WEAPON

*T*he sun blazed mercilessly, casting its relentless heat across Niri's Nnabu Valley. The high humidity made the sweat build up on the exposed parts of **Baron Kriminel Nibo's** hands. His purple undergarment, peeking out from beneath his bronze armor, was already soaked, adding to his discomfort. It was early afternoon, with no clouds for miles in the brilliant blue sky. The absence of wind, which had once offered a reprieve from the heat, left the air still and stagnant. Kriminel wiped his forehead, his hand leaving a gleaming trail on his polished breastplate.

"*Fout tonne!*" he cursed under his breath. It had gotten hotter in Vodun, but never this humid. Even the insects were more amiable compared to this relentless assault.

Nearby, Simon, Kriminel's Master of Arms, assertively directed his men. Short in stature with a distinct baldness, Simon invariably donned a leaf-metal plate on his head, insisting it enhanced his intellect—making him the camp's brightest. Lately though, Kriminel wondered if prolonged detachment from home was eroding Simon's sharpness. He wore circular glasses almost as big as his head. Raised by a blacksmith who forged swords for Ghede Ghadou Loa's father,

Simon held an aloof attitude toward such basic weaponry, considering swords beneath him.

Simon's men, their once-white clothes now stained brown and black, scrambled to assemble a massive structure. The wooden and steel frame rose to twice the height of a man, its hollow heart and imposing width commanding attention. A worker, his raggedy shirt clinging to his sweat-soaked body, ascended a ladder with a bag of sharp, metallic objects. At the base, another man worked a complex system of ropes and pulleys. The metallic clangs and the creak of strained wood filled the air, a symphony all too familiar to Kriminel.

Kriminel watched with resignation and faint hope, wondering if the outcome would be any different. His mind wandered to Ghede Ghadou Loa's words: *Broaden your horizons, deepen your insights.* He had arrived in Niri filled with ambition, determined to prove himself worthy of climbing the ranks within the Vodun order. But, with Amadioha's forces advancing and the land in rebellion, Kriminel questioned his choices.

In time, the workers retreated from the structure, save for one at the top and another at the base. As the bottom worker seized the lever, a resounding click echoed.

Simon rode toward him, and Kriminel felt his impatience growing. He wanted to get back to his other administrative duties. "These men should be training their sword skills, not building these contraptions," Kriminel said.

"To what end, Mesye?" Simon asked. "We have seen what Amadioha has done to all the other Vodun strongholds in Niri. Our Loa has suffered worse losses than Radha Rhamirez."

Just because one solution does not work doesn't mean you try something more foolish. "Great losses? And we waste our time on carpentry?"

"We have twenty builders, Mesye. We have been working day and night for weeks on end."

"Yes, that's what you said the other ten times. And we are yet to see any results."

"It is hard to build with the wood here in Kwale. The builders were not used to the porosity. We have adjusted our technique to account for it."

Simon was always so naïve. If they were to meet their end, they should not spend their last days on foolish conquests. "Shut it down," Kriminel said. "Have the men pick up their swords. We will drive this rebellion back the way the Vodun army has always done." They were Vodunese warriors, not carpenters.

"Mesye, you need to trust me," Simon pleaded.

Kriminel's irritation grew. He regretted agreeing to observe. He should have gone with his gut and ignored the request. The failed experiments only worsened morale. "No more."

"Then we might as well dig our own grave," Simon said. "Ten thousand men. The Niri have four to five times that. And the moment the civilians hear their liberators are near, every one of them becomes yet another potential enemy soldier."

Simon was right, but Kriminel was not about to let him know that. He would rather march the army back to Gede Mysters and face the wrath of his Loa for abandoning their station than go down this path. There was no honor in that, but was that a consideration? How could it be dishonorable to abandon your post when your Loa had abandoned you for almost two years?

"You said this contraption would reverse the odds twenty to one? And you have twenty men? Join your carpenters and face two hundred of our prisoners in open field. Those would be favorable numbers. If you can defeat them, you can continue with this," Kriminel said.

Shock filled Simon's face.

Let him be the one to see the errors of his way.

"Mesye, anything could go wrong," Simon said.

I already know this. This is why I am the baron and not you. "And if we use the weapons in battle against Amadioha, maybe his army will pause the swipe of their swords when your weapons malfunction?" Kriminel mocked.

Simon chewed his lip. "Open field. Bring the prisoners," he said defiantly.

Kriminel let a laugh escape his lips. If Simon thought he could bluff him, he really had been spending too much time with hammers and nails. "Don't be foolish, you will die."

"My father and grandfather were blacksmiths and weapons makers. I will fulfill my duty or join them in the next life as a failure." Simon said.

He was serious... No, he wasn't. Surely. But if he rejected Simon's request, what would they do? Simon was right; they would be sitting ducks if the rebellious army approached, and they would die anyway. But what if it worked? They could be the ones to end the rebellion—a rebellion that humbled Radha Rhamirez Loa. A rebellion that wiped out many other barons of Ghede Ghadou Loa. Tales of their victory would spread across Vodun.

"Very well then," Kriminel conceded. He was already clutching at the straws of victory. False hope. That is what he didn't want for himself or his soldiers.

He motioned to a man to his right. "Two hundred of the strongest men in the prison. Bring them in. And all the rest of the carpenters responsible for building this weapon. Swords or spears for each of them," he demanded. "*Kounye!*"

It took a while as they baked in the scorching sun, but a disturbance ruffled the line of soldiers, making way for about fifteen men.

"Second thoughts?" Kriminel asked, half hoping Simon would say yes and half hoping he would say no.

Simon shook his head as the men, armed with swords, were ushered to the back of the weapon before others nearby joined them.

"Twenty of your men then," Kriminel said.

"*Kounye!*" the soldier nearby shouted at the wall of the army. He signaled again, and more men were brought through the sea of soldiers. They had chains on their hands linked to each other as they walked in single file. Their hair was unkempt. Some had light bruises —most needed showers.

"These men have violated their oath to their nation. All two hundred of them," Kriminel said. "We have an approaching army and

The Eden Ruse

cannot continue to waste our food and resources on them. A successful test will solve two of our problems."

"By the gods of Vodun, this will work," Simon said with a lot less confidence than when he had agreed.

We will need more than gods today. "Dismount from your horse," Kriminel said.

Simon slid to the ground with shaky legs.

Kriminel approached a guard, drawing the man's sword gleaming in the sun. He glanced at Simon and threw the sword at him. "Your contraption will work today," Kriminel said. "Or you will meet your ancestors in the afterlife. And maybe we will all join you soon."

Ever so stubborn, Simon grabbed the sword and rushed to his builders, where he immediately issued orders. The men inspected the device, making sure they had configured everything correctly. The man orchestrating the ordeal gave a signal. Ahead, soldiers unchained the prisoners and handed them weapons.

"Prizonye, Prizonye! Hear this message of Ghede Loa via your holy Baron Kriminel," the soldier said as he rode back and forth in front of the line. "Your baron has given you a chance for absolution. If you succeed, we will free you from this camp, and you can go anywhere. You will have no absolution from any other punishment, but you can be sure we will not go after you. At my call, attack the contraption." He paused and pointed toward Simon. "If you can kill them all, you have your freedom."

"Is this some kind of joke?" one man shouted.

"I can assure you, your baron is not in a joking mood today," the soldier said. He smacked his horse and rode back to where Kriminel was. Kriminel felt guilty, but Ghede Ghadou Loa had answered none of his calls for help. He had no other option.

Even from this distance, he could see the sweat drenching Simon's face as he displaced the man at the bottom of the device and pushed him backward. Simon turned around to glance at Kriminel, their eyes locking for a brief second. With heavy eyes, Kriminel looked at the man he had called a friend for many years.

"Attack!" the soldier near the prisoners shouted. The prisoners, some confined for months, others for years, charged at Simon and his builders. Fervent rage replaced their diminished strength and hope.

∼

SIMON'S CHEST heaved as he drew a ragged breath. The thundering footsteps and battle cries grew louder, signaling the rapid approach of the charging prisoners. He turned to the men behind him. "Our swords won't save us!" he bellowed. "But this weapon, forged with our sweat and blood, will not fail. By Ghede Ghadou Loa, we are the best in Vodun. Today, we show it!"

The air was thick with tension as Simon's men stood in eerie silence, their faces masks of fear and disbelief.

"Everyone, to your positions!" Simon commanded. "Drop your swords and man the weapon!" Three men scrambled up the ladder while the rest took their places around the contraption. "Wait for my signal. Not a moment sooner!"

The enemy prisoners charged, covering half the distance before Simon's voice rang out again. "*Dife!*" The moment of truth had arrived.

The builder nearest the lever yanked it down with all his might. A sickening snap echoed across the battlefield. The charging prisoners hesitated, uncertain. Simon's heart plummeted as he realized the sound signaled another malfunction. This weapons test had failed spectacularly, and now they would pay the price.

Seeing no threat, the prisoners resumed their advance with renewed vigor, brandishing their weapons.

"Why isn't it firing?" Simon's voice cracked, panic evident as sweat stung his eyes.

"The cable snapped!" a builder shouted.

The approaching men were so close that the ground rumbled with their steps. Simon spotted the thread connecting the main lever to the rest of the weapon that had snapped. He ripped off his shirt, tying the broken ends together. "Unwind it!" he shouted.

The builder worked feverishly on the firing mechanism. "*Dife!*" he yelled.

Simon jumped up and pulled the lever down once more. A deafening *whoosh* split the air as a single spear tip erupted from the machine. It struck an oncoming prisoner in the neck, decapitating him with terrifying ease. The body cartwheeled through the air before landing with a sickening thud, the head following a heartbeat later.

A collective gasp arose from Simon's men. The prisoners faltered, stunned by the gruesome display. Two more metal spikes hurtled from the device. A builder kicked the base, unlocking the rotating mechanism. The weapon swung from side to side, unleashing a barrage of projectiles that tore through the advancing prisoners. Screams filled the air as spikes ripped through flesh and bone. Most of the prisoners turned to flee, but the relentless weapon showed no mercy. In less than a minute, the carnage was complete.

Simon shuddered at the efficiency of his creation. It was a brutal choice—their lives or his—but one he had to make. His builders stood unscathed, having never raised a sword. One final prisoner, a former mountain of a man, had nearly reached the weapon. Missing a leg and with a metal spike buried in his shoulder, he dragged himself toward Simon, agonized cries escaping his lips. Simon gripped the sword his baron had given him, plunging it into the back of the man's neck. The prisoner's struggles ceased.

~

FOR THE FIRST time that day, **Kriminel** cracked a smile. He urged his horse forward, then turned to face the rest of his army. "Every soldier, man, child, and woman—place them under Simon's command. Every able body should either be producing food or building more of these weapons."

"Yes, Mesye," the soldier to his right said.

"No more training, no more war exercises. Any woman not with child will join the men and work. We must produce as many of these as we can."

"Yes, Mesye. Understood."

Kriminel spurred his horse forward a few paces toward the assembled soldiers. "Soldiers of Ghede Loa! Soldiers of Vodun! Soldiers of Kriminel!" he said as he rode down the line.

"Aye, aye!" they boomed, an excitement in their voices he had not heard for a long time.

"Why are we here?"

"Because our baron demands it!" they chorused as one, stomping their feet.

"And what is it that your baron demands of you?"

"To fight against all who oppose us, to defend the sacred honor of Vodun until our final breaths!"

Kriminel nodded, a fierce grin spreading across his face. He raised his fist high. "What are you prepared to risk in this glorious battle?"

"Everything!" came the resounding reply.

"Will you hold anything back from our cause?"

"Nothing!" they thundered, beating weapons against shields, stirring their shared passion into a frenzy.

Kriminel's voice dropped low, his tone deadly serious. "And if you should fall..." He paused, meeting their eyes. "If the Niri should strike you down, what then?"

The warriors' voices rose in a chilling oath: "Then, in the afterlife, we shall hunt them down and avenge our glorious dead!"

The soldiers' collective roar surged through the air, electrifying the atmosphere and filling Kriminel with adrenaline. He pulled his sword out from its sheath and thrust it into the air, and the men followed. The metal swords sliced through the air, sending a *whoosh* into the skies.

He noticed Simon had stayed near his weapon, seated with his back on the contraption and his head buried in his hands.

Ever a sensitive man. He was mourning the loss of the prisoners instead of celebrating they had just saved the lives of every Vodunese in Nnabu Valley.

Kriminel rode to him. "Our scouts say the Niri army is about two weeks away," he said. "They are expecting ten thousand men. We will give them the might of two hundred thousand."

Simon lifted his head, tears glistening on his cheeks. "Yes, Mesye," he whispered, his voice barely audible above the noise from the soldiers.

Kriminel smiled as he leaned in closer. "When we return victorious, all Vodun will herald us as heroes. And your role in this triumph shall not be forgotten."

"Yes, Mesye," he said. "We will crush the rebellion together." A cautious smile spread across Simon's face.

12

THE NIRI ARMY

*I*nside the tent, candlelight cast shadows on the faces of those seated around the stone table. Maps and parchment scrolls covered the table's surface. The air was thick with leather and sweat.

"Eze Agha of Niri," Ojukwu Wume's voice resonated, captivating everyone as it echoed around the tent. Even when their army stood at over twenty thousand, he could give a speech everyone could hear. If "commanding presence" was mentioned anywhere in Niri, Ojukwu's name would follow shortly after.

There were eight Ezes in the tent, each wearing long white robes and red caps that matched the beaded necklaces hanging on their necks—eight of them and **Amadioha's** wife, Ijele. By the letter of the law, she should not have been there. But Amadioha was not a man who liked to follow the rules, nor did Ijele. She had often proven valuable, and having her directly in the conversations was useful.

As on most days, Ojukwu's bare chest was on full display. Amadioha felt he did it to assert dominance over the other Ezes. Ojukwu's skin sometimes transformed from flesh to a rocky substance, a metamorphosis as sudden and stark as a smile turning into a frown.

"Eze Niri, we hail you," intoned everyone, including Amadioha. They pounded their hands on the table in unison. No man batted an eye as the wine from their full cups spilled on the table. Each Eze took a sip of the drink and put it down. Ijele raised her cup and put it back down without drinking.

"Eze Agha of Niri. The doubters said we could never form an alliance," Ojukwu said. "They said Niri could never unite. They said we could never work together. They thought we were incapable of kicking out the Vodun infiltrators."

With fiery conviction, Achebe shouted, "They thought wrong!"

Everyone in this room also wondered if we could form an alliance until I forced their hands after my assault on Rada Mysters. Now, they all act like it was the plan they wanted all along.

Everyone pounded the table again, spilling more wine.

"Through your prowess and might, we have defeated almost every Vodun stronghold in Niri. And we have done it while sustaining minimal casualties. *Otuto diri* Chineke!"

"Every Niri who has died is resting at the feet of Chineke!" Amadioha shouted. "For every one of us who dies, one hundred of them have fallen."

The pounding on the table grew louder, a stormy rhythm of tension. Amadioha's cup teetered, then tipped over. As the wine poured off the table toward him, Ijele reached out her hand. A soft, blue light emanated from her palm, creating a barrier that halted the liquid in its tracks. She then cupped her hand, pushed back, and the liquid reversed direction and traveled back into the cup. Amadioha stole a glance at her and smiled. Her eyes were a luminous shade of brown. A black tattoo of various curved shapes covered half of the left side of her face.

"For every Niri who falls, let one thousand of them fall!" the Ezes repeated.

Ijele grabbed Amadioha's knee under the table and dug her finger into it. He looked at her with disdain and returned his attention to the table. She knew him well enough to know he was about to say something to upset the mood, but not well enough to accept that she could not stop that from happening.

Ekwensu, a lanky man, got up from his seat. "Yet as we celebrate our last victory, there is one more battle we must fight." As on any other day, he had white chalk around his eyes, making them appear sunken and swollen. Otherwise, he looked to be about half of his actual age.

"We cannot celebrate until Nnabu Valley... until our capital is free." Ojukwu pounded his fist on his chest. The skin around his torso briefly transformed into solid rock, sending the crash of stone on stone reverberating through their room. "When we bring our army right outside the rim of the Narrow Path, they will surely know they will lose the battle and surrender. We will ensure they all leave this land and return to Vodun."

A score of murmurs filled the room as different Ezes whispered to one another. Raising his eyebrows, Ojukwu scanned the room with a look that betrayed he had expected all the men to agree.

Amadioha's breathing increased. Each word Ojukwu had spoken was like a bullet piercing his skin. Ijele sensed it. She gripped his knee again. He put his hand underneath the table and swatted hers away as he stood.

"Let them leave this land and return to Vodun?" Amadioha's brows furrowed. "Is that what we give to the people who ravaged our lands and cities for decades? The people who raped our women, who murdered our men, who stole the future from our children?"

"We will win the war and drive them out." Ojukwu's eyes flashed. "We've exacted our revenge on Vodun and conquered every stronghold they have had." He raised his hands in the room to rally the other Ezes again, but they were mostly silent.

"The right punishment for their actions is death," Amadioha said. "Misplaced mercy is a seed for tomorrow's chaos. We must not yield. We will bring pain up from the ground and down from the skies on them!"

Ojukwu scanned the room, seeking the reactions of the other

Ezes, and received cold stares. "Attack, attack, attack. That is always Amadioha's plan." He gestured dismissively.

"Attacking is better than snatching defeat from victory's hands," Amadioha retorted with a sarcastic hand gesture. "It's certainly better than showing weakness."

"*Otuasi!*" Ojukwu said. "You call my actions weak, but your actions only cost lives. How many died when you raided Rada Mysters? How many have died since this war began? I want to take back our home without risking the lives of more of our men and children."

"You are Eze Niri. You tell us how many died since this war began," Amadioha mocked. "Then tell us how many died before Rada Mysters? Chineke! I ask you, how many of us lived before that? What lives did our women and children have? What lives did our men have?" There were more grumbles among the Ezes. Some even nodded at Amadioha's words.

"As you have called out, I am the leader of this council, not you," Ojukwu was flustered and angry. It was obvious he was doing everything in his power to stay calm, but the entirety of his torso had turned to stone. He raised both hands, and they smashed clean through the table, leaving two gashes where his fists made contact.

The room was silenced. Shock covered all their faces. All except for Amadioha and Ijele's.

"Eri of Eze." Amadioha looked around with an aura of confidence. "I say Eri of Eze," he repeated, and pointed.

"Eri of Eze!" the men shouted in unison. But Ojukwu's silence screamed louder than any of them, his eyes dark with unspoken rage.

Amadioha's stance softened. "You are Eri, yes," Amadioha said. "Erizu, legal expert for all matters." Amadioha turned to face Erizu. "Our laws allow a supermajority of Ezes to override military decisions. Do they not?"

"Our laws allow it." Erizu nodded.

"I move for a vote," declared Amadioha. "Shall we let these invaders escape unpunished for their crimes against us, against our children, and future generations? Or do we reclaim our capital and exact the justice they deserve?"

"Even though it is the law, it is customary for the Eri to endorse all votes." Erizu's eyes probed Ojukwu, seeking an acknowledgment of his words.

He has no choice but to recognize the vote. He must.

After a long silence, Ojukwu spoke. "We shall have the vote."

The final vote was six to two in Amadioha's favor.

"It is done then," Amadioha said as he sat back down. "Eri of Eze. Will you recognize our vote?"

"We have barely won the war and already choose to destroy the alliance we have built?" Ojukwu asked.

"Have we not followed the law?"

"*Ewu!*" Ojukwu roared, clashing his fists together before slamming one into the table and leaving another hole. He stormed out, leaving a heavy silence in his wake.

∽

THE WALLS OF CANIS MAJOR, the administrative heart of Canis, gleamed orange. Ever since Amadioha had risen to the title of Eze at the war's onset, he had staked his claim on the domain. Inside, exposed bricks showcased the building's concrete foundation. Spanning two stories, the section linked to the primary structure through a narrow overground passage. On the ground floor, Amadioha had gathered two of his trusted confidants around a table. Having just returned from Kwale to Canis, his army needed the solace of reuniting with families before facing another battle.

Amadioha leaned forward, his palms flat on the table. "We must strategize our attack on Nnabu Valley."

"We don't have the numbers." Damballa shook his head.

"Numbers have meant nothing in our previous battles," Reebell interjected.

"The rebels in Ikora have targeted key Vodunese locations, serving as a useful distraction," Damballa began, "but funding them has emptied our coffers. We have resorted to stealing from other Ezes. If they discover this, we will face dire consequences. This is the crisis we should be worried about."

"We will continue raiding Vodun outposts for funds," Amadioha said.

"That strategy lost its edge months ago," Damballa countered. "The Vodunese heavily fortify their outposts now."

"Perhaps Sango can assist?" Reebell asked.

Damballa laughed. "Nago Sango? We should be happy he has not declared war after what he claims Ikenga did to his daughter."

"A snake does not give birth to a stick," Amadioha scoffed. "Remove Sango from your mind. We need another solution."

"Your political maneuvers have yielded results, more than your martial feats, for once. Yet, Ojukwu is a man of pride," Damballa said. "His motivations differ from ours. If he senses betrayal, his actions will be unpredictable."

"So we backtrack?" Amadioha asked. "Show mercy? The alliance we have formed against all odds would go out as a whimper."

"You are a war hero, not a uniter," Damballa said.

"What disrespect!" Reebell's voice rose to a shout.

Amadioha raised a hand. "Let him finish."

"While your warrior skills are unmatched, Ojukwu was the glue binding our nation," Damballa said. "We succeeded because of him, not despite him. Underestimating his influence is a grave mistake."

"How much money has Ojukwu paid you to side with him? Or is it the Vodunese at the capital lining your pockets?" Reebell accused.

"Is your vision only limited to what is directly in front of you?" Damballa said.

Reebell, hand gripping his axe, snapped, "Your Vodun heritage shows. *Damballa Weddo!*" he said, spelling out all the syllables in Damballa's name. "Shall I remind you of real warriorship?"

"My name is worth one hundred times what yours will ever be! I will not let you question my loyalty again."

"If Canis is to be destroyed, it will not be by those in my court!" White sparks flew out of Amadioha's eyes as both men reluctantly relented. *If cracks exist in my court, how can I hope to keep my other men focused?* "Devise a strategy for Nnabu Valley together or find your way out of my court. The farms are eager for more hands."

Both men nodded.

Even though Damballa's words were wise, he could not let those Vodunese soldiers have safe passage back to the place they called home.

∼

"I should be Eri, not him. His tactics… they reek of fear," Amadioha lamented. Having advanced to the easternmost part of Canis, their army settled in makeshift tents. Dim torches flickered around the room's edges, casting soft shadows that danced lazily on the walls. Amadioha lay on a bamboo bed, his head resting on a pillow as he watched Ijele massage his legs. His body always felt sore after war, and those moments made him better.

She picked up a bottle of fragrant oil, poured it over his feet, and let her fingers glide as she massaged him. The semi-transparent cloth wrapped around her torso and legs left little to the imagination. Her firm hands kneaded his legs. "Ojukwu is the reason those same Ezes formed an alliance," she said.

Amadioha's smile faded. "I am the reason we have won every battle against the Vodunese. Left to Ojukwu, we would still be battling Ghede Loa's barons in Anaku, trying to negotiate."

"The burden of being Eri goes past winning battles. One distracted by those concerns has less time to think about military strategies."

Amadioha's face furrowed in a deep frown. "Whose side you are on?"

She squeezed his feet with more pressure as she worked through his toes. "I just want you to understand the cross Ojukwu carries."

"You sound just like Damballa. If you want to be with him, you can leave and go to his tent."

Rising, Ijele swayed toward him, the candlelight accentuating the contours of her body through the sheer dress. "The only place I will be is right where I am," she said as she sat on the bed beside him.

"From the sound of your words, I do not know if I believe that."

"You claim you want to carry the burden of being an Eri, but you cannot control your emotions."

Bright white sparks of electricity leaped from Amadioha's eyes. He slapped her across the face, sending her sprawling to the floor beside the bed. He grabbed her by the wrists and threw her onto the mattress; the thick padding cushioned her drop. She let out a squeal as he ripped off the sheer garment she had on. He pulled down his pants, and within moments, his arms gripped the sides of the mattress as he thrust in and out of her. She gazed deep into his eyes, like she wanted to touch his soul. Electricity sparkled between them and from his chest. It bounced off an invisible shield as it traveled toward her face. She put her hands on his chest and pushed him back. Then she curled her legs back, placed her feet on his lower abdomen, and hurled him off her. He flew into the air and landed on the bed with a loud crash. The legs at the head of the bed gave way, and it slanted down to the ground.

Before he could move, she scrambled up and mounted him. She slid him inside her and moved her hips up and down forcefully. He tried to reach up to touch her breasts, but she smacked his hand, then slapped his face. Their moans synchronized with each motion. Her hands covered his neck, squeezing harder and harder until he could barely breathe. They came together violently as they slid off the bed and landed on the floor.

They took a few moments to catch their breath.

"Why settle for Eri when you can dream much bigger?" Ijele asked.

"Bigger? What is much bigger than the ruler of Niri?"

"Vodun is bigger than Niri."

Amadioha let out a laugh. "Vodun? If there is any benefit to this war, it is that it made you funny."

Ijele kept her eyes on the ceiling. "There is more to being Eri than war. Let Ojukwu carry that burden. For now."

She got up, grabbed an incense stick from the corner of the room, and lit it with the lantern. When she placed it at the edge of the bed, the aroma, mixed with the smell of sex, created an intoxicating sense in Amadioha's head.

She sat cross-legged at the foot of the bed, the incense smoke curling around her. "After we take Niri, we do not stop there," she said. "You will suggest we take our army all the way to Nana and strike at the heart of our enemy."

"In Niri, we have the advantage that this is our home. If we take our army into Vodun, we lose all of it. That would be a suicide mission."

"That is what you told me about Rada Mysters," she said, "and you took it all the same."

"We were lucky. We had the element of surprise. They will see us coming from a mile away."

"The man I married had a bigger vision than this."

Amadioha furrowed his brows. "Even if we take it, they will never allow us to hold it."

"Vodun has many enemies. Inside and out. Once they smell blood, they will strike. They will be embattled in wars on multiple fronts. Their army will never recover."

Amadioha hummed in thought, rising to sit on the bed.

"In the meantime, this unlikely alliance of Ezes is shaky," Ijele said. "You must make amends with Ojukwu. We must stand together until we reach the capital."

"Now, you are back to making me upset." He raised his hand to slap her. She raised her hand and opened her palm. Dim blue light shot out and knocked his hand back. He groaned in pain as he grabbed his shoulder.

"You have a lot to think about," she said. "Save your energy."

Amadioha's Journal: The Weight of Legacy

The weight upon my chest grows heavier with each passing moon. Today, as I watched the children of Canis play in the marketplace, I felt a pain so sharp it nearly brought me to my knees. Chineke, why do you test me?

Ijele and I have tried everything. Yet, our home remains silent, devoid of the cries of a newborn. The emptiness mocks me, a reminder of my failure not just as a man, but as an Eze.

Last night, I dreamt of my father. He stood before me, his face a mask of disappointment. I awoke in a cold sweat, Ijele's concerned eyes searching my face in the darkness. How can I tell her that I fear failing not just her, but all of Canis?

The whispers grow louder each day. I see the sidelong glances and hear the hushed conversations that stop when I approach. They wonder if Chineke has turned his back on me. Some even suggest I take a different wife, as if Ijele were to blame. The very thought sickens me.

Ijele, my rock, my everything—how does she remain so strong? She smiles and says that Chineke will bless us in time, but I see the pain she tries to hide. Each month brings renewed hope, only to crush it mercilessly.

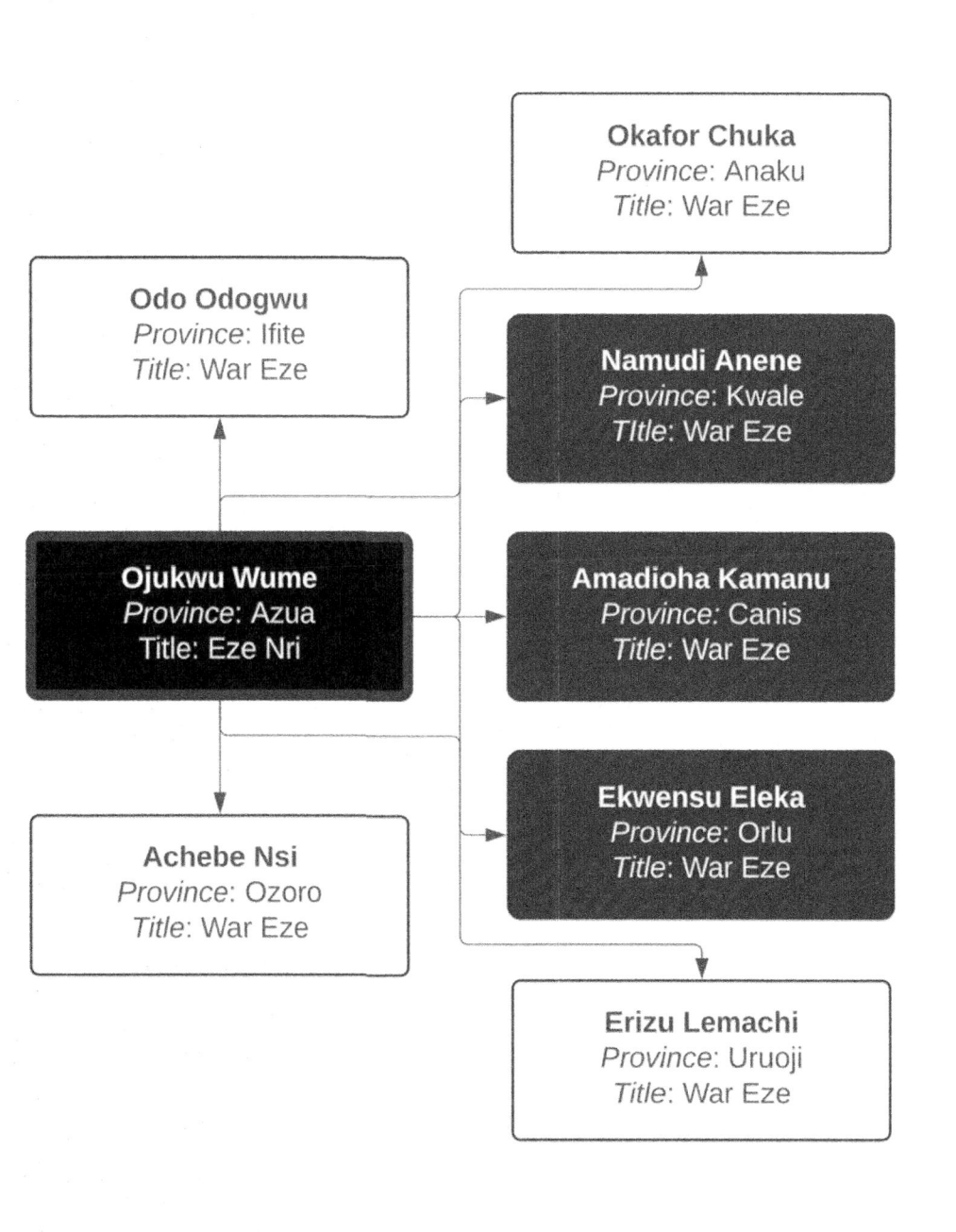

```
                                    ┌─────────────────────┐
                                    │  Okafor Chuka       │
                                    │  Province: Anaku    │
                                    │  Title: War Eze     │
                                    └─────────▲───────────┘
                                              │
┌─────────────────────┐             ┌─────────────────────┐
│  Odo Odogwu         │             │  Namudi Anene       │
│  Province: Ifite    │             │  Province: Kwale    │
│  Title: War Eze     │             │  Title: War Eze     │
└─────────▲───────────┘             └─────────▲───────────┘
          │                                   │
┌─────────┴───────────┐             ┌─────────────────────┐
│  Ojukwu Wume        │────────────▶│  Amadioha Kamanu    │
│  Province: Azua     │────────────▶│  Province: Canis    │
│  Title: Eze Nri     │             │  Title: War Eze     │
└─────┬───────┬───────┘             └─────────────────────┘
      │       │                     ┌─────────────────────┐
      │       └────────────────────▶│  Ekwensu Eleka      │
      │                             │  Province: Orlu     │
      ▼                             │  Title: War Eze     │
┌─────────────────────┐             └─────────┬───────────┘
│  Achebe Nsi         │                       │
│  Province: Ozoro    │                       ▼
│  Title: War Eze     │             ┌─────────────────────┐
└─────────────────────┘             │  Erizu Lemachi      │
                                    │  Province: Uruoji   │
                                    │  Title: War Eze     │
                                    └─────────────────────┘
```

13

KRIMINEL'S STAND

*P*erched on the top floor of the Sant Komand building, the room crowned a corner with vast windows that offered a panoramic view. The gentle hum of the city below crept into the room, and the blend of spices from the Abate market, the busiest and most vibrant in the Nnabu Valley, wafted up to **Kriminel**. The distant cries of Niri sellers reached him as they hawked spicy foods, colorful household items, and intricate art pieces. Below, the rhythmic march of his patrols echoed, having recently doubled in frequency.

Kriminel had conscripted every able-bodied man to either build the new weapons Simon was overseeing or stop a potential rebellion by the city dwellers. Whispers of liberation passed from one local to another, their eyes shining with a newfound hope that replaced the weariness they wore just a few weeks prior.

Kriminel, flanked by his trusted court members, sat around an ornate table. Carved in the intricate likeness of Vodun, its cool, polished surface was strewn with various maps, each telling a story of its own. Simon, his fingers grazing the map, said, "We are almost done positioning our weapons." A proud smile curved his lips, but it vanished as he added, "We have been pushing hard, given the challenges."

Kriminel eyed the map. There was only one obvious way into Nnabu Valley, but the land was vast.

"These weapons are insufficient," Kriminel said.

"We went as fast as we could." Simon's smile faded further. "The wood in the forest is hard to harvest. And the locals are less cooperative."

"You gave us assurances."

"Even with half the area covered, the damage we will inflict on Amadioha is enough to make any army think twice," Simon said. "The journey here is long. They will be tired, and watching their brothers fall will kill their morale."

Kriminel's gaze remained fixed on the map, processing Simon's words, the weight of their implications pressing on his chest.

"The plan the master of arms has put forward is sound," the head of army logistics said. His face was as solemn as his voice.

Simon smiled but just as he started to speak, a jarring bang from outside resonated through the room, cutting him off mid-breath. One of Kriminel's personal guards opened the door and rushed in. He bent his head to the ground and dabbed his hand across his forehead. "Mesye, apologies for the interruption."

"What is it?" Kriminel stood and pressed one hand on the table, his other on the hilt of his sword.

The guard turned toward the doorway and barked. "Bring him in!"

The atmosphere tensed as two more guards marched in, clutching a man by the shoulders. "We found this one lurking near the trees by our outpost." They thrust the man forward, causing him to stumble to the floor.

He approached Kriminel's table and the guards tensed. "Stop right there!" they shouted, drawing their swords in unison.

The man's features were defined—a long, chiseled face framed by wild, curly hair that had a life of its own. And then there was that persistent, maddening smirk, permanently imprinted on his face. A smirk that was hard to forget once you had seen it the first time.

"Kokou?" A deep frown covered Kriminel's face. "What is Brigid's errand boy doing in my territory?"

The man smiled wider, if that was possible. "Baron Maman Brigid sends her regards."

"Her regards? Or a spy to meddle in my business?"

"This is no way to treat the chief scout of your fellow baron."

Kriminel pulled out his sword and pointed it at Kokou. He moved closer until the tip of the blade barely touched Kokou's chest. With an icy glint in his eyes, Kriminel hissed, "Choose your next words wisely, chief scout. I will not think twice about spilling your blood here for trespassing."

Kokou raised his hands in the air. "She sent me ahead of her army to ensure things here were... suitable."

"Army?" Kriminel glanced outside, but the market dwellers were still going around their business as normal. "What army?"

"The one that should be outside your camp at any moment."

I should use my blade and make his smile permanent.

"Do not toy with me, boy." While Kriminel's words still hung in the air, the distant ruffling and murmurs from outside became more pronounced.

The doors burst open and another guard, his face pallid, rushed in, gasping for breath. "Mesye," he began, kneeling and pressing his fist to his chest in respect. "Sorry for the—"

"Kounye! Get on with it!" Kriminel said.

"Sir, Baron Brigid is outside our camp. She has come with a large army in the thousands!"

Kriminel's heart skipped a beat, the sheer number echoing in his mind. Sheathing his sword, he strode toward the guard. He grabbed his shoulder and whispered in his ear. "Find out how she got here with no one noticing."

The guard sweated as he stammered, "Mesye... they came in through the Dead Forest."

The Eden Ruse

THE OPPRESSIVE HUMIDITY clung to the surroundings as Kriminel emerged from the Sant Komand. Even though it was mid-afternoon, the dense, overcast skies painted a scene closer to dusk. Each step radiated his unbridled fury. An uneasy knot tightened in the pit of his stomach. *She couldn't have come here to attack, could she?* That was ridiculous. *But then, why is she here?* The Dead Forest was on the camp's east side. When he neared it, he found most of his army had assembled in battle formation.

At the forest's edge, Brigid sat atop a white horse, its head adorned with a sharply tipped spear. The intricate plate shielding her neck seamlessly blended into her ensemble. The patterns accentuated her dark-rimmed eyes against her rich brown skin, all framed by coiled hair cascading from beneath her crown.

With a determined grip on his reins, Kriminel rode past his soldiers, halting at the tense midpoint between the two armies. The smug smile on her face grew as she approached him, only rivaled by Kokou's. She dismounted her horse and approached on foot when she was a few feet away. He did the same. As they neared, the clouds above roiled and thickened, casting a shadow over them. The distant murmur of soldiers and the soft rustle of the forest were the only sounds in the heavy silence that separated the two barons.

With a tilt of her head, Brigid remarked, "For barons reuniting after so long, this is not the warm reception I imagined."

"State your intentions," Kriminel demanded.

Brigid arched an eyebrow, forming a playful smirk. "Feeling threatened?" she teased, her laughter light and taunting. "Spending so long in Niri is making you fidgety."

"I have no time for games."

"Life has a peculiar way of steering us onto unexpected paths, often revealing things we haven't dared dream of." She retrieved a parchment sealed with wax from beneath her armor and extended it to him.

The air thickened as Brigid's hand lingered in the void between them.

"Enough games!" His fingers grazed the cold hilt of his sword.

"Are you afraid to see what Ghede Ghadou has written for you?"

Ghede Ghadou! Nervousness traveled through him as he grabbed the note with newfound hurriedness. He scanned the parchment, each word sinking deeper: *"Baron Brigid is to assist all affairs of Nnabu Valley until further directive."* The signature beneath was unmistakable —*Ghede Ghadou Loa.*

Kriminel crumpled the letter and tossed it to the ground. "For two years, Ghede Loa remained silent, ignoring our pleas for reinforcements. And now, you appear in his stead?" he seethed through his teeth. "We are no longer in need of help."

"That's not what Kokou tells me."

"The spy we caught? He will face judgment."

"Kokou has been going in and out of this camp undetected for months," she said. "He should train your men how to do their jobs."

"Fout tonne! You seek to make me look like a fool."

"If we were Niri rebels coming in the night, you would be a dead fool."

Kriminel's anger simmered just below the surface, his clenched fists aching from restrained force.

"The enemy is not here. Yet," she said, "Ghede Loa knows about your new weapon. He is interested in learning more about it after we quell this rebellion and return his name to grace among his peers. Accept my help. You need it." A half-serious smile traveled across her face. "But also, your Loa has ordered it."

"I will accept your offer. But I need you to understand that I am in command."

A bashful smile spread across her face. "Of course you are." She took a step toward him and extended her hand.

Pulling her close enough to feel her breath against his skin, he whispered, "Don't make me regret this."

"Regret is a word not usually found in situations you do not control," she whispered.

A unified clang echoed as soldiers from both sides raised their swords, their voices melding into a powerful chant that rumbled across the field.

∽

Simon's voice resonated, unwavering, throughout the room. "With Baron Brigid's soldiers added to ours,"—he let the weight of the statement settle—"our position is more fortified than ever." His voice dripped with anticipation. "The defeat of the Niri army is already written."

Inside the Sant Komand, burning incense wafting in the air, Kriminel's closest court huddled, faces aglow with the fervor of an imminent victory. Their hearts yearned for a triumphant return to their homeland, where tales of their conquests would echo through the ages. With it being a market rest day, the usually bustling view outside was silent, revealing abandoned tables and wind-tossed baskets. A map of Nnabu Valley covered the table they huddled over.

"Except that we are not waiting for them to come." Brigid's voice caused all heads to turn. Kokou accompanied her, stepping in with an aura of silent authority.

"What are you doing here?" Kriminel's voice pitched higher than usual.

Clad in the same armor she arrived to camp with, it shone brilliantly, every scuff and stain meticulously removed. Her coiled hair cascaded down, catching hints of sunlight. "We will not wait for Amadioha to come here. We are going to him."

"Three days you've been here, a shadow unseen and unheard," Kriminel's voice mixed exasperation with challenge. "And now you think you can waltz in dictating terms?"

With a piercing gaze, she responded, "While you were in here, complacent, I have been out there, doing what leaders do—assessing our position, understanding our enemy."

With a silent nod from Brigid, Kokou, hesitating just a moment, spread out a different, more expansive map over the one Kriminel's court had been engrossed in. The parchment's edges crinkled, the inked territories revealing much more than the valley.

Kriminel scoffed.

Kokou shifted a bit but pointed to a location in Canis. "Amadioha's army split from the rest of the camp three weeks ago," he said. "They traveled through the long road back to Canis."

Kriminel frowned, genuine confusion clouding his features. "Why would they do that?"

Kokou waved a dismissive hand, eyes on the map. "Forget the 'why.' It's the 'where' that should concern us."

"We have spent weeks devising our strategy! After fortifying our position, you expect us to leave because of some foolish conjecture?"

Kokou's ever-taunting smile grew as he jabbed a finger at the map. "The rest of the Niri army is still three weeks south in Kwale. If we can intercept Amadioha's men and overwhelm them with numbers, losing the face of their rebellion would be sure to end the war."

"Attack Amadioha head-on? Are you mad?" Simon asked. "We have the perfect position here. Why would we give that up?"

"An entire army slipped past you, yet you think this position is unassailable?" Brigid said.

"Yes, you have pointed that out many times," Kriminel said. "Now we have scouts in the forest, and we have another army, thanks to you."

"My scouts tell me an attack from the mountain is risky but viable. Your weapons are pointing toward the narrow path and the forest."

"She has never heard of people turning weapons around," Simon said. Most of the soldiers surrounding the table let out laughs.

"They will take refuge in the city and fortify themselves with the residents. When your weapons face them, what use will they be? Will you then be protecting the forest or the city?"

Kriminel stopped laughing as he pondered her words. He spat on the floor and slammed his hands on the table. "I—"

Brigid's voice hardened. "My scouts have come and gone as they pleased for months. You have grown complacent. Let your pride guide you, or make the right choice."

"She comes into our territory and disrespects us in front of her pet! We cannot let this stand," one man around the table said.

Kriminel's eyes darted between Simon and Brigid, his jaw clenching. A low growl escaped his throat. A swordless battle was being fought in the room, and he felt like a spectator. "We have heard your concerns and will consider them in due time."

Brigid turned and commanded, "Bring him forth!" The room fell silent, all eyes on the door.

Guards hauled a bare chested man with a powerful build in. His piercing dark-brown eyes took in the room, defiance clear. The sides of his head were shaven, making his appearance fiercer. Vibrant red cloth wrapped his wrists, highlighting sinewy muscles.

"Koca ci!" the man shouted as he cursed, speaking the local tongue.

"Our scouts caught him a few miles from Amadioha's location," Kokou said.

"What is Amadioha doing in Canis?" Kriminel asked.

The prisoner smirked. "Waiting for nightfall to fuck your wife!" The boot connecting with his abdomen echoed, and he doubled over, crimson staining the floor as he spat.

A guard advanced, his hand lingering over his sword's hilt. "Speak to him with respect," he demanded.

Defiance sparkled in the prisoner's eyes as a mischievous grin spread across his face. "Maybe he'll want to join in on the excitement once Amadioha is done fucking his wife."

The guard's boot connected with the prisoner again, and rhythmic thuds filled the air as the baton relentlessly struck the prisoner's back.

"Your life hangs by a thread. Answer me. What is Amadioha doing in Canis? How many men does he have?" Kriminel asked.

Brigid's eyes, ever watchful, flickered to Kriminel. Her smile was muted, yet it spoke volumes of the silent calculations in her mind.

"Well, there is Amadioha, your mother, and your wife. So three," the man said.

The guard pulled out his sword and placed it on the man's neck. He hesitated mid-swing, his gaze locked on Kriminel.

"I prefer my floors unsullied," Kriminel said. Switching to fluent Vodunese, he ordered, "Remove him."

"Yes, Mesye!" the guard said.

"You will all die soon," the man laughed.

The words, coupled with the doubt Brigid sowed, filled him with discomfort. With a withering glance at her, he declared, "Your little show gave us nothing." He leaned in. "Outside. Now."

∼

"Even our fortified positions have vulnerabilities. You must see the weight of this opportunity," Brigid pressed on outside the room. "One missed spot. One minor mistake and things could turn. Attacking our enemies directly is the Vodun way."

"Your strategies and plans mean nothing when you belittle me in my court!" Kriminel hissed. "The Vodun way has led to nothing but massive losses for our Loa."

"You surround yourself with incompetents with no battle sense and tinkerers obsessed with their toys." Brigid remarked, "Kokou's strategy is reasonable. If we can kill Amadioha before the Niri army gets there, we kill their spirits. And if we don't kill their spirit, they will have something else waiting."

Kriminel scoffed. "Perhaps I should send you and your scouts back to Vodun. Why were you not here from the start if you are superior?"

"It is time we stop playing defense and show Niri the power and might of Vodun."

Kriminel grabbed her shoulders and pushed her to the wall. "Fout tonne!" She put her arms around his waist and smiled. He recoiled at the touch. "It would take too long to move the weapons there. They are too heavy."

"Not if we go through the forest," Brigid countered.

Her eyes sparkled with mischief, a trace of triumph. She had played her cards expertly, each move calculated to corner him. She had presented the facts, discredited his current plan, and then finished by saying it was his choice to accept or reject. In reality, he had no option but to go with it. His Loa had sent her, and hearing his first task was to push her away would not go well.

He turned around and brought his mouth next to her ear. "We do it your way—this time. As soon as this battle ends, you will immediately march your men back to Vodun. All ten thousand of them can deliver the news to our Loa."

Pulling back, he met her eyes, aflame with defiance and desire. "As you wish, Mesye," she teased, her tone dripping with irony.

∼

"I do not take visitors the night before an advancement," Kriminel said.

Brigid smirked. "I would know this."

A soft lunar glow bathed the room, casting silver sheens through the window. Five tall torch sconces lined the walls, their flames dormant, leaving the room in eerie quietude. Draped in white pants, Kriminel stood shirtless, the moonlight highlighting the chiseled lines of his lean physique. A scar crossed his chest diagonally where a sword had sliced him in one of the many battles he had fought.

"What are you really doing here?" he asked.

She stood near the room entrance, her hair packed up on top of her head. She wore a fitted garment, leaving no part of her shape to the imagination. A circular choker around her neck attached to the body of the dress. The center was purple, but the top and bottom were black leather.

"Our Loa commanded me."

"You misunderstand my words," Kriminel said. "What are you doing in my room right now?"

Her eyes widened. "There was a time when you would welcome my company in these moments." She moved toward him.

"You are a snake in the bushes where I piss," Kriminel said. "Ghede Loa would not send you on his own. Unless you asked him to."

"Are you saying our Loa does not have a mind of his own?"

"I say no such thing!"

She placed her hand on his bare skin, the warmth of her palm seeping into him. There was a calmness from the familiarity, one he tried hard to reject. Before he could protest, she had shifted to the bed behind him, her fingers kneading the tension from his shoulders. The world blurred as her lips, soft yet insistent, found his, pulling him into a moment he'd long resisted. He lifted her dress and pulled down her underwear.

"Yes," her voice trailed off.

She was lying face down. He was inside her. Flashes of past pleasures filled his mind. He lost himself in time for a few moments before coming back to the room.

"Control is what you want," she said in between moans. "This is what I want."

The words infected his pleasure and killed it. He went limp. He pushed away from her and stood, looking down at his flaccid manhood.

She turned around coyly. Her eyes dimmed. "I can help you with that."

"Get out of my room," Kriminel's eyes darkened. "I want no more of this."

She let out a coy laugh and motioned for him to come to her.

"Get out!" Kriminel barked. "Before I have my guards take you out."

Brigid rose, adjusting her attire with an unruffled poise. Her face remained inscrutable, though a flash of irritation sparked in her eyes. "Our Loa has big plans for Niri. When the seats of power reshuffle, I wonder where your position will be."

Kriminel looked at her in confusion, wanting badly to ask her what in the world she was talking about. But his pride kept his mouth shut. *Fout Tonne!*

With one last lingering look, she produced a sealed paper from within her dress and laid it on the bed, ensuring he saw every move before sweeping out of the room.

Kriminel eyed the paper as if it were a coiled snake. With a deep breath, he picked it up. As the first roll she had given him, it also had their Loa's seal. He broke it and unrolled the paper.

Baron Brigid is to assume complete control of the operations in Nnabu Valley. Baron Kriminel will be placed directly under her command to facilitate orderly operations. It was as emotionless and matter-of-fact as the first order.

... Complete control...

For over a year, his Loa had not responded to his calls for help.

... directly under her command...

And now this? Ghede Ghadou Loa would pay for it. Brigid would pay for it. Once they had taken care of Amadioha, they would all pay. She had known that from the beginning and had hidden it from him. Desolation washed over Kriminel, and he sank to his knees, his fingers clawing at his hair, the gravity of betrayal bearing down on him. *I have done everything right. I have done everything asked of me and more.*

He pounded his fists on the bed and buried his eyes in the softness.

∽

KRIMINEL SWATTED YET another relentless fly from his face, cursing silently. While they called it the "Dead Forest," it was pulsating with life, every crevice teeming with unseen creatures. As the soldiers marched, rodents and other animals scurried away on the forest floor. They had taken off at dawn, but the overgrown branches overhead made it feel like night. There was a thick smell of soil, the kind that permeated your nose after heavy rain.

"You know," Brigid said, "it was not my idea to come here."

They rode side by side, close to the front of the advancing soldiers. *Everyone knows I have been demoted. Their eyes are filled with disdain.* He sighed in defeat. "What does it matter?"

"Don't get me wrong," she said. "Taking the upper hand and seeing you falter was quite the thrill. It reminds me of those old days when the tables were turned."

No, you are wrong! I was better than you then. And I am better than you now.

"I would never have wanted to leave my assignment to come to this *monte kaka*." She let go of her reins and patted her horse's side. "Ghede Loa is not happy with you. Demotion will be the least of your worries if things don't go well."

Would another Loa regard my loyalty more?

"How many barons have we lost in Niri?" He avoided her gaze, choosing instead to fixate on the distant horizon.

"Too many," she said, her voice hinting at sorrow.

"After all this time, why send you now?"

The rustling leaves, and distant bird calls filled the silence as she began. "Even with our imminent defeat of Amadioha, our ranks have dwindled perilously." The subtle bitterness in her tone was evident. "Rumors once whispered about Radha Loa, target our Loa—portraying him as feeble, ineffectual." She paused, taking a shaky breath. "Look at me!"

He kept his face looking forward.

Her voice grew colder, carrying an edge. "I can request again, or I can command it."

"You just don't know when to stop, do you?" He said, turning his head.

"We will change the narrative. You have been stubborn, but our Loa does not have to know. I am sure he will reinstate you after our success."

"I planned to stay in Nnabu Valley and fortify our position. This is your battle."

Brigid shook her head. "Wait and see? The same military strategy that has lost us control of almost all of Niri."

"My finest soldiers toiled for weeks, forging weapons, building machinery, preparing for this very battle with patience and determination!" He took a sharp breath, his fingers touching the hilt of his sword. "And yet, our calls for help fell on deaf ears when we were most desperate. Those weapons are now stuck near the forest entrance because they are too heavy. Maybe we would not have lost so many barons if he had sent help a year ago when we needed it."

"While you lamented here, invoking your Loa's mercy, we faced relentless raids from Ikora, Aksum, and Kush. Do you believe we have been idle, merely lounging on our thrones?" Her voice faltered, words hanging in the air, replaced by an eerie silence. Almost simultaneously, they turned to the faint rustling of leaves, a whisper of movement in the thick foliage around them. Kriminel's horse neighed. An uncomfortable feeling traveled through him. They were just under an hour into the forest. His heart pounded in his chest as he scanned the trees. He calmed his horse and placed his other hand on his hilt. More neighing from the other horses followed. They were not alone.

"You fool!" he shouted at Brigid. "You led us into a trap."

His keen eyes caught a fleeting shadow blending into the verdant backdrop. The faint glint of a dark arrow's tip betrayed the enemies position.

"Attack formations!" Kriminel shouted, usurping Brigid's authority. He hopped onto the top of his horse and dove for Brigid, connecting with her body and tackling her off the horse as a half-dozen black-tipped arrows flew where she had been. A few more went into the horse, causing it to buck and neigh. It took off running into the forest. Kriminel's gaze locked onto the spectacle ahead; the forest breathed, trees metamorphosing into warriors whose cloaks had melded seamlessly with the woodland. As they moved, only their weapons and their eyes gave them away.

"Attack!" Kriminel screamed over the ensuing panic.

He and Brigid pulled out their swords. A barrage of Niri soldiers charged at them with leaves meticulously adhered to their body, creating a quilt of greens and browns that disguised their presence. Their forms, chiseled and unyielding, radiated strength. Their hair flowed behind them, mostly locked. Some were clean-shaven. The men carried swords, axes, and spears, but the most formidable weapon they brandished was the burning fury in their eyes. The Niri moved with breathtaking agility through the dense forest.

As his men launched their attack, the Niri responded with fluid twists, sharp turns, and nimble dodges. They moved as if they knew what was happening before it happened. Every rustling leaf, each moss-covered rock, and the bark of the ancient trees seemed to whisper secrets to the Niri, aiding them in their dance. One of Brigid's soldiers sliced his sword down on an advancing Niri. The Niri warrior twisted and sidestepped it. He moved close to the soldier, planted the bottom of his wrist at his neck, and stole his sword all in one motion. Before the soldier's body kissed the forest floor, the Niri warrior had thrust the stolen sword, burying its cold steel deep within the man's skull.

"We can't hold them off much longer!" Kriminel shouted, his eyes wide with urgency. "We must retreat!"

"Vodun does not retreat!" Brigid roared in defiance.

Soldier after soldier surged forward, only to meet the brutal efficiency of the Niri, their fates sealed almost as soon as they stepped forth. The thick, metallic scent of spilled blood mingled with the acrid smell of torn flesh, overpowering the forest's natural aroma. A distant rustling, growing louder with every heartbeat, signaled a vast number of Niri reinforcements closing in. Kriminel and Brigid's numbers had meant nothing in the dense, muddy forest.

The Niri soldiers were fast, strong, and agile. But Kriminel noticed that the Vodunese who came with Brigid didn't move or fight like regular soldiers. They seemed a second slower, their movements less polished, as if they were untrained.

One Niri soldier, about the same height as Kriminel, got past the scuffle in front of them. Kriminel refocused on the man whose eyes, ablaze with a fiery rage, reflected a madness driven by sheer hatred. He advanced toward Brigid and swiped at her with his axe. She blocked it with her sword. He followed with another quick swipe. She dodged that, too, but slower. In a heartbeat, with a display of raw power, he had Brigid pinned beneath him, the forest floor unforgiving against her back.

Kriminel rushed over and swiped his sword at the man's head. It took it clean off just as the man was about to bury his axe in Brigid. His limp body fell on top of her, blood from his neck painting her face red. Brigid, gasping for breath as her face smeared with dirt and blood, shoved the dead weight off her and staggered to her feet.

"There are too many of them! We need higher ground, now!" Kriminel pleaded. Brigid's stubbornness, usually a mere annoyance, threatened their very survival.

"Vodun does not retreat!" she yelled back.

Driven by desperation, Kriminel's hand formed a fist and struck her across the face. She staggered, then collapsed, unconscious. Without hesitation, he lifted her limp form over his shoulder, his muscles protesting under her weight. He sprinted away from the advancing soldiers, shouting as he went, "Retreat! Back to the base! Now!" For a moment, time froze. Then the retreat horn filled the air, a signaler near him hearing his command. Like a wave rolling back, his men heeded the call and started retreating toward the camp's safety.

He reached a horse, carefully positioning Brigid on its back, and spurred the animal into a gallop toward the forest's boundary. Urging his horse faster, Kriminel narrowed the gap while arrows and spears flew past them, harbingers of death. The haunting chorus of screams and cries in the background told a grim story; many would not live to see another day. *Vodun does not retreat.* Ghede Loa had said those words too.

I am not ready to die. Not today.

With blood and grime streaking through his hair, they reached the forest edge. Simon's weapons would await the advancing Niri army. They would feel his wrath.

Brigid stirred, her face a grimace of pain. Kriminel had desperately hoped she would remain unconscious until they were safe. She shook when she realized what had happened. The forest's edge was near, so they stopped their horses and dismounted.

She put her hand on her head and rubbed it. "You will pay for this when we get back."

"Great words to the man who saved your life twice." Kriminel cast a glance over his shoulder. He caught glimpses of his men, some retreating, others not so fortunate.

"If you had just listened!" Kriminel spat, breathless from their mad dash.

"Fout tonne! Keep talking to me like that, and your punishment when we return will increase," she retorted.

For a fleeting moment, Kriminel's mind danced with the forbidden thought: would it have been better had he not pulled her onto the horse? There were very few witnesses to Ghede Loa's order. He would have two armies if he came home with a victory against Amadioha and no Brigid. Ghede Loa would have no reason to demote him. But he could not ignore Ghede Loa's role in a dangerous game. His hand, too, had shaped their fate.

The weapons, the huge wooden contraptions Simon had intricately engineered, loomed at the forest's edge. His retreating soldiers had halted a few hundred feet ahead casting wary glances around.

At that moment, Kriminel realized he had not heard the Niri army in pursuit. In fact, apart from when they fled the first time, he had not heard them coming after them. Then he noticed something more disturbing. The man on top of the machine nearest to him was not a Vodunese soldier. He wore red pants with a bare chest. A golden crown with red gems embedded around it rested atop his head, casting elongated shadows over his face. His blue eyes and bushy hair gave him away. They locked eyes for an eternity. His eyes crackled with an electric intensity, resembling bolts of lightning trapped within their icy depths. With a voice that carried the weight of doom, he commanded, "Fire!" in the guttural tones of their native language.

Amadioha!

The metal projectiles fired as Kriminel scrambled to take cover behind the nearest trees.

The world around him erupted in chaos, and a vivid memory surfaced: himself as a child.

He held his father's sword up and claimed to be a fearless warrior. His mother laughed and told him he was a cute boy.

Amid the harrowing sight of his army being decimated by his ruthless machinery, the soothing memories of childhood served as a fleeting refuge. But only for a few seconds. The last thing he heard was someone shouting, "Protect your baron!" Without hesitation, loyal soldiers darted in front of him and Brigid, their bodies intercepting the deadly projectiles intended for him. Even in such dire moments, their unwavering respect for his title pierced his heart, regardless of the disgrace the Loa had imposed upon him.

PART IV
AN INVESTIGATION

14

PRISM
REALM OF HELL

*T*he shadowy division of Internal Intelligence was in overdrive, decoding encrypted transmissions and documents seized during the high-stakes operation against Lamech. The information garnered had brought many a rogue operative to their knees, dismantling the insidious Sons of Lamech network. Yet, an accolade or nod from General Gadreel was as elusive as a mirage in the desert. Perhaps his silent concession was letting her walk free. On the other hand, the investigation into the dual assassination of the president and Lucifer had hit so many brick walls their elite operatives looked like rookies. The corridors of power in Masina and its neighboring states whispered about their incompetence.

Lilith's office held little by way of personal comfort. Vines resembling those in a rainforest adorned the walls, casting illusions in the light. Hues of amber drenched the room, painting her skin with shades resembling a sunset masterpiece. She reached for the high-tech console on her desk. A trio of micro-needles shot out, drawing a speck of blood. A holographic emblem of *PRISM* underscored by an inverted pyramid emerged.

"Update," she ordered.

PRISM operated in the deepest shadows of covert operations—so secret no line in any official ledger recorded its existence. It was an omnipotent surveillance tool, collecting data on everyone of note, including the late president. Its existence was a ticking time bomb, the revelation of which could bring down the entire Masinian establishment. But for Lilith, it had been worth every stolen penny. The tool, crafted by a handpicked team, had been her silent partner. It was perhaps the only thing beyond the grasp of General Gadreel's hawkish surveillance. Her loyalty to Masina was unwavering. She would not let her homeland be compromised, not by red tape or politics. She was prepared to make the hard choices for the nation she loved.

"Naval Vessel three four one. Mutiny. High priority," said PRISM in a computerized female voice.

Lilith waved her hand to her left through the hologram. It switched to a question mark. She had read through her notes from the raid and recalled the lingering memories of Lamech. "Port four five nine," she said.

"Possible trade fraud. Port four five nine. High priority."

"More info." Her eyes opened wide as she sat up.

"Not found," the voice said.

That can't be right. "Port four five nine," she said.

"Not found."

"PRISM," she said. "Pull up information on port four five nine."

"Not found. Port four five nine does not resolve."

She swiped down, and the hologram disappeared. She picked up her phone and called Eligos's direct line.

"Eligos here," he said, punctuating his words with a sleep-heavy yawn.

"Port four five nine. What is it?" Lilith said.

"Lilith? Is that you? What time is it?"

"Port four five nine. I need more information on this."

"Should be a simple system check?"

"Too many prying eyes."

"Got it." He mumbled something, then went quiet for a few seconds. "Used for civilian shipments. Came online about a month ago."

The wheels in Lilith's head spun. *Why did PRISM not have this information?* "Can you get me a manifest of everything that has gone through there?"

"If I do that, it gets registered. If avoiding prying eyes is your objective—"

"Backdoor it," she interrupted. Her analysts had rerun their simulations and confirmed the seven-year timeline for Hell being uninhabitable was accurate. They had re-assessed that as a best-case scenario. What was the chance that everything happening wasn't connected? She had a gut feeling that the time she had to figure out the puzzle was less than it appeared. A lot less.

"It will still show up on an audit."

He was right. But the audits happened every few months. Lilith weighed her options for a moment. "Forge the access credentials for me." She needed to figure out what was happening before her superiors ended her career.

Silence filled the line, and the faint sound of shuffling papers was the only evidence Eligos was still there. Lilith scratched her thumb as she waited.

"There has only been one shipment. Not itemized, but looks like a big one. Went out about two weeks ago. Destination was Sasobek."

"Wouldn't something like that need clearance from Homeland?" she asked.

"Usually, yes. But I don't see records of that here. The docket shows up as incomplete."

"What names are on the sending docker?"

"The first one is Daeva Isrut. Elijah Ferro is the second."

Daeva. That name had popped up again.

Lilith ran Elijah Ferro through PRISM. He was ex-Masina military. Kakuten. He moved to Sasobek many years ago. Multiple sources listed him as deceased. The only problem was that the day of his death showed up as over a year ago.

Dead people rarely receive or send shipments.

She made a mental note of his last address and entered Daeva Isrut. The hologram also listed her as deceased. Lilith peered into the eyes of the face in front of her. She hovered her arm as more information surfaced. Daeva was buried in a class three facility in Prejudice Triangle in Sasobek. Class three facility meant that it was top security.

Daeva Isrut, who are you?

~

"Urgent flare warning! Stay inside for all non-essential travel," the high-pitched voice blasted over the room's sound system. Her watch buzzed and displayed the same message. At 156 degrees, they expected the Flares to have one of many anticipated peaks tonight.

The scorching heat from outside baked her skin, helping calm her by distracting her from all the thoughts in her head. The window hummed and closed. A thick metal sheet dropped, effectively tombing her into her home. The temperature fell almost immediately. She let out a deep breath and gasped for air. Her body welcomed the coolness as her breathing returned to normal. She picked up her phone and placed a call to Bez. A hologram of him in a white cloak appeared over her desk. The seal of Sasobek pinned the cloth to his shoulders. From the background, he looked like he was in the Sasobek Embassy in Masina City. Her problems dissolved as his image materialized, if only for a few fleeting seconds.

He smiled. "I have been thinking about you,"

She smiled back. "I have been following a lead. A dead girl. Maybe. Sasobekan. I need to know where she is buried."

A faint look of surprise crossed his face. "Sasobekan? Do you have a name?"

She hesitated and contemplated how much information she wanted to share. After all, he was a politician, not an intelligence officer. The relationship between Sasobek and Masina had been strained since the assassinations. "Daeva Isrut."

"Who is she? What is the connection?"

His curiosity was reasonable, but irritating. "The less I tell you, the better."

"I am worried about you. You have been more stressed these days."

Lilith scoffed. *If he only knew.* "War is brewing. The ones not stressed need your worry, not me."

He recoiled, like her words had struck him.

"I am just trying to make sense of all of this," she said.

"Sometimes, your snappiness gets to me," he admitted. "But I know where your heart lies."

She smiled. When it was all over, she had plans for both of them.

"Wait one second." He pulled out a device and searched for the information she asked for.

"Daeva Isrut..." he said, "looks to have died almost two months ago."

Two months! But PRISM said a year, and Eligos had her sending shipments recently. "Where is she buried?"

"It's a class three morgue in Prejudice Triangle."

"Which one?"

"Don't tell me you are thinking of doing what I think you are?" A concerned look crossed his face.

Bez, why do you always do this? "Which one?" she asked again.

"Faragua."

"I need as much information as you can get on it,"

"Let me handle it. Tell me what exactly you are trying to do, and I will have my people look into it."

Lilith shook her head.

"Be smart here. Prejudice Triangle borders No Man's Land."

"Bez, I love you dearly, but my least favorite part of this is when you want to tell me what to do."

He raised his hands in surrender. "I could never convince you to do anything you didn't want to,"

"So, why do you keep trying?"

He sighed. "When are you planning to go there? How are you going to do it?"

"I need a couple of weeks to figure it out."

She waited for his response, a few seconds ticking by in silence. "After all this is done, let's go somewhere," she said. "Away from Masina and Sasobek. Remote. Just the two of us."

A warm smile spread across his face. "Just the two of us."

15

ELIAKIM'S FUNERAL

The scene was somber, set under a canopy of wispy gray clouds that threatened rain but never delivered. Muted hues of green and brown, where trees stood tall, their thick branches knitting a webbed canopy overhead, painted the cemetery. Their leaves whispered secrets to the wind, creating a soft symphony that seemed almost respectful of the mourning crowd gathered. Under the shadow of the oaks, mourners clad in black stood with their heads bowed in reverence. A single marble tombstone, gleaming white, had been freshly erected. The name engraved on it read "Kapten Eliakim Seres."

Lilith approached slowly, her boots digging into the soft ground. Her gait was hesitant, each step heavier than the last, weighed down not just by the burden she carried. The eulogist, an old friend of Eliakim and a mentor to many, began with a deep, resonant voice. "— In life, we often cross paths with those who leave an indelible mark on our souls. Kapten Eliakim Seres was one such man—" Whispers of agreement echoed among the crowd. Her eyes roamed over the gathering but were inexorably drawn to Eliakim's wife. Dressed in a mourning black gown contrasting her pale skin, his wife stood with their four-year-old daughter.

His wife's voice, icy and sharp, broke through the ambient murmurs. "Why are you here?"

Lilith met her piercing gaze, searching for a hint of warmth. "To honor him, to face what happened," she said.

Her laugh was bitter. "By attending his funeral?"

The eulogist continued, undeterred or perhaps used to such outbursts in his long career. "—Eliakim was a beacon of hope, a man who believed in the goodness of humanity even in the darkest of times—"

Lilith took a steadying breath. "I can't change what happened. I wish I could. He was my responsibility, and I failed him." Lilith hesitated. "I... I had to pay my respects. He was my comrade."

"You mean your subordinate. He died following your orders."

Lilith wasn't officially on the mission, but the information leaked to his wife was not surprising. Every fiber of her being urged her to walk away, but she held her ground. "Yes, he did. And I will live with that burden every day of my life."

The eulogist continued, ignoring the tension building between the two women. "—In our hearts, we know Eliakim lived and died as he wished, defending Masina, his family—"

Eliakim's wife's eyes welled up again, but her gaze didn't waver. "You might carry the burden, but you are still breathing. My husband isn't."

He died for Masina just like many other soldiers before him, so your family and others could have the lives they did, was what Lilith wanted to say. But she instead kept a solemn expression on her face and turned around, putting distance between them. A man, dressed in all black, stood alone under a tree a few hundred meters away. She wanted to believe her eyes were deceiving her, but Abbadon's face was unmistakable.

∽

"Abbadon? I thought you... I mean, the last report said you were still in critical condition..."

His gaze was icy, his blue eyes piercing her. "Maybe the reports were exaggerated? Or perhaps you never cared to check?"

The words stumbled out of her mouth. "Things have just happened so fast. I—"

"They must have."

"I—"

"Save it," he said. "Today, we mourn our dead."

"I need to say—"

"I heard what you did," Abbadon interrupted. "I know you risked your life against protocol. But do you know what hurts me? It was the mission, wasn't it? That was and has always been your prime directive. Complete the mission at all costs. What happened to me didn't matter once the mission ended."

"No!" she said, a little louder than expected. The demon giving the eulogy stopped. He and Eliakim's wife both glanced at her with a curt expression. Lilith covered her mouth. He continued talking.

"I care about you, Abbadon," she whispered.

"You cared about the mission first!"

"Masina first, above all? Yet we can still have space for one another."

"And that was why you did not check in?" his face filled with dismay. "You were busy saving Masina?"

"I—" She could tell him about everything she had been doing. But he would not understand. She sighed. "I would never put you in that position again."

"I would never let you," he smirked and turned away from her.

The mission first, Abbadon's words rang in her mind. The truth of his statement was more painful than her betrayal of him.

∼

LILITH DISCOVERED SENET IN SOLITUDE, her silhouette a lonely figure beside an unmarked grave, a few hundred meters detached from the cacophony of the ongoing funeral.

"Every grave here is unmarked," Lilith said. "But you know the name of the corpse underneath each one. Don't you?"

"Not everyone," Senet replied. "Major."

A weary smile found its way to Lilith's face. "Our mission in Sharik Hora has left my mind crowded."

"The council may not see it, but your efforts were exceptional, Major."

Lilith frowned, considering her words. "Things haven't added up lately."

"What do you mean?"

"Let me tell you a story." Lilith clasped her hands behind her back. "Five years, six months, and three days ago, Aamaris and Qataban teetered on the brink of war. The region braced for chaos as peace treaties unraveled."

She paused, hands crossing over her chest. "Yet days before declarations of war, the king of Qataban died in his sleep. Officially, a heart attack. Investigations showed no foul play."

Senet nodded. "I remember. We worked hard to remain neutral, but war seemed inevitable."

"Funny how luck intervenes sometimes," Lilith mused. "Another example of luck is being pinned down by snipers in Sharik Hora and having a scout who can listen to bullets to triangulate them."

Senet's neutral expression faltered almost imperceptibly. But Lilith caught it—the fleeting hint of unease.

"Your reputation made the story believable," Lilith continued. "But imagine if a class eight Navigator slipped into Qataban undetected, assassinated the king, and vanished. The right toxins could mimic a natural death."

She stepped closer to Senet. "That same person could Navigate into the building in Sharik Hora, maybe even a partial Navigation, and identify the sniper positions. After that, she could pretend she figured it out through sound."

Senet laughed. "Major, that's absurd. There has been no known class eight Navigator for years."

"Mere theories until now," Lilith said quietly. "But your reaction confirms my suspicions."

"Assassinations?" Senet scoffed. "Preposterous." But her eyes darted uneasily. Lilith had trapped her, and they both knew it.

"You served your country and diverted an imminent war we would get drawn into. You saved the lives of Masina soldiers. That is commendable," Lilith said. "But how have you honed your skill so well and kept it secret?"

"Major," Senet said. "You must be mistaking me with someone else."

Lilith's impatience grew. A partial frown covered her face. The funeral would soon wrap up, and she needed to be as far away as possible from here before Abbadon and Eliakim's wife were let loose. "I am a forward thinker," she said. "Not an idealist like you. I know why you did what you did. I would do anything for Masina too. But do not mistake me for someone who wastes her time. If you will not help me, I have no use for letting your secret stay secret."

Senet retreated a few steps. "Kalla! I did what was necessary, as you have done many times, even if it meant bending the rules." Her voice quivered with rising anxiety.

"There we go," Lilith said with a nod. "Progress."

"I had to keep my abilities secret. The scrutiny I would get from Masina, our allies, and even our enemies..." Senet turned away. "What do you want?"

"I need to Navigate to a Sasobek military morgue. Class three facility."

"Class three? That is impossible. No one can do that. We would end up between walls or in the ground!"

"Qataban was impossible. Sharik Hora was impossible; since when did you allow the impossible to stop you?"

"No one has ever successfully Navigated into a class three structure. Qataban was a cakewalk compared to this." Senet had a genuine nervousness on her face, which unsettled Lilith. "Can you do it? Or not?"

"Anti-Navigation I can handle," she said. "But I would have to guess the plan of the structure when we get there. I would be going blind. We could end up inside someone else."

"Can you do it? Or not?" Lilith asked again.

A long silence descended between them, punctuated only by the distant eulogies whispered by the wind. Senet's pensive face was half-cast in shadow; her brows knit together.

"What if I say I can't?"

Lilith locked eyes with hers. "Is that what you are saying?"

"Three months to plan," Senet said

"Two weeks," Lilith responded.

"That would be insane!" Senet said. "Too many things could go wrong."

"I'll be straight with you. I have many people watching me," Lilith pressed. "I have been looking in places I'm not supposed to. Once General Gadreel gets wind of this, it will be over if I don't have something to show him."

"Major, that goes beyond acceptable risk tolerances."

"I came here because I thought you were the best Navigator in Masina. Did I make a mistake?"

Senet paced as she kept shaking her head. "Seven million Mira," she said

"What?" Lilith frowned, taken aback.

"Seven million Mira."

"You think I should compensate you for serving your country?"

"From where I stand, I am serving you. Fourteen if I don't make it back alive."

"There is too much scrutiny on me. I can't get you those funds now."

"Then I am sorry I can't help you."

"Seven," Lilith said.

"Yes, seven million," Senet replied.

"Seven years."

"I don't understand."

"Two months ago, someone tried to kill me," Lilith said.

Senet's jaw dropped. "Major, I had no idea."

"Then I got a troubling report that with the rate of acceleration of the Flares, Masina will be uninhabitable in seven years. Maybe sooner, maybe later. Then, our president was assassinated shortly after. Do you think that these are all coincidences?" Lilith asked.

"Uninhabitable in seven years?" Senet repeated, her eyes opening wider.

Lilith walked Senet through the debrief she had received and gave her all the details.

Senet chewed her lip for a second.

"So when I ask you to help me chase a lead, you are serving Masina, not me." Lilith paused for a second. "Will you derelict your duty?"

"Tell me more about this mission."

PART V
COLLIDING REALMS

16

THE USURPER'S DREAM
REALM OF KIRINA

Today, our land is filled with death.
    Into the streams, it sheds tears of blood.
Yet tomorrow, it is not our bodies that embrace its soil.
It is the defeat of the cancer we bask in.
We will dance in the sunset at dusk.
We will dance through the night at our victory.
We will dance and not stop till the early morning.
—Amadioha

AMADIOHA STOOD near the heart of Nnabu Valley, his gaze sweeping across the rugged mountains that clawed ambitiously at the sky. A relentless downpour shrouded the day, each drop of rain drumming a rhythmic symphony, harmonizing with the distant thunder. Water trailed through his hair, meandering along his jawline and dripping steadily from his chin. On an average day, the valley air would be rich with the scents of rain-kissed soil and lush grass. However, the stark odors of death and blood covered and replaced them.

His strategy had been flawless. Ghede Loa's latest barons lay defeated, with the Niri army sustaining minimal losses. But unlike the previous Loa that fell, this win came with no euphoria. Across the valley, his unilateral action would displease Ojukwu and the other Ezes, yet they would inevitably revel in the outcome. *Vodun is bigger than Niri.* They had liberated Niri. However, Ijele's haunting words had planted an uneasy thought, growing like a relentless tree, its implications branching out in his mind.

Nearby, Baron Kriminel knelt in defeat. With arms bound, the baron was a picture of capture and surrender. Beside him, three soldiers and a woman, another baron named Brigid, mirrored his defeated posture.

Amadioha's command sliced through the rain's heavy curtain. "Put their heads on the blocks." There was a momentary pause and a heartbeat of hesitation from Damballa, who glanced at Amadioha before nodding in solemn acknowledgment.

"Touye prizonye san zam se kont konvansyon lagè Vodun," Kriminel said.

Amadioha approached, crouching beside him. "I know you speak the local tongue."

"We are unarmed. It is against Vodun war conventions to kill us," Kriminel said in Niri.

Amadioha smiled. He understood the baron well the first time, but enjoyed the spectacle. "We are not in Vodun."

"Take us to your commander," Kriminel demanded.

"Spare us! Have mercy," a white-haired man next to him said. "We can give you whatever information you need. Have mercy."

"Mercy is for Chineke." Amadioha stood and drew his axe from behind him. The blade glistened as raindrops collected and fell from its edge. "Your vile blood will feel the edge of my blade last." A dark thrill coursed through his veins. "So you will understand what it is like to lose everything before you die."

Kriminel ceased his struggle, turning to face Amadioha. "We are the stewards of this land. You have forgotten your place," he said. Spittle flew from his mouth, but Amadioha shifted his head quickly to the right. It missed his face and flew past him. "All of you will pay.

The entire Vodun force will rain down and burn every village to the ground." Kriminel said.

"You spit just as well as you fight," Amadioha said. "Hold his head steady," he ordered. He collected as much phlegm in his mouth as he could and released it all in Kriminel's face. Then he smeared it with his axe. The Niri men all burst into laughter. Amadioha used the blade's sharp edge to draw an X in the center of Kriminel's forehead. Kriminel winced in agony as his blood dripped.

"By my power as Eze, I sentence you to death for crimes against Niri," Amadioha's voice echoed in authority.

Kriminel's eyes bore into Amadioha's, defiance burning in them. "Our faces will haunt you for the rest of your life."

Amadioha glanced at him. "Mine will haunt you in the afterlife."

"Stay your action, Amadioha."

At the sound of the commanding voice, Amadioha whipped around. Standing tall, Ojukwu wore blue overalls. The chiseled texture of stone peeked out from the exposed part of his neck.

"This is not your concern," Amadioha said.

"As the Eri, everything is my concern."

The three men accompanying Ojukwu stood a few paces behind, their eyes cold and calculating, lips drawn tight, yet they held their ground, not advancing.

"You dare disrespect me in front of my men?" A spark of electricity danced in Amadioha's eyes, illuminating the fury within. He gripped his axe harder.

"Consider your next moves properly, Eze," Ojukwu said.

The men behind Ojukwu touched the hilts of their swords, eyes narrowing, and watched every move with hawk-like precision, yet their blades remained sheathed.

"We are not in a council meeting where you can lobby the other Ezes to follow your lead."

'Pick your battles,' urged Damballa's voice.

'He embarrasses me in front of everyone,' Amadioha thought back.

'This is not the place or the time to address this.'

Amadioha's fury intensified, sending brilliant arcs of electricity crackling from his eyes, casting eerie shadows across the ground. "The Vodunese would give us no such grace," he said to Ojukwu.

Ojukwu's voice took on a softer but firm tone. "We are not Vodunese." He took two more steps toward Amadioha and placed his hand on Amadioha's shoulder. "We have emerged victorious from a brutal war. Now is the time for unity, for celebration, not further bloodshed."

'Pick your battles,' Damballa's voice entered his head again.

The stiffness in Amadioha's shoulders lessened. With a wave of his hand and a voice that echoed with finality, Amadioha commanded, "Lock them up. Now!" Ojukwu extended a placating smile to Amadioha, who managed a terse smile in return despite the storm of anger brewing inside him.

⁓

The echoes of Niri's rebellion against Vodun still rang fresh. Yet the hall buzzed with a euphoria Amadioha had never sensed. Everywhere, men and women, once worn by war, moved with a dance in their step, their spirits buoyed to new highs. As he wove through the crowds, warriors, their eyes shining with respect, snapped into salutes. Their smiles radiated pride and admiration.

"The champion of Nnabu Valley, the man who both started and ended this war," Namudi declared.

Ekwensu, seated next to him, clicked his cup with Namudi before taking a large gulp of wine. Namudi had pitch-black skin and a blemishless face with almost no creases, which made him look at least a generation younger than he was. He had no hair on his face, not even over his eyes. He slid an extra cup from the center of the table to Amadioha, motioning for him to drink.

"To Niri," Amadioha said.

The men clinked their cups and took a gulp.

"To the curing of the long disease," Ekwensu said. His regular bushy hair was even more scattered. His deep eyes were the first, and sometimes only, thing one noticed when they met him. They clanked cups and drank again.

"To the defeat of the armies of not one but two Loas!" Namudi said.

They cheered again, emptied their cups, then slammed them down.

"I have known you for many years, nwanne." A nervous look crossed Namudi's face. "Closer more recently. You do not have the look of a man who has won."

Amadioha chuckled. A look of concern crossed Ekwensu's face as he realized Namudi was right.

"Winning a war against Ghede Loa's army does not erase what Vodun did to our people," Amadioha said.

"Nothing can erase it. We can only hope the next generation does not suffer through it again. You have done that," Namudi said.

"Our work is not done," Amadioha said.

"The same fire that burns in your ass, the one that makes you a great warrior, sometimes shows itself in less pleasurable ways," Namudi said. "Now is the time to spend time with your wife and family."

Amadioha wanted to agree. But Ijele's words and the pain from his brother's loss haunted him. "But Vodun is still there," he said

The color drained from Namudi's and Ekwensu's faces. "Are you saying what we think you are?" Namudi asked.

"We cannot rest until we have cured the disease from the source."

Ekwensu grabbed another cup from the center of the table and drank it in a few seconds. "You took on Nnabu Valley without telling us," he said. "What you did... that was not the plan."

"The window of opportunity was too short," Amadioha mused. "I saw an opportunity before me and had to act decisively."

"And you have your victory," Ekwensu conceded, glancing at Namudi. "But the support in this room may not be as strong as you think."

"Do you support me?" Amadioha asked. He looked at Ekwensu square in the eyes.

Ekwensu looked at Namudi. Namudi shrugged. "Of course I support you. But—" Ekwensu started.

"Do you support me?" Amadioha said again, but he was looking at Namudi.

"I would follow you to the hottest parts of *Ebe Oku*," Namudi said.

"Then I have all the support I need." Amadioha's posture relaxed.

"Don't be foolish," Namudi said. "Vodun is wide and expansive. There is no military prowess that will multiply our men."

"Your trick with the forest may have worked, but we would fight the battle on enemy terrain," Ekwensu said.

Amadioha drew his axe and traced a circle around the table with its sharp edge before planting it in the center. "We kill the beast by striking at its heart."

"Our alliance is weak," Namudi said. "Even if we support you, we push Ojukwu further away. It is a miracle we have kept this coalition for so long. Let us not snatch defeat from the jaws of victory now."

These men do not possess my conviction yet.

"There is wisdom to your words, nwanne," Amadioha said. "I will take your counsel to heart." He removed his axe from the center of the table, then grabbed another cup of wine. "But our children can never be free if Vodun exists in its current form. If our alliance is weak then we must strengthen it. Not disband it. Otherwise, nothing will remain to push them back when the Vodun army returns. As you said, this one was a miracle." He took a sip of wine and wove through the crowd.

○

AMADIOHA MOVED through the Omoge farmlands, each barn casting a looming shadow in the dim light. Raindrops pounded on the tin roofs, a rhythmic backdrop to the otherwise quiet night. But amid the rainfall, the faint echo of footsteps reached his ears from distant corners. Every rustle of leaves or distant murmur made his heart race and his palms sweaty. Although certain he wasn't being followed, his past kept his senses on edge. His fingers brushed the rough wood of a barn door, finally landing on the two subtle scratches on its bottom right. On the left, a solitary elongated mark marred the surface. The door creaked as he pushed it open. When it clicked shut behind him, darkness enveloped him. The pungent mix of horse droppings and the nauseating stench of decay clawed at his nostrils.

A velvety voice pierced the stillness. "We can talk in the dark."

He jerked around, fingers wrapping around the handle of the axe. Though the darkness was near complete, his eyes discerned a familiar silhouette. Zara. Though the long waistcoat obscured most of her form, Zara's allure was undeniable. Silken curls were bundled into a bun, with a lone braid accentuating its edge. Two more braids cascaded from her left, framing her face, while the rest of her tresses flowed freely.

"It feels like ages." Her voice had a softness laden with memories.

Amadioha blinked, realizing he had lost himself in a reverie, caught in her gaze. "Just yesterday, I saw you at the victory parade," he murmured, struggling to find a footing in the present.

She came out of the shadows, every step deliberate, "That is not what I meant."

Every fiber of Amadioha's being urged him forward to close the distance and touch her, but he held back. "I will make a case to the other Ezes that we take our army to Vodun and bring down the capital."

Her eyes sparkled with mischief, lips curling into a teasing smile before she laughed. "Have you discovered humor since we last met?"

A shadow passed over Amadioha's features, his jaw tight. "I am not joking."

Her playful demeanor faded, replaced by genuine concern. "Even in your wildest dreams, Ojukwu would vehemently oppose it."

"That's precisely why I need your influence with the Anwasi council."

"My influence on the council has waned since Chief Umoren's death. Regardless, Ojukwu does not listen to the council. They could never make him do what he doesn't want to."

"They can't make him say yes. But they can make it difficult to say no. The council can also have sway over the other Ezes."

"Attacking the capital of Vodun is suicide."

His eyes darkened, irritation clear in his stance. "Focus on your strengths, and trust me with the military strategy. We each have our roles."

Her posture stiffened. "You are asking me to risk my reputation. If Ojukwu gets wind of this, then what?"

"Use your finesse, your art of persuasion. I trust you to keep things discreet."

"And what reasons should I present to them?"

Amadioha smirked. "Given you know the deepest secrets of the land, I'm sure you can come up with something persuasive."

She took measured steps closer, her eyes searching his. "This means everything to you, doesn't it?" Her fingers grazed his cheek.

His gaze dropped to the ground. "It does."

"Then, I'll do it."

Relief surged through Amadioha. "You have my deepest gratitude. I won't forget this."

"There's something I want in return." Zara's voice held an edge.

Amadioha looked back at her. She unbuttoned her coat, revealing more than he expected. He felt an urge to flee, yet found himself rooted in place. "I can't."

"This is what I need."

"We can't do this!" Amadioha protested.

"The almighty Amadioha fears what Ojukwu would do?" she asked in a cocky voice.

"Koca ci!" He wanted her. Badly. But he had promised himself he would be a better man.

If I have her, no one will know. No. I will know.

"You forget I am married, just like you. What would Ijele do if she found out?"

"Ijele will understand you did what you had to do to accomplish her mission." Zara took a couple of steps back and sat on a nearby bench. She spread her knees and lay back.

"How dare you mention…" His voice caught, recalibrating. "How did you know about Ijele's involvement?"

Her smirk was knowing. "It's clear when an idea bears her signature. This isn't you."

Amadioha frowned. "We cannot do this. I will contact you as planned."

"Do you think you can forget us?"

"There never was an 'us.' There's only me and Ijele. And you? You have Ojukwu."

Her eyes glistened, a lone tear falling. "Very well," she murmured, rising from her perch and reaching for her coat.

"Don't do this," he said.

"The choice is yours, almighty Amadioha," she mocked. Despite her manipulations, her face had undeniable vulnerability, an innocence that belied her actions.

∽

Ojukwu's voice rose, resonating with an intensity that electrified the air. "Ego Kwenu!" he bellowed. When viewed from certain angles, the distinctive arch of his back resembled the silhouette of a hedgehog. His powerful voice echoed across the mountain's expanse, perhaps reaching neighboring towns. He raised his sword with each proclamation, slicing the air for emphasis.

In perfect unison, the ground-shaking chant of tens of thousands of soldiers responded, "Ke Kwenu! Ke Kwenu!"

Amadioha's gaze descended to the sea of warriors. The vast, unified force was the embodiment of true power. Doubters had once questioned their ability to amass such a force, yet they were fifty thousand strong, with twice that number stationed throughout Niri.

"Against all odds today, we have taken back our capital from the grasps of our oppressors," Ojukwu said. "Ego Kwenu!"

"Ke Kwenu! Ke Kwenu." The voices were louder this time. The mountain shook as the entire army roared to Ojukwu's words.

Damballa Weddo's voice intruded into Amadioha's thoughts. *'You are less happy than expected.'*

'Leave my thoughts,' Amadioha retorted, casting a wary glance at the rear of the podium.

"We have purged the blight of the Vodunese in our confederacy!" Ojukwu declared. "Ego Kwenu!" With a fierce determination, he clashed his right fist into his left. As they collided, his upper body petrified into stone. The solid thud of rock meeting rock resonated, magnifying his voice's echo against the mountain. "We did not ask for pity. We made no apologies for our revolution; rather, we proclaimed with pride the certainty of our struggle, the indestructibility of our people, and the assured finality of our success."

'While we revel in today's victory, Nana beckons us,' Amadioha thought to Damballa. Tuning out Ojukwu's thundering voice was hard.

'So, you still harbor ambitions for the capital?' Damballa probed.

'Vodun still lives. And within her, hundreds of thousands of enemy soldiers,' Amadioha thought.

'The goal was to liberate Niri. We have liberated Niri.'

'How can Niri be liberated when the Vodun state still stands?'

Ojukwu's sudden and piercing voice jolted Amadioha from his mental discourse with Damballa. "You will address our soldiers?" Ojukwu asked.

Amadioha spun his head as the entire mountain went silent. "Of course," Amadioha replied. He advanced to the podium's forefront with measured steps, standing shoulder-to-shoulder with Ojukwu.

By age-old custom, every War Eze had the honor of addressing their troops after a victory, a symbol of unity and shared triumph. Amadioha knew Ojukwu would call him first so they would forget whatever he said by the end.

Damballa Weddo's voice rang in his mind. *'Don't do it!'*

Summoning every ounce of strength, Amadioha bellowed, "Niri people! Ego Kwenu!" Though his voice lacked the booming depth of Ojukwu's, its fierce intensity reached every ear.

"Ke Kwenu! Ke Kwenu!" they shouted.

Surveying the vast landscape, he marveled at the disciplined formations dotting the mountain's slope. Compact units, the backbone of the Niri army, stood at attention. To his left were the Canis—warriors by his side during the assault on Rada Mysters. A bond forged in battle, they would march to the ends of Kirina at his command. In the heart of the left flank stood the formidable Kwale, their numbers nearly tripling the others. Their armors bore the distinct sigil of Namudi, signaling their fierce loyalty. The men from the other Ezes scattered around the center and the right.

"Niri brethren! Today, we shattered the chains of darkness! Tomorrow, we shall bask in the glory of dawn!"

Thunderous screaming and applause carried through the mountain. Amadioha took a deep breath.

'Don't do it!' Damballa warned.

With a stern voice that resonated with authority, Amadioha declared, "Mark my words, we will not rest till every Vodunese soldier has paid. We cannot rest until every Vodunese soldier sees the might of Niri. We cannot rest until the cure for the disease is permanent." Without a backward glance, he sensed Ojukwu's shadow looming close, the air thick with his barely contained fury. "Niri warriors, Ego Kwenu!" Amadioha's voice rang. An uncertainty clouded the soldiers' faces, the weight of his words sinking in. He had told them the war they thought was over was just beginning.

Breaking the brief silence, the fierce Canis shouted, "Ke Kwenu!"

Men from the right glanced at each other for a second.

"Ke Kwenu," Namudi shouted. His men followed right after.

"Ke Kwenu! Ke Kwenu!" Ekwensu said.

All the other War Ezes shouted it back.

The tension in the army released. All the soldiers raised their swords and shouted.

"For Niri!" Amadioha shouted.

"For Niri!" the thunderous voices boomed.

"We will cure the Vodunese disease!"

"Or we will die trying!"

Amadioha wheeled around. Ojukwu's towering presence was mere inches from him. Although blazing with unspoken rage, his eyes were trapped behind a veneer of forced calm. Amadioha had audaciously redrawn the lines of power for all to witness.

17

BARTHOLOMEW
REALM OF NOWHERE

*I*n the heart of the chamber, the sight seized **Ikenga's** senses. For the first time, he saw a demon face to face. The demon bound to a towering bed was much fairer than any man Ikenga had seen. His hair, sleek and straight, was shorn at the sides while flowing in a cascade atop his head. Iron chains shackled his limbs and encircled his torso in a metallic embrace. A labyrinth of tubes wove across his form, some siphoning his blood, others infusing unknown liquids into his veins. He looked human.

"Where are we?" Ikenga asked.

"Somewhere in Nowhere." Legba said.

Two figures with ghostly white hair sat behind desks at the room's distant end. Their bodies were frail, like they stood on the cusp between life and death. "The demon's appearance is uncannily human," Ikenga remarked, his eyes fixed on the creature before him.

Legba nodded, his expression grave. "Indeed, they share many similarities with us. However, do not let their looks fool you. These beings possess strength and speed that surpasses the average person, a lesson we learned at a great cost. And their wings, a defining feature, can protrude from their backs at will."

Intrigued, Ikenga leaned closer to the demon, searching for any sign of the mentioned wings, but he found none. The demon's back appeared smooth and unblemished, betraying no hint of the appendages supposedly beneath the surface.

Sensing Ikenga's confusion, Legba continued, "When they retract their wings, the appendages meld seamlessly with the skin on their backs, effectively vanishing from sight. It is a mystery we have yet to unravel."

"Hmm..." Ikenga mused, his brow furrowed in contemplation as he turned back to Legba. "This is the—"

"This is the demon whose memories will become yours," Legba interjected, pointing again with an urgent insistence. "The process you are about to undergo is nothing like what happened in Nowhere. You will assume all the demon's memories, even some it may not remember." His gaze locked onto Ikenga. "A normal mind would crumble under such a burden. But yours is special."

A chill ran down Ikenga's spine. *Special.* A mix of pride and apprehension swirled within him.

"You must focus on a powerful memory to anchor you to this world while assimilating the demon's memories. Otherwise," he warned, "Ikenga will be lost forever. You would become Bartholomew."

A strong memory. Ikenga closed his eyes and thought of Moremi. When he opened them, he was no longer in the room.

"You should not have come here," Moremi said.

He jerked his head to the side, his eyes widening in the starkness of a small chamber. It was a study in minimalism: stark white walls devoid of windows or doors. But mysteriously, a soft, ambient light filled the space. Moremi sat at the other end, draped in a flowing red dress that accentuated her form and revealed her scarred, burnt legs.

As Ikenga struggled to sit up, a dull ache throbbed through his skull. He reached for his pocket, only to realize he was naked.

"The Vodun man is luring you into a trap," she warned. *Her face was gorgeous despite the dire message.*

Memories of the past flooded his mind again. He just wanted to hold her. "If he wanted to kill me, there would be much easier ways to do it," he said.

She looked at her feet. "Why do you think death is the ultimate punishment?"

Her words sent a pang of guilt through him. "What would be his aim?"

"I don't know," she said in a lighter voice.

"I don't even know if you are real."

"You are the one who should be here, not me." Tears filled her eyes.

His stomach sank. "I would trade places with you without any thought."

"But you can't, can you?" she screamed. Her face distorted, the red dress faded, and her body deformed.

"I cannot live alone in the shadows of what I have done," Ikenga said.

"You are not alone. You have me. Let us go back to Niri. To Orisha. We will play in the mountains and bushes of Akesan just as before."

The last words sounded all too familiar. Eshm's sick laugh followed. Moremi had completely transformed into Eshm's solid white form. "Come and touch my heart," Eshm said, but with Moremi's voice.

Ikenga breathed heavily. He put his hands over his eyes and closed them. "Go away!" he shouted.

When he opened them, he was back in the room with Legba, a mixed feeling of relief and loss coursing over him.

"Did you hear anything I just said?" Legba asked in an irritated tone.

Ikenga was uncertain whether the scene unfolding before him was reality or another layer of an intricate dream. Moremi's warnings resonated in his mind; he had no substantial reason to trust Legba. And yet, it was this very enigma, the Vodun man, who had given him a long-lost ember—hope. Would he choose to live burdened by the regret of having discarded it?

"Back in Abisina, how did you find me?" he asked.

"We needed someone capable of withstanding an immersion," Legba said. "One of our spies embedded with Ghede Ghadou told us about you shortly after you escaped Nago Sango's grasp. We have been looking for you ever since."

Two years evading both Vodun and Orisha. The brief moment of pride was a welcome distraction from the heaviness of the current situation. "What else is there but to proceed?"

Legba pricked Ikenga's skin with various needles. Two tubes were attached to the big oval container into which the demon's blood flowed.

Legba placed his hands over the oval container. The blood inside it pulsed. Ikenga watched as it traveled through the tubes toward him. The redness filled them as the fluid covered the distance. He realized he was holding his breath. He let out a loud sigh. As the blood reached the needle in his hand and entered his bloodstream, the room faded before coming back into focus.

His vision flashed. A surge of energy coursed through his body. Images, sounds, and emotions bombarded his mind. He wrenched free from the chains binding him to the chair. As he collapsed onto the cold floor, he clung to his head, the sensation of his mind expanding against its physical confines near unbearable.

Bathed in the welcoming glow of a sun-drenched day, he reveled in the solar caress, the radiating heat oddly comforting. He looked down at his tiny feet encased in worn leather shoes. He ran through the forest. Joy and freedom filled his heart. He spotted his companions, children who shared his joyous escape, their skin as fair as the demon he had previously glimpsed on the table. With a shift, he found himself in a room, standing before a man, a demon crowned with towering, light-gray wings.

"Mastering your wings is the inaugural lesson for a young demon," the demon stated.

Ikenga inspected the room and saw a dozen demons beside him. He looked at his hands. His skin's whiteness made him jerk. His body felt alien, estranged from him. The room's edges blurred, shimmering as his mind pushed against the invasive memory. Then everything plunged into darkness. A surge of fear gripped him. When the world blinked back into existence, he was in Sasobek amid the hot, dry air of the bustling city Prejudice Triangle. Fire blazed from large, round holes scattered between the roads and towering structures. The buildings were constructed from molten rocks from the volcanoes surrounding them, making them look like extensions of the mountains and not something artificially built. Absent of doors, windows, and signs, it would have been impossible to tell the difference. Apart from their hair and sometimes fair skin, demons looked like the men and women of Kirina.

Ikenga snapped out of the memories and back into the stark reality of the room. He tried to get up from the ground, but his trembling legs failed him. He raised his head, leveling a determined gaze at Legba. "I will make you pay," he vowed. The feeling of hate toward the man felt natural and justified.

The pair of white-haired men closed in on Legba, their footsteps echoing in the silence.

Legba raised his hands. "Se Mewn, Ikenga," he said.

"I need to kill you," Ikenga said.

"Remember what I said!" Legba said. "Anchor yourself to a memory."

Ikenga understood his words this time.

"Kkisa nou ta dwe fè," one of the white-haired men said.

What is this strange language they speak?

"Tann! Listen to me," Legba continued. "Your feelings right now are not yours. Push them aside and anchor to your true self."

"I am hungry." Ikenga struggled to get upright, but fell again. An image of bloody, raw meat made his stomach churn. Yet, an alien part of him salivated, craving the raw flesh.

"Focus on the real you," Legba shouted.

The faces of the two white-haired men blanched, their eyes wide and frantic. They still spoke the same weird language. He was fading as he struggled to anchor himself.

"You are Ikenga. Son of Amobi Umoren."

"I am Ikenga. Son of Amobi Umoren."

"You are from Niri."

"I am from Niri."

"You are the reason your beloved Moremi is dead." The words were an anchor that pierced his skin. It sent unbearable pain throughout his body, but pulled him back to himself.

Legba spoke again, but Ikenga did not understand what he said.

"Your words are still gibberish," Ikenga spat. Then realization dawned on him—he could understand the white-haired men. "The experiment has failed yet again," muttered the one on the left.

"Your brain's understanding of the languages is still split," Legba said, his face creasing into a broad grin. "You must train it to recognize the dual thoughts not as yours but memories. Then you can understand both at the same time."

"I feel him inside me, a presence, foreign and insistent," Ikenga admitted.

"Good," Legba said. "Now, tell me: where is Daeva Isrut?" His eyes bored into Ikenga, intense and unblinking.

Ikenga searched the demon's memories. "He does not know."

"If that demon knew, you wouldn't be necessary." A note of irritation crept into Legba's voice. "He is close to the resistance. If he wanted to find her, how would he do it?"

Ikenga chewed on the words. It came to him naturally. "In the heart of Prejudice Triangle, there is a place called Ode to Babel," he began, "And a demon there, Zepar, who can find her."

18

IKENGA IN HELL
REALM OF HELL

Whenever Ikenga thought about Hell, burning fires, not drinks and dancing, came to mind. Ode to Babel's interior throbbed with a vivid display as the lights danced from a murky red to a moody green. The air vibrated with the bass from eclectic music, blending with the murmur of hushed conversations. The scent of spiced cocktails and the warmth of crowded bodies filled the air. Around the center, standing tables, interspersed with red-velvet-clad booths lining the walls, offered a plush embrace to their occupants.

At the room's heart stood a circular bar, an island amid the lively crowd. Behind it, two demons presided, deftly serving an array of drinks. **Ikenga** knew they were the demons to approach first in his quest to locate Zepar. He navigated the sea of bodies, aiming for the bartender at the far end.

A voice as smooth as silk yet infused with undeniable authority interrupted Ikenga's focus and brought him to an abrupt standstill. "I didn't give you permission to walk past me," she declared, her words hanging in the air like a challenge. Startled, Ikenga turned to face the source: a demon whose height barely reached his shoulder.

"I'm just—"

With a mischievous glint, she pulled Ikenga close. Gently pressing a finger to his lips to hush him, her other hand embarked on a daring exploration under his shirt, her fingertips skimming lightly over his torso. "Quid is facia ame," she whispered. As her hand ventured lower, Ikenga's reflexes kicked in; he grasped her wrist and extracted them.

Ikenga inhaled, steadying his racing thoughts amid the overwhelming sensory overload. The language he absorbed from the demon swirled chaotically in his mind, mixing with the sights, sounds, and smells around him. "Hold on," he shouted in the local tongue, his voice barely cutting through the music and chatter. He muscled his way back, only for her to respond by closing the gap again. He knocked her hand out midway.

A flash of confusion crossed her features, eyes narrowing as they flickered to anger. She freed herself from his grip as her lips twisted into a scornful sneer. "You look ugly anyway!" she said before vanishing into the sea of bodies.

Sasobek has always been full of surprises, he thought. Or was that what the demon thought? For a moment, he wondered if the blood memories would wear off and what would happen afterward. He turned around to continue his mission to the bar and bumped into another woman, spilling her drink all over her top.

"Kalla! Watch where you are going!" she said as her plastic cup landed on the floor. About the same height as the last girl, she wore a cropped top that exposed her toned arms and shoulders. Her face was like someone made half of it and used a mirror to create the rest. Even her eyebrows had perfect symmetry.

Ikenga grunted an apology. "Didn't see you there." He raised his hand to calm her before she made a scene.

She tilted her head, her eyes fixing on him with a challenging gaze.

Ikenga opened his hands in a placating gesture, his eyes earnest. "It was an honest mistake, I promise."

She pointed to the ground. "What does that do to my drink you spilled?"

Two people turned around to them.

"Let me make it up to you at the bar," he said, eager not to draw any more attention.

Her expression softened. She looked at the cup on the floor and back at him. "After that, I will decide if that's enough." A hint of a smile played at the corners of her lips.

"After you," Ikenga said and pointed to the bar. To his surprise, she burst through the crowded space with remarkable ease, parting the crowd like it was second nature to her. Ikenga followed, impressed by her confidence.

"Give me whatever she's having," Ikenga told the bartender as they found seats.

Just one drink and the effect had already hit. His human body was not as used to the alcohol produced there. It relaxed his posture and made him uninhibited, yet the conversation remained coherent and spirited. Her words inspired him. Worthy of an essay or even a book, she had emigrated to Sasobek from Masina City in search of new opportunities and had become a clothing material broker for some of the more prominent local manufacturers. She led a unique manufacturing process using material mined in the city.

"What time does this place close?" he slurred.

She regarded him with a playful tilt of her head. "Is there somewhere else you need to be?"

Ikenga cast a fleeting glance at the clock clinging to the far wall. The hands pointed starkly past midnight. If he returned early in the morning, he could find Zepar before his rendezvous with Legba. He thought he saw Moremi in the crowd, but he dismissed it, feigning a casual scratch on his head. "I am going to need a bathroom."

"Down the stairs around the back. The ones on this floor are closed."

"I just realized I never got your name."

"When you come back, I will tell you." The capricious lights of the bar played over her features, casting her in a momentary glow of perfection, highlighting a beauty Ikenga had sensed from the start.

Only upon rising did he grasp the depth of his drunkenness. The room swayed around him, a churning sea of bodies and noise. He steadied himself, striving not to be swept away by the tide of drunken revelers. "Don't go anywhere," he said into her ear as he passed her.

"I have no other place to be," she whispered.

A childlike grin lit up his face as he stumbled down the staircase. The emptiness of the ground floor amplified every sound. His heart raced. The anticipation of seeing the mystery demon again filled him. Zepar became an afterthought, a distraction. He staggered to the sign of the bathroom door toward the end. He had barely made it there when a shadow eclipsed him. Something behind him piqued his sense of danger.

Formless was in the shape of a penknife today. He put his hand inside his pocket and grabbed his weapon as he turned around. Two of the three demons looming behind him stood so tall their heads nearly grazed the ceiling. The one in the middle landed his fist smack into Ikenga's forehead. His vision blurred with the image of Formless, torn from his grip, spinning in the air before he passed out.

∼

IKENGA'S EYES SNAPPED OPEN, a sharp pain throbbing in his temples. Gradually, the blurred contours of a wall came into focus, jarring his senses into alertness. His forehead pressed against the cold, hard surface of a table while two pairs of powerful hands held his arms down, iron-like in their grip. Beneath his frenzied thoughts, Ikenga squirmed and writhed, struggling against the overpowering grasp of his captors.

"He's conscious, boss," grunted the brute, clenching Ikenga's left arm.

"Get off me!" Ikenga shouted, his breath heavy. Blood and saliva dripping from his mouth stained the table.

Moremi was right—the Vodunese man betrayed me. How was I so blind?

"What is your name?" the voice came from someone in front of him.

"Bartholomew," Ikenga said.

"Bartholomew?" the demon echoed with skepticism. "Where are you from?"

Ikenga considered admitting he was from Sasobek, Bartholomew's true home. But he maintained the lie he had spun at the bar. "Northern Gimaa. I am here on business."

The pressure on his neck increased as the demons pushed him harder onto the table. The demon in front of him walked into focus as he picked up Formless.

"How did the Eden Protocol find us?" his hand brushed against the blade as he spoke.

Eden Protocol? Ikenga searched deep into Bartholomew's memories but came up blank. "What is *that*?"

One demon restraining him jabbed a knee into his side, eliciting a pained squeal. "You are making a mistake," Ikenga said.

"You speak our tongue, yet you come from the land of man," the demon observed.

How could he know this?

"They are moving faster than we thought," the demon before him said.

"I have never heard of the Eden Protocol," Ikenga pleaded. Once he got back to Kirina, if he got back, he would find Legba and make him pay. He was so foolish and naïve to fall for this. "Let me go! I—"

"Chop off his right arm," the demon interrupted.

"Ok, boss!" The voice from Ikenga's left was disturbingly excited.

Ikenga wrestled and wiggled, but they were too strong.

"Wait!" he said. "I... can't... talk properly... like this," he managed between ragged half-breaths.

"Behemoth..." the demon in front of Ikenga said, "raise his head slightly."

"Ok, boss," Behemoth responded.

He pulled Ikenga's head until he stared directly at his interrogator.

The bartender from upstairs!

Ikenga seized the opportunity. Summoning his last reserves of strength, he drew in ragged breaths. His eyes ignited with white fire, zeroing in on his target.

As shadowy flames streamed from his eyes, a cold metal clamp seized his neck, snuffing out the fire. The collar seared his skin as it heated. He tried again to direct the white flames, only for the metal to burn hotter in reprisal.

"Foolish Dominions!" the demon across from him bellowed. "I said tilt his head slightly, not raise it fully!"

"Sorry, boss! I try again," Behemoth said.

He slammed Ikenga's head into the table, the loud crack of splintering wood sending a wave of excruciating pain down his spine. He let out a loud grunt. The demon pulled Ikenga's head back up, but only a little.

"No, you imbecile! Don't pull him up again. Put his head back on the table."

"Zepar, I don't like I make you upset," Behemoth lamented. "I just do what you tell me.

Zepar! The name settled like a weight in his mind.

"Sometimes, I get confused," Behemoth muttered, sulking like a scolded child. He slammed Ikenga's head back onto the table with a resounding thud, maintaining relentless pressure. Ikenga would pass out from the pain if they continued.

"Forget it!" Zepar said.

"We know you are not a demon," Zepar said. "You are not Bartholomew. And you are not from Gimaa." The statement from Zepar floated in the air. "One last time, how did you find us?"

"I didn't come here to kill anyone," Ikenga said, each word a struggle. He ought to have said, *'I came here seeking Daeva Isrut, guided by Bartholomew's memories. He, by the way, is likely dead since we drained all his blood.'* Yet such a statement would make his predicament worse.

"Do it," Zepar said to Behemoth.

Do what?

Ikenga thrashed, lashing out with his leg in a blind attempt to strike Behemoth. He heard a sickening crack before the searing agony radiated through his body. Sweat streamed down his face, mingling with the warm trickle of blood from the gashes on his head. Through blurred vision, he glimpsed his right hand lying at an angle that defied nature.

"Koca ci! You broke my shoulder!" he shouted in Niri; the searing pain overloaded his brain, forcing it to disassociate Bartholomew's memories and his.

"I said cut off his arm, not break his shoulder!" Zepar scowled.

"Arm?" Behemoth inquired.

Zepar crouched low to Ikenga's eye level. "As you can see, he is not very bright. Next time, I tell them to give you a back rub, and they might chop off your head."

Laborious and inconsistent breathing, coupled with overbearing pain, meant Ikenga barely processed the words.

"For the last time..." Zepar's voice cut through the fog, "Eden."

"Bartho... Bartholomew," Ikenga forced out as the room blurred in and out of focus.

"Bartholomew?" Zepar asked.

Pain surged through Ikenga's body. He had a sinking feeling that if he passed out, he would never wake up. "He said you could help us... help us find... he is my friend," Ikenga mumbled. "I was... I was looking for someone. He told me you could help me."

Laughter, cold and mocking, erupted from Zepar. "If he sent you to me, he was no friend of yours."

"He said you could... help find someone," Ikenga said.

"Find who?"

"Daeva," Ikenga said, "Isrut."

"For what purpose?" Zepar pressed.

Words failed Ikenga; his energy was a dwindling flame. Beneath him, a chilling, wet patch spread, a mix of blood and sweat.

"This one is useless," Zepar said as he got up from his crouching position. "Chop off his head and clean up this mess. We must leave."

"Which one is the head?" Behemoth inquired.

"I'll do it myself," Zepar snapped, reaching for the knife.

"That's enough for today, Zepar," a female voice called from across the room.

"This one is bad news," Zepar argued.

"He's mostly truthful," she countered in a soothing voice. "I spent hours talking to him at the bar. He is a terrible liar."

"What do we do, boss?" Behemoth said.

"He is mine," Zepar said to her. "I outrank you."

"Are we going to do this again?"

Zepar mumbled something under his breath. "That won't be necessary," he said. "Let him go."

Ikenga half-expected them to kick him in the groin, but they all let go simultaneously. He dropped to the floor, clutching his shoulder in pain. He turned to see the lady he'd spent the last few hours talking to. Her hair, freed from its wig disguise, revealed a striking blend of deep red and vibrant scarlet. Some strands shone with an unnatural brightness, while others were so dark they bordered on black.

"Sorry, they were not as hospitable as they should have been," she said. "The Eden Protocol is dangerous and well-connected. We had to be sure."

"You... you are—" he said.

"Daeva," she said, "Daeva Isrut."

19

MAAD A SINIG
REALM OF KIRINA

The warm hum of conversation and rhythmic clinking of cups echoed through the wine parlor, the air rich with the tang of malt. A bar of aged oak, polished to a soft sheen, ran the length of one wall, with rows of gleaming bottles reflecting the light and taps oozing drinks. The bartender, a broad-shouldered man with a bushy beard streaked with gray and intricate tattoos snaking up his muscular arms, filled pint glasses for a steady stream of thirsty patrons.

Amadioha and Omoro, his chief magician, had Navigated to Sine a few hours prior after sending word to Amadioha's brother for an urgent meeting. He shifted in his seat at the rectangular table, the worn wooden surface rough beneath his fingertips. "Brother," Amadioha said, his voice cutting through the noise in the tavern.

"Brother," Chinedu replied, leaning back in his chair, which creaked under his weight. His eyes mirrored Amadioha's, their resemblance unmistakable. But despite their close age, the lines on Chinedu's face made him appear a decade older. Chinedu stole a glance at Omoro, who silently sat next to Amadioha. Omoro's eyes glinted blue in the dim lighting as he gazed at the brothers like a father watching his children.

Amadioha reached for his mug. "How is the farming going?" he asked before sipping his drink.

"We are expanding," Chinedu said. "Now supplying a good part of the south. You would know if you visited more."

"I have a war to fight," he snapped. "But perhaps I should have run away like you did when the Vodunese killed our brother."

Chinedu's jaw clenched, and he leaned forward, his elbows resting on the table. "The Vodunese did not kill our brother. You did," he said.

Amadioha's eyes flashed with an electric intensity. "Do not slander his memory."

"You still have the marks from the beatings I gave you when we were little. Do you want me to add more?" Chinedu smirked.

"How about we go outside and see?" Amadioha challenged.

Omoro's hand shot out, gripping Amadioha's arm. "Enough of this," he butted in. "Or I tell everyone in this tavern my experience cleaning both of your arseholes when you were young. Might I add till you were much older than I should have been doing that?"

Amadioha clenched his jaw and lowered himself into his chair, taking time to steady his breathing. "I need to meet the Maad A Sinig in secret. Do you still have a way to get to her discreetly?"

Chinedu scoffed. "You call me on short notice, then insult me. Why should I help you?"

Amadioha pointed an accusing finger at his brother. "Because you know in your heart, you are a coward for letting Vodun get away with what they did, with what they did to our friends, with—"

"I have heard this one hundred times. One hundred times too many." He leaned forward. "The Maad A Sinig is married now. If she is to see you in the Djibo, it must be an official visit." Amadioha opened his mouth to protest, but Chinedu cut him off. "I am not finished, baby brother."

Amadioha seethed, a spark of electricity dancing between his fingers under the table.

Chinedu jerked his head toward a door at the far end of the

tavern. "She is in the back. Go through those doors. She will be in the second room on the left."

Amadioha glanced around the tavern, lowering his voice. "So you knew what I wanted all this time?"

Chinedu smiled, raising his mug to his lips. "Such is the joy of watching you squirm when angry."

Amadioha cursed under his breath, the words lost among the tavern's chatter as he rose. After taking two steps, he turned to see Omoro still seated. "You are not coming?" he asked.

Omoro shook his head. "It's better you see the Maad A Sinig by yourself," he said. "Besides, I hear my godchildren have grown so big." He turned to Chinedu, his smile widening.

Chinedu raised his mug, sloshing some of the wine onto the table. "My wine is tastier than what they have here!" he exclaimed. "They would be happy to see you. You too, baby brother."

Amadioha's nostrils flared, and he took a deep breath. "Do not call me 'baby brother' again."

Chinedu grinned, his eyes glinting in the tavern's light. "Ok, *baby brother.*"

Amadioha clenched his fists, doing everything he could to keep his response to himself as he turned and headed for the door, weaving through the crowded tables and boisterous patrons. As he reached the door, the realization that the Maad A Sinig was expecting him cast a shadow of unease over his thoughts, putting him on the defensive. She had known far enough in advance to inform his brother before he arrived, and the knowledge settled heavily in his gut as he pushed open the door and stepped into the hallway beyond.

∼

WITHOUT BOTHERING TO KNOCK, Amadioha reached for the doorknob.

The room exuded warmth and comfort, the gentle glow of a flickering lamplight enhancing its ambiance. The scent of aged wood mingled from the roughly hewn log walls that transported one to a secluded, rustic cabin. A solitary window, set high on one wall, allowed moonlight to filter in. Through its clear pane, the inky sky shimmered with countless stars. A plush, angled couch hugged the wall in the room's corner. Against the opposite wall was a comfortable-looking bed adorned with a cozy quilt and piled with pillows.

Aissatou Mbaye, the Queen of Sine, reclined on the couch's edge. Atop her head rested an ornate crown, its opulence mirrored in her ensemble and the tinkling of her accessories. Red diamonds interspaced other expensive-looking stones that matched her earrings. Similar jewelry covered her neck and most of her forearms. Intricate braids cascaded from the left side of her face, woven into the rest of her lustrous hair, which shimmered under the lamplight.

"Oha," she murmured, her lips curving into a smile that felt like a soft embrace, both warm and inviting.

She was the only one who dared to call him 'Oha.' A flicker of irritation flashed in his eyes. "How did you know I was coming?" he demanded.

"You always ask the wrong questions."

"You looked into my future."

Her laugh was soft with melancholy. "If divining the future was that effortless," she sighed, "I would have known you would leave me before it happened many years ago."

"I—" he stopped himself.

"You have come a long way," she said. "You should have a seat."

He unraveled the scarf from his head as their eyes locked. "I shouldn't have come here," he said. "It was a mistake."

"Action and reaction," she said. "That is the way of life."

Her eyes, a striking shade of green that contrasted with her olive skin, captivated him. Those eyes held a wild, untamed ferocity, making her appear as though she harbored dangerous secrets.

"I need your help," Amadioha whispered in desperation. "I have started down a path I cannot stop."

She raised an eyebrow. "Indeed. Attacking the Vodun capital was not our arrangement."

"Our plans have changed."

"*Your* plans have changed, is what you meant to say," she said.

The Eden Ruse

"There can be no peace while Vodun exists."

"Do not sell me the same lines you sold your War Ezes." she dismissed his words with a flippant wave.

Amadioha's face contorted in frustration. "Since you know everything, why don't we cut to the chase?"

With a composed grace, she crossed her legs and leaned back into the plush cushions of the couch, fixing him with a pointed look. "You should sit and gather your thoughts."

"I don't want to sit do—"

"Sit!" Her voice was sharp, yet her body remained relaxed. Amadioha hesitated for a heartbeat, his frown deepening, before relenting and settling into his seat.

"I don't need visions to decipher your dealings with the Ezes nor the weight of your promises," she began. "And just as clearly, I have always known your burning ambition, that thirst for revenge, would lead you here."

Amadioha lowered his gaze. "There can be no peace," he murmured, "not as long as Vodun casts its shadow."

"In Sine, Salom, and Baol, we've known peace," she began. "Decades of it, even after the secession. You requested my resources to fund rebel factions, to posture, to spread the Vodunese defenses thin. And I complied, orchestrating the Loas' distractions, setting up your win. If you destroy the Vodun capital, it will destabilize the region in ways not seen before. That does not benefit Sine."

"It may not be today, maybe not in our lifetime. But they will return. I know it. You know it! Do not lie to yourself," Amadioha said.

"A butterfly's graceful dance upon a fragile bloom can influence the very winds of fate. Such is the intricate weave of cause and effect," Aissatou mused. "Action and reaction."

"Stop the riddles!"

"You talk about lifetimes and generations. How do you know destroying Vodun will not birth a darker future for Niri? Maybe a bigger threat emerges from the ashes."

"I am bound by the present! I act on what stands before me, not the uncertainties of tomorrow!" Amadioha's voice cracked, his inner turmoil seeping through.

"At least the blind man acknowledges his darkness rather than pretending to see," she countered.

"My patience wears thin," Amadioha declared, a hard edge in his voice. "With or without your blessing, Vodun will face my wrath. But if you possess insights, if there's a glimpse of my fate, share it now."

Aissatou uncrossed her legs, placing her hands on her thighs as she leaned forward, her gaze unflinching. "If you move to take the capital, you will find pain, then you will find death."

"Whose death?"

"That is not how this works."

"So, will I fail?"

"You will fail, or you will succeed."

"You always frustrate me!"

"And yet you always come back."

"Will you help me?" he pleaded.

She stayed silent. He stared at her for a moment longer before standing. "I knew I wasted my time coming."

"You are a stubborn man, singularly focused, willing to burn every bridge to achieve your goal."

"I would burn everything to destroy the enemy of my people."

Aissatou shook her head. "From dust we came, and to dust we shall return."

A chill coursed down Amadioha's spine, though he strived to keep his expression unreadable. "Thanks for your time, Queen Mbaye," he said with a curt nod. He turned on his heel and strode out of the room without another word.

∼

THE MOMENT AMADIOHA emerged from the tavern's dim interior, three men standing in the shadowy recesses met him, waiting for him. Scarves obscured their faces, with only their eyes—piercing and watchful—visible. Amadioha took a step back and clenched his fists. "You don't want to do this," he warned.

"The Maad A Sinig will not help you. But she has asked us to deliver a message," the man in the middle said.

Relief crossed Amadioha's face, though his eyes remained narrow with suspicion, watching their every move. "Speak it."

"If you attack the castle, Omoro must ride directly behind you."

"Why is that?" The request was odd.

"Those are her words." The man removed the scarf covering his face to reveal a young, boyish face. The other two followed. Triplets. In an eerily synchronized tone, they responded, "It is not our place to question the ways of our queen." Their grave and unwavering expressions matched as they intoned, "Tell no one about this meeting."

"Send her my gratitude for nothing," Amadioha said.

The central triplet nodded. He smiled as if he failed to understand the sarcasm. "From dust we came, and to dust we shall return," he said before covering his head and disappearing into the tavern.

PART VI
DECEPTION

20

LEADS

REALM OF HELL

Nothing in PRISM or from **Lilith's** off-book contacts had a hit on the Eden Protocol. It was like a wisp of smoke, dissolving each time she attempted to grasp it.

Her watch beeped—the front desk. She tapped twice, and a woman's face flickered on the hologram. "Major Lilith, you have a visitor."

She froze. "Visitor?"

"General Gadreel." The woman's tone was deferential.

Lilith's heart fluttered. She swiped off PRISM and glanced around her room, checking for imaginary cameras. "I'll be right there."

"Please hurry, he seems very impatient," the woman said before ending the call.

Lilith's thoughts raced. Why was he visiting her privately? She tidied herself hurriedly. The general only made personal visits when the situation was dire. Something big had happened behind the scenes.

THE LUMINOUS GLOW of city lights trickled through the gaps of the half-drawn curtains of the common area of Lilith's residence. She pictured herself lying on her plush bed and relaxing to hide her nervousness from General Gadreel.

He sat upright, the stars on his uniform glistening in the overhead light. Even sitting down comfortably, he exuded an aura of being in charge.

"General," Lilith said.

"You have been missing from the Dome lately." He stood from his seat and gave her a curious look.

"I feel like I am being monitored," she said.

"You are," he said flatly.

At least he is honest. "I've been—"

He swiped his finger in the air. "This is not a personal visit."

Oh, perfect. Nothing like a cold, professional visit to brighten the day.

She wondered if he had found out about PRISM. But if he had, he would have had her arrested already.

"We have important matters to discuss. Walk with me." Without waiting for her response, he strode toward the exit. She fell in step without a word.

They traversed the hushed city streets, the shadows of skyscrapers looming around them, before ducking into an unassuming three-story building, its neon sign blinking *'Food.'*

Densely packed tables filled the interior, leaving little space between each one. No one else was there except the owner, who recognized them.

"Coffee," General Gadreel said.

Lilith gave the server a nod, signifying she would have the same.

Navigating through the narrow maze of tables, they eventually found a spot far from the entrance, their chairs grating against the floor as they settled. An oppressive silence engulfed them as they engaged in a prolonged, wordless staring contest. Eventually, the coffee came, and the server disappeared behind a door at the other end.

"Lucifer's funeral is in two weeks."

Lilith all but choked on the coffee in her mouth. "Two weeks?"

"At the Eredise in Aamaris. The military arm of the United Nations met yesterday and decided a quick funeral would be necessary to keep the peace. Show the world a sign of unity and placate any uprisings."

General Gadreel's words left a disquieting echo in her mind, a discordant note she couldn't place. "Unity and peace? Did they miss the part where our president also got killed?"

The general sighed. "Your raid in Ebos... our techs cracked the encryption on more data we retrieved. We moved the data processing offsite to keep whatever we say away from prying eyes."

A smile crossed Lilith's face.

"That location was hit this morning," he said.

Her short-lived smile transformed, and her jaw dropped. "How is that possible? It would have been—"

"Level 8 clearance only," he interrupted. "They have hit us twice in too short a time."

"Someone from the inside has to be in on this," Lilith said.

"There is no this." General Gadreel locked eyes with her. "And if there were, it's not your concern. Rumors circulating say we killed Lucifer." He leaned in close. "Most Upper and Lower Council members will attend; gather intel on the location, but keep it quiet—you're running point."

Lilith frowned. "Martial law could spark more problems than it prevents."

The general's voice lowered further. "I'm not here for strategic advice. Just gather the intel."

"In two weeks? That's impossible." Lilith exclaimed, "The risk is too high."

With a startling crash, General Gadreel's fist connected with the table. The sound echoed, causing their server to dart out of the kitchen in curiosity and alarm. Lilith jerked back and almost fell off her seat. "Let me rephrase that. Most of the leadership in Hell will be present. And in case you didn't realize, I just gave you a direct order."

Doubt gnawed at her as she chewed her lip. Their relationship was running on fumes. Still, his outburst was unprovoked. "What about Major Jagan? Wouldn't we need someone to handle intelligence here in Masina? Someone is leaking information to our enemies."

"I wouldn't trust Jagan with a bag of bricks, let alone the top leaders of Masina."

She wanted to tell him about the intel on the Flares she had dug up. But some of their methods were illegal. *I can tell him later.*

"I—"

General Gadreel raised his hand to stop her. "This is risky," He echoed her words, letting them hang in the air before continuing. "Short notice. You said that too. That is why we need to own security. As many of our undercover operatives as possible in Sasobek, Qataban, and Aamaris must be involved. You can decide to become part of the problem, or you can choose to be part of the solution. You wanted to get out from behind the desk. Well, here you have it,"

He must be desperate to come to me like this. After a long, tense moment, she finally broke the silence. "Consider it done."

"I leaned into General Adramalech to put your name forward. You are reckless, but the most qualified, given the short notice," he said. "The Upper Council will expect a full security briefing in three days."

He stood and headed for the exit. "Three days."

With a sense of impending urgency, she pulled out her phone and dialed Senet's number. She answered before the first ring even finished. "Change of plans. We leave for Sasobek tonight."

∼

THE ROOM MATERIALIZED around them in a timeless flux, stretching and compressing in a way that was both as eternal and fleeting as five seconds. A surge of food rushed up Lilith's esophagus, threatening to spill out. Before her stomach could revolt, Senet darted to her side. She clamped a hand over Lilith's mouth, forcing the surging bile back down her throat. Shock flared in Lilith's eyes as she choked on her protest.

"Swallow it," Senet demanded.

Were it not for Senet's hand, Lilith would have yelled a curse at her. She settled with giving her a stare.

"Swallow it," Senet said again. "The less we leave here, the better."

Fighting her gag reflex, she forced the bile down. But the action nearly made her vomit again.

The sharp scent of formaldehyde penetrated the morgue's otherwise sterile atmosphere of labyrinthine hallways. Faint, silvery overhead lights flickered, casting shadows across the ground and creating a chilled ambiance.

"Someone left the fridge door open," Senet muttered, her breath visible in the cold air.

"Let's just find what we need and get out," Lilith said.

If we are caught here, General Gadreel will be the least of our worries.

The numbers on the doors decreased as they went on: 1987 FGH, 1986 FGH.

"We are looking for 1960 BN," Lilith said. "If we run into anyone, we keep to the story."

A facility like this would be low-traffic, but nothing had been happening as it should have recently. They would pretend to be Sasobekan Secret Service investigating a case. When asked for details, they would stress it was classified. If whoever they met didn't buy it, they would have to neutralize them and terminate the mission. The numbers continued: 1970 FGH, 1969 BMN then finally 1960 BN.

"No one has been in here recently." Senet glanced around inside the room.

Lilith searched around, wondering what they may have missed. "Check the compartments."

Senet unlatched the handles on the sides of the drawer on the far right wall. A gut-churning stench erupted from within as she cracked the seal.

"Kalla! What is that?" Lilith asked in disgust.

Senet took the brunt of the smell. She held her nose and mouth to stop from spewing. "It's empty."

Lilith walked over and peered inside. "This can't be." She moved to the next compartment, yanking it open to reveal another hollow space. The smell from it was worse. She slammed it shut and opened two more—same thing.

"Time to leave," Senet said.

"It's time to leave when I say it is," Lilith said, flashing her an angry look.

"I have a bad feeling about this," Senet said.

"A bad feeling about what?" a third voice came from behind them. The demon placed his right hand on a gun hanging from his waist. From his slouched posture and slender frame, he could not be military.

"I am Agent Razel. This is my partner, Agent Veron. Secret Service," Lilith said.

He studied them, his fingers twitching with visible tension. "I'm going to need some identification."

"Unfortunately, we cannot do that," Lilith said. "But we can patch our superiors in, and you can tell them why you wasted our time."

His grip on his pistol tightened a fraction. Lilith assessed the distance and her opponent's readiness, confident she could disarm him before he could react.

"What is your name?" Senet asked.

"Morgua," he replied, straightening with an air of importance.

"Listen Morgua, we are looking for a body that should have been in this room. Daeva. Do you think you could help us with that?" The confidence in her tone made Lilith believe Senet was, in fact, agent Veron.

"Daeva Isrut?" Recognition sparked in Morgua's eyes. "You are from South Division 7b? You should have led with that." He moved his hand away from his pistol and a smile crossed his face. "Your colleagues were here a couple of days ago. They ordered us to move the body. You must not have been notified."

"It appears we were not," Senet said.

The Eden Ruse

"Of course, I understand. Follow me. I'll take you there immediately!" He turned around and walked out the door.

Lilith turned to Senet, giving her a silent nod of approval.

The body had been moved to a completely different section of the morgue. They moved through the labyrinthine facility, sharing wary glances as they ventured deeper into the icy heart of the building. As they went through numerous secured doors, Morgua's access card saved them from the mess they would be in from lack of planning.

"Do you know why the other agents moved the body?" Lilith asked.

"Your people are always stingy with words," he said.

The title "South Division 7b" wriggled in Lilith's memory like an alien. She was well-versed in the Sasobek secret service divisions—yet she had no recollection of a 7b. There was a covert unit operated under the moniker "South Division Seventy," yet the utmost secrecy shrouded their presence. They would never self-identify themselves to anyone, let alone a mortician. Even the King of Sasobek didn't know about them.

He pulled the body out of a vault. All three of them hovered over it and looked at the lifeless form before them.

"How long has this body been here?" Lilith asked.

"A little over three months,"

PRISM had her at the docks about a month prior. A puzzle piece was missing; a secret Morgua seemed to clutch tighter with each passing moment. He trusted them more now, but she could not tell how far it went.

"Hold him down," Lilith said to Senet.

Senet darted a glance at Lilith. She had a "What?" look on her face.

Morgua, equally baffled, mirrored her confusion. But then, understanding flickered in his eyes, and his demeanor shifted dramatically. Like a cornered animal, his instincts kicked in, and he made a sudden, desperate lunge for the weapon at his side.

Senet knocked his hand away, sending the gun clattering to the ground. She followed with a blow to his stomach, then she wrapped around him from behind and put him in a headlock.

"Let me go immediately," Morgua said, struggling to free himself. "I have done nothing wrong."

Senet's eyes shot a question at Lilith, silently seeking guidance as Lilith advanced on their captive.

"Never speak of this to anyone," Lilith said as she stepped closer.

"I won't tell anyone, I promise!" Morgua pleaded.

"That wasn't meant for you." She opened her mouth. Her two canine teeth elongated, sending a look of shock through Senet's face.

A primal terror took hold of Morgua, making his heart beat visibly through his shirt like a frantic drum against his ribs. He kicked back at Senet, but his feet landed on the wall behind them instead.

"You are hiding something from me," Lilith said.

"I told you everything! What else do you want to know?" he screamed. "Get away from me!"

She sank her teeth deep into the vulnerable flesh of his neck. He let out a short-lived scream before his body went lifeless. The glands in her teeth secreted fluid directly into his blood and sedated him, rendering him unconscious. His lifeblood pulsed into her, carrying a cargo of memories along its crimson current. They were a jumbled mess, scattered and disorganized. He was filled with fear. She used that to her advantage and scanned the memories, trying to find the source of the apprehension. Visions of the demons flickered through her consciousness like an old, grainy film reel; three husky, tall demons. Their uniforms were police, not military. Division 7b, indeed. She made a mental note of all their faces. PRISM would give her more information later.

"Where is the camera's location?" one demon asked Morgua. His accent was strange. Sasobek. But closer to the south, she thought.

"We only have cameras in the east wing," Morgua responded.

"These bodies are part of an internal investigation," the demon said. "I need you to move them for me."

"I can work on the paperwork and see what I can do," Morgua said.

"Tonight," the demon responded.

Why would they be so eager to move the body that quickly? Her question was answered immediately.

"We are going to need a direct link to your surveillance." The demons flashed a piece of paper at him. It was a court-ordered request. A forgery, she thought.

"Of course, sir," Morgua responded.

A phone rang, the shrill tone cutting through the tension. Lilith's senses honed in on it like a hawk spotting its prey. The sound of the other person was slightly audible. "Ode to Babel," the man said.

Withdrawing her teeth from Morgua's neck, she rose to full height, her teeth slowly receding from their unnatural state.

"What did you just do?" Senet's voice wavered as she took a tentative step back, her eyes wide with shock.

"You are not the only one holding secrets," Lilith said, wiping Morgua's blood from her mouth.

Senet pressed her lips together, her brow furrowing as she took another cautious step back. The air between them hung heavy with tension.

"When I taste blood, I can see memories. Flashes of thoughts, emotions, experiences—all flowing into me like a river of consciousness," Lilith said.

"How is that possible?" Senet asked, her feet rooted to the ground again.

"How is Navigating possible? It just is. The Masina military might consider it a national security problem if they knew I could do this. I need assurance I don't have to kill you to hide mine."

"Why do you think you could kill me if you tried?"

"Maybe you win in a fair fight," Lilith conceded with a slight shrug. "But we're going to be in close quarters over the next few hours. All it would take is one moment of vulnerability."

They stared at each other for another moment before bursting out laughing.

"Remind me to transfer far away from Masina City once I get back," Senet joked.

Lilith let out a measured laugh as she crouched next to Morgua. She pressed two fingers against his wrist, finding his pulse slow but steady.

Daeva's body connected the raid on Lamech with the mystery shipment at the port. And it somehow led all the way to Sasobek. She had no concrete evidence, but Lilith was more than sure that it had something to do with the assassination of their president and Lucifer.

She sat Morgua up and slapped him hard on the right side of his cheek. His eyes flickered open, a fog of confusion clouding his gaze as he blinked at his surroundings.

"We need an autopsy. Now," she commanded.

His eyes had a glazed, faraway look in them while he grappled with the surreal reality of his predicament. But the expression of horror on his face showed his memory was returning. He tried to crawl away, but Lilith grabbed his leg and forcefully turned him on his back. "I won't ask you again."

~

THE ROOM HUNG in a stifling silence, the air thick with antiseptic and the heavy burden of anticipation. Morgua's hands trembled as he made an incision into Daeva's lifeless form. Sweat beaded on his forehead, his hands never stilling in the endless dance of dissection. The minutes stretched into hours, each passing second thick with suspense. He removed organs, inspected them, and toyed with various chemicals.

"There is a bullet hole in her head," Senet pointed out. "I don't understand why we are wasting our time."

"Stop distracting our expert mortician," Lilith said. She had gone down an endless path, grasping at any straw she could. One tenet of the art of war was never to be desperate. But her demeanor was the antithesis.

Senet pouted and walked to the corner before sitting on the ground.

Sometime later, Morgua emerged from his examination, meeting Lilith's gaze over the dissected body. "Multiple organ capitulation."

"Plain words," Lilith said.

"Her liver has necrosis. Lungs seem to have had reduced capacity with some scarring on the inside." He motioned for her to come closer and showed her the inside. Blackened lesions marred the tissue, though Lilith lacked the knowledge to discern whether it was an anomaly or norm.

"The heart was very weak, close to the time of her last breath."

"And the bullet hole in her head?"

"She was already dead."

Senet sprang to her feet, curiosity magnetizing her toward the dissected body. "After she was already dead?"

"Yes. Like a—"

"Coverup," everyone said concurrently.

"So she was poisoned and then shot?" Lilith asked.

"That's what I thought initially," Morgua said as he bit his lip, "but the scarring in her liver says different. Her organs have been failing for a long time. If someone poisoned her, they played a slow and gruesome game of waiting."

Lilith's mind raced. "So, she died of natural causes, then someone who knew this shot her post-mortem and dumped her body here." What piece of the puzzle had she overlooked? A thought struck her like a bolt of lightning. "Pull up all the cases from the past two months," she ordered.

Morgua removed his gloves and moved to the keyboard on the side wall. He tapped into it, and a hologram appeared in the center of the room. A few of the names that scrolled died of gunshot wounds, stabbings, and similar tragedies. "How many of these cases did you get before the last two months?"

He manipulated the hologram. "Two."

"And in the last two months?"

"Fifty."

"That one," Lilith said. "We have one more autopsy to perform." That demon had died of a similar gunshot wound.

In the clinical light of the morgue, Morgua stood over the cold steel autopsy table. Each corpse, he found, told the same tale of death—a silent but lethal cascade of multiple organ failures. A little more digging and they realized all the dead bodies that had come in the last two months had the same issues.

"Bio-weapons research," Lilith proposed, her tone grim.

"There is no way this could happen without us knowing," Senet said.

Lilith bit her lower lip.

First, the assassination of Lucifer, then an attempt on my life, and now this mystery. The troubles piled up without pause. Her mind was full of disconnected thoughts, suspicion, fear, and countless dead-ends—a puzzle with an elusive missing piece.

"There is something you should know," Senet said.

"What?" Lilith opened her eyes wide.

"This looks like the Blight. There have been multiple cases in Masina. People not healing from injuries. Kapten Eliakim had symptoms before he died."

"What?" Lilith exclaimed.

"It was all unconfirmed rumors." Senet glanced at the ground. "I did not think it was relevant until now." She relayed the whispers of a strange ailment slowly pervading Masina, rumors she'd initially dismissed.

"This is far graver than I expected," Lilith murmured, barely above a whisper.

She twisted her wrist, bringing up a holographic interface on her watch. With a flick of her fingers, a three-dimensional model of Ode to Babel, the name she had gotten from Morgua's memory, materialized. "We need to go here. Now," she commanded, her finger tracing the spectral image.

"We had a deal. Get in, get out," Senet said. "I have held up my end. We should take this information to Masina City. Bring others in."

"And say we illegally broke into a military morgue of our allies?" Lilith scoffed. "How well do you think that is going to go?"

"What are we going to achieve by following this lead?"

"I don't know yet. But we need to—"

"Go there." Senet rolled her eyes as she completed Lilith's sentence. "Got it. What about that one?" Senet pointed to Morgua.

His eyes widened in surprise, mirroring his naïve hope that he might have slipped their attention. Cornered and fearful, Morgua attempted to claw his way out, but the stark, unyielding wall behind him offered no reprieve.

"You will not remember this when you wake up," Lilith said as she grabbed his neck with both hands. Terror crossed his face as he struggled. He was weak from the previous blood draining, so she didn't need Senet to help hold him. When she sank her teeth into his neck, she focused on his most recent memories and drained them into her. He would remember nothing that had happened over the last few days when he woke up.

Senet had a less surprised look. However, an uneasiness forced its way into her posture. "Naaga is far. Embarking on two extensive journeys in such quick succession would drain me of my strength."

"Masina needs you." Lilith said.

21

THE EDEN PROTOCOL

*I*kenga slumped into the seat, his hand pressed against his throbbing, injured shoulder as he leaned back in the worn leather booth. They had brought him two levels lower, but the muffled hum of music still filtered down the stairs at the far end of the wall.

Zepar and the two other demons stood near the staircase, guns in hand, their postures alert and watchful. The door next to them creaked open, and the sharp click-clack of high heels punctuated the tense silence. Daeva strode in, her vibrant red hair catching the light. A metal flask swung from her hand, the contents sloshing faintly.

She slid into the booth beside him. "Please forgive the rough introduction," she said, her voice smooth as silk. "Lots of people are after us, and most of them have less noble intentions than yours."

Ikenga let out a sharp, humorless laugh that quickly turned into a painful cough. "Noble intentions? Those brutes nearly sent me to an early grave."

Daeva shot Zepar a pointed look, her eyes narrowing. "They can be a bit... enthusiastic sometimes. Their strong suits are more physical." Her expression turned serious. "You are bleeding internally. Faster than your body can heal."

The coppery tang in his mouth confirmed her words.

"Here." She unscrewed the top of the flask and placed it on the table, the metal clinking against the surface. She hesitated for a moment before sliding it toward him. "Drink it."

He flashed her an angry look, shoving it back.

"It will heal your shoulder," she insisted.

"My shoulder will heal itself."

"As you wish," she conceded, lifting her hand in mock surrender. When she reached for the flask, Ikenga caught her hand, his palm encircling her wrist. A faint tingle passed through him at the touch of her skin.

"Wait." He peered into her eyes, pretending he could discover her agenda by looking at them. He slid his hand off hers, tracing a path down to her fingers. Then he snatched the flask, uncapped it, and swallowed its contents in a single, hasty gulp. Gagging, he spat on the floor.

Daeva laughed out loud. "It's an acquired taste."

"Kalla!" Ikenga shouted, feeling something foreign invade his body. His veins throbbed as his shoulder pulsated, bones realigning, flesh knitting together. He screamed in agony. "What's happening to me?!" He tried to move but couldn't.

Daeva's expression remained calm, but her eyes held a glimmer of concern. "Don't fight it," she urged, her voice steady. "Let it work."

Ikenga stared at his hands in horror and disbelief as black flames flickered to life at his fingertips, dancing across his skin. "Get away from me!" he shouted, panic rising in his chest. "I don't want to hurt you."

The calm on Daeva's face dissolved into an expression of deep worry. She jumped up from her seat and backed away from the table. Zepar and the other demons gawked at him with their mouths open in awe.

"Calm yourself! Don't fight it!" Daeva cried out.

But it was too late. An inferno of black flame roared to life, engulfing Ikenga's body. The searing pain intensified as the fire consumed his skin, his screams echoing off the walls. Then something inside him snapped. The built-up pressure released itself in a violent burst, the flames exploding out in all directions, lighting up the room with an eerie, otherworldly glow.

As the flames neared Daeva, massive, white-feathered wings erupted from her back, ripping through her top as they unfurled. She dropped to one knee, and her wings formed a protective cocoon around her. Zepar and the other Dominion followed suit, shielding themselves as best they could. But Behemoth stood frozen, his jaw slack with shock.

The black flame devoured everything, reducing flesh, bone, and wood to ash within seconds. When the inferno finally died down, the room was a charred ruin, the air thick with acrid smoke and burnt flesh. Ikenga slumped to the floor, his body sprawled across the blackened remains of the booth.

Daeva stood, her wings flapping gently as the last flickers of fire and dust dissipated. She rushed to Ikenga's side, Zepar close on her heels.

"I told you not to mess with that stuff!" Zepar shouted in anger.

"He was going to die!" Daeva retorted unapologetically.

"What did you give me?" Ikenga croaked. He yearned to gesture at the charred remains of Behemoth, but found himself too weak to lift a finger. His consciousness ebbed away, retreating like a tide that might never rush back in. He closed his eyes. The end was coming. It was only a matter of time.

Daeva put her hands on his chest. "You are still alive," she said, as if declaring a mathematical fact. A faint smile graced her lips. Ikenga yearned to mirror it, but his body remained frozen, unyielding to his will. Yet, his senses were painfully acute; each nerve electrified, buzzing with a raw intensity. It was good he could not move because he may have cried and screamed in front of her. The only thing that would have stopped everyone upstairs from rushing down was the booming music.

"I'm not usually the type of girl to make the first move," she said. "But we will make an exception this time."

His gaze locked onto hers, the world slowing as her face neared.

What may have lasted mere seconds stretched out endlessly. He closed his eyes and opened them, but the moment had not passed. Their lips touched. Even though he could not move, his heart beat faster. Her kiss sparked a surge, rippling through him like lightning. He jerked as she forced her tongue into his mouth. She violated him. The sensation was intoxicating. Her taste was a complex blend of tart lime and sweet apple, a contradiction he found irresistible. Her arms gripped his sides gently but firmly as her kiss intensified. He jerked more. Motion slowly returned to his hands, then his toes. A surge of energy rushed through him. She was pushing herself, or something else, into him.

His mind raced, struggling to comprehend the sensations coursing through him, like the heady rush from the mysterious potion he'd drunk but devoid of its punishing aftermath. Summoning every ounce of his remaining strength, he fought against an inexplicable weariness to raise his hand. His muscles protested, but he persevered, placing his hand on her head and drawing her nearer. At that moment, he could not fathom why he acted so impulsively. He felt an illusion of control, yet his actions were driven by an unseen force. As their kiss continued, more movement returned to his body. Then she placed her hands on his chest and shoved him back to the floor.

"No, don't stop!" His plea filled the air as he tried to stand, an effort to close the sudden distance. When he got close to her, she put her hand on his chest and shoved him back to the floor again.

A low grunt escaped him as he assessed his shoulder, a surprising vigor surging within him. Regaining his voice, he stammered, "What did you... what did you do?"

"Save your life," she said. "What you just did will attract unwanted attention. We must leave."

The fire in his hand had burned black for the first time.

"Every second we waste puts our lives at risk." Her voice was a whisper, yet the undercurrent of determination was unmistakable.

He was tired of being jerked around by people who always acted like they knew more than he did. "I'm not going anywhere."

She looked at him in bewilderment. "Do you want to die? Or do you want to live?"

"I want the truth. All of it."

"If Zepar and I walk up those stairs, you will not last in this city," she said.

"If you could leave, you would have already," Ikenga said.

She shifted on her feet, then crouched low next to him. "What do you want to know?"

"We don't have time for this!" Zepar exclaimed.

Daeva flashed him an angry glare. "Do you have a better way to get him to come with us?"

He shrugged and stepped back.

"Is it true that demons are plotting with Loas in Vodun?" Ikenga asked.

"Yes," she said

It was the answer he expected, but it still took him aback. "To what end?"

"Hell is dying. Some of its inhabitants plan to invade Kirina and take your home."

"Invade Kirina?" It was a similar story to what the Vodun man had said. *Maybe he had not lied. Or perhaps they were working together.*

"Yes, that is what I said," she snapped, irritated.

"How many demons?"

"I don't know."

"I don't believe you," he countered, finally rising from the ground. "Why would the Loas betray their realm, their people?"

"I don't pretend to understand the inner workings of your kind. I have been in hiding for over six months. Many things could have changed," she muttered.

"Convenient," Ikenga said.

"About a hundred miles north of here, in Aamaris. Asmodeus rules the United Hordes of Aamaris. He united over ten thousand clans. You understand that significance, coming from a nation where many tribes could never work together until recently." She picked up a board from the ground and snapped it in two. "Asmodeus's ambition has not always translated into results. But no one here or in your realm rivals it."

"You are an excellent storyteller. The way you string words together."

"How—" she started.

"I may not be a Navigator, but I know no living being can move that many people across worlds. And the Brokers would never agree to help him."

"My task was to stoke division in Kirina, cause unrest, and start a civil war," she said.

Ikenga raised an eyebrow. "Amadioha's rebellion?"

Nodding, she exhaled. "It's not just Niri that yearns for independence from Vodun. Fear holds many back. Amadioha was one of several we identified as potential chaos agents to destabilize your realm. We scoured Vodun for vulnerabilities, discreetly passing on what we found to select individuals."

Disbelief washed over Ikenga, his jaw slackening. He struggled to digest her words, reluctant to accept them as truth.

"All the water that flows through Rada Mysters goes through a single source," she continued. "We covertly informed one of Amadioha's scouts about this. Amadioha's fury took over from there. He believes his battle is for Niri, but in reality, he's serving our cause."

"If what you say is true, we must go back now. You must tell them everything you have told me."

"The first place we need to go is out of here before someone comes looking for us," she stressed. She tossed the broken board across the room. "We can talk more upstairs. We need to figure out our plan of escape."

Ikenga nodded. He didn't trust her. Not in the slightest. But he didn't have any other options. Legba would know what to do. But now that he thought of it, he didn't trust Legba either. He strode past her, stopping abruptly just two feet away. "Don't presume for a moment that this conversation is over."

SENET'S VOICE WAS NONCHALANT, her eyes roving, methodically inspecting everyone occupying the bar. "If you tell me what we are looking for, I can help you find it," she said

Inside Ode to Babel, they had staked out their corner for nearly an hour. The bar hummed with an infectious energy as patrons floated in and out.

Lilith rubbed her temples, her brow furrowed. "I'll let you know when I figure it out myself," she muttered.

Senet shrugged. "The law of averages," she said. "Someone will—"

A tall, dark, solidly built man entered the bar and stole her attention. Leather strips wrapped around his waist and chest. He glanced around inquisitively before heading to the bar.

"Him," Senet said.

"Him what?"

"Him is who you are looking for."

"How could you possibly know that?"

"There's a story in everyone's eyes. His reek of anxiety and unfamiliarity," Senet said. "I could see he is nervous and not from around here."

Lilith perked up. "What is he doing here?"

"Probably something in relation to the thing you are looking for, but I don't know."

The man bumped into a girl, got into a mini-altercation, and eventually made his way to the bar with her.

"Our alive-and-dead demon has stitched herself together since the morgue," Senet said.

Lilith gawked as the man talked to the same demon they had just dissected. The man occasionally glanced around the room, but Lilith made sure not to make eye contact. "We need to intercept now."

Senet arched her brow. "What about an airstrike while we're at it?"

Lilith gave her a wry look.

"We're flying blind here," Senet persisted, her fingers tapping restlessly on the table. "There are too many unknowns."

"I will be the judge of that," Lilith said.

"So, what is your plan?"

"Your constant stream of words is interrupting my thoughts."

Time ticked by as they watched the bar's comings and goings, their whispered arguments punctuating the lulls in conversation. Despite their best efforts, a consensus eluded them.

"We can wait till he leaves and apprehend them outside," Lilith said.

"Have you forgotten we are part of the Masina Military?" Senet asked.

They lapsed into a cycle of bickering and observation, their attention divided between their quarrel and the patrons enjoying the music. The man got up and walked away from the bar toward the back before disappearing downstairs. Daeva followed soon after.

An hour might have passed when they felt a muffled but perceptible shake. The loud bass music nearly masked it, but there was no mistaking the vibration.

Lilith started to ask for confirmation, but Senet was already nodding, confirming she had noticed it too. For the first time that night, they were on the same page. They rose from their seats and wove through the crowd, pushing their way to the back of Ode to Babel, where the stairs were located.

"In and out," Lilith said.

"I've heard that one before." Senet rolled her eyes.

The stairs led them down a winding path, the air growing colder with each step, their footfalls echoing softly in the stillness. Lilith's nerves were on edge, every shadow a potential threat.

Couches filled the ground floors, and dim lights lit the room. At the end were various bathroom doors. It was otherwise empty. There were voices coming from down the stairs.

"One level down," Senet said.

They headed down more cautiously. The voices got louder as they neared the ground floor.

The undead Daeva and the man stood with two other demons. Lilith recognized the military bearing in their stances. She put her hands to her lips, facing Senet, and motioned to move to the left of the room. Boxes around the center helped to conceal them in the shadows.

Barely a few steps to the side, she knocked over a stray can she had missed in the darkness.

The group turned to face Lilith and Senet in unison.

"Who are you?" one demon demanded. Then, for a moment, no one moved. The demon went to his holstered gun. Lilith reacted instantly, her own weapon already in hand. She fired, the bullet finding its mark on the demon's head.

Kalla! Things were about to get crazy.

∼

BOTH WOMEN HAD RED EYES, almost as bright as Daeva's hair. **Ikenga** watched in shock as one demon, the shorter one, drew her weapon and fired a bullet straight into the head of Zepar's companion. The gruesome sight sent a chill down his spine, and Bartholomew's memories reminded him that a well-placed shot from such a weapon could end his life—an outcome he might have embraced mere weeks ago, before his newfound sense of purpose.

Ikenga brought his hands together, conjuring black flames that burst to life between his palms. As he pivoted, he thrust his arms forward, unleashing the inferno upon the two demon intruders. The blaze roared with an intensity that matched his resolve. As the black fire surged toward the female demons, their wings unfurled from their backs, forming a protective barrier. The flames swirled and danced around their wings, yet the demons emerged unscathed.

Daeva and Zepar followed, opening fire on the intruders. The demons' wings provided some protection against the onslaught of bullets, but the relentless barrage forced them to seek cover behind the nearby boxes.

"Take cover!" Daeva grasped Ikenga's hand, and they sprinted for the far end of the room, desperately seeking refuge from their exposed position.

The air filled with deafening gunshots as Zepar and the intruders engaged in a fierce gunfight. Amid the mayhem, Ikenga's heart nearly stopped when Daeva screamed, not once, but twice. He turned to her, his pulse pounding in his ears, just in time to see her crumple to the ground, blood spurting from her wounds.

Without hesitation, he lunged for her, dragging her across the floor toward safety. Mere moments before reaching cover, a searing pain tore through his leg as a bullet found its mark. White-hot agony coursed through his veins, but he gritted his teeth, determined to bring them both to shelter.

Ikenga's voice strained as he yelled over the relentless hail of gunfire, "We're trapped! Who are they?"

"Eden Protocol!" Daeva shouted back. "More will be coming."

The gravity of their situation hit Ikenga like a freight train. Without hesitation, he hoisted Daeva up, and they hobbled deeper into the room, seeking any semblance of safety.

As he witnessed Daeva's uncharacteristic vulnerability, unfamiliar emotions surged through him, feelings he couldn't grasp or untangle in the heat of the moment. More bullets flew through the air, followed by Zepar's agonizing scream. He was down, leaving Ikenga and Daeva alone in their desperate fight for survival.

"Do you trust me?" Amid the ensuing chaos, Daeva's whisper grazed Ikenga's ear, her words a fervent plea.

"Do I have a choice?" Ikenga's heart raced as he replied.

"I need you to open your heart."

Confusion and fear gripped Ikenga. "What does that mean?"

"Open your heart!" Daeva pressed. "Or we both die. Release all your inhibitions and let me in." With a determined yet gentle touch, she slipped her hand beneath his shirt, her palm resting against his chest.

An unfamiliar sensation washed over Ikenga as if Daeva were merging her very essence with his, intertwining her being with the very fibers of his soul. His body resisted instinctively, unsure of the foreign presence attempting to forge an intimate connection.

"Let me in," Daeva whispered.

Ikenga risked a glance beyond their makeshift barrier, his heart pounding as the two female demons charged toward them, their weapons lowered. The realization that they wanted him alive sent a chill down his spine, fear gripping him more tightly than the threat of bullets.

Taking a deep breath, Ikenga surrendered to Daeva's touch, embracing the warmth that emanated from her, reminiscent of their kiss. Her essence intertwined with his, as if she were simultaneously pushing herself into him and pulling him out of his physical form.

"They are getting away!" one demon shouted.

The room blurred around them, and the bullets whizzed past, but their physical forms had already started dissipating. At that moment, comprehension struck him—Daeva, like Legba, was a Navigator.

Senet's voice rang out with urgency as Daeva and the man slipped away, their forms fading into the ether. "We need to stop them! I can follow their Noise."

Lilith's instincts warred with the desire to give chase. "It's too dangerous," she cautioned, her eyes narrowing. "It might be a trap." Her gaze shifted to the lone demon crawling on the floor, clinging to life by a thread. A calculating smile played across her lips. "Plus, we have what we need right here."

Senet's expression hardened. "Do it quickly," she said. "The music upstairs is loud, but someone could have seen us."

Lilith's teeth sank into the demon's flesh, and a flood of memories surged into her mind, transporting her to a distant place and time.

She found herself in Aamaris, standing amid a sprawling military compound. Row upon row of barracks stretched before her, each one filled to the brim with soldiers. They used buildings built from Krinote rocks, similar to what she had seen in Sharik Hora. The sheer number left her breathless—hundreds of thousands, ready to march at a moment's notice.

She learned the demon was called Zepar. Lilith focused her attention on a specific memory, one in which Zepar stood before a man who could only be Asmodeus, the King of Aamaris himself.

"Do you understand your mission?" Asmodeus asked.

"Yes, commander! Our forward team is already in Masina."

"Excellent," Asmodeus said.

Ten other demons stood around Zepar—military-trained but not part of regular Aamaris military.

As Lilith emerged from the memory, shock coursed through her veins, chilling her to the bone. *Invasion? But who was the target?* She glanced up at Senet, who was watching her intently.

"I don't think he can take much more," Senet warned, her eyes flicking to Zepar's convulsing form.

Lilith knew Senet was right, but the unanswered questions burned within her. With a determined set to her jaw, she sank her teeth into Zepar's flesh once more, delving deeper into his memories.

The skies above were clear, but the sun hung low on the horizon. Judging from the scenery, they couldn't be too far from the location of Lucifer's funeral. A nagging doubt tugged at Lilith's mind—why would Asmodeus need such a vast army if his plan was merely to attack the funeral? There had to be something else at play, a larger scheme she had yet to uncover.

Frustration mounted as Lilith realized Zepar's rank was too low to provide the crucial information she sought. She traversed his memories in vain, gleaning only fragments of his life and training within this secret camp. That they had kept such a massive operation hidden from Masina's watchful eyes only deepened the mystery.

As Lilith withdrew her teeth from the demon, she turned to face Senet, her expression grave. "This is bad. Very bad."

"Level with me." Senet's brow furrowed.

Lilith took a deep breath. "They have been assembling a secret army for decades now. Their numbers are in the hundreds of thousands."

"How did we miss that?" Disbelief flashed across Senet's face.

Lilith shook her head, her mind racing as she contemplated their next steps. "Their stealth technology is far more advanced than what we saw at Sharik Hora. We must take this to the Upper Council."

"Did you forget this is a rogue mission? We would get court-martialed immediately."

"The future of Masina is more important than ours," Lilith said. "If our military careers end, so be it."

∽

THE WORLD around them snapped back into focus and **Ikenga** stood amid an unfamiliar landscape of soaring peaks and craggy slopes. A blast of hot air hit him, the temperature a lot higher than he had ever experienced.

Gasping for breath, Ikenga choked out, "I can't... breathe."

Daeva cast him a worried glance, her confusion apparent. "Flares!" she exclaimed.

Leaning against a boulder, Daeva steadied her wavering form. Her labored breathing was evidence that her condition was not much better than his. She grabbed Ikenga's hand and dragged him along a narrow path. Being so close to her made him tolerate the environment better. With each breath, he inhaled her essence directly.

Once they sought shelter under an overhanging cliff, Daeva extended her wings, their impressive span blocking out the already scant light.

"Come closer," she urged.

Ikenga moved closer. Her wings curled around him like a protective cocoon. He carefully removed his shirt, their skin making contact as she pulled him closer. The world outside vanished as she enveloped him.

Ikenga forced himself to steady his breathing, each inhalation drawing in her essence.

The intimacy of their proximity, his face resting next to hers, filled him with a tranquility he hadn't experienced in a long time.

22
THE NIRI ALLIANCE
REALM OF KIRINA

The flickering light from a solitary lantern inside the tent cast eerie shadows over the assembled faces. Ojukwu, having called the War Ezes together for an urgent late-night gathering, was absent, leaving a heavy shroud of tension in the air. **Amadioha**, Namudi, and Ekwensu stood apart from the rest, who scattered themselves, deeply engrossed in their discussions.

Namudi sighed, running a hand over his weary face before murmuring, "These past two weeks... they have been unlike any hell we have ever faced."

Ekwensu nodded. "The losses we sustained since leaving Niri surpass those of the entire secession war."

"I do not wish to hear things I already know," Amadioha snapped.

"There are grumblings," Ekwensu said. "Ezes are losing their faith in your mission."

"We are at war," Amadioha said. "I want the Ezes to fight, not worship."

Ekwensu's voice softened. "Have you already forgotten our shared struggles? Just this week, Vodun forces ambushed us twice. Your brazen tactics do not work well when we are far from familiar terrain."

Amadioha's gaze shifted, locking onto Ekwensu with an intensity that pierced through the dimness. "Is it the rest of the Ezes, or the two of you, who waver in your convictions?"

Deep lines of concern creased Ekwensu's forehead, his eyes darting nervously. He sought reassurance from Namudi, but the latter's stoic silence and unwavering gaze only intensified the heavy atmosphere. "We have many scouts who have not returned; our rations are dwindling, and our men are not as sharp anymore. We want to go home. It has been a grueling journey. Every extra day we stay, we tell another wife, husband, and child that their loved ones will never return."

"Every man in our army should be ready to die. Every Niri baby will be born free, knowing it is better to die for freedom than to live in slavery. Something we long forgot before this war. We must stand here strong now and forever."

Ekwensu motioned like he was about to respond when a jarring commotion erupted outside. The coarse shouts and frantic pounding outside the tent silenced him.

Amadioha and Ekwensu stepped out first.

Ojukwu, standing some distance away, lashed out in a fit of rage, sending a stand of gleaming spears crashing to the ground, their clatter echoing the palpable tension. Two men, their distinct Anaku tribal markings clear, rushed forward, arms outstretched to pacify him. As they got closer to him, Ojukwu saw Amadioha just as Amadioha saw Zara. Amadioha and Zara's eyes locked for a fleeting moment, a silent exchange so profound it was an eternity's worth of conversation. A storm of emotions swirled in her gaze—pain, confusion, perhaps even a trace of bitterness.

With a roar, Ojukwu lunged at Amadioha, his approach reminiscent of a bull at full charge. With each step, more parts of his skin turned from flesh to rock. He knocked away everything in his path, including one man from his camp. By the time Amadioha's brain had fully processed the scene, it was too late. Zara's haunting confession cut him deeper than any blade.

This world really hath no fury like a woman scorned.

Ojukwu's imposing, stocky frame, with muscles rippling under the skin, often misled foes into underestimating his agility. Amadioha made no such mistake. Yet his brain took too long to assess the situation. By the time Ojukwu's fist reached Amadioha's face, he had just inched backward. Ojukwu's hand turned to rock as it connected, sending Amadioha flying into the air. He broke his fall with his hand, but the pain radiated through his body. Instinct took over as he rolled across the floor to regain his composure.

Ojukwu jumped and slammed his two fists into where Amadioha had just been. The ground quaked, yielding a deep imprint where Ojukwu's stone-clad fist struck with formidable force. After that, it was punch after punch. Amadioha was ready for the first few and blocked and parried them, but the next one came too quickly, and he was flying again. He landed on the floor, breaking his fall a little better. Crimson blood and a chipped tooth stained the ground.

Amadioha's eyes crackled with building power as Ojukwu swung his granite fist again. He released a torrent of white lightning, but it barely staggered the hulking man with an upper body of hardened stone. With a guttural roar, Ojukwu gathered himself and lunged again. Amadioha thrust out his hands, blasting his foe with a bigger burst of electricity. The discharge slammed Ojukwu to his knees, skin smoking. But he resisted the onslaught, struggling back to his feet. Step by agonizing step, Ojukwu marched through Amadioha's lightning, weathering it through sheer fury. Amadioha's power lagged. He had to end it before Ojukwu's unfathomable rage overcame him.

"Stay your hand!" Amadioha demanded.

"You will die for what you did," he retorted.

"I stand accused of a crime I do not know."

"You have done what no man should ever do to a woman. And now you have stained my wife's honor. For that desecration, you will pay dearly."

Why would she do this?

The words hit Amadioha hard. He had suspected she had told Ojukwu about their adultery. But he never thought she would lie. It was a momentary lapse in concentration—enough for Ojukwu to pick up momentum. The second hit, on the other side of his face, was harder than the first. Amadioha flew into the air again. Too winded to break his fall, he landed straight on his shoulder with a loud crack. In a primal fury, Ojukwu leaped, driving Amadioha's head into the unforgiving ground, the sickening cracks echoing the severity of the impact. Ojukwu raised his hand to finish him. Amadioha's life flashed before him as the hands came down. He was supposed to die a warrior's death, not be killed by his brethren. Just as Ojukwu's hands began their deadly descent, a blaze of blue light burst forth, illuminating the space and arresting his motion. The force catapulted him away from Amadioha, causing him to tumble across the ground.

Ijele stepped over Amadioha's head, stood tall, and faced Ojukwu. Standing defiantly with her chin lifted, her voice resonated with authority, "Have we become mere beasts, or do we still stand as a nation governed by laws?"

"That wretch you call a husband violated my wife's honor. By every right, I should end his life."

"In which court has this been proven? Are you judge and executioner?"

Ojukwu growled, his breath coming in ragged pants, evidence of his physical and emotional exertion; the toll of wielding such raw magic had profoundly drained his vigor.

"Koca ci! To hell with rules. You and your wretched husband... if our paths cross again, I swear on the souls here and those to come. He is a dead man." He stormed off in the opposite direction.

Ijele turned and crouched beside Amadioha. Blood and saliva mixed as he spoke, each word a labor.

"You saved me," he said. Pain lanced through him, more pronounced than he first thought. His hand, trembling and smeared with dirt, reached out, silently begging for her help.

Her eyes, usually so full of warmth, searched his for truth. "Did you do it?"

"Of course, I did not soil her!"

"That was not the question I asked. Did you do it?"

Amadioha sagged, a lump forming in his throat that he struggled to clear.

A solitary tear escaped, trickling down her cheek. She stood, casting a lingering, sorrowful glance at him before heading opposite Ojukwu's path. He reached out, yearning to pull her back, but a sharp, searing pain in his shoulder forced his hand to falter and drop. "Wait," he rasped.

~

"GET ME... THOSE THREE OVER THERE." The voice was distant, like a soft echo carried by the wind. Amadioha opened his eyes to see Ijele's blurry face leaning over him. She massaged his forehead ever so gently. He closed his eyes again and tried shifting his body. He didn't have control of his legs.

"The green herbs, not the blue!" Ijele corrected.

Her eyes were wider than normal, and there was no tattoo on the left side of her face. He realized it was Afua, his head healer, tending to him. He turned his head to the left. Needles delivered various fluids to his hands and legs. Metal stands propped up the bags.

"Ah, you are awake," Afua's lips curled up awkwardly, revealing a lopsided grin.

Amadioha tried to form words, but a sharp stab of pain cut him short.

"Save your energy," she said as she patted his head. "You came out of a one-on-one fight with Ojukwu and are still alive. That itself is cause for celebration." She replaced a bag feeding yellow liquid into his abdomen.

"How bad am I?" he said.

"Your injuries are extensive. Fractured ribs, a cracked skull, and even some pierced organs," Afua paused, eyeing him, "the base of your spine was also crushed."

Amadioha grunted and looked toward the other side of the room.

"Thankfully, I got to you early," she said. "You should fully recover, but your legs won't work for a while."

As memories and thoughts swirled in his head, Afua's words became a distant murmur to Amadioha, but he mustered the energy to give her a weak nod. When the blurriness in his vision receded, the ambient sounds grew sharper—the soft rustle of Damballa's clothes, the distant echoes of footsteps outside.

Afua continued talking to him, but he tuned her out.

'There were moments when I believed we had lost you.' Damballa's thoughts resonated in Amadioha's mind.

'You will not get rid of me that easily,' Amadioha thought back.

The corners of Damballa's lips turned slightly, an amused glint in his eyes.

'Afua is optimistic about my recovery.'

'I noticed.'

'When does the army move?'

'You need rest,' Damballa thought. *'We can discuss these details when you are better.'*

'Do not treat me like a child ever again. I might be bedridden, but I am still your Eze.'

Damballa nodded. *'The army is not advancing.'*

'Ojukwu! He took advantage of my absence to take control of the council.'

'Ojukwu left with his army shortly after your fight. The other Ezes left and followed him home of their own accord.'

'Which Ezes?'

'All of them.'

"You are lying," Amadioha said out loud. He used his hands to push his torso up.

Afua protested and tried to pull him back down. "Do you want never to walk again? This is not the time to be stubborn!"

"Leave us!" Amadioha shouted.

She glanced at Damballa, who nodded. With her head bowed, she hurried out of the room.

"Tell me you are lying," Amadioha said.

"All the Ezes are gone. Your fight re-solidified the alliance. Unfortunately, against you."

Darkness crept at the edges of Amadioha's vision, the room spinning as a wave of dizziness overtook him. "Zara fed Ojukwu lies and poisoned his mind," Amadioha said.

"Lies? Maybe. But it was a push to have the others move in a direction they already wanted to go."

"What about our people? Have they left too?"

"The warriors of Canis are loyal and awaiting your command," Damballa declared.

Amadioha breathed a sigh of relief. He lay back down, his gaze fixed on the ceiling. The sting of defeat gnawed at him, a shadow he hadn't danced with before. His men may have stayed, but he would lose his legacy and respect if he walked back to Niri with his mission abandoned. Word would spread. He would be weak. They would be weak. What did that mean for them and Vodun? Yet retreat was still somehow better than death.

"What is our next move, my Eze?" Damballa's voice was thick with concern.

"What would you do?"

"I am not Eze."

"I know that, you fool. But if you were, what would you do?"

"The reason I have no ambitions ever to be Eze is because I never want to have the burden of leadership," Damballa said.

"Koca ci!" Amadioha waved him off.

"Even with the entire Niri army, taking the castle would have been hard. What plan will you pull out of your arse this time?" Damballa asked.

"We cannot retreat. We cannot show weakness."

"We have two impossible options."

In the corner, a lonely wheelchair sat, its metallic surface gleaming faintly. "I need to consult with Ijele. We will talk tomorrow."

"But what will I tell the men?" Damballa asked. "Without direction, they are testy, nervous."

"Tell them nothing. They can be testy and nervous for another day."

Damballa nodded and pushed the wheelchair toward him. With a grimaced motion, Amadioha pulled out the needles embedded in his side and stomach. Depending on Damballa for assistance, gnawed at his pride even for a moment. Once outside the room, Afua protested they should leave him there, but they ignored her.

∼

As Amadioha wheeled into his tent, an unexpected emptiness greeted him. Ijele was gone. Not only was she missing, but so were all her things—clothes, weapons, medicine—she had removed everything of hers from the tent. The space, devoid of her familiar scents and the memories they shared, was alien and unwelcoming.

"I am sorry," Damballa said.

At the entrance, Damballa watched as Amadioha, in his wheelchair, frantically sifted through the belongings, seeking any trace of her.

"I didn't know how to tell you, so I thought you should see for yourself," he said. "She left shortly after all the Ezes."

The news thrust a cold dagger into Amadioha's heart. "To go where?"

"She ordered us not to follow her."

"And you just let her go?" His voice roared with betrayal, eyes flashing with electric fury lighting the tent. The pain from magic consumed him. He took a deep breath and toppled onto the floor. Damballa rushed to help him up, but Amadioha swatted his hand away.

"How could you let her go?" Tears streamed down his face, each drop echoing his heartbreak.

"I sent our best trackers after her. But her skills were unparalleled; she lost them."

23

KAL MYSTERS

The campfire had burnt out, emitting only wisps of smoke but no warmth. At the peak of the night, moonlight bathed the forest, casting an eerie silver glow on the trees. A chill permeated the air as the temperature continued to drop.

Damballa leaned against a towering ferra tree, while Ironsi, Omoro, and Reebell sat on fallen logs around the dying fire. They had stopped to rest in a small clearing within the dense forest. Omoro, the chief magician, wore a pensive expression. Ironsi, the chief scout, clutched his weapon, eyes scanning the woods.

"It's been five days now," Reebell said, breaking the silence. "Amadioha still hasn't shown himself."

Omoro and Ironsi nodded grimly, clearing their throats.

"He will appear when the time is right," Damballa replied, an unusual weariness in his voice. His typically spiked hair hung limply around his face. A full beard obscured his strong jawline, resulting from many sleepless nights. Though Damballa hid his torment well, he had suffered the most while waiting for their leader.

"Koca ci!" Reebell burst out. "Is Amadioha even alive? How can we trust a leader who abandons us in enemy territory for five days? We are vulnerable out here, yet he cowers and refuses to show his face!" Reebell seized a stone and hurled it violently into the dark forest.

"At any moment, the Vodun army could descend upon us!" Ironsi warned.

Damballa raised a silencing hand, his gaze cold and hard. "Think before you speak further. Remember your oath."

Ironsi's voice quivered in resentment. "Our loyalty, our allegiance, was promised to our Eze. Not to an absent leader."

Damballa, nostrils flaring, countered, "Amadioha is the Eze you vowed to serve!"

Ironsi leaned in closer. "Join us, side with our vote. We have the strength to overthrow him," he said.

Damballa's eyes flashed as he unsheathed an axe, its blade glinting. "You tread on perilous grounds."

Reebell chuckled. "Ah, Damballa Weddo, ever the staunch protector of Amadioha," he said, smirking. "You would spill our blood for treason yet remain blind to a leader who has left us vulnerable."

Omoro's eyes, a vivid blue mirroring his hair, shimmered with unshed tears. "We owe it to our people, to Canis, to Niri," he said, rising from his seat. "You would silence those who dare challenge his flawed leadership?"

"There is always a plan, even if it's hidden from our sight."

"A plan, you say?" Reebell leaned in until his face was inches from Damballa's. "Perhaps a strategy of prolonging our inevitable defeat? To protect his pride?"

"Everything Amadioha does, he does for his ego," Ironsi said.

A simmering rage bubbled inside Damballa, directed at the defiant men, at his helpless situation, but mainly at the elusive Amadioha. The very leader who'd kept him in the shadows, making him feel as lost as the rest. Yet, he would bite his tongue before revealing that vulnerability.

"Each of you has stood by Amadioha for years. Reebell, how many have you served?"

"Five," Reebell muttered.

Damballa turned to Omoro. "And you? You served his father too, didn't you?"

Omoro nodded. "Seven with Amadioha, and many more with his father."

Damballa looked at Ironsi expectantly.

"A decade of knowing him, many more beside him," he said.

Damballa's gaze swept over them. "Together, almost twenty years. Remember Rada Mysters? Remember the naysayers? Had we heeded their fears, where would we be now?"

With a heavy sigh, Reebell retreated a step, letting himself collapse onto a fallen log. His voice cracked with bitterness. "Everyone else has left us in the lurch. Even his wife."

Damballa cleared his throat. "Nwanne, our vows to each other are stronger than any in marriage. It is tied in blood."

Ironsi scoffed, "So, what are you saying? We should wait here indefinitely while he plays with his balls?"

Damballa locked eyes with each man. "One day. That's all I'm asking. Then I will consider everything, including your treasonous ideas."

Reebell's gaze searched Omoro's face for agreement, then shifted to Ironsi, their eyes locked in an unspoken debate. He moved to Damballa and outstretched his hand. "One day."

"And both of you?" Damballa implored, his eyes darting between Omoro and Ironsi. They rose, their boots crunching on the ground as they approached. They shook his hand and disappeared into the forest.

Damballa pressed his back to the tree, the rough bark biting his skin. His heart hammered in his chest, a frantic rhythm against the eerie silence. He took a series of deep, deliberate breaths, steadying himself before even thinking of approaching Amadioha again. Reebell, with his ever-shifting eyes and secretive meetings, had long harbored ambitions to wrench the rule from Amadioha by force. Damballa knew because it was his job to know. He had promised them a mere twenty-four hours, but uncertainty gnawed at him in the depth of his heart—would he ever find the words, or the chance, to reach out to Amadioha?

~

IN THE MOST secluded corner of the settlement, where the pungent aroma of burning firewood hung heavy in the air, Amadioha's tent stood apart from the others. Eight men formed a protective ring around it, their eyes gleaming with alertness. As he neared, they put their hands on their weapons but didn't draw. Their eyes traced his every footstep as if they were predicting the exact patch of grass he would step in next.

"I must see him now!" Damballa's voice carried a desperate edge, his eyes wide with urgency. He could fight them and lose. But maybe that would get Amadioha's attention.

"He has been awaiting your arrival," the taller guard said, his tone hinting at a smirk. They shifted, clearing the entrance.

Damballa gaped at them in shock. "Expecting me?"

The guard who had spoken frowned and stood back at attention.

Inside the tent, Damballa's breath caught as he took in the sight before him. Amadioha, far from the broken leader he'd feared, was a picture of vigor and vitality. Clad in his distinct red pants, the ceremonial markings on his chest and around his eyes signified his readiness for battle. He had fastened two smaller axes to his belt. In front of him was a map of Vodun with a circle around Kal Mysters, the capital. The presence of Ikenna, a scout, surprised him the most. Without shifting his focus from the map, Amadioha finally acknowledged Damballa. "You are just in time. Ikenna and I were planning our strategy to attack the Mysters."

"Attack?" Damballa's eyes widened. He glanced at Ikenna. "You were discussing a plan of attack with him?"

"Gather the men," Amadioha said. "We march toward the city tonight. With our smaller numbers, we can use the forests for cover and make our way undetected."

Damballa could not hide his confusion. "I thought... I thought we would order a retreat home."

"Retreat?" Amadioha narrowed his eyes. "When we have not yet won the war?"

Damballa's voice wavered. "With whom we have left, you must know an attack would be suicide." Hurt sharpened the edge in Damballa's voice as he directed an accusing glare at Ikenna.

"That is what people said of Rada—"

"Enough about Rada Mysters!" Damballa snapped. "That is what we keep talking about. That was not the capital. Rada Mysters was not expecting us. And we were not as outmatched as we are now. This is Kal Mysters, the home of the Bondye." A gnawing doubt took root in Damballa's mind: had Amadioha lost his wits, or had Ikenna fed him dangerous notions?

Taking a measured breath to calm the rising tension, Amadioha gestured toward Ikenna. "Share with him the intel you brought me."

"Yes, my Eze," Ikenna said. "Petro Perou Loa has requested assistance from the Bondye to deal with a rising insurrection up north. Kal Mysters has deployed most of the army to MawuLisa."

"Why would the Bondye desert his castle when our army is still here?" Damballa asked.

"The cowardly retreat of the other Ezes has served as an unintentional ruse," Amadioha said. "The Vodunese believe we have abandoned our mission. They do not know the fierce warriors of Canis still stand strong."

Damballa's breath caught in his throat, and an uneasy feeling traveled through his gut. "The Vodunese detected our retreating army, and they just let them go?"

"Of course not," Amadioha smirked. "Most of what remains of Ghede Ghadou's army is chasing them through Hohos, trying to intercept before they reach Niri. The thought of attacking Gede Mysters even crossed my mind." Amadioha let out a laugh. Ikenna followed.

Damballa's expression remained stoic as he did everything in his power to contain his frustration. "You must give the order. We have to rush to their aid."

With a stern frown and an imperious wave, Amadioha challenged him, "Who is the leader of this army? You or me?"

"We cannot abandon our nwanne," Damballa said.

"The same kin who turned their backs on us?"

"We were not about to—"

"Ikenna, tell him the rest," Amadioha interrupted.

"Even if Ghede Ghadou catches them, they should be able to beat him easily."

"You cannot risk their lives on speculation!"

Amadioha raised his hand, silencing Damballa. He seethed under his breath, but remained silent.

"When we take the castle, Ghede Ghadou will be duty-bound to turn around and re-take it," Ikenna continued with an annoying smirk.

"If we take it," Damballa interjected.

"Doubt is a fire that ravages a forest," Amadioha snapped. "Remove that from this room."

Ikenna looked to Amadioha, who nodded in approval for him to continue.

"Ojukwu and the Ezes are too far for us to help. Taking the castle is the only way to help them," he said.

"You see," Amadioha said to Damballa, "the element of surprise is on our side yet again."

"This is Kal Mysters, not a random Vodunese outpost! You sentence all of us to die," Damballa said.

"Chineke does not favor any warrior entering battle plagued with thoughts of defeat!"

"I..." Damballa tried to hold back his words. "I... I want to talk to you in private."

"Leave us. We shall reconvene later," Amadioha said to Ikenna.

Ikenna nodded. When he passed Damballa, he walked near the edge of the room and kept as much distance as possible.

"Tell me you're doing this for Niri," Damballa implored, "and not for your pride."

Amadioha's face flustered. "How dare you question me?"

"How dare you! You disappear for five days. Left me to deal with all of this... Then you come back with this crazy plan to take the capital and abandon the rest of the soldiers who fought with us during all the other wars? How dare you!"

"When we spoke last, you told me you did not want to be Eze. You said you were too weak to carry the burden." Amadioha moved around the table, closing the distance between him and Damballa, asserting his authority with every stride. "Well, I am Eze. And I have my burden to carry. And as long as I am your leader, and you are my subordinate, you do not question me like that."

Damballa's gaze dropped to the floor, a storm of emotions swirling within, yet the fiery anger still burned in his eyes.

"If you want to save the warriors who fought with us, do what I command and rally the army. Let us begin our move to take the capital."

Biting back his resentment, Damballa managed a strained, "Yes, my Eze," his words barely escaping through his gritted teeth.

~

THE FIRST RAYS of dawn crept over the horizon, bathing the imposing walls of Kal Mysters in a warm amber light. **Amadioha** stood at the edge of the forest, inhaling the morning dew as he gazed upon the stronghold. Massive walls encircled the fortress, broken only by an immense gate that stretched nearly to the parapets above. Sentry towers marked two corners, each looming twice as tall as the walls. A vast plain lay between the castle and the forest, with three roads converging on the stronghold. Perched atop a hill, Kal Mysters held the high ground against any assault. Its single gate was the only way in or out. No doubt the guards in the towers had already spied the Canis army at the forest's edge.

Amadioha, Reebell, Ironsi, and Damballa stood bare-chested,

their muscular torsos glistening in the sunlight. A cool breeze whispered through the trees, making their red pants rustle against their skin. White chalk marked their faces and bodies. An intricate crown sat atop Amadioha's head—the same one he had worn when Rada Mysters fell.

Damballa narrowed his eyes. "How are we to take that castle with a mere thousand men?"

"Our insider confirms only a handful of soldiers defend the place," Reebell said, adjusting his sword.

Amadioha chewed his lip. "How many exactly?"

"No more than a hundred," Reebell stated.

Damballa flashed with disbelief. "Are the Vodunese so foolish as to think such meager numbers can defend their capital?"

Amadioha shook his head. "Arrogant, yes. But never mistake them for fools."

"A hundred of our men have already infiltrated the city disguised as traders. They will dispatch any archers and open the gates for us. Kal Mysters falls today," Reebell declared.

"What about those sentry towers?" Amadioha asked. "We did not account for those."

"They were not there the last time our scouts assessed the defenses," Reebell admitted. "But they are too high for archers. I would not worry about them."

Amadioha's warm smile barely scratched the surface of the stormy sea of thoughts churning beneath. He glanced back for a second. The metallic ring of swords and axes being sharpened echoed across the forest, punctuated by occasional laughter and friendly banter, as most of the army made final preparations for the imminent war. Ever since they had set up camp at the forest's edge, Amadioha frequently cast glances back along the path, a knot of hope and regret in his chest, yearning for a glimpse of Ijele's return, hoping to see she had seen the error of her ways. But there was no sign of her now, as there was no sign of her then. She had planted the seed in his head and abandoned him as it grew.

Amadioha addressed his comrades. "Reebell, Damballa, Ironsi, remember when, many years ago, I asked you to join me on this quest to free our people from shackles? You were unwavering. Now, only this vast expanse of whispering grass stands between us and our destiny."

Reebell stepped forward. "In our very bones, we know our birthright: freedom. And we would do it again a thousand times more."

"After tonight, we will all go back to our families." Amadioha paused as his mind returned to Ijele.

"On the souls of my men, those fallen and those not yet born," everyone intoned. "I swear my allegiance until my life departs from this realm or our mission is complete. For our ancestors, those alive today, and those not yet born."

A surge of excitement coursed through Amadioha. Ojukwu and all the Ezes who had forsaken them would soon recognize their mistakes. It would be Canis seizing the castle, not Niri. And Ijele, she would beg to come back and stand by his side.

Amadioha's gaze sharpened, and with a fire in his eyes, he ordered, "Get the men in formation! We march to the wall, now!"

In minutes, the synchronized stomps and clattering armor announced that all thousand warriors were aligned, ready for the march.

"Kwenu!" Amadioha shouted.

"Kwenu!" The sheer power of their unified voices sent leaves rustling from nearby trees.

"Ke Kwenu!" Amadioha shouted.

"Ay ay ay ay!" all the men replied.

"My people of Niri, of Canis," Amadioha said. "My people of the Canis rebellion. Day after day, week after week, city after city, we have conquered. Today is the day we send the ultimate message."

"Ay ay ay ay ay!" all the men replied.

"If a snake fails to show its venom, little children will use it to tie firewood," he said. "Today, we will show Kal Mysters our venom!"

"Ay ay ay ay ay!" all the men replied.

"Our nwanne have left us." He swallowed hard. "My wife has left me." His tone of voice dropped. "Yet in the ashes of every letdown, a bird flaps its wings and flies! My people, will you answer my call?" Amadioha asked.

"With blood and anger!" they replied.

"We march forward!" He pointed his sword at the city walls. Urging his horse with a gentle prod, he backtracked to join Damballa and Reebell, allowing the frontline men to lead the march. Once the first file was ahead, the trio and the men behind them followed.

∼

THE THUD of hooves echoed across the expansive plain, their rhythm pulsing through Amadioha like a primal heartbeat. His gaze swept over the horde riding at his side, their faces set with grim determination. The raw energy of impending battle crackled in the air, raising the hair on his arms. Omoro rode just a hairbreadth behind him. Queen Mbaye's request made no sense, but he had learned not to doubt the words of someone who had glimpses of the future. Side by side, Damballa and Ironsi set the pace, leading a single file of soldiers, each brandishing a flag in one hand and a sword in the other. Their destination loomed ahead, so close Amadioha could taste it—a bittersweet mix of excitement and trepidation thick on his tongue.

Because of a shortage of horses, nearly three hundred men trailed behind on foot, their progress slower but no less determined.

As they closed in, the formidable stone walls of the Mysters grew from a distant smudge to an imposing barrier blocking the sky. Amadioha's ears caught the groan of hinges as the massive doors of the Mysters swung open. The Vodunese soldiers stationed at the forefront broke their formation. Their orderly ranks dissolved like ants as they retreated, their armor clanking as they scrambled for the dubious safety of the castle.

"See how they scatter before us, the cowards!" Amadioha let out a bark of laughter, his lips curled in a smug grin.

Reebell's smile was predatory. "Those walls will offer them no protection!"

Amadioha laid out the plan. "Once within the mages' range, they will—"

A searing flash of blue light severed his words. Three of their vanguard disintegrated before his eyes; their agonized screams cut short as their bodies dissolved into smoky wisps that drifted in the wind. Horrified gasps rippled through the ranks. Another flash, another trio of warriors gone, as Damballa's alarmed cry pierced the air. "Chineke!"

"The towers!" Ironsi shouted, his face pale as he pointed at the menacing black stone structures that loomed above the walls. His warning was his last act; the next flash targeted him, disintegrating him despite his futile attempt at a defense.

Amadioha saw a surge of blue light hurtling toward him—the harbinger of his end. But a hard shove sent him sprawling to the ground before it could claim him. Gasping, he rolled onto his back, blinking away the daze. Omoro stood over him, feet planted wide, his entire body rigid with effort. White light pulsed from his palms in rhythmic waves, each pulse making his arms tremble. Where his energy met the blue beams, the air crackled and hissed. "Sound the retreat!" Omoro's voice was strained, each second costing him energy. "Sound the retreat! Now!"

Amadioha struggled to his feet, his head spinning and ears ringing. The battlefield had transformed into a nightmare of flashing lights and screaming men. Through the chaos, Omoro's desperate shouts finally penetrated the fog of shock and confusion that gripped him.

"Fall back!" Omoro shouted. "We'll cover your retreat!"

Blue light from one tower continued to pound Omoro's shield, weakening him but allowing the other fleeing soldiers some reprieve. Amadioha was torn between his instinct to fight and the grim realization that they were outmatched. "Retreat to the forest!" He screamed at the top of his lungs.

What had been an orderly charge devolved into a frantic rout.

Horses wheeled and reared, their riders struggling for control. The foot soldiers turned and ran, some trampled in the panic. The other magicians moved with them, their faces strained as they poured their energy into a flickering barrier that stretched over the retreating army like a soap bubble ready to burst.

The relentless barrage from the towers took its toll. One by one, the mages faltered, their strength spent. Amadioha watched in horror as a searing blast punched through a weak point in the shield, turning a young warrior to his left into a cloud of glittering dust. The man's scream cut off abruptly, the sudden silence more terrible than any sound.

Amadioha risked a glance over his shoulder, his heart sinking at the sight of the dwindling number of mages. Omoro stood at the rear, his face a mask of grim determination as he poured every ounce of his power into the fading barrier. Another mage crumpled, his body disintegrating into dust that blew away in the wind. The shield contracted, barely covering the remaining survivors as they neared the edge of the forest.

Amadioha's mount reared suddenly. He clung desperately to its mane, but a blast of heat from a near miss sent the horse into a final panic. It bucked, throwing Amadioha clear. He hit the ground hard, the impact driving the air from his lungs. Stars burst in his vision as he rolled, momentum and blind luck carrying him into the relative safety of the trees.

From their new vantage point, Amadioha watched as another flash of light reduced a dozen more men to swirling clouds of ash. The entire field looked like a sandstorm, visibility clouding as the remnants of his warriors filled the air.

Through the haze, he saw Omoro appear at Damballa's side in a flash of white light. The mage's hands blazed with energy as he threw up a shield, deflecting a beam that would have reduced Damballa to dust. Omoro's knees buckled, his strength clearly waning from the constant exertion. He gripped Damballa's arm and in a blink, they vanished, leaving only a crater where blue light pounded the ground they'd occupied a heartbeat before. They reappeared at the forest's edge, Omoro's face ashen, his eyes rolled back. He collapsed into Damballa's arms, unconscious.

"This is your doing, Amadioha!" Damballa's voice was sharp with blame. "You have led us into the arms of death!" Around him, he could hear the wounded groans of the survivors mingling with furious mutterings. The rumblings of discontent grew, a wave of anger and despair threatening to crash over him.

Amadioha fell to his knees, the weight of what had happened finally crashing down on him. The taste of dust, the remnants of his men, was bitter in his mouth as he choked out, "How many? How many are left?"

Damballa met his gaze, eyes clouded with anguish, but he kept silent.

Amadioha's shoulders slumped, his hands trembling as he clutched at the ground beneath him. A strangled cry escaped his lips, echoing through the battlefield. His body shook with silent sobs, the weight of the lives lost crushing his spirit. The once-proud leader knelt there, broken, as the remnants of his army looked on in stunned silence. The victory they had been so sure of just hours ago now felt like a foolish dream, replaced by the bitter taste of defeat and the weight of lives needlessly lost.

∼

AMADIOHA TIPPED THE CUP, draining its contents for the fifth time that night. Each burning swallow of the potent brew brought a fresh wave of numbness, muffling the ache inside him. Reaching for the bottle to pour another, he found it empty. His court wanted to dethrone him, likely led by the ever-duplicitous Reebell. They were justified.

The tent flap rustled open, revealing a guard who strode in and halted.

"More wine!" Amadioha demanded.

The guard did not respond.

"I said more wine!" he repeated, and he turned around. Through the haze of his intoxication, the detailed patterns on Damballa's shirt swirled and blurred, melding into confusing patterns. "Damballa! Go get me some more wine," Amadioha shouted. He flung his cup across the room.

Damballa tracked the cup's flight with his eyes as it struck the tent's back flap, then clattered to the ground. "We have the final count," Damballa said.

"How many?"

"Over five hundred souls lost."

A guttural, strangled "No" tore itself from Amadioha's throat. He crumpled to the ground, clutching his neck as if the very air around him had turned into a choking fog.

"Many have abandoned camp. All the ones that snuck into the castle are dead. The Bondye hung their corpses over the wall of the Mysters," he said. "Barely three hundred of us remain."

Amadioha coughed. He crawled on the ground toward the other end of the tent. He gaped at the dirt and smashed his head down twice. A trickle of blood flowed down his forehead. The question clawed out from his soul, hanging in the silence, echoing in his ears. "What have I done?"

"Now is not the time to lament. Our men are desperate."

"I cannot be strong. I cannot lead them anymore." Tears poured from his eyes.

"You are still their Eze," Damballa said. "That is your duty."

"Ijele, why did you leave me?" Amadioha asked as more tears fell down his face. "Ojukwu, why did you leave me?" He turned back to Damballa. "I wanted to save my people. But I have killed them all. How can you expect me to lead them?"

"Petro Perou Loa's troops have arrived at the Kal Mysters with the rest of the Bondye's troops. It appears they played a little trick of their own. Deceiving us into thinking the palace was unguarded. The only reason they have not come for us is because they fear a trap. But that will not save us for long."

Damballa approached and crouched beside Amadioha, meeting his gaze. "We are disjointed. The scouts are non-existent; most died in the attack. Morale is low."

Amadioha stared at the flames. His head swayed, drawn by the hypnotic dance of the fire. His breathing was fast. Tears streamed from his eyes like a relentless river. "My place is not with them anymore," he whispered, his voice breaking. "You must lead them back to Niri."

"You are the—"

"I am nothing! I have lost everything. And I cannot bear to see the men, as they have lost respect for me."

"A leader is not someone who only thrives in times of success."

"I am no leader," Amadioha said.

Damballa opened his mouth to protest, but Amadioha raised a hand, silencing him. "I swear to the ones born, the ones who have died, and the ones who will come, I relinquish my power as Eze. As the second in command, you are now Eze."

"No," Damballa said.

"You always had the people's heart. Lead them back home."

"You know that if you do this—"

"I know what it means!" Amadioha snapped.

"What will you do?"

"I will follow you," Amadioha said. "I will be two days behind, but I do not know what I will do when we arrive in Canis."

"So be it," Damballa straightened, opening his shoulders with acceptance, then lowering his head in reverence. "I accept."

∽

AMADIOHA LOST himself in the dance of the flames, their flicker reflecting the turmoil within. He adorned his body with the same white markings from the day he attacked Rada Mysters. The first time he attacked her, fear and excitement had surged through him, a sensation he hadn't felt since. He wanted to feel it again—one last time.

"Radha Loa," he chuckled. "Ghede Loa." He had wanted to destroy all nine of them. The weight of his tears gradually gave way to a newfound lightness. A clarity settled within him, illuminating his path. He knew what he had to do. A wooden beam in the middle held up the tent. He went to his makeshift bed and pulled up the sheet, fastening it into a rope. He checked the knot to make sure it was strong enough. It was. He dragged a chair from the side of the tent and placed it next to the beam. Then he buried his axe at the top of the wood and fastened the makeshift rope at the end of the handle.

Confronting the inescapable truth, he acknowledged that there was no path ahead. Damballa, he realized, would be a capable leader. The era of conflict had ended; now was a time for healing, for his people to mend. With a heavy heart, he secured the rope around his neck. He gave the rope one last tug, ensuring its steadfastness. Gazing downward, he prepared to kick the chair away. But in that critical moment, a flicker of hesitation held him back, a silent question lingering in the balance of his actions.

Petro Perou Loa was at the castle. He could attack them. Kill some Vodunese soldiers before he died. But then, he could not give them the satisfaction of killing him. He could sneak inside undercover. But if they got him alive, he did not want to think of his fate. He took a deep breath and released his mind from its bonds. He let everything go. For a moment, he had no worries. Not Ijele, not Ojukwu, not Vodun. Nothing. He kicked the chair from under his feet. There was a small crack as the rope tightened around his neck. He didn't struggle as he stopped breathing. A solemn look spread over his face. He stared at the calmness of the flames across the room. He slumped as life left his body.

∽

Queen Aissatou Mbaye's Journal: Fearful thoughts

The flickering lamplight casts long shadows across my chamber as I sit here, my thoughts as chaotic as the sea during storm season. My husband sleeps peacefully in the adjacent room, unaware of the turmoil in my heart.

Amadioha has come and gone, leaving behind a trail of unease and a bitter taste of inevitability. The man who once held my heart now treads a path that may lead to his ruin—and perhaps to mine.

Oh, Amadioha. My Oha. Your future is no longer clear to me—hazy and uncertain, shrouded in death and dust. I see blood, I see ruin, but I cannot discern whose. This troubles me more than I care to admit. Will my beloved Sine be drawn into this violence and chaos you seem determined to unleash?

I find myself second-guessing my actions. Should I have revealed more to you? Would additional knowledge have swayed your decision or hastened our descent into conflict? The weight of this choice bears heavily upon my shoulders. And yet, even as I ponder these what-ifs, a grim realization settles over me like a shroud.

The darkness I glimpse on the horizon is not solely of your making. Your intervention may have hastened it, but I suspect it would have come eventually, regardless. Our realm stands on the precipice of change, and I fear it may not be for the better.

I know you will heed my request to have Omoro ride behind you when you attack Kal Mysters. I know it will save your life in that moment. But I fear that may end up changing nothing, even for you. I fear I do not know anything with certainty anymore. Perhaps I never did. I find myself afraid—afraid of the future, afraid of the consequences, afraid of my powerlessness.

From dust we came, and to dust we shall return.

24

NO MAN'S LAND
REALM OF HELL

When **Ikenga** opened his eyes, Daeva was gone. In her place sat Moremi, clad in black. Her face was a mask of simmering anger.

"What do you expect to gain from this demon?"

"To save Niri," Ikenga responded.

"Liar! You only crave her body."

"She saved my life," Ikenga shot back.

"You can't trust her. It has only been so long, and you have already moved on to another... another thing! She is not even a real woman."

"Don't be ridiculous! You know I would never do that to you!"

"The same way you told me you would protect me?"

"Must I pay for this again and again?" Ikenga's voice trembled in frustration.

"You're in love with her!" Moremi accused.

"And if I am?" Ikenga's shout surprised even him.

Moremi's expression crumbled, a deep anguish in her eyes, previously unseen by Ikenga. Her sobs filled the room. "How could you? You promised to be my husband. The father of our future children. And yet... another betrayal."

"Stop it!" Ikenga shouted. "You're not real, and still you torment me!"

Rising, Moremi advanced toward him. "You might betray me, but denying me? That you'll never do."

With a shake of his head, he shut his eyes against the painful scene.

When they fluttered open, the rocky terrain and Daeva greeted him again.

Although shielded by the shade, stray beams of light ricocheted off the rocks, piercing his eyes. Ikenga found Daeva beneath him, her wings splayed on the rocks. Her naked torso rose and dipped as she breathed. Guilt gnawed at him as his gaze lingered on her breasts, yet he couldn't tear his eyes away from her mesmerizing form. She lay there, the very picture of tranquility and innocence. His eyes dropped to his pants, desire surging through him.

As her eyes opened, they met him with an innocent gaze.

"I want..." The words that left his lips were foreign to him.

"What do you want?" she said.

"I want you."

"I am ready," her gaze pierced his, as intense as an army storming a castle. She reached into his soul, capturing more than just his physical desire.

He leaned in and kissed her neck. She quivered. Her breath hit his face. His body quivered. He kissed her shoulders before his tongue slid down to her nipples. She moaned in his ears. His mind was going to explode.

"What do you want?" she whispered to him.

"I want... absolution," he said, "for Moremi, for Utaka, for Niri, for Orisha." A sad look crossed his face. "I want redemption."

A soft moan escaped her lips. "Is that all you want?"

"I want..." His voice faltered, caught between the fire of his desire and the chilling void of his losses. "I want to go back home."

"What do you want?" she asked.

He met her gaze once more, taking in the fiery hue of her hair. With a deep breath, he dropped all inhibitions like a king who saw an army storming his castle, but simply opened the gates. He let everything in. "I want to... I want to be inside you," he said.

"Be inside me."

He wanted her, needed her. For a brief second, he thought he saw Moremi standing by the rocks, looking at them.

What are you doing? His mind raced.

Daeva raised her hips and pulled him closer to her. He moved fast, like someone was chasing him. In an ideal world, she would do everything he wanted. They would travel together across realms. They would birth new empires together and destroy old ones. He needed more than one life to fulfill the potential of their destinies. Ikenga looked into her eyes and saw stars destroyed and reborn. He entered her slowly. It was electrifying. If her essence filled him before, now it consumed him.

"I want your soul," she said. "Give it to me."

He was bare, flesh to flesh. She was on top of him. Her wings flapped as her body moved up and down. He could never imagine them ever being apart again.

Take my soul. The thought wanted to fly from his head, but he held it back. He had no energy, yet all the energy in the world.

"I have never felt things like this before," Ikenga said.

She bent forward and whispered in his ear. "We are all experiencing things for the first time."

He came inside her. As she screamed, loose stones and sand traveled down the rocks around her. Her body collapsed on top of him. Her wings served as a blanket, protecting them and keeping them cool. His breathing matched hers. They were in sync. They were together where they were supposed to be.

∽

DAEVA SAT CROSS-LEGGED, her delicate hands resting on her knees as she leaned against the rough wall, weathered rocks digging into her back. Ikenga gazed at her, transfixed, his body frozen as if under a spell. The darkness shrouded them, but a glimmer of tears shone in her eyes.

Endorphins surged through his veins, the lingering memory of their intimate encounter still fresh in his mind. The euphoria was quickly followed by guilt gnawing at his conscience. He half-expected Moremi or Eshm to materialize from the shadows, their voices stern and disapproving, ready to admonish him for the sin he had committed. But the forest remained silent, and the guilt slowly ebbed away, replaced by a growing sense of contentment.

Daeva's eyes met his, and a soft smile graced her lips. She crawled toward him until she was close enough to rest her head on his shoulder.

"How are you feeling?" Her voice was barely above a whisper. She peered into his eyes with an intensity that made him feel like a specimen under examination, as if she were unraveling the mysteries of his soul.

Ikenga struggled to contain his smile, but it was a losing battle. "You remind me of a little garden, so bright and red with a little rose," he murmured.

"If you read me a poem, I might melt," she teased, her eyes sparkling with mischief.

Her smile, her scent, her touch—it was all too much for him to bear. "Its mornings of purity, its nights of tranquility—" he began.

But Daeva silenced him with a finger to his lips. "I am still healing," she said. "I need to rest."

A wave of rejection washed over him, but he pushed it aside. Daeva needed him, and he cursed himself for being so selfish. Her well-being was all that mattered now. "We can Navigate somewhere?" he suggested.

"You saw what happened the last time," she looked at him, her eyes filled with tenderness, and kissed him. Then, her gaze drifted to Formless.

"How does it work?" she asked.

"I have a bond with it," Ikenga explained. "It's like it's alive. When we are connected, I pass my will into it, and it answers, transforming into whatever shape I desire."

"Any shape at all?" She inquired with wide eyes.

"The bigger the shape, the more energy it requires. Once, I passed out trying to transform it into something too large."

"May I?" Daeva asked, her eyebrows raised in curiosity as she motioned toward Formless.

Ikenga hesitated, then picked up the weapon and handed it to her. It was the first time someone other than he had held it since he received it from his father. To his surprise, the blade pulsed, as if acknowledging Daeva's presence. Ikenga's eyes widened in awe—Formless had never responded to anyone outside of his lineage before.

His attraction to Daeva intensified, a magnetic pull that he could no longer resist, even as a small voice in his mind warned him to be cautious. "I want you," he said.

"Have me."

Ikenga rushed at her, his heart pounding in his chest, his breath coming in short gasps. The last thing he remembered was her telling him, "I want your soul. Give it to me." And him telling her to take it, to take all of it, to take all of it forever.

25

AIR STRIKE

Chancellor Moloch narrowed his eyes as he fixed **Lilith** with a piercing gaze. "An elaborate story," he said. "How convenient that you come forward with this just as your court martial approaches."

The irony of a court-martial, as she was overseeing security for the funeral, was not lost on her. They were willing to extract usefulness from her and discard her after. She stood before the assembly of the Upper Council, having just recounted the harrowing events that transpired in Sasobek, including her unsanctioned infiltration into the neighboring state. Despite the looming threat of her court martial, Lilith's rank still commanded some attention, and the council members were obligated to listen when she invoked matters of national security.

General Ko'ron, known for his hawkish tendencies, seized the opportunity to push his agenda. "We should consider an air strike against Aamaris," he declared. "Just to be sure."

The council exchanged weary glances, all too familiar with Ko'ron's perpetual eagerness for military action. Most of them had grown accustomed to his warmongering and paid little heed to his suggestion.

"You would consider an air strike against your wife just because she made you upset," General Yigit's attempt at humor cut through the tension, eliciting a wave of laughter around the room.

Lilith, however, found no amusement in their levity. Anger seethed within her as the council members treated her dire revelation with dismissive nonchalance. Frustration boiled over, and she could no longer contain her outrage. "I have just informed you Aamaris is concealing a massive army, and you respond in jest?"

The laughter died down, replaced by a heavy silence. Angry stares bore into Lilith, the council members' amusement giving way to irritation at her outburst.

General Ko'ron spoke up. "I vote to throw her in prison," he declared. "Then we can continue discussing more important matters."

General Gadreel, ever the voice of reason, interjected. "They deserve to go to prison," he acknowledged. "But the council must regard their sworn statements, regardless of the circumstances under which they collected the information."

"Statements meant to delay their fate," General Ko'ron argued.

"I can prove it," Lilith said.

He scoffed. "How?"

Lilith turned to Senet and gave a subtle nod. Senet, in response, tossed a rectangular disk onto the table. It hovered above the surface, slowly rotating as a holograph flickered to life above it.

"Coordinates alpha delta, 1454, 3423," Senet said. The hologram obeyed, zooming in on the specified location.

The council members leaned forward, focused on the holographic display. At first glance, the area appeared to be nothing more than a barren landscape, littered with rocks and devoid of any signs of life.

"I said it!" General Ko'ron exclaimed triumphantly. "Nothing but rocks. Nothing exists in that region of Aamaris."

"Please let us finish," Lilith said in a voice that was a little too loud.

General Ko'ron's anger was evident as he glared at Lilith, his teeth clenched. "Remember where you are," he warned.

"How about an air strike against Major Lilith?" General Yigit joked, eliciting a round of laughter from the council members. Although the humor was at General Ko'ron's expense, it eased the tension in the room.

General Ko'ron cursed under his breath and sank back into his seat, his anger simmering just beneath the surface.

The leaders of Masina are making a mockery of me.

"Get on with it," General Gadreel urged.

Senet tapped her watch. "De-noise visuals with infrared. Counteract distortion," Senet said to the hologram.

As the holographic image sharpened and the distortion dissipated, gasps of shock and disbelief filled the room. Before their eyes, a sprawling military encampment in Aamaris came into focus, its presence previously concealed from their satellites.

General Ko'ron, his eyes wide with astonishment, couldn't contain his surprise. "How did they do that?" he asked.

"They can distort the images our satellites pick up," Senet explained.

The council members exchanged glances. The room buzzed with a newfound sense of urgency as the council grappled with the implications of the shocking discovery.

"Impossible. Even we do not have the technology." Yigit said.

"Look at the building structures. Krinote rocks, similar to what we saw in Sharik Hora. They have been amassing this for decades." Lilith said.

More gasps of shock and realization filled the room as the council members comprehended the scale and duration of Aamaris's secret operation.

"We must strike immediately!" General Ko'ron declared, turning to face Chancellor Moloch. "Chancellor! What do you say?"

A chorus of voices joined him, each council member chiming in with their arguments for an immediate strike.

Chancellor Moloch raised his hands and silenced the room. He rose from his seat and stepped closer to the holograph. "The army is too far from Masina for an invasion," he mused, his brow furrowed in thought. "And they would not need five hundred thousand to attack Lucifer's funeral."

A murmur of agreement filled the room as the council members considered Moloch's words.

"No secret army of five hundred thousand controlled by Aamaris will lead to good outcomes, regardless of the objective." General Ko'ron said.

"I recommend a small team to go in for reconnaissance first," Senet said.

The room fell silent, like a private making such a recommendation offended them.

"Major Lilith, Private Senet, thank you for your service." Chancellor Moloch said. "You can wait outside while the council discusses. Dismissed."

∞

LILITH's inner monologue raced as General Gadreel exited the council room. *Don't even think about talking to me. Just keep walking.*

But as if he could read her mind and chose to do the exact opposite, he halted right in front of her and pivoted to face her.

"You are an excellent soldier. Your quick thinking and resourcefulness are unmatched," he began, meticulously smoothing out an imaginary crease in his uniform. "But when it comes to following orders and respecting the chain of command, you fall short."

His words hung in the air, a backhanded compliment Lilith saw right through. She didn't believe for a moment that his statement held genuine praise.

She rose from her seat, squaring her shoulders as she faced him. "Sir," she said, using the formality to buy herself a few precious moments to choose her next words carefully.

"You do not thrive in times of peace. That is why you persistently seek chaos. It's what your soul craves, what allows it to grow.

And today, you have made this abundantly clear to the entire council."

"Sir," Lilith repeated, her tone steady. "Permission to speak freely?"

"Go on," he nodded.

She took a deep breath before speaking. "With my discovery, I may have just saved our nation, some of our allies, and perhaps even the entirety of Hell from the destruction Aamaris threatens to bring. How can the council not see this? How can you not recognize the importance of what I have uncovered?"

His expression remained unchanged. "Perhaps you have," he conceded. "But you have also shown the council something they may fear even more than Asmodeus himself. You've revealed yourself to be a soldier they cannot control. And someone as resourceful as you? That terrifies them more than the looming threat in those mountains."

"Sir—" Lilith started.

"We are leveling the site in two days."

Of course, they ignored the recommendation for a recon mission first. Two days would be the same day as the funeral. "Sir, am I still on point for security for the funeral?"

"No."

Her breath caught in her chest as she digested his words. "Having our top leadership in Aamaris at the funeral as we stage a direct assault on them is not a wise military choice. We will deploy decoys —look-alikes for both the Upper Council and the Lower Council—to attend the funeral in our stead. Our security needs have been... adjusted accordingly."

∼

Lilith found herself lost in thought as she pored over the aerial maps of the Aamaris military camp spread out on her desk. Questions swirled in her mind: How long had the camp existed? How much time and effort had gone into its construction? She felt trapped and restricted by the very organization she served. Despite consistently delivering results, all she seemed to receive was more criticism and admonition. General Gadreel's words echoed in her mind—the council would fear her resourcefulness.

Absurd. Aren't we all working toward the same goal?

A sharp, solitary knock on her office door jolted her from her ruminations.

"Come in," she called out.

Senet entered the room, her red eyes catching the light from the overhead lamp, giving them an eerie glow.

"Have a seat." Lilith gestured to the chair opposite her desk.

Senet hesitated, then lowered herself into the chair, perching on its edge.

Lilith took a breath, preparing to speak. "I—"

"The answer is no," Senet interrupted.

Taken aback, Lilith furrowed her brow. "You assumed I brought you here to ask for a favor?"

"The answer is no," Senet repeated, crossing her arms over her chest and leaning back in the chair.

Lilith leaned forward, her eyes locked on Senet's. "You know this is the right thing to do," she insisted.

Senet shook her head. "I don't know anything about anything."

"Don't forget, I am still your superior officer," Lilith snapped, her knuckles whitening as she gripped the edge of the desk.

"Is this an official visit? Are you about to give me an order?"

Lilith's fingers drummed against the wood. "We found a Sasobekan working with a man. A man! When was the last time you saw someone from that realm here? And then they are tied to the secret base in Aamaris."

"It stinks," Senet admitted. "But we are going to level that site in two days."

"I haven't made a request yet."

"I don't think whatever you say will make a difference."

"We need to go in, gather intel, and get out before they blow up the site."

"I must admit, I was not expecting something that ridiculous." A humorless chuckle escaped her.

"What is the plan with a secret army that big?" Lilith asked. "Invade Sasobek? Invade Qataban? You must admit that none of these makes sense."

Senet shrugged. "When we blow it up, it won't matter what the plan is."

Lilith shook her head. "Blowing it up will just be hiding the evidence. If we are missing something, we could endanger our nation."

Senet rose from her seat and paced the room. "Before our mission in Sharik Hora, I heard many stories about you. How effective you were, how you always got things done. Permission to speak freely, Major?"

Lilith's lips curled into a slight smirk. "Only if you intend to say yes to my request."

Senet ignored the jab and continued, "That is both your best and worst characteristic."

"I've heard that a few times recently," Lilith sighed.

Senet stopped pacing and faced Lilith. "I'm not doing it this time. This thing, going all out against my superiors, it's not my style. I am not like you."

"You are so much better," Lilith said. "Hell may not even be here in a few years," Lilith continued. "We have gotten so far. We can't stop now."

Senet's shoulders slumped. "How will we get in and out without Navigation? My secret will become public," she said.

Lilith's gaze bore into Senet. "Do you want to save your secret? Or save Masina?"

Senet turned away, "Kalla! Why do you keep making me do this?"

"We must leave asap. In and out. Before anyone notices."

Senet shrugged as a resigned sigh escaped her lips.

THE MILITARY ENCAMPMENT before Lilith unfolded like a metallic organism, stretching across the barren landscape. Silvery structures, their surfaces gleaming under the harsh orange embrace of the sun, formed a labyrinth of regimented rows. Launchpads and landing strips cut through the terrain, their outlines shimmering like mirages in the oppressive heat.

Infiltrating the complex proved less challenging than expected. The anti-Navigation measures in place were less sophisticated than those at the morgue, suggesting that most of their security focused on maintaining the secrecy of the location itself.

As Lilith and Senet surveyed the area, they noticed the ground patrols were sparse, typically comprising pairs of soldiers. Most of the personnel moving between buildings had purposes other than security.

"Those two," Senet whispered, her keen eyes locking onto a pair of soldiers who resembled them in terms of build and stature. "They'll do."

They emerged from their hiding spots and approached the unsuspecting patrolmen with calculated movements. Lilith drew her tranquilizer gun and fired two shots, striking the soldiers in the back of their heads. They crumpled to the ground with a muffled thud.

Dragging the unconscious soldiers proved to be a bit of a challenge, but they maneuvered them into a secluded corner near one building. They stripped the soldiers of their uniforms and donned them themselves, taking care to ensure a perfect fit. As a precautionary measure, Lilith administered two additional tranquilizer doses to the incapacitated demons.

"We don't even know what we're looking for," Senet said.

"We need to find someone who looks important, steal their memories, and then get out."

They wandered through the complex, blending in seamlessly with the occasional passerby. The facility's sheer size worked in their favor, as it was unlikely for everyone to know each other personally. Despite a few curious glances, no one paid them any undue attention.

"That building," Senet said, pointing to an unmarked structure featured noticeably fewer windows compared to the surrounding buildings.

Lilith nodded. "It's a good start," she agreed.

As they entered it, an unsettling stillness greeted them. The interior was devoid of any signs of life, with empty corridors stretching out before them. The soft hum of electronics and the muffled echoes of their footsteps were the only things to break the eerie silence.

Exchanging puzzled glances, they explored the building, their senses on high alert for any potential threats or clues. Room after room revealed nothing but bare walls and abandoned workstations, adding to the growing unease that settled in the pit of their stomachs.

Finally, they stumbled upon a room that stood out from the rest. When they entered, their eyes were immediately drawn to the large holographic display that dominated the center of the space. The image that greeted them, however, differed from what they had expected.

Instead of the familiar landscapes of Hell, the holograph depicted a realm both foreign and unsettling. At the heart of the image was a nation labeled "Vodun," surrounded by unfamiliar territories and landmarks.

"What is this?" Senet whispered. Confusion and apprehension filled her voice.

Lilith stared at the holograph. "I don't know," she admitted, her eyes scanning the details of the mysterious realm. "But that looks like the realm of man."

The revelation hung heavy between them, raising more questions than answers. Why would a secret military complex in Aamaris have a detailed holographic map of the world of man? What was the connection between Vodun and the Aamaris army?

"Hands behind your head! On the ground now!" Six soldiers burst into the room, their hulking forms rendered more ominous by the scant light. One hung back, ceding the forefront to his comrades. Lilith spun around, her thoughts racing for an escape, but there was only one exit from the room. Brandishing batons, not firearms or swords, their intent was clear: capture, not kill. The scenario darkened.

"This might be a good time to Navigate out of here," Lilith said.

Senet grabbed Lilith's hands and closed her eyes. But instead of the room fading away, Senet screamed and fell to the floor, clutching her ears. "It's... it's some kind of anti-Navigation device," she gasped through gritted teeth.

The soldiers smiled. "On the ground. Now!"

"If you back out now and leave, we may not hurt you," Senet said in defiance.

The remaining three soldiers unsheathed their batons, closing in with predator intent.

"We will get out of this," Lilith's words were calm, but her perspiring forehead told the actual truth.

The closest adversary lunged at Senet, swinging his baton at her head. She deflected the blow and twisted his arm into a punishing lock. The sickening crunch of dislocated joints echoed in the confined room. A brutal punch to his shoulder sent him sprawling, his screams ricocheting around the room. She pressed down on his injured shoulder as he withered in pain.

The other demons exchanged bewildered glances. "Are you witless?" the one on the floor roared. "Subdue them!" With a shared nod, they lunged at Senet in a coordinated attack.

While Senet held her own, Lilith found herself overwhelmed. She incapacitated one demon, but the other two proved too much. They seized her arms and legs, their combined strength crushing her resistance. Within moments, she found herself face-down on the floor, a heavy knee pressing between her shoulder.

Through the haze of pain, Lilith glimpsed at Senet. She had dispatched her attackers and was now sprinting toward her.

"I don't think so," growled the demon pinning Lilith. He pulled out a gun and fired it at Senet's chest. She dodged by twisting to the side. He fired again, twice in quick succession. The shots hit Senet in the torso and leg, needles piercing her flesh as an unknown substance invaded her bloodstream.

The effect was instantaneous. Her legs gave way, sending her crumpling to her knees. She crawled with her hands to get closer to Lilith. The demon fired another two rounds into her back. Her head crashed to the floor, her entire body devoid of motion.

Lilith broke her neck out of the lock from the demon's knee and raised herself slightly.

"You have no idea who—" Lilith's defiant words were cut short as he fired another shot, the round striking her squarely in the forehead. The needle delivered its substance into her blood. She went unconscious before her head hit the ground.

∽

Lilith startled awake to the bone-numbing chill of the warehouse. The soft glow of a dozen monitors cast flickering shadows, displaying satellite views that exposed every corner of Hell in intrusive detail. The ominous sight spurred her pulse into a panicked rhythm.

In the background, the low thrum of helicopter blades powered up. She spotted indistinct silhouettes of several demons finishing the Loading of nondescript crates into the chopper's belly. The helicopter displayed a cheerful logo from a catering company, but the dissonance only heightened her distress. Instinct told her whatever was in those choppers was heading for the funeral. And it wouldn't be good.

Senet jerked against her restraints, eyes wide with mirrored alarm.

Most of the men continued their task, indifferent to their captives. But one figure paused his loading duties to stalk closer, his posture radiating coiled menace. As he approached, the incongruity of his Aamaris police uniform and combat boots kindled a spark of recognition.

He crouched before her. Up close, his features held a ruthless edge.

"You've made a grave mistake," she said.

He assessed her with narrowed eyes. "We'll see."

"Who are you?" she demanded.

"Rimmon."

"What's in those crates?" She kept her voice steady.

Rimmon leaned closer, his breath ghosting her ear. "Let's play a game. I answer one question, then you answer one of mine."

Lilith tensed, but nodded.

"What are you doing here?" he asked.

She weighed her options. *Reveal myself and risk cover, or protect my identity at all costs?*

"The same thing everyone else is doing. Protecting the mission," she said.

Rimmon's smile held no warmth. "I don't think so, Major Lilith Saeon."

Lilith froze, pulse exploding. He knew far too much already. She had to turn the game to her advantage. Quickly.

"I require you alive, not whole," he remarked. "Private Senet... I can't say the same." His menacing gaze drilled into her.

"Masina will retaliate. Everyone you've ever cared about will suffer. We'll—"

His slap cut her off, silencing her.

Lilith thrashed against her chains in desperation. Panic overwhelmed her, obliterating reason. *Has this all been a trap? It couldn't be. There is no way they could know we would come.*

"Almost finished here! Hurry," the third demon yelled from the helicopter.

Rimmon pulled out his knife and took a glance at Senet. "Last chance."

"Kill us both. I will never talk." Lilith said with defiance.

"We can't be late for our delivery," the other man said.

"Fine. We will handle them later." Rimmon replied.

The third demon approached Lilith, drawing a familiar gun—the same one used to sedate them earlier. He aimed at Senet first, firing two shots that made her collapse. Then he turned it toward Lilith, discharging two more into her chest.

When Lilith regained consciousness, she found herself in a confined space. Blinding lights bore down on them as cacophonous music tore at their senses. Time warped—seconds felt like hours, and days were indistinguishable. Desperation and despair gnawed at Lilith as she clung to shreds of sanity.

Had they missed the funeral? What day was it? What month? They were still alive, so the air strike couldn't have happened. Or did the attack fail?

"How long have we been out?" Lilith asked Senet.

"My legs feel weak," Senet said.

Lilith closed her eyes, but the brightness of the overhead lights passed through her lids. "Save your strength and be ready when the moment comes," she said.

Who am I fooling? We are done.

Rimmon burst into the room, his associate in tow, and they dragged Lilith and Senet across the ground to the expansive, shadowy interior of the warehouse. The ominous clinking of chains binding their ankles echoed as they were left lying on the cold concrete floor.

Rimmon leaned in. His hot breath rasped in Lilith's ear. "Your fate is sealed, but your friend's life hangs by a thread. Worry about her."

"How long were we sedated?"

Rimmon's eyes opened with a smile. "Two days," he said.

The air strike can happen any minute.

His associate pressed a knife to Senet's throat, drawing a bead of blood.

"No! Don't hurt her!" Lilith begged. "Just tell me what you want!"

Senet's eyes blazed. "They'll kill us regardless! Say nothing!"

The demon next to her rammed the bottom of the blade into the side of Senet's skull. "Quiet!"

"The access code for PRISM. Give it to me," Rimmon demanded.

Lilith's breath caught in her throat. *PRISM? How could they know about it?* "I don't know what that is," she lied.

"Five seconds," Rimmon said. The knife edged closer to Senet's jugular.

"Please, I'm begging you!" Lilith cried.

"Three," Rimmon said, ignoring her.

Lilith's mind raced. "This act of terrorism will destroy countless innocent lives, including your own people's! Stop this madness!"

Rimmon's eyes were chips of flint. "One."

"Voice activation!" Lilith exclaimed. "The code changes. You need me to speak into it."

Rimmon lifted his hand, and his associate lowered the knife. "No tricks."

"Why wage war on Masina? What is your goal?"

Rimmon tilted his head, intrigued. "You think this is about Masina?"

"Then what?" Lilith asked.

Rimmon lifted his phone in response, hitting the speaker. "The code. Now."

"Closer," she said in a whispery voice. He obliged.

Close enough.

She took a deep breath and bent her core, raising her torso. She bit the phone out of Rimmon's hand. When the glass on the screen cracked, she sucked the broken pieces into the back of her mouth. The edges sliced her gums and tongue, sending a wave of pain from her mouth down her spine. She sucked air into her chest and spat out two pieces of the broken screen into his eyes.

He screamed in pain, blinded as he swung helplessly at her. "My eyes!" he cried.

The second demon ran toward her, but she bid her time for two more seconds. She lurched again and took the deepest breath she had taken in her life, then spat the rest of the glass into his neck. A piece went right through the front and out the back. Blood sputtered everywhere as he lurched to the ground. She rolled over to him and dug her teeth into his neck. He struggled and wailed, but she held firm. A lot of useless information filled his mind.

He was a soldier performing the orders he received, one of a few demons who had to deliver the boxes in the warehouse to Lucifer's funeral.

Finally, it all clicked into place—the dead bodies in the morgue, experiments, the rushed funeral. Someone was trying to take out all the leaders in Hell silently. The army had to be for the chaos that would ensue after. It was a theory, but it still made little sense with the holographic images of the realm of the man in the room they had found.

Her mind pivoted back to the funeral. The Upper Council had sent decoys, but Bez would be there. She rolled away from the demon and focused on Rimmon, still writhing and screaming out in pain.

Lilith scrambled upward, still bound behind her back. She looked at the gun attached to his hip and the chains bound to Senet's hands.

Time to improvise.

∽

"THAT PAYLOAD SIZE," Lilith and Senet scoured the warehouse as she spoke. "They don't go missing from Masina without someone noticing. They shipped it here before sending it to the funeral."

"Wouldn't it be safer to manufacture it here?" Senet asked.

"This way, it becomes a Masina operation."

Lilith's mind raced as fragmented memories of her confrontation with Lamech surged to the forefront. The pieces of the puzzle fell into place, revealing a sinister plot orchestrated with meticulous precision. Lucifer's and President Khandoz's assassinations were nothing more than a calculated ploy to gather Hell's leaders in one place—the funeral. Every move she had made had been anticipated by an adversary far more cunning than she had ever imagined.

"If our fingerprints are on the attack on the funeral," Senet began, her voice trailing as the realization dawned on her.

"And we bomb this site," Lilith continued, her eyes widening with understanding.

"No one will believe it was an Aamaris operation," Senet finished, the gravity of their situation sinking in.

The warehouse shuddered as a deafening explosion ripped through the air. Lilith staggered, her ears ringing. A second explosion followed in quick succession, the ground heaving beneath her feet. Beams holding up the ceilings creaked as part of the roof fell, exposing the night sky. The acrid stench of smoke and burning metal filled her nostrils.

Sirens wailed, piercing the night sky. Hundreds of smaller warheads rained from the sky, their purpose to overwhelm any air defense systems that stood in their way. The real payload, the one that would deliver the crushing blow, would follow shortly after.

Lilith's eyes stung. The smoke and debris made it difficult to see. She blinked rapidly, clearing her vision, and spotted Senet across the room. In that moment, their eyes locked, a silent understanding passing between them. They had mere seconds to act, to seize a chance to escape before the next wave of missiles struck.

Senet lunged forward, her hand outstretched, desperate to reach Lilith. Lilith's hand shot out, their fingers intertwining as they clung together like a lifeline. They both held on to a desperate hope that the initial strike had disabled the anti-Navigation systems. Their forms dematerialized as the room erupted into flames, narrowly escaping the inferno.

From a safe distance, they watched Masina rockets rain down upon the military camp, reducing it to rubble and dust. An elation washed over Lilith, knowing Asmodeus and his army had been destroyed. Yet, an unsettling feeling gnawed at her, a premonition that the worst was yet to come.

"How are we going to stop the funeral attack?" Senet asked, tapping her watch to bring up a holographic display.

Lilith's gaze fell to the ground, her mind racing. "We need to radio it in. Alert the funeral security."

"No need," Senet said.

Lilith glanced up, confusion papered over her face.

"Levitate," Senet commanded, and the top of her watch lifted, hovering. A live broadcast of the funeral materialized, revealing a scene of devastation. The Eredise had been reduced to a pile of rubble.

Lilith's heart sank, her thoughts immediately turning to Bez. Was his dead body trapped under the remains of the Eredise? Her fingers trembled as she tapped her watch, manipulating the hologram to access PRISM.

"Funeral invite list. Search for Senator Abezethibou," Lilith instructed.

His name and photo appeared on the screen.

"Verify attendance," Lilith demanded, her heart pounding in her chest.

"Subject not present," the mechanical voice confirmed.

A wave of relief washed over Lilith, and she released the breath she had been holding. "How many senators from Sasobek were present?" she asked, dreading the answer, yet needing to know the extent of the damage.

"Two hundred and sixty-one," PRISM answered. The names of the Sasobekan senators scrolled across the holographic display. Lilith's eyes darted over the list, noting a fifth of them were marked absent. A sense of relief settled over her. "We are going back to Sasobek."

Senet's eyes widened in disbelief. "Sasobek?"

"Bez was not at the Eredise. I have to find him."

"Bez?"

"Senator Abezethibou," Lilith clarified, her mind already racing with the possibilities of what could have happened to him.

Senet's brow furrowed, and she placed a gentle hand on Lilith's shoulder. "This is not the best time for that."

"I could not think of a better time." Lilith tapped her watch, activating a hologram that sprung to life between them, projecting a detailed 3D map. She manipulated it until it came to a small area covered by trees near Bez's location. "Take us here. Give me two hours. Leave if I am not back. If I reach out again, do not respond. Do not come to my aid. It will be a trap."

Lilith stretched out her hand, waiting. Senet reached out and grabbed it. They faded. A sensation of weightlessness enveloped them, and an encroaching darkness soon swallowed them.

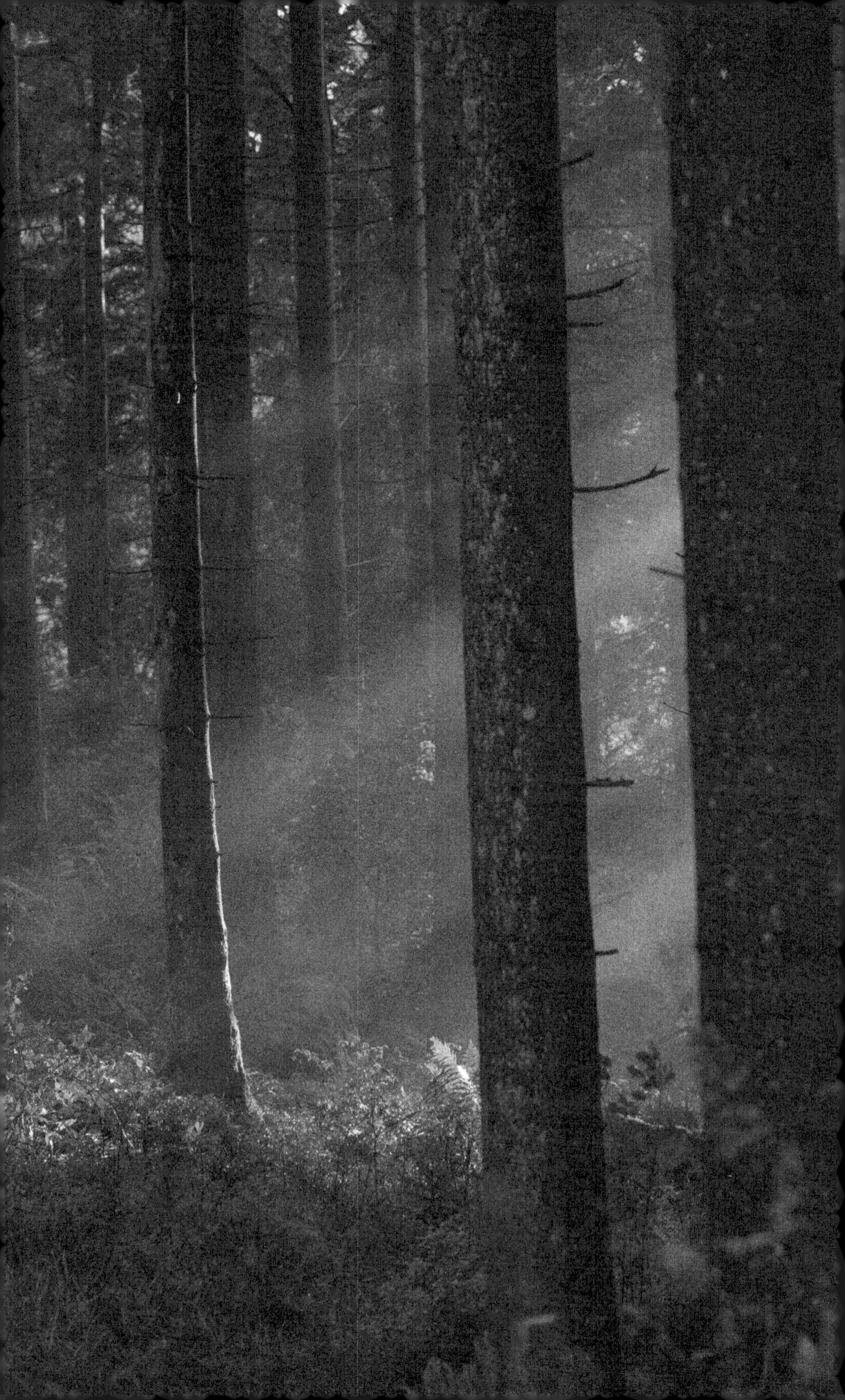

PART VII

REVELATIONS

26

DEATH
REALM OF KIRINA

The room had an ethereal blur, like someone had draped a loose cloth over **Amadioha's** eyes. A misty haze hung in the air, rendering the world soft and indistinct. He looked up at the tent's roof, his gaze drawn to his axe still buried in the ceiling. His body lay on the floor a few feet from the entrance, a lifeless shell that once housed a warrior's spirit. Ijele leaned over him, her frame shaking with the intensity of her efforts. She was trying to breathe life back into him, her hands compressing his chest in a rhythm of hope against hope, willing his heart to beat again. Her face was a canvas of anguish and determination, covered with the pain of loss and the fierce refusal to accept it.

The realization that he was dead was almost inconsequential compared to the deepening ache seeing her again caused. *'You were my heart. If only you had come a day sooner.'*

Damballa crouched next to her, his usually stern face softened by concern. Amadioha thought he might have seen the beginnings of a tear in Damballa's eyes, a rare glimpse of vulnerability.

"Amadioha Kamanu of Canis, it is time." The voice behind him brought a chill that permeated the very air of the tent.

He turned to see an unexpected visitor, a woman who towered a foot taller than him. Fiery red markings dappled her alabaster skin, glowing as though she was lit from within. Her white hair cascaded down in a waterfall of darkness, almost brushing the floor, contrasting strikingly with the dark gown draped around her form.

"Who are you?" Amadioha asked. She had a sense of majesty about her that demanded respect, yet a strange familiarity he couldn't place.

"I am the echo in the void, the beginning and the end. And now is your time."

Death.

"You are not what I imagined," Amadioha remarked, a hint of amusement shading his tone.

With a secretive smile, Death raised her hand, summoning a scythe with a glistening blade and a long, sturdy handle. "I can assume whatever form makes this process easier."

"My entire life's journey cannot end this way. Not here, not now," Amadioha whispered.

"You have already made your choices."

A door materialized across the tent, spilling forth a blinding white light that engulfed everything.

He felt the powerful urge to take a step closer to Death, after which a strange sense of tranquility washed over him.

A distant whisper reached his ears, Ijele's voice barely more than a breath, "Mutant... mutant."

Torn between Death and his lifeless body, a tumult of uncertainty raged in his eyes. "What is she saying?" His eyes darted back to Death; her smile tinged with a hint of something predatory.

"The matters of the living are of no concern for the dead," she declared with a chill of finality.

He turned back to his body and stared at Ijele once more. "You came back," he said, as if she could hear him. He continued to Death. "I have people who depend on me."

"You sealed the fate of your people and pushed away those you love. You have lost everything, including your life, Amadioha Kamanu."

Each word was a dagger, leaving an abyss of regret and pain.

"But am I truly dead?" His voice was a whisper.

"You were told the road to the capital of Vodun would lead only to death. Your life's warnings fell on deaf ears. Do not make the same mistake here," Death advised. But Ijele's strengthening cries of "Mutant!" drowned out her words.

He turned around and took a step toward his lifeless body. An indescribable pain surged through every nerve in his body. The magnetic pull of the open door challenged his resolve, but he fought it.

"Enough with this foolishness!" Death's voice soared.

If Death could force me through the door, then why is she still talking to me?

"If you could coerce me, you would have already," he retorted as a newfound courage surged through him.

Death shifted, the air around her crackling with tension. She donned a hood, obscuring all but an impenetrable void beneath, while her scythe, more menacing than before, cast an ominous shadow.

"I will have what is mine." As Death's words reverberated, the pull of the open door grew, its' beckoning nearly irresistible. The raw desperation in Ijele's cries clawed at his very soul, anchoring him from the precipice of the void. He made a mad dash for his body with a sudden resolve. He stumbled, an unbearable pain radiating from within as he crumpled to the ground, hands clutching his head. With raw desperation, he cried, "Make it stop!" His voice, filled with anguish, echoed hauntingly in the silent tent.

"It will stop when you join me."

"I can't," Amadioha gritted. "I need one more moment." His journey to his body was an agonizing crawl.

Death reappeared, a towering barrier between Amadioha and his lifeless body. Gathering every ounce of his will, Amadioha steeled himself, closed his eyes, and plunged fearlessly through Death's ethereal form.

"Your defiance will seal a fate of calamity for those you hold dear, echoing through generations," Death intoned, a chilling calm in her voice.

"If you cannot stop me in the land of the dead, how can you interfere in the land of the living?" Driven by a determination that defied comprehension, Amadioha summoned the depths of his strength, his every muscle screaming in protest as he forced himself upright. He launched toward his lifeless form, a grimace of defiance etched across his face.

From the depths of his haze, a distant voice exclaimed, "he is breathing!" A sharp pain passed through Amadioha's chest, like a knife piercing through his lungs.

"Keep going!" urged another voice.

A familiar scent filled his nose. Lips pressed against his, forcing life-giving air into his lungs. His eyes fluttered open in a blur. Yet, even through the haze, he recognized her instantly.

"Chineke!" Ijele shouted.

His vision returned slowly, but he still couldn't move. Ijele crouched over him. Her hand held his nose shut as she continued trying to resuscitate him. Damballa pushed on his chest again. A little too hard. Another sharp pain sickened him in his chest—another broken rib.

"Let him breathe!" Damballa said.

Ijele let go of his nose and moved her mouth off his lips. "Oh my God," she said again. "Why would you do this?" she whispered. Dark ink framed her eyes, smudged and streaked by her tears, leaving rivulets of sorrow on her cheeks.

Amadioha tried to talk, but coughed out droplets of blood. His chest heaved. Each breath was painful because his broken ribs dug into his lungs.

"Make sure no one comes in here," Ijele said to Damballa. "No one else can see him like this."

"I cannot leave him," Damballa said.

"You are of no use standing there," Ijele retorted.

Damballa nodded and walked outside.

Summoning his remaining strength, Amadioha wrapped his arms around her. The familiar touch and scent were both comforting and disorientingly surreal. His voice barely above a whisper, he said, "You came back... for me. Why?"

"The end is always good," she sighed. "If it's not good, it's not the end." She kissed him on the neck. "You are arrogant, and you were unfaithful. But you are still my heart."

"I owe you my life. I owe you the world. And I owe you a debt I can never pay."

"You owe yourself the biggest debt."

"I lost the alliance, the war, you," he said. "There was nothing to go back to but shame and loneliness. How could I continue living?"

Stepping back, she extended her hand to him. He allowed her to pull him to a sitting position. A black headwrap encased her head, its dark hue seamlessly merging with the flowing black gown that draped her form. "How does your body feel?" she asked.

"I am here with you," he said.

She leaned forward, delivering a sharp slap that stung his cheek. "Next time you try to kill yourself, I will let you die." The warmness of the threat calmed him even though he wasn't sure she was joking. She leaned forward and kissed him again. All his nerves amplified. As their lips locked, he felt like he was dying and being born at the same time.

∼

AMADIOHA OPENED HIS EYES, meeting the concerned gaze of his healer, Afua. As he tried to sit up, a sharp residual pain in his chest restricted his breathing, causing him to wheeze in short, shallow spurts.

"Well, look who's finally awake," Afua remarked with a hint of sarcasm.

He coughed, his attention drawn to the nearby poles holding

transparent bags. Each bag contained different-colored fluids, which dripped through tubes connected to his skin.

"How bad is it?" he asked.

Afua glanced at him like a mother would a troublesome child. "Nearly every rib in your chest is broken, and you have a collapsed lung. But other than that, you're as good as new." A wry smile played on her lips.

"Like a newborn baby," he mocked.

"Your wife and Damballa might have been aggressive during resuscitation, but they saved you," she remarked.

Visions of his struggle with the reaper flashed in his mind, and he realized the weight of Afua's words.

"In a few days, you should be on the mend. But we need to be cautious. Administering too much medicine, even to someone as resilient as you, can be dangerous."

"Where is Ijele?" Amadioha asked.

Afua stepped out, then returned with Ijele.

"I am sorry," he said as she walked closer.

She sat next to him and took his hand.

"I don't deserve your forgiveness," Amadioha murmured, shaking his head. "I should have been stronger."

"You are not alone," she said. "We all have our moments of weakness. But as the leader of your army, your responsibility is to your people. As a husband, your responsibility is to me and your family. But as a wife, mine was to you. And I left you when you were at your lowest."

"Do you remember when we were betrothed?" he asked. "I was so young, I knew nothing about this world."

"I remember you having eyes for my other sisters," Ijele said as she playfully brushed his face.

"Four of them," he admitted. "All beautiful, yet I knew it was you that was my heart."

She smiled as her shoulders softened.

"I will seek absolution," Amadioha vowed.

"The time for absolution is not now. We need you to get better. Three hundred men out there still wait for your guidance."

Locking eyes with her, the fear of a life without her clear, he whispered, "Do you still love me?"

Ijele rose from her seat, taking a momentary step back, creating a distance. The action made Amadioha's heart sink. She stood there for a few long moments before she turned around. "I'm pregnant."

A wave of emotion crashed over Amadioha, an epiphany dawning. He realized his earlier confusion. He had misheard her words as *mutant*, when she had been telling him she was *pregnant*. Those words he did not understand had drawn him back to this world, and maybe that was what drew her back to him. She approached and pressed a tender kiss upon his lips, the gentlest they had ever shared. At that moment, their hearts beat in unison, though he wondered if it might be the lingering effects of the drugs.

27

LAST RESORT

Amadioha's council convened around a massive wooden table. In his brief absence, they had shown resilience, fortifying their position and erecting makeshift buildings using timber from the adjacent woods.

"Damballa, Reebell, my friends. I have made a grave mistake, falsely believing being a leader meant projecting only strength. But true leaders also show vulnerability, confiding in those they trust most," Amadioha said. "I hold each of you dearly. My blind ambition has cost the lives of too many of our brothers and sisters, alienating us from the very alliance we struggled so hard to build." Raising a toast to fallen comrades, Amadioha proclaimed, "To Ironsi." He placed a hand over his heart, offering a deep bow.

"To Ironsi!" they all shouted.

"To all the other brave warriors that have given their lives so that we can live free, so that our children can live free, so that our children's children can be born free.... to all those brave warriors!"

"To all of them!" they all shouted.

"As your Eze, I make one final request. Let us end this reckless war against the Bondye and return home. My quest for revenge drove us here. I am resigning my post. I urge this council to lead in my absence."

Reebell leaned into Damballa, covering his mouth as he whispered into his ear.

Amadioha's discomfort, seeded by his vulnerability, escalated. "What is this secret gossip?" he asked.

A silence settled. The council members' expressions revealed Amadioha was the punchline of a joke he had yet to comprehend.

"Well? Go on! Speak!" he demanded.

Damballa leaned in, his teeth gleaming white in a smug smile. "Perhaps you have forgotten, but I am Eze now."

Amadioha gave a strained laugh. "You are right. So much has transpired; I forgot what happened."

"Our assault on the capital, despite its disastrous outcome, sent shockwaves through Vodun and the entirety of Kirina. Whispers of Sine and others entering the war slither through the sand."

Amadioha thought about Queen Mbaye. She had promised to help. But she had also told him death would fill the path to Vodun.

"The more reason we should go home. Where they need us," Amadioha said.

Reebell shook his head. "You misunderstand," he said. "Ojukwu made it back to Niri, but Ghede Ghadou has redirected his forces to block our escape through Hohos. And Dan... we cannot risk a clash with Radha Loa." A wry smirk flickered across Reebell's face, belying his grave words. "Grand Bois Loa has also redirected some of his soldiers here. Within a week, the armies of three Loas will surround us."

He retrieved a rolled map from a sheath by his side and unfurled it onto the table. "Retreat is not a viable option."

"Regardless of your self-doubt, we cannot allow you to abandon your position," Damballa said.

"Now is when we need you the most," Reebell said. "Now is the time your people need you the most."

"You have told me our fate is sealed. What use am I?"

"We must stage another direct assault on the Kal Mysters," Reebell said with a determined gleam in his eyes.

Amadioha narrowed his eyes. "With just three hundred men? We might as well wait for the army of Grand Bois to finish us here."

"That is not a warrior's death," Damballa said. "When we make our last stand at the Mysters, from our ashes, the fight of many brave warriors around the realm will rise."

"Sacrifice ourselves for the sake of everyone else," Amadioha said, scratching his chin.

"Is it a sacrifice if no other options remain?" Damballa asked.

Amadioha settled onto the table, his gaze drifting into the distance. For a fleeting moment, haunted by the weight of his choices, he imagined the specter of Death looming. *'You will pay for this.'* Her words had imprinted on his mind. The choice lay before them: confront Kal Mysters again with even fewer soldiers, or take their chances fleeing through Vodun like cowards.

~

THE GOLDEN DAWN touched the horizon, breathing life into the vast battlefield between the Canis troops and the combined forces of the Bondye and Petro Perou Loa. From Amadioha's distance, the distinct features of the Vodun army blurred, but he felt the might of all the souls guarding the castle. What remained of his army had split in two. Mounted warriors occupied the vanguard, their bare chests glistening in the sun, while the rest of the soldiers on foot stood a few feet behind them.

As Amadioha moved through the ranks, his horse's hooves left indents in the dew-kissed grass. Each soldier met his gaze with fiery resolve, prepared to pay the ultimate price. He made a point to remember each face, knowing the gravity of the battle ahead.

He patted his horse, steering it toward Ijele and Damballa.

'Is there conviction in your heart?' Damballa projected to Amadioha.

'You have access to my thoughts,' Amadioha responded. *'You tell me.'*

'I see your mind, not your heart.'

'My heart holds conviction,' Amadioha assured him. He nudged his steed, urging it to move across the ranks of his troops. "Brave warriors of Canis!" his voice echoed. "Kwenu!"

"Aye," they roared in response, their voices sweeping the field.

"This cause we embark upon, for our nwanne, Kwenu!"

Their affirming shouts resounded.

"Petro Perou Loa's forces have come from the north to join the Bondye in defense of Kal Mysters. We will destroy them all for our sisters, Kwenu!"

Their roar vibrated in the morning air.

"For Canis, Kwenu!"

"Ke Kwenu! Ke Kwenu!" The rallying cry echoed, each soldier lifting their axe skyward.

"For Niri!" Amadioha asserted.

As his horse reared on its hind legs, he held his axe toward the heavens. A surge of electricity sparked from the tip, branding the sky. The clouds swallowed the light before expelling it in a dark, temporary gloom. Their voices rumbled, competing with the ensuing thunder's roar. With a determined tap on his horse, he urged it into a gallop toward the looming fortress. Ijele and Omoro flanked him, their pace matching his as they bore down on their destination. Damballa lagged, maintaining a safe gap.

"So it begins," Amadioha stated with finality. His army surged behind him, moving like a relentless tide.

~

"This must be the desperate act of a madman," said Baron Hougan, the head of security for Kal Mysters. "Charging us in open terrain?"

Petro Perou's face, painted and stoic, was accented with gold lines that mirrored the glint of his feather earrings in the sun. He groaned as the matching chains around his neck shifted with the motion. The weight of his armor was suffocating; he longed to shed it and sink into a bath. His men had numbers and weaponry that far exceeded those charging toward him. But he did not read that confidence when he looked into his soldiers' eyes. Turning his gaze to his second for counsel, he received only a shrug.

"The towers will take care of them," Baron Hougan said. "Maybe we can retreat closer to the wall?"

"Another word of doubt from you, and I will pin your tongue to the top of your mouth," Petro Perou said.

His men shifted uneasily, fear plain on their faces.

"Instruct the towers to fire on my command!" Petro Perou bellowed. "When we are through, only dust will remain of these dogs. We will feast in the Mysters by nightfall!"

"Yes, my Loa," replied the head of security. His eyes darkened, and his head tilted back, signaling his communication with the towers. As his eyes cleared, he nodded toward Petro Perou in confirmation.

∽

SIXTY SECONDS until they were in range of the magic towers.

Amadioha's heart raced, the headwinds drying the sweat on his brow instantly. To his left, Ijele rode with an unwavering gaze, radiating a conviction that even he struggled to match.

Fifty-five seconds.

He tugged his horse to slow it, allowing Omoro and Ijele to pull ahead. The two magic towers emitted a blue light. Amadioha felt weary in his bones, the weight of the journey already affecting him. They spoke no words, but Omoro swerved his horse beside Ijele. Amadioha picked up speed and moved to his left.

Thirty seconds.

In the middle, Omoro raised his hands and touched Amadioha and Ijele's horses. They rode so close that the legs of their animals would intertwine with one wrong step. His eyes turned black as he chanted, "The powers of those before us flow through me. May the strength of a thousand flow through you."

Twenty seconds.

The light from the towers illuminated the area ahead as he continued his chant.

Ten seconds.

Omoro removed his hands from their horses. Amadioha felt a surge of energy from his horse. Just as they crossed the threshold, all their horses picked up speed, moving almost four times as fast as before. By the time the light from the tower hit the ground, they had already traveled past it. Hundreds of strikes rained from the sky, but their horses moved too quickly. Amadioha looked behind him to see dust clouds rising along the path they had passed.

In front of them, the archers of the Vodun army had pulled their bows, ready to fire. Within seconds, they would be raining down arrows.

"Ijele! Now!" Omoro screamed.

He pulled his horse back as Ijele rode to the middle. A black cloud of arrows descended upon them. Ijele's brow furrowed in concentration, hands raised as she deflected the deadly volley. Her magic batted arrows aside in streaks of azure, sending them hissing into the dirt.

But the archers' barrage intensified, a relentless torrent of whistling wood and steel. Ijele gritted her teeth, the cords of her neck taut with the strain. Arrows slipped past her defenses, hungering for flesh.

Amadioha cried out when a razor-tipped arrow grazed his shoulder, slicing through his skin. Blood trickled down his arm as flaming pain bloomed. Moments later, an arrowhead buried deep into the meat of his thigh, wringing another agonized shout from his throat. He gripped the shaft, blood slicking his fingers as he struggled to break the wood.

"There's too many!" Ijele screamed. Her arms quaked as she barely waved another swarm aside. "We'll never make it!" The next burst from the tower hit in front of them.

"Vary our speed! They are getting smarter!" Amadioha shouted.

He lifted his hand toward the brooding skies. Electricity crackled in his palm as he called forth his power. Lightning shot from his fingers into the dark clouds above. The clouds convulsed, birthing crackling arcs of lightning that pounded the ground between the riders and Kal Mysters. Thunder shook the ground as the electric sparks struck, sliced through the airborne arrows, and gouged smoldering craters in the plain. Clouds of dust and grit exploded, rapidly melding into an obscuring fog.

"Now!" Amadioha bellowed, seizing the opportunity that presented itself. Digging spurred heels into their mounts, they plunged headlong into the concealing haze at a reckless speed. The soil drank the blood from Amadioha's wounds as they raced through the veiling murk toward Kal Mysters's towering walls.

～

Petro Perou stepped back from the wall of dust roiling toward his position.

"They release their arrows without sight!" he shouted at Baron Hougan. "Command the men to conserve their ammo!"

The rest of the Niri army had stopped advancing just short of the range of the magic towers.

What scheme drives this attack?

"Attention!" Petro Perou shouted. All the men stamped their feet and straightened. "Draw your weapons!"

The sound of steel slicing the air filled the skies.

"Form up!" he shouted.

The galloping grew close. A single sweat bead trickled down Petro Perou's forehead. He could not wait till the start of the next day. Perspiration formed around the hilt of his sword.

To his astonishment, three horses emerged from the thickening cloud of dust—each without a rider. With a quizzical arch of his brow, Petro Perou was about to ponder their fate when Baron Hougan exclaimed, "Our archers struck them down!"

Some men cheered, but Petro Perou wore an uneasy smile.

An electrifying blast struck the magic tower on their right, halting their celebration. As they turned around, two more lightning strikes hit the tower. Shortly after, a blue light emanated from the top.

"They are in the tower!" he shouted, realization coming too late.

The Eden Ruse

How could he have been such a fool? How had he not seen it? Amadioha was never planning a direct attack. They just wanted to get close enough to bypass the anti-Navigation defenses. "Target the compromised tower now!" Petro Perou screamed at Hougan. "Do it now!"

Hougan cocked his head, and his eyes turned black. But it was too late. A burst of light shot from the first tower and hit the second one right in the center. Ten, twenty, maybe even thirty more strikes followed, reducing it to rubble and dust.

"To the walls! Retreat!" Petro Perou's shout wavered with desperation. The growing cacophony of the Niri's approach filled his ears, forcing him to glance back.

But before they could find safety closer to the wall, the looming tower unleashed its wrath, erasing his men from existence, one after the other. Blue light rained from the sky as everyone scrambled. In mere moments, the dust from his obliterated men enveloped Petro Perou, blinding him to everything but the few inches before his eyes. By the time the Niri army would arrive, none of his men would remain.

28

THE BONDYE

The floors of Kal Mysters gleamed, adorned with intricate patterns of black and brown serpents coiling endlessly. Stone animal heads protruded from the walls, their eyes and nostrils ablaze with red flames casting an eerie, wavering glow across the hallway.

Unlike Rada Mysters, Kal Mysters boasted a more substantial civilian population, primarily grunt workers responsible for the mundane aspects of Vodun and its illegitimate territories. Acutely aware of the unfolding events, most had sought refuge, hiding from the advancing Niri soldiers.

Amadioha's pulse quickened in anticipation, the rhythmic echo of their footsteps reverberating through the cavernous halls. Flanked by Damballa and Omoro, he strode toward the throne room, a fierce determination burning in his heart. Kal Mysters and its ruler would fall to their knees. They pressed forward, encountering civilians who shrank into the shadows, their whimpers barely audible over the sound of the advancing group.

Amadioha smirked as he observed the terrified civilians. "Look at them, hiding like frightened rats," he scoffed. "By day's end, we will sear our names into the memory of every one of them."

'Stay Focused.' Damballa's voice echoed in Amadioha's mind, accompanied by a pointed glance.

'You are one to talk, always raining on my parade,' Amadioha mentally retorted.

'Better a damp parade than a dead one,' Damballa countered.

As they pressed forward, the corridor widened, unfurling into a grand antechamber. At its far end loomed the throne room's entrance: a pair of colossal doors. Intricate carvings adorned their gilded surfaces, each detail thrown into sharp relief by the dancing torchlight.

Inside, the Bondye lounged on his throne, alone and smug. His regal attire and the ornate bracers on his muscular arms emphasized his stocky build. He regarded the intruders with a contemptuous sneer, utterly unfazed by their presence.

A menacing double-bladed weapon leaned against his throne, its presence as impossible to ignore as the Bondye himself. The weapon's handles were mere stubs, barely enough for a double-hand grip, yet the blades extending from them were anything but diminutive. Each one was as long as a man's arm, their crescent shapes honed to an edge that glinted with deadly promise. Atop his head sat an elaborate crown shaped like a spear, its base gold and peaks tinted with amethyst hues. Amadioha, Omoro, and Damballa closed around him, each step measured and purposeful.

"Amadioha Kamanu, here in my throne room," the Bondye remarked as he sipped from a glass of wine. "When you attacked Rada Mysters, the Loas wanted to unleash their full might on Niri and obliterate her," he continued, his tone thick with condescension. "It is solely because of my mercy that your nation still exists."

"You dare speak of mercy?" Amadioha's eyes blazed with fury. "Your brutal occupation of my lands, spanning decades, is what you call mercy? The Vodunese soldiers who abused, tormented, and destroyed families—that is your idea of mercy?"

The Bondye let out a mocking laugh. "Niri leaders oppressed their people long before we arrived. Your factions were at each other's throats. You speak of death, but have you forgotten the countless Niri lives you've taken in your pathetic attempt at a rebellion? And how many more will perish when we reclaim what is ours?"

"They died with honor," Amadioha shot back.

"They died following a fool's orders," the Bondye sneered and took another sip of his wine.

"It is over. Kal Mysters has fallen. We have seized the seat of power."

"The true seat of power in Vodun is not Kal Mysters. It is me. And I have not fallen."

Amadioha waited patiently until Damballa and Omoro were in position, having successfully distracted the Bondye long enough. The time for action had come. In a burst of energy, a blast of light erupted from Omoro's hands, striking the Bondye's throne just as he vanished from his seat. The heavy chair screeched backward, and the Bondye's glass of wine shattered on the floor, sending red liquid everywhere. His weapon clanged on the floor, sending echoes through the room.

Amadioha received a blow to his back as if struck by a hammer, sending him tumbling onto the floor. As he scrambled to his feet, the Bondye stood behind him, a menacing presence. Damballa hurled an axe through the air. Omoro thrust his hands forward, unleashing a searing beam of energy. But the Bondye shimmered and vanished, leaving Damballa's axe to slice through empty air before clanging against the stone floor. The Bondye materialized behind Damballa in a heartbeat, sidestepping his swing with preternatural grace before driving a fist into his stomach. Damballa crumpled, gasping for air.

Omoro unleashed another burst of light, but the Bondye's speed was unmatched. He grabbed Damballa and used him as a human shield. The light stuck, sending Damballa crumpling against the wall. In a flash, the Bondye reappeared on his throne, a mocking smile taunting his attackers with his power.

"Shall we try this again?" He squeezed his fists, and the shards from the shattered cup rose, reforming the glass as if it had never broken. The spilled liquid followed, pooling off the ground before flowing back into the cup. The Bondye took a leisurely sip and settled back into his lounging position, exuding an air of nonchalance.

Amadioha's eyes burned in fury as he spoke through panting breaths. "You will pay for what you have done."

"We brought prosperity and order to the lands we stewarded. Before Vodun came, what was Niri?"

"Mighty before and mightier after."

The Bondye's laughter echoed through the room. "Little child, what do you even know of your people's history?"

Power surged through Amadioha, his eyes blazing with energy as he hurled a bolt of lightning at the Bondye's throne. The Bondye vanished, the glass of wine falling to the floor and shattering again. Bracing himself for another punch, Amadioha tensed, but the blow never came.

Instead, Ijele's voice rang out. "I can't hold him much longer!"

Amadioha turned to see the Bondye frozen in space, with Ijele straining to maintain her hold on him. It was barely a second before he broke free from her, the reverse impact sending her stumbling backward. But those precious seconds were enough. Amadioha unleashed a surge of electricity, striking the Bondye's leg and sending him tumbling to the ground. Before he could recover, Omoro sent another burst of light at his body, causing him to slide across the floor and slam into the wall with a sickening thud.

"Again, Ijele!" Amadioha shouted, electricity surging through his veins, his body humming with power.

Ijele's brow furrowed in deep concentration as she channeled her power, to keep the Bondye immobilized. Three more Niri soldiers poured into the throne room, ready to aid in the battle against the invincible ruler.

However, the Bondye's strength proved too much for the weakened Ijele. With a defiant roar, he raised his hands and slammed them on the ground, creating a shockwave that sent everyone tumbling, their bodies tossed to the ground in the chaos. A cloud of dust billowed through the throne room, obscuring their vision and adding to the confusion of the intense battle.

The air shimmered and distorted as the Bondye materialized beside his throne, his face a mask of rage. "Enough of this nuisance!"

The next few seconds were a blur to Amadioha. Each breath he took was like an eternity. The Bondye seized his weapon and spun it in dizzying circles, advancing on Omoro with inhuman speed. Omoro unleashed another surge of blinding light, but the Bondye's rotating weapon deflected it easily.

The Bondye swiped downward, cutting through Omoro's leg like a hot knife through butter. Omoro staggered backward and screamed in pain. The Bondye released one hand from his weapon and slammed it into Omoro's chest with devastating force. The impact sent Omoro crashing to the ground, his limp body landing with a sickening thud.

Amadioha barely had a moment to process the scene before the Bondye dashed toward Damballa, his weapon poised for a deadly swipe at his head. Damballa raised a hand and jerked his head back, desperately trying to evade the blade. But the Bondye's aim was true, and the blade sliced cleanly through Damballa's right arm, severing it at the elbow. The Bondye leaped into the air, delivering a powerful kick that sent Damballa crashing against the wall behind him, his body crumpling upon impact.

The Bondye whirled around, his gaze locking on Ijele. Amadioha's heart plummeted in that moment, consumed by the overwhelming urge to reach her, to save her from the Bondye's wrath. But the Bondye's attention shifted, his piercing eyes fixed on Amadioha, and he surged forward with terrifying speed.

Fear replaced the momentary relief Amadioha felt as the menacing figure closed in. Electricity crackled and surged from Amadioha's eyes and hands, a desperate attempt to halt the Bondye's advance, but the spinning weapon deflected the bolts, not even slowing him down.

As the Bondye drew near, he brought his blade arcing toward Amadioha's torso, intent on cleaving him in two. Amadioha leaped back, but the blade's tip grazed his stomach, drawing a thin line that welled with blood.

Amadioha hit the ground hard, his body tumbling from the force of the Bondye's attack. He looked up in horror at the Bondye looming over him, the deadly blade poised to strike. With a powerful thrust, the Bondye drove the blade straight toward Amadioha's heart, his eyes burning with raw fury. Amadioha unleashed a surge of electricity, the crackling energy enveloping the blade, slowing its descent. But despite his efforts, the blade inched closer and closer, the Bondye's strength unrelenting.

"Your ancestors await you." The Bondye's words rumbled like distant thunder, his eyes gleaming with murderous intent.

As the blade forced its way through the electricity surging from Amadioha's eyes, his strength waned, his body growing weaker with each second. The realization that his end was near washed over him like a cold, unforgiving wave.

The blade pierced Amadioha's skin, sinking deeper into his flesh. Then, something strange happened. The Bondye's eyes turned pitch black, a look of shock and disbelief crossing his features. "No, it can't be," he muttered, his voice barely above a whisper. For a brief instant, the Bondye's grip on the weapon loosened. Then, without warning, he vanished, leaving nothing but a whisper of air in his wake. Amadioha lay there as the echoes of the Bondye's final words hung heavy in the air.

∼

AMADIOHA WALKED through the throne room, taking in the aftermath of the intense battle. The once grand chamber was littered with debris, shattered tiles, and goblets crunching beneath his boots with each step. The opulence of the room, with its portraits of conquered leaders and depictions of triumphant Loas in radiant splendor, repulsed him. He approached the throne and hesitated before seating himself upon it, a triumphant smile gracing his lips. The weight of the moment was not lost on him, nor on those who had fought alongside him.

Ijele, her face beaming with pride and loyalty, knelt before him with a smile even more radiant than his own. "My king," she whispered, gently kissing his outstretched hand.

"All hail, Amadioha!" one man shouted.

The men in the room chanted in unison, their voices filling with a resounding chorus, "Hail! Hail! All hail Amadioha Kamanu, Son of Thunder, War Eze of Canis, King of Vodun!"

As the chants continued, a surge of victory coursed through Amadioha's veins. Yet, even in his moment of triumph, a nagging uncertainty gnawed at the back of his mind. The mystery of the Bondye's disappearance still lingered, a question that would need an answer in the days to come. For now, however, he allowed himself to bask in the glory of their hard-fought victory and the loyalty of those who stood with him.

29

THE EDEN RUSE
REALM OF HELL

*L*ilith cautiously entered Bez's opulent living room, her eyes immediately drawn to the grandeur of the high ceilings and the intricate artwork adorning the walls. Cascading vines of velvety red plants draped from the ceiling, their sweet, musky scent filling the air and creating an exotic jungle ambiance. A massive TV dominated one wall, prominently displaying her face with the label "mastermind" beneath. According to the broadcast, she was the lead operative of the funeral bombing, acting on behalf of the Masina government.

It kept flashing to images of the Eredise bombing and back to her. Interestingly, the news articles mentioned nothing about Asmodeus's secret military complex. She ambled through the room, moving further away from the bathroom she had entered through. She had used an open vent in the ceiling to access Bez's place.

A muffled sound reached her, the hint of a conversation coming from a room in the distant corner. Her heart raced, every beat resonating with hope and dread. She dropped her bag on the floor and hurried toward the room. All of Hell had seen her name paraded as the alleged mastermind behind the Eredise bombing. Why did she think he would believe whatever alternate story she told him? Something inside her told her to turn around, go back to the bathroom, and climb up that vent.

She pressed her ear against the smooth surface of the door, straining to catch fragments of the conversation within. "Don't tell me you still haven't found it..." Bez's voice hinted at frustration. "You had three weeks... This was not our agreement..." he continued, then paused.

She opened the door and stepped into the room. He whipped around to face her, eyes widening in shock, his usually tanned complexion pale as if he'd seen a ghost. "Lilith," he gasped.

From the other side of the call, a voice demanded, "What did you say?"

"I'll... I'll call you back," Bez said.

"You're alive!" his voice cracked, a vulnerable tremor betraying his disbelief. "I feared you were dead." He got up from his desk and hugged her. She hugged him back. And for a moment, everything on her mind left. Everything was okay.

"They said you blew up the funeral! That Masina blew up the funeral!"

"Bez, you must believe me when I say they are all lies."

He grabbed her face and kissed her. "I believe you."

She kissed him back like she never had. He rushed to unbutton her pants, pulling them down, and her gun and knives clattered to the floor. She stopped him when he tried to remove her top. "Who was on the other end of that call?" She asked.

Bez sighed, rubbing his neck. "Things are getting dicey. The government is teetering on collapse. We lost half our senators."

"What was it they had not found?" she pressed.

"What are you talking about?" He shifted his weight, avoiding her gaze.

"Before I came in. You said something about not finding something after three weeks."

"Oh, that? It was nothing. Don't worry." He waved a hand dismissively. "What matters is clearing your name immediately."

She relaxed and sat on the couch near his table. "I need a drink."

The clink of glass resonated in the tense silence as he reached for a decanter, pouring a clear liquid into a finely cut crystal glass.

Her eyes shimmered with unshed tears. "I thought you were gone forever."

"I thought I lost you, too." He kissed her neck.

"All my life," Lilith said. "Being seen as less than and mistreated because of what I was. I was drawn to you because I trusted you." His breathing sped up. "We broke so many laws and conventions being together. Even though I served Masina with everything I had, you were the place I always made an exception."

He chuckled, "My charm knows no bounds."

Even though she couldn't see him, she knew his cheeky smile played on his lips. "You were always my haven because I always knew when you were lying."

"What do you mean?" He let go of her shoulders and took a couple of steps until he stood by her pants.

"The missed calls, the almost botched mission to the Sons of Lamech." She got up from her seat.

"Wait a minute," Bez said and raised his hand to stop her.

"When I heard someone bombed the funeral, you were the first person I thought of. Why would a third of the senators be missing from the Eredise?"

"Last-minute things came up! Are you accusing me of being involved in the bombing? Why would I do that?"

"I don't know what you did or didn't do. But there is much more you are not telling me," she said. "Bez, you need to tell me the truth." She took another step toward him. He bent down and picked up her gun, then pointed it at her.

His voice broke with desperation. "Don't come any closer!"

"You would rather shoot me than tell me the truth?"

His hand trembled. "I can help you. Just... stay back." Ignoring his warning, she took two steps closer. A wild panic flashed in his eyes, his finger trembling on the trigger for what felt like an eternity before he pulled it. But instead of a deafening bang, there was a hollow click.

Tears glistened in her eyes, betrayal constricting her voice. "It was you all along."

"You don't know what you're talking about!" He hurled the useless gun at her. She dodged it and advanced another step. He bent down and grabbed two blades off the floor.

When she approached, he thrust a blade at her chest. But he was a senator, not a soldier. Lilith sidestepped right and seized his wrist, bending it back until the blade buried deep in his leg. He screamed in agony, the other blade clattering to the floor.

"If I tell you anything, they'll kill me!" he pleaded desperately.

"I'm the one you need to worry about right now," she said, twisting the blade.

She forced his neck to the left and sank her teeth in. He tried to scream, but she covered his mouth with her hands. As his blood flooded her, so did the memories.

The man delivered the chilling order. "She's getting too close to us. Your mission is to eliminate her, permanently."

Bez scoffed, his eyes narrowing in disbelief. "That's absurd. She's nothing more than a persistent dog chasing a bone. For years, she's dug into the Sons of Lamech, and what has she uncovered? Nothing of consequence."

"Hold on a moment." the demon stepped closer, his eyes locked onto Bez's face, searching for any hint of emotion. "Don't tell me you've developed feelings for her. Real feelings?"

Bez's heart skipped a beat, but he maintained his composure, forcing a mask of indifference onto his face. "Of course not," he lied. "This is merely my job. The grand schemes of the Eden Protocol supersede all else."

"That is good. Because if you did, then we would have two problems."

The memory forwarded to Bez, talking with another demon.

"This intel you provided," Bez said. "Are you certain it will lead nowhere?"

The man's grin was unsettling. "They will uncover nothing of value," he assured. "However, the surprises they stumble upon should be more than enough to throw her off the scent and derail her investigation."

Bez's gaze drifted to the map of Sharik Hora, its surface littered with a constellation of red dots, each one marking an area riddled with deadly cluster munitions.

He had sent her to die in that forest. No. He had assumed she would not be on the mission since they had moved her to internal intelligence. Another memory. Another revelation. *The room, unmistakably in Aamaris, was a military establishment. Bez was engaged in a heated discussion with three other Sasobek senators.*

"I have my doubts about the Aamaris operatives," one senator, standing close to Bez, confided in a low voice.

"It's a bit too late for misgivings." Bez said.

He glanced up, his eyes drawn to the other side of the room where Lucifer stood, deep in conversation with Asmodeus. Even from a distance, Lucifer's presence was commanding and unmistakable. His towering figure dominated the space with a face as pale as moonlight chalk. His raven-black hair cascaded down, nearly brushing the ground, resembling an endless river of darkness flowing from his head.

She found herself lost in the memory, the revelation taking a moment to register fully in her mind. As the pieces fell into place, a stunning realization struck her: Lucifer was alive! The memory was a mere week old.

Bez's body hit the floor with a sickening thud. He dragged himself to the far corner of the room, leaving Lilith stunned and motionless.

Her voice trembled as she spoke. "Lucifer... he's alive."

Bez's cry of horror pierced the air. "What have you done? What are you?"

Lilith stepped toward him, her gaze locked intensely with his, never wavering for a moment.

Tears streamed down Bez's face as he poured out his anguish. "I tried to keep you out of it! The tip I gave you was a cover. They assured me it would be a low-level sting. Just enough to placate you. But they lied to me. And you... you learned too much. You wouldn't let it go! I tried to stop you, but you refused to listen."

Lilith's gaze turned to ice, her voice a chilling, emotionless whisper that cut through the air. "You're pathetic."

Bez's voice cracked with desperation. "I love you, Lilith. But our realm is dying! The only way to save ourselves is to unite. As a soldier, surely you understand the necessity of unwavering dedication."

Lilith's internal struggle was clear as she contemplated Bez's deception. The Flares and the Blight were locked in a race to destroy them, and she had kept it from him. Was she just as culpable? No, she reasoned. She hadn't sacrificed him or left him to die.

Tears streamed down her face as the weight of his betrayal crushed her heart. "All my life, the world judged me, but you saw me, cherished me. Was it all a lie?" Each step she took toward him was deliberate.

"My love was never an act," Bez pleaded. The truth of his words only intensified Lilith's pain. Despite his genuine feelings, he had done nothing to stop the attempt to kill her in the name of furthering the Eden Protocol's mission. The irony of the moment struck her—he had inadvertently shown her just how alike they were in their unwavering dedication.

"That's what makes your betrayal even more painful," she whispered. "Knowing the man who held such deep feelings for me would still do this."

He choked on his words, desperation clawing at every syllable. "Just one chance. Let me make things right."

She sunk her teeth into him again and drained his memories, focusing on every moment they had spent together over the last three years. She erased herself from him. He did not deserve to know her or who she was. Whenever he thought back, there would be time gaps; details would be elusive, on the border of his mind but out of his grasp. It was the only thing she could do other than kill him.

The Eden Protocol had made Masina everyone's enemy. She could return home and help steer the nation through the chaos that would ensue over the coming days. But she knew where Lucifer was going next. Yes, Masina was everyone's enemy now, but enough people were already taking care of that problem.

She was going to make Lucifer pay for what he had done to her world first. Then, every other soul that was part of his ruse would come next.

30

AAMARIS

*W*here military buildings, residences, launchpads, and landing strips had once stood remained collections of rubble. **Daeva** felt sick in her gut as she looked at the remnants of the Masina missile strike. Metal rods poked out of the destroyed krinote walls of the buildings. Small fires still burned. A strong smell of metal and chemicals filled the air.

She walked through the rubble. Bodies were everywhere, incinerated or buried under crumbled buildings. Tears flowed down her eyes as her anger seethed. Her mind went to the encounter at Ode to Babel. She was responsible. She had let the Eden protocol down.

Ahead, a hand extended from another rock—a child. She crouched low and forced it off to find the crushed remains of the girl. She had tried to use her wings to protect herself, but the falling concrete was too strong.

"Hands up! Stand slowly!" Daeva's heart raced from the commanding voice behind her. Her mind assessed her options, concluding that attempting to flee would be foolish. With a heavy sigh, she raised her hands, the grit and dust from the rubble clinging to her skin as she stood up.

"Turn around now! No sudden moves," the voice demanded.

Daeva complied and pivoted to face her confronters. Five demons stood before her, their faces obscured by scarves and visors, their guns trained on her.

"Option nineteen?" the demon in the middle remarked in recognition.

The Eden Protocol had dispatched eighty-five operatives, each entrusted with a separate mission to determine how to transport hundreds of thousands of demons to Kirina. In the aftermath, each operative was only referred to by their number.

The demon in the middle removed his visors and scarf. He was a lifer, born and raised within the decimated base in ruins around them. The lifers had never known anything beyond the confines of the camp, their entire existence revolving around a singular, all-consuming purpose. In a way, Daeva envied the simplicity and clarity of their focus. With nothing else to live for, embracing death in the service of their solitary cause came easily to them. She couldn't imagine the unbearable pain the lifer must have felt, witnessing the destruction of the only home he had ever known.

Despite the grim circumstances, seeing at least one familiar face warmed her. "What happened here?"

"You need to come with us," he replied. His words held a hint of pain.

Daeva detected an accusatory hint in the latter part of his sentence. The implications of his words hung heavy between them. It was understandable that he suspected her involvement in the catastrophic events that had unfolded. He would suspect anyone he met who wasn't there during the attack.

"I hope you understand, but I am going to have to restrain you," he said, confirming her suspicions.

She nodded, offering no resistance as they secured her wrists.

The crunch of debris beneath their feet as they moved through the rubble was a somber soundtrack to their journey. A car awaited them at the edge of the ruins, its exterior coated with the same rocks used to conceal the buildings from prying eyes.

A short distance away, the transport veered into an opening carved into the rocks, shielding them from any unwanted attention from above. As they exited the car, the lifer approached a seemingly innocuous section of the rock face and knocked three times, placing a keycard against what appeared to be a random spot on the stone surface.

A hidden door opened, and a humming of shifting rocks filled the air, revealing a secret concealed from Daeva throughout her years at the base. The realization that Asmodeus, the king of secrets, had kept it from her all that time left her stunned and in awe of his ability to maintain such a covert operation.

"I lost friends, young ones, hundreds of thousands gone," the lifer said as the elevator descended.

Daeva shared his anger, emotions swirling within her, but she remained silent. The guilt that had gnawed at her since she saw the rubble. Despite the overwhelming odds stacked against them, she couldn't help but wonder how they could still succeed despite such devastating setbacks.

When the elevator doors parted, Daeva's jaw dropped. Before her was an entire underground city, its massively high ceilings stretching as far as the eye could see. Doors, sub-buildings, and long hallways extended in every direction.

"Asmodeus? Is he still alive?" Daeva asked. Asmodeus was the king of the United Hordes of Aamaris and the face of the Eden Protocol.

The lifer met her gaze. "You need to check in with the Recordkeeper."

∼

THE RECORDKEEPER'S office commanded an unobstructed view of the sprawling underground complex. They had excavated hundreds of feet of rock and erected beams to hold up the ceiling of the mini-city. If one didn't look up, they would never know they were underground. It was incredible. She had spent most of her time off base. It would have been easy to have the right people come to the surface whenever she came back for a check-in.

The room was sparse, its walls adorned with maps and strategic diagrams, the only concession to comfort being the well-worn leather chair behind the imposing metal desk.

"Soldier," the Recordkeeper said as he glanced up from a sea of paperwork. The office was orderly, disciplined, without a hint of unnecessary embellishment, just like the person who occupied it. "Report." He reached for a mug, its contents obscured, and took a casual sip, his gaze never leaving her.

The lifer stood at the edge of the room. The others with him had left. Maybe they didn't consider her a threat after all. She wondered how many were still alive in the underground city.

"Sir! I am here to report option nineteen is a success," Daeva said.

The mug halted midway to the table as the Recordkeeper choked, a mist of liquid arcing through the air. "What did you just say?" his eyes widened in bewilderment.

"Mission success," Daeva reaffirmed.

He abruptly stood, his chair scraping loudly against the floor in the tense room. "Option nineteen succeeded?" His eyes bore into her, seeking confirmation.

"Affirmative!"

He pushed a button on his desk, his fingers dancing over a holographic interface that sprang to life. Text labeled "Nineteen" materialized, followed by an image of Daeva.

"The Brokers," he mused. More manipulations conjured an image of Ikenga framed against a backdrop of Niri's topography. "Is the child of Eden dead?"

Ikenga. She hesitated. "My mission is complete."

The RecordKeeper's eyes narrowed. "That is not what I asked you, soldier."

Daeva knew his uncanny ability to detect lies made him indispensable to Asmodeus. Her heart beat faster, but she did everything she could to hide it.

The Eden Ruse

Ikenga is dead to me. Dead to me. So he is dead. Dead. Dead to me. She repeated on and on in her head.

"The child of Eden is dead," she said. *To me.*

He studied her for a moment longer. Then his expression softened into a smile. "This is... impossible... amazing... impossible," he said. "Why is she restrained?" he shouted to the lifer. "Take them off at once!" He got up and scrambled out of the room. She knew exactly where he was going.

∽

IN THE HEART of the oval room, Asmodeus presided over the gathering from his central position at the table. The mesmerizing dance of holographic displays illuminated the chamber, their glow mingling with the soft light caressing the polished walls.

Around him sat three distinguished figures. One was clad in the crisp uniform of an Aamaris military official. Another was a senator from Sasobek, his brazenness underscored by the choice to wear official tunics with no attempt at disguise. The last two were from the realm of Man—Ghede Ghadou Loa and one of his associates.

The Loa wore an intricately woven overall with geometric patterns too colorful for Daeva's tastes. He had no crown. Asmodeus would not allow it in his presence. Daeva lingered near the doorway, waiting to be acknowledged as they conversed.

"The time for us nears," one senator proclaimed, gesturing toward the luminous dots scattered across the holographic map that dominated the table. "Their Loas are scrambling, reeling from the Niri rebellion." His finger paused over a bright cluster. "Kal Mysters remains a formidable force, but there's another. Rada Mysters is amassing strength, as if they expect our arrival."

"How is that possible?" Asmodeus asked, his eyes drilling into the Ghede Ghadou Loa beside him.

Daeva observed Ghede Ghadou Loa's subservience, and a pang of unease twisted in her gut. How could someone so readily betray their people for personal gain? The thought brought memories of her role in the Eden Protocol's subjugation of Hell's leaders.

Everyone believed themselves to be the hero of their story, no matter the cost to others.

Ghede Ghadou stuttered. "It can't be. Radha Rhamirez knows nothing of what is happening."

The senator pressed on, undeterred. "Their numbers are swelling. Defense structures are moving. Someone in your camp must have leaked the information!"

"Leaked?" Ghede Ghadou asked. "Impossible!"

The senator scoffed. "Then what is this incompetence?"

"You want to talk about incompetence? Above this bunker, a pile of rubble has replaced what used to be a military base. I hear half of the soldiers are dead. Is this mission even still viable?"

"Kalla!" Asmodeus cursed. "Go back to Vodun and ready your forces to attack Rada Mysters."

"Attack Rada Mysters?" Ghede Ghadou's eyes widened in surprise. "Exposing our alliance would be a disaster. I cannot risk that."

"You said it yourself. We have lost nearly half of our soldiers—hundreds of thousands gone. The replacements will come from you."

"I... I cannot order my men to attack another Loa. I will be the enemy of all Vodun."

"Better off being the enemy of vanquished Loas than the Eden Protocol." Asmodeus peered into Ghede Ghadou's eyes, making him peel back into his seat like the gaze was a knife.

"Understood," Ghede Ghadou said with a grumble.

Asmodeus nodded, his strategic mind surely already turning.

"What about the Bondye and Kal Mysters?" the senator asked, leaning forward. "How do we deal with him?"

"Lucifer will handle the Bondye. If his luck is to be held, the Niri will take care of him before the second army arrives."

The senator nodded. "We all have faith in the Eden Protocol mission." With that, he stood and strode out of the room, the Loa and his own man trailing behind him.

Asmodeus shifted his attention to Daeva, beckoning her with a subtle yet commanding gesture. "Your success has been so important at this pivotal moment," he said. "The brutal destruction above... as you can see, our enemies will not tire until they stop us."

Daeva stepped forward. Her posture was straight, but she hid her inner turmoil beneath a veneer of confidence. "I trusted in your vision, and it has yielded results," she said.

He nodded. "I sent many out, but only one, only you, succeeded. You have done well. The operative outside will show you the way to Limbo. You know what to do."

"Yes, commander," Daeva said, although a storm of thoughts raged within her, twisting her gut. Even Asmodeus, with all his power, had not secured an audience with the Brokers. And yet, he had chosen her for the task. It underscored her importance, but also highlighted the gulf between desire and duty.

So why is it so hard to ask what I want?

Asmodeus's keen gaze pierced her contemplation. "Is there something else you need, soldier?"

"My sister," she started, her voice barely above a whisper. "I was wondering if I could see her."

"In due time," he said. "She is very sick, but we have the best people on her. Now is the time to focus on phase two. Do what you do best and let the doctors do their work."

Daeva's heart clenched at his words. Asmodeus's wisdom was not to be questioned. Completing her mission was the quickest path to reuniting with her twin.

"Of course, commander," she replied.

"The lives of all demons depend on you," Asmodeus said.

"I will not fail you," Daeva said. She knew her sister would understand the sacrifices she made in the shadow of a larger cause.

PART VIII

INVASION

31

THE BROKERS
REALM OF LIMBO

The dense, clammy fog shrouded everything in the realm of Limbo, the moist air chilling **Daeva's** skin and restricting her vision to a mere few steps. A gentle breeze momentarily parted the fog, revealing glimpses of the path. Beneath her calm façade, every nerve in her body screamed, betraying the fear simmering inside. Clad in a sleeveless top and white pants, she moved with purpose. She had pinned her hair up, baring her shoulders and readying herself for what she might encounter.

Her boots were not the only thing contacting the marble floor. From the moment she entered the forsaken realm, she felt the eyes of the Guardians on her, always lurking out of sight. They were the fierce protectors of the Brokers, nearly as dangerous as their masters whom no being, not even archangels, had harmed. She took a few steps before stopping in her tracks. More footsteps. At least three more Guardians had arrived.

"Show yourself!" she shouted, her voice teetering on the thin line between demand and plea.

"What is it you seek here if not death?" the voice rumbled, a chilling blend of beast and man, its echo coming from everywhere and nowhere. If they attacked, she would be dead in seconds.

"Guardians of Limbo," she retorted with a hint of disdain, "the mightiest ever, yet you choose to hide from me?"

The gentle gust halted, leaving a suffocating silence as the fog dissolved.

There were rumors that hundreds wandered around Limbo. She found herself encircled by five. Their heads resembled ferocious lions with snarling fangs atop towering, muscular humanoid bodies carved from stone. Gleaming armor encased them with vicious spikes protruding from their broad shoulders. A dark fire, as black as the abyss, burned in the hollows of their chests, its wild flames mirrored in the depths of their predatory eyes.

The Guardian before her drew a long, wicked blade, its edges consumed by the same hellish fire raging within him. "State your case, demon."

Daeva trembled, her words a constant juxtaposition of the feelings traveling through her body. "If you were not curious why I came, you would have cut me down already."

The Guardian scrutinized her, its feline eyes narrowing with suspicion. "What you do or want is of no consequence to us."

They were curious.

Her audacious solitude in the treacherous realm intrigued them, yet there was no guarantee of how long that would keep her alive. "I seek passage through Limbo for my people," she said. Navigators were rare in Hell and even in Kirina. The Brokers were the only thing stopping her from opening the door to save Hell.

"What passage?" the Guardian demanded.

"From Hell to Kirina."

The other Guardians whispered. The fire in the eyes of the one talking to her burned more ferociously. "Demons have no place in Kirina," it hissed, its intense gaze piercing her.

"Kirina is home for the children of Eden as much as it is for us." A bead of sweat trickled down her forehead.

Stick to the plan!

The nervousness enveloped her like a cloud of smoke. Maybe she could explain what she wanted, go into the details, and convince them to grant her an audience. Or maybe they would just kill her.

Stick to the plan!

The Guardian's blade expanded as wide as its formidable frame. That was all she needed to break out of her indecision. She sprinted at the Guardian on her left. It remained still, its face a mask of confusion rather than fear. Unfurling her wings, she spun midair, flapping to generate more speed. It caught her leg with one hand as she attempted to kick its head. It clamped its hand around her foot, squeezing and compressing the bones in her ankle. She screamed in pain as it slammed her to the ground. She gasped for air, the crushing force stealing her voice and winding her.

It drew its blade, the fire in its eyes intensifying, promising doom. As it swung down to end her life, she grabbed the pin in her hair and pulled on Ikenga's essence. Formless recognized the bond and grew into a long sword.

The Guardian's weapon clashed against hers with a resounding clang, surprise flashing in its lion-like eyes as the flames within dimmed briefly. That was her chance. She slashed at its standing leg. It jerked back, but her blade tore through its armor, leaving a burning gash on its limb. An unearthly scream erupted from its maw as the fire in its chest blazed, nearly consuming its body. It plunged its sword into her foot, pinning her to the ground. A primal scream escaped her as the sword's fire consumed her leg, creeping flames radiating from the wound, slowly charring her skin ashen black—each second an eternity of agony. Stepping with its unwounded leg, the Guardian kicked Formless from her grip.

When its foot hovered above her face, intent on delivering a fatal blow, the lead Guardian's shout cut through the air. "Stop!" It approached and picked up Formless, examining the weapon with intense scrutiny. "How did you not sense this weapon?" the Guardian demanded his subordinate, eyes still fixed on Daeva.

"It is a sacred weapon," the other retorted. "How can a demon possess this?"

"Solac will have questions," the lead Guardian mused, eyes narrowing. "Keep her alive."

Yes.

"We should kill her now. Her sin against me marks her," the other Guardian retorted.

"Or maybe you deserve death for such incompetence," the lead Guardian said.

With a curt nod from its companion, the Guardian wrenched its blistering sword from Daeva's leg. She choked back a scream, teetering on the brink of unconsciousness as fiery agony overwhelmed her. It sheathed its blade, then seized Daeva by the hair. Thick mist enclosed them once more, the world blurring before her eyes, leaving her in disorienting blindness as it dragged her across the ground.

It was a close call, but part one of her plan had been successful. The next two parts would be *much* harder.

∽

THE BOUNDARY ROOM was a marvel of otherworldly architecture, melding contrasts so jarring that they unbalanced the senses. It was like Daeva stood at the threshold of a paradox, where the suffocating pressure of a claustrophobic cavern clashed with the endless expanse of a boundless meadow. At the epicenter, seven seats arched in a commanding semi-circle.

On either side of Daeva, a towering Guardian stood watch. One still held a swath of her hair in an iron grasp. Six of the seven seats cradled figures known as the Brokers. Towering above even the Guardians, their stature was immense. Their skin, a pale milky hue, was translucent and luminous. Their eerily humanoid faces resembled sculptures carved from marble—beautiful yet intimidating.

Daeva took in her surroundings as a tension gripped her. Her heart raced, thudding in her chest, and a knot of cold, piercing fear constricted her gut. There she was, ensnared amid beings of unparalleled power, and though she was the center of attention, she was infinitesimally small. Yet, against all odds, she had achieved the unthinkable: something even Commander Asmodeus had failed to do. She had secured an audience with the Brokers.

Stick to the plan! Trust it! The words repeated over and over in her head.

One Broker spoke, its voice echoing like an icy wind through the vast room, making the ground tremble. "Before you so much as dare to utter a word, marvel in the presence of our brilliance, then absorb the weight of your predicament. The last mortal who occupied the space you now desecrate has been languishing, broken and tormented, in our dungeon for millennia. Those who defy us soon beg for death's mercy." The words carved into the top of the magnanimous chair it sat on read "Solac."

Their arrogance is unmeasurable. Tears forming in her eyes, Daeva pleaded, "My people are dying. We must leave Hell; otherwise, we will be no more."

"Your lives are a speck, dust in a desert storm, barely noticeable in the grand working of the cosmos," Solac said.

Yes, I have heard this line before. "My sister slowly fades from this world." She flinched, casting a fleeting, agonized glance at her leg. The once spreading black scab had halted its advance, yet the searing pain it radiated was immense. She turned back to the Broker and spoke. "Yet you would call the future of my race inconsequential. How can life have meaning to you, the most powerful beings, yet you spend all your time sitting in this room?"

"Insolent child!" Solac roared, his eyes blazing with a menace that could freeze one's soul.

In the blink of an eye, the majestic boundary room evaporated, replaced by an oppressively intimate, windowless chamber. It defied natural law—though devoid of any visible light source, every corner, every crevice was illuminated. On a stark plain bed, Daeva found herself seated, staring at Eshm. His silhouette was tangible and solid. Like twin beacons, his eyes glowed with a fury that mirrored a raging inferno within. It was his first appearance since she stole the spirit from Ikenga.

"What madness is this?" *Eshm's demand cut through the silence.*

"What must be done." Daeva mentally fortified herself, repeating her mantra internally: *Stick to the plan.*

"How can you contain my power?" Eshm's voice echoed with surprise.

"You really don't know, do you?" Daeva met his gaze. *"Why did the Brokers betray you?"*

Eshm stared at her, realization dawning on his face. *"No... it can't be."*

Daeva nodded. *"They tried to eliminate your offspring, viewing any cross-breeding as an abomination. But you hid one, didn't you? A child born from your union with a common angel."*

Eshm's laughter filled the air, a sickening, guttural sound. *"You are my descendant?"* His laughs continued.

"Many generations removed, but your blood flows through my veins," Daeva confirmed.

"How could you know this?" he demanded.

"For thirty years, Lucifer and Asmodeus scoured every realm, pored over ancient texts, and sought wisdom from countless sources. They searched tirelessly for a way to persuade the Brokers to grant demons passage through Limbo." She paused, letting the weight of her words sink in. *"When I tried to steal you from the child of Eden, I risked my life. If we were wrong, it would have killed me."*

"Ah. Ikenga," Eshm said. *"He was much more fun than you."* Another sickening laugh followed as he walked around her, observing her like a specimen. *"What you say is true,"* he confirmed. *"But my kin were right. You are still an abomination."*

"Once they learn I harbor you within, they will undoubtedly devise more inventive methods of inflicting agony. You spent a millennium in rest. We will spend the next in torture. Together. And then we will die."

"I cannot die. A millennium is a mere dot in time for me."

"How do you know you are immortal?"

"Because I have lived long and have never died."

"Everything alive has never died."

Eshm narrowed his eyes into slits of contempt. *"You tread on dangerous ground."*

"Release your full power to me. Have your revenge on the ones who betrayed you. You will find your peace one day. But that day is not today."

The Eden Ruse

Eshm's eyes blazed with a dark fire, and he lunged toward her.

She focused within, imagining heavy blocks of rock forming a wall around her mind and fortifying it. "Not so fast," she whispered, raising her hand in a commanding gesture. He halted, the power of her will binding him. "I know this room is only in my mind. I only must believe you have no power over me here."

Though laden with disbelief and desperation, his voice was almost a hiss, "You cannot—must not—do this."

"Help me, or we will both suffer for eternity!" Daeva said, forcing him backward with her mind.

"They are still my kin. I will not side with a demon against them."

"I am your kin!" Daeva said. "I have made my choice. You must make yours." Daeva snapped, and the familiar, dizzying vastness of the boundary room returned.

She scanned the grandeur of the Brokers, her gaze pausing at the names carved in reverence atop each seat: Akoman, Indar, Nanghait, Solac, Tauriz, Zariz. The final, vacant throne was engraved with a singular, resonating name: "Eshm."

She drew a shuddering breath, whispering more to herself than anyone else, "The circle of life," she said, and her eyes became windows to a cataclysmic storm. A surge of black flames, fierce and relentless, exploded from her being, turning the boundary room into fire and fury. There was a momentary second when the eyes of the Brokers widened with the realization of what was happening. But it was too late.

∼

DAEVA CONVULSED AS A RAGGED, wet cough tore from her throat. Hot blood sprayed from her lips, spattering the pristine marble floor beneath her with red, the metallic taste clinging to her tongue. It felt like a serrated blade was twisting inside her, carving her organs into shreds with each excruciating movement. Using that much energy should have killed her instantly. But, by some hellish miracle, she still clung to life.

She stumbled toward the boundary room's sole entrance with every ounce of her fading strength. Grunting, she threw her weight against the towering twin doors, the stone's cold, unforgiving surface biting into her palms. They swung shut with a resounding thud, an ominous echo weaving through the chamber. Ignoring the primal screams of her body begging for preservation, she reached deep within, summoning more of Eshm's power.

She focused every ounce of energy on the doors. Black fire left her fingertips. The stone hissed and bubbled, edges glowing molten orange before cooling into an impenetrable seal. The acrid scent of scorched stone filled her nose as she welded the doors shut.

Mere seconds after she finished, a deafening bang erupted from the other side. The vibration was so abrupt it sent Daeva falling back onto the hard floor. Her heart hammered. Death would be mercy if the rest of the Guardians reached her. More resounding bangs came, one after another: more Guardians. Daeva's breath caught in her throat as the sealed entrance creaked under the assault. But it held for the moment.

She got up on her feet, wobbly. She spat on the floor—more blood.

Time to finish this.

Behind the seats of the Brokers was the Ogg Vorbis, the portal opener. It could channel the power of a Navigator, allowing them to open portals an infinite number of people could use.

The moment her fingers brushed it, a torrent of raw energy lashed through her, amplifying her agony. Every cell in her body screamed in protest. The device was meant for the most powerful beings, not her. She was a mere mortal, vulnerable, yet defiance blazed within her.

She focused, pushing away all the pain and ignore her body's survival instinct. "In my mind and body, I am committed," she declared. *When she prepared for the mission, they told her opening a portal should be like Navigation.* It was one hundred times worse. She tuned her senses to the exact location in Aamaris. Asmodeus and the rest of the army would be waiting.

The Eden Ruse

Near her, the air quivered like the disturbed surface of the water. A rectangle, spanning twice her height, emerged from the stillness, rippling as though reality was bending. It looked like a thick mist, a door. When it solidified more, a searing pain in her insides sent her crumpling to the ground. Blood streamed from her nose and eyes, a veil of agony.

Another bang, and the door creaked. The seal was failing. She got up again and placed her hands on the Ogg Vorbis. Every ounce of energy in her body focused on the portal. Her eyes filled with blood, blinding her almost completely. Every nerve in her body lit up, but she refused to stop. "I yield my mind!" she screamed. "I yield my body!" she coughed. "I yield my soul!" she whimpered.

There was a loud crack. Through the blood-soaked haze, she witnessed the doors shatter, fragments flying in slow motion. Shadowy figures loomed—the Guardians had arrived. She collapsed on the floor again. As she wiped her eyes, the humanoid beings passed through the entrance. Ferociousness filled their eyes. Swords with black fire extended. But before they crossed the halfway point, there was another sound—footsteps from behind her. From the solid, quivering anomaly of the portal, a surge of military soldiers stormed forth, their determined faces set in grim lines.

Heavy machine guns, archaic in design, were strapped over their shoulders. Electrical components would not survive a trip through a portal. Their weapons, menacing in the half-light, were loaded with their scarce composite diamond bullets—each a precious shard of hope against the near-invincible Guardians. It had taken them over a decade to mine just enough bullets for this mission.

"Open fire!" A demon shouted.

She watched in stillness, her body incapable of much movement. The Guardians dodged the first few bullets or blocked them with their swords. But no matter how fast one was, dodging continuous bursts from thirty-plus machine guns was impossible. The bullets ripped through their limbs, separating them from their body. Guardians kept coming through the door, even when they knew they were running toward certain death.

The Eden Protocol soldiers kept firing. Amid the smoke and echoes of gunfire, Daeva's gaze lingered on the fallen Guardians. Enemies they were, yet in their sacrifice, she saw a mirrored valiance that tugged at her respect and regret. Eventually, no more came. The shooting stopped.

"Secure the entrance," a demon barked, urgency sharp in his tone.

Two soldiers sprinted forward, boots pounding on the marble, agilely navigating the gruesome aftermath strewn across the floor. They stepped into the hallway and shouted, "Clear!"

Two more soldiers emerged from the portal, maneuvering a towering piece of artillery that dwarfed any handheld armament. Its formidable structure rolled forward. They put them on either side of the room and pointed it at the door.

"Room secure!" the demon said.

Another soldier nodded before going back into the portal. After an agonizing minute, Asmodeus made his grand entrance. He approached Daeva, his face breaking into a rare, genuine smile.

"You have served beyond the call of duty, soldier," he said.

Daeva wanted to salute, but her arms would not move. She wanted to say *'Thank you, sir,'* and ask about her sister again. But her strength betrayed her, and she crumpled to the floor, breathless, her back against the cold marble. The ceiling looked as high as the sky, yet she could see every intricate detail.

32

OLD FRIENDS

*L*egba lingered in a shadowed corner of the boundary room, surveying the horrific aftermath wrought by the demons upon the Guardians. He may have seemed like an illusion to the casual observer, his form only becoming distinct when one focused intently on his specific place. He rapidly Navigated through many locations in Limbo, lingering only briefly in each spot, too quick to be caught by the naked eye. His constant shifting gave him an ethereal quality, as if he were simultaneously present in multiple places yet tethered to none.

The scorched markings and looming presence of Daeva whispered a bitter truth—his assumptions had been gravely mistaken. Bringing Ikenga and Daeva together unknowingly caused the very thing he had tried to stop.

While sympathy for the son of Umoren tugged at him, Kirina's fate dominated his thoughts. The demons were opening ten portals. Ten portals intended for nine Loas and the Bondye, some of which Amadioha had already defeated. Most of the others had sent their army to aid the Bondye or to deal with other uprisings and rebellions, leaving their Mysters poorly guarded.

Radha Rhamirez Loa was already making defensive preparations.

She stood the most prepared in Kirina, yet the imminent invasion loomed closer than anyone had expected. Legba faced a daunting choice: venture through the portal to Hell to gauge the full might of the demon forces or follow Daeva's Noise to locate the Son of Umoren. But the demon had stolen Eshm and his weapon, rendering him useless to Legba's cause. Yet still, Legba had a sense of responsibility to the man.

As he ruminated, a drop of blood fell from his nose. The little trick he played was draining his energy quickly. What should he do? He hated deciding, so he chose the third option—the riskiest of all.

He Navigated to the room's center near the doorway. As he materialized, he raised both hands, his mind locking on two daggers falling through the Abyss in Nowhere. They solidified in his grasp, drawing puzzled stares from the demons.

"Intruder!" the one who was most likely Asmodeus shouted. "Kill him!"

Two demons closest to Asmodeus seized their firearms, unleashing a hail of bullets. Another pair dashed toward the room's perimeter, intent on commandeering the mounted heavy guns to turn the tide.

As bullets whizzed from their barrels, Legba Navigated again, materializing inches from Asmodeus. He lunged, aiming for Asmodeus's neck, his left blade slicing through the air. But Asmodeus, his reflexes almost otherworldly, parried with an upward motion. His counterattack, a fierce blow to Legba's face, could have ended the fight there and then. Yet Legba Navigated away, reemerging in a crouched position by Asmodeus's right leg. He swung his other hand in an arc, but the demon evaded with astonishing speed.

Time to improvise!

Legba Navigated in front of him and swiped at Asmodeus's shoulder again. Before his arm had traveled half the distance, he Navigated, appearing beside him. The ruse caught the demon off guard, allowing Legba's blade to nick his shoulder before he could react. The wound was barely noticeable, but Legba had his blood and, thus, his memories.

He tried to Navigate again, but a defensive punch from Asmodeus's left arm clattered with his face, sending his body tumbling next to Daeva. Every instinct screamed at Legba to flee. But he could not abandon the son of Umoren.

Daeva, who had momentarily shifted her focus from the Ogg Vorbis, was vulnerable. Legba banished his blood-stained blade to the Abyss of Nowhere and swiped his second blade at her leg. But in an instant, she vanished. She was a Navigator! How could he forget?

He Navigated away from his position just as a barrage of bullets hit the ground where he had been. He moved toward Daeva, a few feet behind him, and lunged again. She vanished just as his blade neared her neck. He closed his eyes and focused on her essence, tracking her movements as her body Navigated to the other end of the room.

Summoning his dwindling strength, he followed her Noise, keeping up with her as she transported across the room. She materialized next to the entrance of the boundary room door, but he was there a fraction of a second after. His sudden appearance caught her off-guard, her eyes widening. Before she could react, he sliced her thigh, drawing her blood. And in the blink of an eye, he vanished, leaving only a whisper of his presence behind.

~

A LOUD SLAP jolted **Ikenga** awake, his eyes snapping open to Legba's looming figure. Disorientation flickered across his features, replaced quickly by recognition.

"Legba?" Ikenga asked.

Legba took a step back and turned around. "Put your clothes on," he said.

Ikenga laboriously pushed himself up, his muscles screaming in protest as he searched for his clothes. They were folded neatly by the side of the rocks. Two needles protruded from his arm, tethered to a pouch of mysterious liquid at his side. Each movement was a struggle, his body protesting with sharp stabs of pain as he dressed.

"Where is Daeva? What are you doing here?"

"Are your clothes on?" Legba inquired, his tone masking an undercurrent of concern.

"Yes," Ikenga said.

As Legba pivoted, his long, flowing jacket billowed around him, grazing the ground. Beneath the layers of fabric, glimpses of his exposed chest could be seen.

Coughing, Ikenga rasped, "Where is Daeva?"

"I suspect you may know the answer to that question," Legba said.

Ikenga shifted. "We have to find her," he said.

"I know the full plan now," Legba whispered. "Unfortunately, it's too late."

"Stop it. No," Ikenga said as poignant memories from the previous night flooded his senses. The moments felt so real. He had to find her.

"All the Brokers are dead. We must return to Kirina," Legba urged. He paused, his eyes unfocused, lost in a sea of distant thoughts.

"Dead? How can they be dead?"

Legba raised his hand, summoning a gleaming sword, and lunged at Ikenga, brandishing it high. Ikenga instinctively raised his palms in defense. But something was missing. He tried to use his magic to bring out fire from his hands. The flames that came out were red.

"Daeva needed two things," Legba said, softening his stance. "Your weapon and the spirit inside you. From the first time you met her, everything that has happened was her plan to steal them from you."

"It can't be." Ikenga shook his head. "How would she know?"

"The Vodun Observer who gave you the plans to summon the Esi... that was Ghede Ghadou's man. They didn't expect you to go into hiding for two years."

Reeling from Legba's revelations, Ikenga glanced around frantically, only to realize Formless was missing.

"I was with her when the Eden Protocol attacked, when we came here," Ikenga said.

"You are wrong. Those were Masina operatives trying to stop them," Legba said.

"But she did not find me. I found her!"

"The spy we had in Ghede Ghadou's camp was compromised," Legba said. "They used me to find you and bring you to them. They deceived me just as much as you."

I want your soul, Daeva's words echoed in his mind. A wave of nausea overwhelmed Ikenga as he clasped his hand over his torso, a hollow void gnawing at his very essence. In a moment of blind trust, he had offered her everything, not grasping the gravity of his words.

"Take all of it!" he had told her.

"A succubus can only take from you what you willingly give them. Even the strongest man would find it hard to resist," Legba said. "It is too late to stop the demon invasion. But maybe, just maybe, we can mount a formidable defense."

"No," Ikenga protested in desperation. "I cannot accept that. If we confront her, she will have an explanation. She must." Their connection had felt too real.

"When was the last time you saw her?" Legba said.

"It has to have been just a few hours."

"You've been unconscious for three days. She abandoned you once she got what she wanted. Be grateful you still breathe."

Tears of anger and betrayal glistened in Ikenga's eyes. "You lie!" he roared. "All the elaborate moves... why? She could've taken the sword when we first crossed paths. We've saved each other. How can all that be a mere ruse?"

"Genuine desire. She needed you to trust, to truly yearn for her. Only then could she complete her deception."

"I will kill her!" Tears welled in his eyes as the crushing weight of his anguish and betrayal overwhelmed him.

"We must go to Vodun immediately. If we can get to Amadioha or the Bondye soon enough, we might be able to rescue this situation."

"If what you say is true," Ikenga said. "We have already lost."

"No. You cannot say that." Legba paced on the dark, fine sand, a storm of anxiety replacing his usual composed façade. "We must try!"

Ikenga looked away from Legba, peering into the distance. Nausea settled in his stomach, reminiscent of the gut-wrenching moment he informed Utaka of his father's death. "No," he said

Legba's face dropped in surprise. "No?" he said. "We are not doing this again."

"For most of my life. I have simply blown around without direction, basing my actions on the whims of my current situation. No more."

"You are speaking nonsense, son of Umoren. This is your redemption, and you throw it away."

"I am beyond redemption," Ikenga murmured in resignation. "If I had not chased that spirit, Moremi would be alive. If I had not run, Utaka would not be in prison. And if I had not gone after Daeva, perhaps Kirina would not be on the brink of destruction." There was a calmness within him as he spoke.

"So now you choose to do nothing?" Legba shouted. "We must fix this!"

"If we are in the last days, I will spend it correcting the wrongs with the one I care about," Ikenga said.

"You exhibit the foolishness you did when we first met," Legba advanced closer to Ikenga.

"I will go to Akesan and rescue Utaka."

"You have not been to Orisha in years. Your name has been plastered around the Akesan walls since Moremi's death. Your reward would turn even the most loyal servant against you. They would arrest and execute you long before you got anywhere near Utaka."

"When I met you, you were a stranger," Ikenga said. "Yet I did what you asked. I know I cannot get there myself. I need you to help me. Leave me at the edge of the city. I will take my chances. Then you can go to Vodun and maybe save the realm." Ikenga paused, a surge of emotion overwhelming him. Thoughts of Moremi flooded his mind, drawing tears from his eyes. "If this is how it ends, then so be it. But I have not had this much peace in my heart since my father passed."

33

ORISHA
REALM OF KIRINA

*I*kenga drew a deep breath and savored the scent of the stream blending with the ripe aroma of crops from the farm ahead. Memories of Moremi flooded his thoughts, their weight so poignant it nearly buckled his knees. The owner, Yemi, had shown them hospitality, something Ikenga had found harder to come by in Akesan, the capital city of Orisha, just a mile north. Next to the farm was an open plain of grass that went on endlessly. Ikenga reminisced about how he and Moremi spent hours gazing at the sky. They would talk about what their children would look like and how many they would have. He must have memorized every single constellation over the years.

As memories of Moremi lingered, a shadow of guilt crept in. Daeva's presence surged in his mind, their moments together demanding his attention. Why was he still thinking about her? Were his feelings of anger or hurt? His mind went to the first time they lay together. They had shared an intensity, as if ripping out each other's souls and consuming them. He was not angry. She had left him to die, but he was not angry.

He looked at the ground in embarrassment. At the corner of the sprawling farm stood a quaint single-story house. Its freshly painted façade gleamed in the afternoon sun. That and the just-about-to-be-harvestable acres of planted corn meant someone still lived here. They walked silently, with Legba not having uttered a word since their arrival in Orisha. They knocked on the door. Tension filled his chest as they waited.

Yemi, wearing a loose-fitted shirt that looked like it had once been white, eventually opened the big wooden door. He was slender, but his arms were muscular and oversized from years of farm work. The blood left his face as he saw Ikenga. "Ikenga!" he shouted, words catching in his throat as he tried to say more.

Ikenga smiled nervously, spotting Legba in his peripheral vision, who was ready to do what was necessary.

"Yemi!" Ikenga exclaimed.

Tension hung in the air before Yemi rushed forward and hugged him. Ikenga hugged him back. His massive arms made it hard to breathe for a few seconds. He gasped once Yemi released him.

"You're alive!" Yemi said, his eyes scanning Ikenga. Then, as if a dam broke, his words rushed out. "Where have you been? What happened?" He asked his questions faster than Ikenga could register. Yemi rattled off, his words tumbling over each other.

"We need to catch up on the years," Ikenga said, "But I cannot tell you everything now."

Yemi nodded. "Who is this one?"

"The one who is leaving now," Legba replied, his face utterly emotionless. "Ikenga of Umoren, may your gods guide you." The finality in Legba's tone echoed a farewell more than a simple good luck. He became translucent and then disappeared.

A shocked look crossed Yemi's face.

"He has a flair for dramatic exits," Ikenga chuckled.

Inside, the room was drenched in the musty aroma of fresh paint, intensified by what had lingered outside. Yemi had decorated the walls with the heads of animals he had hunted. Round stones filled the voids where eyes once were.

The interior had changed so much that Ikenga felt he had never been there. "It is so different."

"You have been gone for a long time," Yemi said. "Ale?"

"Just water," he replied, still sick from being unconscious for so long. "And any food you have, if it does not bother you."

"Do birds fly? I'm a farmer!" Yemi exclaimed.

They burst out laughing. Ikenga consumed dish after dish, his fork scarcely leaving his hand before diving back into the plentiful spread.

"At the pace you're gobbling that food, your stomach must think it's in a race," Yemi said.

Ikenga almost choked on the meat he was chewing as he laughed.

"It's good to see you," Yemi said. "But you must know you are a wanted man. Why have you come here?"

Ikenga took a measured sip of water, the merriment fading from his eyes. "I tried to save her."

"Moremi was always stubborn," Yemi said. "Some would say you should still have protected her."

Ikenga looked down at the table.

"After her death, Nago Sango sent his goons here, pelting me with questions like arrows. When they left empty-handed, they escalated their methods. They tried to break my spirit and this sanctuary on their next visit. They underestimated my resilience. This redecoration wasn't by choice." He paused and stood, putting his hands behind his back before facing Ikenga. "King Nago Sango even sent spies."

He pointed out the window. "Right there in that field. Then he sent fake customers and traders to buy my crops. People who would notice any signs of you."

The words weighed heavy on Ikenga. "I am so sorry."

Ignoring Ikenga's apology, Yemi continued, "Then he changed his strategy and offered me ten times the reward for any information. I couldn't lie. The idea of money instead of harassment tempted me. But I didn't know where you were or even if you were alive, did I?" He dragged the chair over and sat down again. His arms landed on the table with enough force to shake the plates. "You are my friend, but I must ask again. Why did you come?"

Words escaped from Ikenga's mouth without a voice. Yemi, Utaka, Moremi, his choices had brought pain to so many. "I thought Utaka was dead," he said.

Yemi had a pained expression on his face. "Yes, that too."

"I need to find him and correct some of my wrongdoings. Just point me in the right direction, and I'll leave."

Yemi laughed. "If I were waiting for you to do that, I would be long out of here and begging on the streets."

Beneath the table, Ikenga's fists clenched, a tremor of self-directed anger coursing through his veins. Yemi got up again and put his hands on Ikenga's shoulder. "You put me through it, but I know the burden you carry is worse." He squeezed.

Ikenga raised his head and looked at him. "When I thought of anyone in Orisha I could still trust, you were the only one who came to mind."

Yemi walked to the kitchen and poured liquid from a clear glass container. He downed it in one gulp. "My expertise is in farming, not information gathering," he said. "I'll make some inquiries in town. But you must leave first thing in the morning."

Ikenga nodded. "Thank you."

"Don't thank me yet. Rest. You look like you haven't slept in months."

∼

IKENGA SUCCUMBED TO FATIGUE, drifting to sleep on the couch beside the crackling fireplace. But even in his state, uncertainty nagged at him: What was his plan once he found Utaka? He had no obvious answer, but an inexorable need to act propelled him.

He jolted awake, his heart thundering in his chest as if he had just been running. Looking out the window, he noticed it was close to midnight. He searched the house, but Yemi was still not back. In his dreams, Moremi had walked in while he lay naked with Daeva. He had frozen, the pain in her eyes turning to anger. He had woken up when they started trading blows.

Seeking solace, he exited the house and wandered the farm. As he meandered through the crops, the crisp scent of dew-kissed grass and trees filled his nostrils. The farm was twice as big as the last time he had visited. He plucked a yellow lime from a nearby plant, biting into its flesh. It had a sweet, tangy taste. He craved more, much like a beggar reaching out hungrily. He devoured four, savoring the juices as they trickled down his throat. A revitalizing energy coursed through him, awakening his senses.

A loud crash pulled him from his reverie. He glanced at Yemi's house from his place among the crops, alarm gripping him as several men converged on it. Even from a distance, one man's distinct short red hair stood out in the moonlight; Ososi Nago, Nago Sango's oldest son. Many others surrounded the building. Among them, Ikenga recognized Dudu Nago. His distinctive swagger was unmistakable, even in the distance. A surge of adrenaline kicked in; Ikenga turned on his heels, racing toward the open plain with desperate strength. As he brushed against the crops, he remembered Legba telling him it would happen. How could he have been so naïve to think otherwise?

"In the fields! Over there!" Ososi's voice echoed across the farmland. Ikenga's shoes pounding on the soil were as deafening as his racing heartbeat. If there was one thing Nago Sango's children excelled at, it was running. Just as Ikenga entered the forest, a vicious kick swept his feet from under him, sending him tumbling forward. The cool grass cushioned his fall, cradling him as he rolled several times.

Ososi leaped into the air, his fist enveloped in a blue light aimed at Ikenga's face. Ikenga rolled aside, narrowly avoiding Ososi's hand as it slammed into the ground. "You will pay!"

Ikenga scrambled as Ososi kicked. He attacked with force but was rash, telegraphing every move. Ikenga could have bested him on a good day. But today was not a good day. And for a brief second, he forgot at least ten other men had been chasing him. A searing jolt exploded at the back of his head. He turned around to see Dudu wielding a baton, a sinister smirk on his face. Ikenga was dazed enough to miss the next flying kick from Ososi, which sent him to the ground. Within seconds, they were both on top of him. They punched and kicked him with eagerness and conviction. Through the daze and pain, he made out a vengeful chant—"For our sister"—as the blows continued to rain down.

At some point, they stopped, leaving him sprawling on the grass. The pungent stench of churned soil mingled with the tang of his blood invaded his nostrils. One eye was bloodshot and blurry. They had spread the punches out evenly, distributing the blows fairly. Every part of his body, from his toes to his head, was bruised. He did not know how long he lay on the grass before the brothers dragged him by his shoulders. He saw Nago Sango's indomitable figure riding toward them at a measured pace on his horse. His expression was solemn, akin to a disappointed father's gaze. Next to him were Yemi and Nago Sango's third son. Though much younger than Ososi and Dudu, his eyes bore the same fiery anger.

With bloodied lips, Ikenga glared at Yemi. "You were family."

"Everything I said to you was true," Yemi said defensively. "But I was not about to allow you to ruin my life again."

Ikenga tried to summon the energy for anger, but his battered body and spirit only mustered a profound sense of disappointment.

"Remove him!" Nago Sango's voice boomed across the field, its raw power vibrating Ikenga's aching bones.

One of the eight men rode toward Yemi and ushered him back to the farm. Yemi started riding away, then stopped. For a fleeting moment, Ikenga caught what he thought was a shadow of regret or disappointment on Yemi's face. Then he turned back and rode full speed away from them.

"For years now, your cousin lay withering away in my cell," Nago Sango said. "I expected you to come for him, but like a coward, you ran and hid." Nago Sango's horse huffed, struggling to support the man's towering frame.

"Had I known Utaka was alive, I would have willingly surrendered myself in his stead," Ikenga's voice trembled with regret.

"You are a coward and a liar!" Nago Sango said.

"I would have traded my life for Moremi if I could."

The Eden Ruse

"Do not speak her name!" Black sparks shot from Nago Sango's eyes. As it flew at Ikenga, Nago Sango's sons barely had enough time to jump out of the way. The sparks struck him on his shoulder, leaving a gaping hole where skin and flesh once lay. Ikenga tumbled back and rolled across the ground. He focused internally and redirected his energy to suppress his pain receptors at the expense of healing. If he were going to die, he would make it as comfortable as possible.

He rose, settling back on his calves. With shoulders slumped in resignation, he locked his gaze on Nago Sango. One hand clamped over his freshly wounded shoulder. The sparks had sutured the blood vessels, so he was not bleeding.

"I am Nago Sango, King of Orisha! For crimes against our kingdom, crimes against me, and crimes against my daughter, how do you plead?" Nago Sango asked and pointed his finger at Ikenga.

Ikenga could feel it. Those were words this vengeful man had waited so long to say.

"It was not Utaka's fault. End his suffering," Ikenga begged.

"I said, how do you plead?!"

Ikenga looked up at the stars, the very ones he and Moremi had gazed upon countless times together. It was a clear, cloudless night. After so many years, he would finally be with her again. "Guilty," he whispered, but the night wind whisked his voice away.

"I sentence you to die!" Nago Sango's voice echoed in the night, and his eyes sparked with lethal intent. A ball of electricity surged, growing into a fearsome force, before hurtling toward Ikenga. He kept his gaze skyward, the familiar scene a final comfort as he braced for the end.

The afterlife was a void. The stars in the sky disappeared, surrendering the night to a profound, unnatural darkness. Then, the breeze made him realize something was flying over him. Daeva landed right between him and Nago Sango with her wings spread wide. The electricity struck her wings, a sparkle igniting in her eyes before vanishing into the ether. Her hair, elegantly secured by a pin, framed her face while her skin radiated a smooth, vibrant vitality, a newfound life Ikenga had never witnessed.

She spun around, crouching low with her eyes trained on Nago Sango. She slowly stepped closer to Ikenga, her wings still fully extended.

Nago Sango dismounted his horse, his boots thudding against the ground as he took a determined step toward her. Dudu and Ososi hesitated, uncertainty shadowing their expressions. They pulled out daggers, but moved away from them.

Accusations seethed in Ikenga's voice as he glared at her. "You lied to me, betrayed my trust!"

"Shut your mouth and stay behind me," she said.

"Name yourself! What is your business on my land?" Nago Sango thundered. He took another step toward her. Electric sparks covered his hands. Ikenga wondered if Daeva even understood Nago Sango's words.

"Place your hand on my back now," Daeva screamed.

Nago Sango, black electricity sparkling from his eyes, had taken another few steps. Dudu and Ososi had found more confidence in their father and advanced.

"Do it now!" Daeva said in a higher voice.

"It is my time to die." Ikenga coughed out blood.

She turned her head around. Her eyes locked onto his. "I am with child."

The words entered Ikenga's ears and reached the bottom of his stomach. Panic, joy, and apprehension surged through his veins. This was another trick. It had to be.

Casting aside their apprehension, Nago Sango and his sons charged at Daeva and Ikenga with unbridled fury. Ikenga's heart pounded against his ribs, his gaze darting to Daeva. She narrowed her eyes at him. He looked into them and lost all reservations. He put his hand on her back. The open fields disappeared immediately—faster than before.

The off-orange colors of the bricks on the walls hinted they were still in Kirina. Most likely in Vodun. The fragile tether to consciousness that had sustained him finally gave way, plunging him into a deep slumber. But as he traveled out of consciousness, her words rang in his ear: "I am with child."

～

A COLD, hard floor barely cushioned by a thin, worn-out blanket pressed against Ikenga. His eyes fluttered open and a pain-laden groan escaped his lips, drawing his attention to the gaping hole in his shoulder—a grim souvenir from his encounter with Nago Sango.

They were in a suffocatingly narrow room. On either side, tables laden with strewn parchments stretched out. The wall opposite bore even more papers, dominated by a map of Vodun. In front of it stood Daeva, her arms crossed as she studied the map intently.

"You are awake," she remarked, not bothering to turn around. "I thought I had lost you."

"I need an explanation. Now," he said.

She spun around, presenting him with a gray flask. "Drink."

He frowned. "Not again."

She bit her lower lip and opened the flask before handing it to him again. "Let's skip the part where you resist this time."

Desperation won over suspicion. He snatched the flask and gulped its contents. The liquid was even more revolting than he remembered. As his body healed, he remembered the crater he had blown into the wall in Sasobek.

"A new formula," she announced with a knowing smile, as if tuned into his thoughts.

A tremor raced through him, each nerve tingling with reawakened vitality. It was an eternity, but eventually, the raw void in his shoulder mended, leaving behind an insatiable hunger. "You betrayed me!" he exclaimed.

Daeva squatted, her face unreadable as she peered into his eyes. "A few years ago, the Blight affected my twin sister."

"The Blight?"

"It halts our natural healing. Minor injuries worsen, leading to organ failure and, eventually, death," she explained, her gaze falling away.

Shocked, Ikenga jolted upright, his eyes widening.

"I was distraught," Daeva continued, her voice choking. "We were inseparable, often switching places for fun. Then came my recruitment into the Eden Protocol. I learned our race was perishing, that we had been distant from heaven for too long. Joining was the sole path to save my sister and our race." She paused. "I did what I felt was necessary."

"How does this relate to saving your sister? And what does Kirina have to do with any of it?" Ikenga's voice trembled in frustration and confusion.

"My sister is dead," Daeva whispered, a lone tear tracing her cheek. Part of Ikenga wanted to embrace and comfort her, but he held back. "I don't know how it comes together. I was foolish for not asking questions, but I jumped at the first opportunity to save the one I loved. The same way you did when you brought Eshm back to this world."

"It's not the same!" Ikenga waved his hand dismissively.

"I don't pretend to know your kind. But you must believe me, your father did not die of natural causes."

"My father was ill!" Ikenga shot back, eyes aflame.

"His sickness was an engineered virus. But his spirit was strong. He still would not die. So they killed him in a much quicker fashion."

Amadioha had said the Vodunese killed his father. Now Daeva said it was the demons. Maybe they both told the truth. It all made sense. He could have avoided it all if he had listened deeper. "How could you possibly know that?" he asked.

"Because they orchestrated the same fate for my sister," Daeva's voice cracked. Her eyes, brimming with tears, spilled over. "She did not succumb to the Blight. They manipulated her symptoms, like your father's. She suspected it, and I foolishly brushed her fears aside. Only recently did the truth come crashing down."

"I am so sorry," Ikenga said as she wiped her tears. Her story put a sinking feeling in his stomach.

"I was the intended target. For over a month, I had masqueraded as her when she first showed symptoms. It was supposed to be me facing death, not her."

Torn between sympathy and anger, Ikenga approached her and, with a deep breath, wrapped his arms around her. She put her face on his shoulder and he patted her back. It was a warm, soothing feeling, a familiar one. Then he remembered how she had left him to die in No Man's Land and jerked back.

"I will not be fooled twice!" Ikenga said. "You have spun stories before, ones I believed."

Daeva wiped her face. Her teary eyes pulled him in, making him want to trust her despite his reservations.

"You were my mission," she admitted. "I needed Eshm, and I needed your weapon. But it was never personal. You had to give them to me. I couldn't just take them."

"And that is that?" he asked.

"That was it. However, I could not bring myself to kill you after I was done. You should have died after we lay together. That happens with my kind."

"Your kind?" he echoed, eyebrows raised.

"Succubi," she whispered.

"Did the others before me meet the same fate?"

Without meeting his gaze, she gazed at the map. "There were no others before you."

Doubt and disbelief raced through Ikenga. "You are lying."

She turned, lowering her top to reveal the left side of her chest. Her hands then moved to her hair, unpinning it and releasing it from its constraints. A cascade of red strands tumbled down her back. She extended her hand toward him and passed him the pin. It was then he first recognized Formless.

"When I took Eshm from you, I did not know it, but I took something else," she confessed, tears filling her eyes again. "Place your hand over my heart," she urged, motioning to her exposed skin.

Doubts swirled in Ikenga's mind.

"Take this," she whispered, holding out Formless.

The moment he grasped it, a familiar warmth surged in his hands, filling a void inside him. Almost immediately, it transformed into a dagger.

"Press it against my throat. Then touch my heart."

He wanted to kill her, but did everything in his power to suppress the urge.

"Feel my heartbeat," she implored, stepping closer. Guiding the blade to her neck, a trickle of blood flowed. He felt the rhythmic thud of her heart, followed by a jolt. In a whirlwind of emotions, she kissed him passionately. His senses spiraled, and he crumpled to the floor, trembling. He gasped for air and managed, "What have you done?"

"Look at your hands."

A black flame enveloped his hands. Eshm.

"You are capable of so much love," she said. "That is why Lucifer chose you. Because those who love the most are those most easily manipulated. That was why he chose me too. When we lay together, that is why I conceived instead of killing you. Love."

"I love Moremi. Not you."

"Love is never about the other person. It is always about yourself."

The words were too much for Ikenga to process. Why did he believe them? "You are really pregnant with my child?" he asked in a resigned voice as the blood left his face.

"Children. We are joined forever." A smile crossed her face as she rubbed her belly. "Asmodeus is on his way to Rada Mysters now. We must avenge my sister and your father. Together."

Shock froze him to his core, stealing his breath as he watched tears stream down her face - a manifestation of his upending world.

34

ESCAPE

$\mathcal{K}$riminel, his muscles aching and slick with sweat, completed his fiftieth pushup in the dim light of his cell. Rising, he wiped his brow and approached a sturdy wooden beam hanging from the ceiling. With determined grunts, he began a series of pull-ups, his well-defined muscles straining from the effort. Months of captivity had whittled his frame, yet each exercise session sculpted him further, revealing the sinewy strength beneath his skin.

The chill of the prison's damp air seeped into his bones. His breath was ragged, punctuating the silent cell. Nearby, Simon, his cellmate, was engrossed in a secretive endeavor. He worked with a conspicuous openness, almost inviting curiosity, but Kriminel knew better than to indulge in the luxury of hope. Instead, he maintained a vigilant routine, using the quieter night hours for rest and resuming his strenuous workouts by day.

The harsh voice of a guard shattered the silence. "Stand back!" A small hatch in the door rattled open, revealing the guard's scarred torso, adorned with two menacing axes.

Startled, Simon jerked upright, his eyes wide with alarm, and scuttled to the farthest corner of the cell.

With a sneer, the guard shoved a tray holding a meager meal

through the hatch: some tepid soup, pieces of stale bread, and a banana to be shared by them. "Dinner is served," he mocked before slamming the hatch.

Despite its blandness, the food was a welcome sight. Kriminel lunged for the banana, his stomach growling in anticipation, only for Simon's unexpected command to stop him. "I need that," Simon stated.

"For what?" Kriminel demanded.

"Phosphorus," Simon said, picking up the banana from the tray. Kriminel cursed under his breath at the loss of his sustenance.

Simon mushed the banana into a pulp and mixed it with a mysterious liquid in a container. Kriminel had watched Simon's strange experiments before, involving various food items and even scrapings from their iron bar. After finishing what was left of the food, he succumbed to a fitful sleep, his dreams haunted by thoughts of escape.

A gentle tap roused him from his slumber. Simon stood over him, a finger pressed to his lips. He revealed the banana mixture, which had transformed into a thick paste. With meticulous care, Simon applied the paste to the lock of their cell and inserted pebbles into it. Kriminel watched in stunned silence as the concoction fizzed and smoked, emanating a pungent, metallic odor. The paste corroded the locking mechanism, shifting the door ajar.

"There are two guards on this floor at night," Simon said. "We need to move quickly and neutralize them before they raise an alarm."

Kriminel, initially taken aback by Simon's newfound assertiveness, nodded in agreement.

The guards, lulled into complacency by the routine monotony of their duties, were sound asleep. Subduing them and securing their keys was an almost effortless task.

In the next cell were four Vodunese, half alert, their eyes narrowing suspiciously at the sight of them.

"Who do you pledge your swords to?" Kriminel demanded as he thumped his chest.

"We pledge our swords to Baron Brigid!" they chorused in unison. Kriminel's expression turned to disappointment, and they moved on without another word.

Approaching the next cell, Kriminel repeated his question. The men inside exchanged bewildered glances, having overheard the previous exchange. "We are loyal to Ghede Ghadou Loa!" they proclaimed.

Kriminel gestured to Simon, signaling to proceed, while the desperate pleas of the men they left behind echoed down the hallway.

Kriminel's question received an instant, fervent response in the third cell. "We are yours, Baron Kriminel! To death and beyond!"

A triumphant smile broke across Kriminel's face, and he nodded at Simon to unlock their cell.

As they drew closer to Brigid's cell, Kriminel's steps faltered, a storm of conflicting emotions raging within him. The temptation to leave her to her fate was strong.

Simon leaned closer, his words a hushed whisper. "The Dead Forest is our only path to Ghede Loa. We need her."

Kriminel gave a begrudging grunt of acknowledgment. He handed the key to Simon, who unlocked Brigid's cell.

Kriminel stepped to the front of the cell, his eyes narrowing as he studied Brigid's disheveled appearance. She sat huddled in the corner, her once vibrant hair matted and dull, her face smudged with grime. She had fared much worse than they had, looking like a shadow of her former self.

"I have had plenty of time to think," he said. "Ghede Ghadou sent you to sabotage my mission, didn't he? I just can't figure out why."

Brigid averted her gaze, focusing on the moss growing on the wall before her.

He looked at Simon and motioned for him to leave before stepping further into the cell. "You have betrayed your people," Kriminel said. "I wonder if a shred of honor is left in you."

"Ghede Ghadou couldn't let you defeat Amadioha," Brigid whispered, her voice barely audible above the dripping water echoing in the cell. "It would have ruined everything he'd planned."

The admission hit Kriminel like a sledgehammer, even though he expected it.

"We have been monitoring you for the last two years, getting reports from spies. He needed the Bondye weakened, and Amadioha was the best person to do that."

"The Bondye?" Kriminel's voice rose in disbelief. "He sacrificed his people? Fout Tonne! His barons? And you... you were willing to risk your life for his madness?"

"The army I came with was mostly peasants passing as soldiers," Brigid said. She turned from the wall to look at him with lost eyes. "We should have been far away before the Niri attacked. But something happened... I don't know. They should not have been in the forest."

I could have taken down Amadioha in Nnabu Valley if not for my Loa's interference, Kriminel fumed. *That was my victory he stole. After everything I've done, he sacrificed me to die?*

"What an honorless pig," Kriminel said and spat on the floor. "You are undeserving of your rank as baron."

"I did what my Loa ordered! Like a baron is supposed to! You are the one without honor!"

Kriminel snorted. "You made the mistake of trusting a manipulator," he said. "All the times we called out to him for assistance, he intentionally left us to fail, like lambs led to the slaughter."

"We need to go back to him. He can explain," Brigid pleaded, her sunken eyes wide with desperation. "Our Loa sees things we can't. You have to understand."

"Understanding is not the problem here."

Baron Brigid struggled to her feet, her tattered robes hanging loosely from her emaciated frame. "I promise we can fix this. Let us talk to Ghede Ghadou." She stepped toward him.

Kriminel's grip tightened on the axe he had stolen from the guards. He stared at her, his eyes filled with a quiet menace.

Her words are as hollow as the empty cell surrounding us. "You can crawl back to Ghede if you want, but I won't join you."

She stammered, "Then where will you go?"

Kriminel's smile was one of sly anticipation. "I will seek an audience with another Loa, one who will truly appreciate our struggle against the Niri." His eyes gleamed with cunning and excitement. "No, I won't waste my time with Gede Mysters. Radha Ramirez Loa will embrace us, and, as far as I know, she needs warriors for her growing army."

35

INVASION PART 1

*L*egba's eyes darted across the shadowy chamber as he leaned in, his voice barely above a whisper. "The attack... it is upon us. Far sooner than we dared imagine." A shudder ran through his usually steady frame. "I fear for the other Loas."

Radha Rhamirez Loa's jaw tightened. "Let us concern ourselves with what happens here."

The Sacred Master trailed behind Legba and the Loa as they hurried through the winding corridors of Rada Mysters. The air grew heavy with the scent of incense, while ethereal blue light pulsed along the walls, casting eerie shadows that seemed to dance and whisper. Their hurried footsteps echoed, a rhythm that matched the frantic beating of Legba's heart. As they approached the ornate double doors, two guards clad in full armor stepped forth and saluted. Legba's gut tightened with an uneasy feeling. Something was off about them. As soon as the Loa approached them, he noticed a slight shift of the head from the guard on the left.

The throne room guards never shift their gaze.

Legba lunged forward, shoving the Loa aside as the guards brought their swords down in a vicious arc. Wicked blades whistled through the air where they had stood mere heartbeats ago. Swords manifested in Legba's hands. Steel met steel in a shower of sparks, the impact reverberating through his arms and driving him to one knee. Gritting his teeth against the strain, he glanced sideways to see Zaka, the Sacred Master, raising his arms. The air crackled with power as tendrils of midnight-black energy erupted from his palms. The beams struck true, boring smoking holes through the men's breastplates. Legba ripped off their helmets after they fell, revealing pallid skin and straight blond hair.

Demons!

More demons emerged from the shadows surrounding them. The throne room door burst open, revealing two more assailants, their blades flashing. The battle was fierce. The Sacred Master blasted the closest demon with rays of light, but its massive wings unfurled, forming a protective shield. Legba danced through the chaos, his flickering blades finding their marks. One, two, then three demons fell before they knocked him down, his senses reeling. The Loa wove among the rest, extending a hand to freeze one, only to cry out as another struck her from behind. The demon raised a spear, poised to strike and end her journey in this life.

Despair rushed through Legba's bones, followed by helplessness. In that eternal moment, a miracle occurred. The demon looming over her stiffened, its eyes widening in shock. Legba blinked, scarcely believing his eyes as he saw a gleaming metal spear tip burst through the creature's chest. An armored knight wrenched his spear free, and the demon collapsed. With newfound hope, Legba swept his attacker's feet and drove a fist into its groin before dispatching it with a blade that materialized in his hand. Another flash of metal caught his eye as he staggered to his feet. Another spear impaled a demon mere inches from him, the force of the blow lifting the creature off its feet and pinning it to the far wall.

Legba's gaze met the visored face of their savior. Even through the helmet's narrow slit, he could see the fierce determination burning in the man's eyes. Intricate runes and sigils adorned the armor—unmistakable markings of one of Ghede Ghadou Loa's barons. The baron pulled off his helmet to reveal an *X* scar in the center of his forehead.

Beside him, a shorter man wielded a wooden contraption, pulling a trigger that launched spear-like projectiles, eliminating the remaining demons.

∼

KRIMINEL MAINTAINED a cautious distance as the skinny man helped Radha Rhamirez Loa to her feet. There was a scar across his face from top to bottom. Her Sacred Master stood gingerly, examining his shoulder as his wounds healed. The baron's mind raced, piecing together everything he knew about these men. Ghede Ghadou's voice echoed in his memory, filled with grandiose plans to conquer Radha Rhamirez Loa's lands—plans that had crumbled to ash when Amadioha's forces had torn through their ranks.

Radha Rhamirez Loa glared at him. "What is a baron of Ghede Ghadou doing in my Mysters?"

Kriminel let his helmet fall to the floor with a clang. "I am Baron Kriminel, but I no longer serve Ghede Ghadou Loa. My army rots in a Niri prison because of him." He dropped to his knees, glancing back to ensure Simon followed suit. "I swear to you, my blade is yours to command."

"How did you infiltrate the castle?" she demanded.

"We arrived under the cover of night. The preparations for an invasion preoccupied the guards, and they let their vigilance slip, perhaps in the same way these demons gained entry."

"I would be a fool to trust anything you say," she scoffed.

Legba interjected, "My Loa, they saved our lives. Perhaps we can determine their trustworthiness later."

"If I suspect even a hint of deception from you, Ghede Ghadou will feel the full force of my wrath. I promise you that."

Kriminel smiled. "My Loa, I would be honored to fight alongside you against him."

∼

Legba took the blood of one of the dying demons and touched a few drops to his eye. The memories flowed.

He was in Aamaris, where this demon lived—an assassin trained by the Eden Protocol. There were tens of them in the memory. Their job was to kill the Loa and any key people, disorganize the resistance, and have the invading army win easily.

Something else caught Legba's eye that concerned him more. Even though nine of them were dead, at least thirty others had made their way into the Mysters, possibly more, but they had snuck in over the last few weeks, just like Ghede Ghadou's Baron had said.

"They will have anti-Navigation capabilities," a soldier said.

"After we destroy it, have our Navigators lead an ancillary force to overwhelm the castle's defenses from the inside."

Holographic imagery was in the middle, showing all the castle's key strongholds.

Legba snapped out of the memory, his heart pounding. "My Loa, we must act now! Assassins have infiltrated the palace, and they're heading for the anti-Navigation chamber."

Radha Rhamirez Loa's expression hardened in resolve. "Zaka, take this deserter of Ghede Ghadou and his pet, round up the Mysters' guards, and eliminate the threat inside. Legba, we are going to protect the palace defenses!"

~

As Legba and the Loa raced down the hall to the anti-Navigation room, the air grew thick with the metallic tang of blood and the acrid smell of sweat. Screams of pain and the relentless clash of steel assaulted their ears. They burst into a massive, vaulted space where the stone walls amplified the chaotic sounds of battle. Tens of demons with wings spread out, locked in combat with more guards, their curved blades blurring as they forced the defenders back.

Legba's heart sank when he surveyed the grim scene before him. The demons swarmed the guards, their superior numbers and ruthless ferocity twisting the tide of battle in their favor. How had so many infiltrated undetected? As he looked closer, he noted their uniformly shaven heads and darker complexions likely chosen to help them blend in. Asmodeus had planned the attack meticulously, Legba realized with a chill.

"My Mysters will not fall again. Not for a second time!" the Loa cried. With an enraged scream, she leaped into the fray, her hair streaming behind her as she crashed into the demons' flank. She whirled and dove through their ranks, her sword lashing out to decapitate one demon while her other hand drew a line of blue light on another's chest. They clawed and snapped at her to no avail, her preternatural grace allowing her to slip through their grasp like smoke.

As he watched, Legba swelled with mingled awe and pride—as well as no small amount of concern. *Reckless,* he thought, clenching his jaw. When she got like that, she was lethal but vulnerable if she faltered, even for a moment.

Legba raised his voice to rally the remaining guards. "Protect your Loa!"

He charged after her. Twin swords materialized in his hands, and he plowed into a trio of demons seeking to surround her. Sparks flew as he parried and redirected their strikes, watching for any opening. There—one overextended. Legba feinted left, then whirled right, his blade shearing deep into its neck. It toppled without a sound.

All around, Legba echoed the song of clashing steel. Spurred by their Loa's fearless example, the guards fought with renewed zeal, even as casualties mounted. Bodies lay strewn on both sides, the stone underfoot growing slick with blood. Legba deflected another blow, then riposted, driving his blade under the demon's ribs to pierce its heart.

A piercing scream filled the air. He spun to see the Loa impaled by a sword, dropping to her knees. He rushed to her, his blade slicing through the air at the demon's head, but another demon's sword pierced her shoulder, and she collapsed. With a single, powerful stroke, he decapitated both demons, their blood splattering as he rushed to her side.

"My Loa!" Legba cried as he cradled her in his arms.

The Loa parted her lips to speak, but instead of words, a rivulet of blood spilled forth, painting her lips a haunting shade of red. The guards formed a protective circle as they took down the last demons. Her sacrifice was enough to turn the tide.

"Legba," the Loa whispered, her voice fading into a whisper. "You have been a good servant."

The Sacred Master and Ghede Ghadou's baron charged into the room.

"Step back!" the Sacred Master commanded. The guards obeyed, parting to make way for him as he clenched his fists. With a surge of black light, the blades piercing the Loa's body extracted themselves, eliciting a heart-wrenching scream from her lips. The Sacred Master kneeled beside Legba while the black light flowed into her wounds, sealing them.

"I have little time," the Loa gasped, her voice barely above a whisper.

"The healers will fix you," Legba insisted, his eyes brimming with desperate hope.

A mirthless laugh escaped her lips, accompanied by another trickle of blood. "No one can fix me now." Her gaze swept across the room, locking eyes with everyone. "All who can hear me, witness this. Because I have no heirs, as the last Loa before me, I pass on my duties and responsibilities to Papa Legba."

Shock rippled through the room, and the weight of her words settled upon them. Legba and the Sacred Master exchanged a look of disbelief, their eyes wide with the gravity of the situation.

"My Loa, what do you mean?" the Sacred Master asked.

The Loa's body went limp in Legba's arms, the last breath escaping her lips as the final spark of life faded away. She was gone, leaving a void no one could fill.

Pain and turmoil built inside Legba. He clenched his fist, looking for someone to release his anger on. The last time he had felt that way was when the Sacred Master had revealed the identity of the man who had taken his sister's life. "She is... She is gone," Legba choked out, his voice barely recognizable to his ears.

The Sacred Master stood beside him, his expression mirroring the same raw emotions courting through Legba's veins. "We have an army of demons outside our castle," the Sacred Master reminded them. "We must defend the Mysters." His gaze locked onto Legba. "You must defend the Mysters."

For a moment, Legba struggled to comprehend the Sacred Master's words. Then, the realization dawned upon him, his Loa's final decree echoing in his mind. "No. I cannot be Loa," Legba protested. "You have stood by her side for many years. You deserve to have it."

"Foute Tonne!" the Sacred Master exclaimed. "She chose you for a reason; we must stand by her decision."

Legba shook his head, his eyes cast downward. "I can't do it," he whispered, the weight of the responsibility crushing his spirit.

"It is not a choice," the Sacred Master declared. He turned to the remaining men. "Get Ogou in here. The rest of you, ready the army outside the castle. Ready them for battle."

"Yes, Sacred Master!" they said in unison and hurried out of the room.

∽

THE PUNGENT AROMA of incense permeated the air, its tendrils weaving through the thick, somber atmosphere. Ogou, the Sacred Master, and a handful of other mages and barons gathered around the body of Radha Rhamirez Loa, their faces filled with grief. A beautiful blue embroidered cloth covered her lifeless form, nestled within the confines of a casket. Despite the stillness of death, her face appeared serene, just as Legba remembered it from their first encounter.

The Sacred Master's voice resonated through the room, "Our Loa has fallen in service to her Mysters. Let us offer words to guide her soul in the afterlife."

Each mourner grasped an incense pot suspended from a delicate chain. In unison, they swirled the pots in a circular motion, raising them toward the heavens. "To the Loa!" they cried out.

One by one, the mages and barons approached the casket, their eyes glistening with tears as they paid their final respects to Radha Rhamirez Loa.

Ogou was the first to speak. "Your leadership guided us through the darkest times, and we will never forget your sacrifice. May your soul find eternal peace in the afterlife." He raised his incense pot and swirled it over the casket.

Ogou stepped back, and another mage took his place, her voice barely above a whisper, "Our beloved Loa, your kindness and compassion touched the lives of all who knew you. Your legacy will live on in the hearts of your people, and we will always carry your teachings with us."

One after another, the mages and barons shared heartfelt words, each sharing her impact on their lives.

Finally, Legba approached the casket, his heart heavy with grief. He kneeled beside Radha's lifeless form, tears pouring from his eyes. "I was lost, and you showed me a way. You gave me what no one else could and made me find another family. Now Rada Mysters is my home, and I will protect it just as you did until you took your last breath." Legba looked at her face, hoping her eyes would open and she would tell him it was all a ruse, but nothing happened.

"An army stands ready to attack, waiting just beyond our walls. We will avenge our fallen leader by demonstrating the true might of Vodun," the Sacred Master said.

Legba's words seethed through his clenched teeth. "Every single one of them will pay."

The Sacred Master turned his gaze to Legba. "Before her soul departed, she anointed you as the next Loa. Do you accept?"

Legba's heart wavered. He was a follower, not a leader, and the prospect of stepping into the role filled him with trepidation. Yet, even as doubt gnawed at his soul, refusing would betray her memory. "I swear to you all, on my life and soul, that I will carry on our Loa's legacy, leading our people with the same strength she embodied. I accept."

The Sacred Master approached, lifted the crown from Radha Rhamirez Loa's lifeless brow, and placed it upon Legba's head. His voice boomed through the room, "All hail Legba Samedi Loa!"

The gathered men echoed the proclamation, their voices rising in unison, "Hail, hail!"

Legba stood tall, his eyes flickering with a newfound resolve. "We will honor her memory with a proper burial. But first, we have an army to conquer."

As one, the mages and barons raised their incense pots high, the fragrant smoke swirling around them like a veil of determination.

∽

THEY BURST out of the Mysters and into the stables, mounting their horses before galloping toward the entrance. When they reached the gates, Legba nodded to the Sacred Master. They dismounted and approached the paired guardian statues flanking the towering gates. They were the statues Legba had stared at in awe the first time he came to the Mysters. Ogou and the Sacred Master each laid a palm on the stone feet of the dormant colossi. They closed their eyes, and their hands shook as they touched them.

For a long moment, nothing happened. Then a resonant groan echoed as the giants shifted. Stone ground over stone with sounds no living throat could utter. The statues tore free of the pillars and facades, standing up straight with their oversized weapons in their hands.

The golems towered over them, their stone bodies fully animated and thrumming with ancient power. Their eyes glowed an ethereal blue, and the intricate carvings on their faces lent them an unsettling human appearance. They kneeled before the Sacred Master, the ground shuddering beneath their immense weight. "We serve you Sacred Master," they rumbled, voices cavernous and grinding like colliding mountains.

Legba shuddered at the sight. The monstrous beasts were on their side, but they were still scary.

"Your time has come. Will you fulfill your purpose?" the Sacred Master asked.

The golems bowed their heads, stone lips and chisel-cut beard plaits scraping the ground. "Command us, and we shall obey," they said

"Defend these walls, defy these fiends from Hell's depths! Destroy all who raise arms against us!" the Sacred Master said.

"We shall obey."

When they passed through the gates, an awe-inspiring sight greeted them: the vast expanse of the plains had transformed into a sea of gleaming armor and waving flags. The Mysters army stood assembled in disciplined ranks, ready for battle.

When Legba appeared, they raised a great cry. "Our Loa! Our Loa!" The chant built like a wave.

Legba scanned the horizon, and his heart sank at the sight of Asmodeus's vast army amassing in the distance. The enemy's ranks stretched as far as the eye could see, their numbers dwarfing the vodun forces. Glints of metal caught the sun—not just swords and arrows, but the far more advanced projectile weapons that fired deadly bullets. The realization of their technological disadvantage settled like a leaden weight in Legba's gut.

"If they want to attack us, let them come!" Legba screamed.

"For Vodun!" the soldiers chanted. "For Rada Mysters!"

"For who do we fight!" Legba shouted.

"For Legba Samedi Loa! For the Bondye!"

36

REUNION

A crushing weight settled on **Ikenga**, his heavy bones pulling him into despair. He wanted to run toward Moremi, but his legs rooted to the spot.

Eshm let out another laugh, a sound so vile and discordant it curdled the surrounding air. Then it turned back to Moremi and ran toward her. As it got near her, its body became an amorphous blob.

"Moremi!" Ikenga screamed. But she was too far gone. He watched in horror as the thing called Eshm absorbed itself into her.

In an instant, movement returned to Ikenga's legs, and he sprinted across the cave toward her with a speed he had never known. Moremi's body convulsed before crumpling to the ground.

He crouched beside her, cradling her in his arms. She stared off into the distance, her eyes unfocused and filled with pain. "What is happening to me?" she gasped, her body wracked with violent spasms.

"I don't know!" he cried. "That thing may have entered you."

As he held her close, a clear liquid pooled from her mouth, her eyes turning a bloodshot red. Seeing her in such a state cut him deeper than any sword ever could. He clung to her as he helplessly looked around the cave.

Eventually, her convulsions subsided, and her eyes fluttered shut. Her body radiated an intense heat, and her breathing grew shallow and labored.

Even in sleep, she found no rest, her body twitching and trembling. Eventually, he succumbed to a restless sleep, collapsing beside her.

He awoke later to a searing heat emanating from her body. He noticed lesions across her exposed arms and neck. Her eyes moved rapidly beneath her eyelids, as if she were trapped in a fever dream, yet the rest of her body remained perfectly still.

"Over there!" the shout echoed through the cave, originating from the entrance. Ikenga's head snapped up, his eyes landing on two armed guards, the white lines on their faces marking them as Orisha soldiers. Questions raced through his mind—how had they found them?—but he pushed them aside. Moremi needed help, and that was all that mattered.

Ikenga lowered Moremi to the ground. "Come quickly! She is very sick," he shouted.

Just before he released her, a strange sensation coursed through his body, a peculiar fullness like his blood vessels had expanded. He shook it off as he waved frantically at the approaching soldiers.

"Step away from her! Immediately." Their voices were sharp.

Ikenga raised his hands in surrender, backing away as the first soldier kneeled beside Moremi, examining her still form. The man's face contorted with fear as he declared, "She is dead!"

"No, she is sick and needs help." Ikenga pleaded.

Ikenga stepped toward her, his hand outstretched, but the soldier's sword flashed in the light, halting his movement. "Step back!" the man commanded, his tone leaving no room for argument.

Ikenga's gaze fell upon Moremi. Horror washed over him. Her body lay motionless. "No!" he cried out. "It can't be."

The second soldier drew his sword. "On your knees!" he shouted

Ikenga complied, sinking to the ground, his eyes never leaving Moremi's lifeless form. The soldiers grabbed him and hauled him to his feet. "You are coming with us!"

As they dragged him across the cave, the strange sensation of fullness returned, stronger than before. His head spun, the pain intensifying until it felt like every blood vessel in his skull was bursting simultaneously.

∼

IKENGA'S MIND reeled as he kneeled on the hard ground, the metal chains that bound his arms to the wooden beam biting into his skin. Nago Sango's men had brought him to an area of the woods a day's walk from his castle, putting him through hours of relentless interrogation. They demanded answers about Moremi, but Ikenga could only offer them the truth.

"I have told you all I know," he repeated. He explained how he and Moremi had ventured into the cave and encountered Eshm. But the soldiers were skeptical, their eyes narrowing with each passing minute.

One soldier slapped Ikenga across the face. The sharp sting of the blow sent Ikenga's head snapping to the side, his cheek burning from the impact. "What kind of ridiculous story is that?" the soldier demanded.

"We should just kill him and say we found her body alone," the other soldier, his hand resting on the hilt of his sword, spoke up.

"You fool! And who do you think Nago Sango's wrath will turn to?"

"Well then, suggest a better alternative!"

A tense silence followed, broken only by the rustling of leaves in the wind outside the tent. Finally, the first soldier spoke. "There isn't one. When he gets to the castle, fear will make him remember the truth."

The soldiers agreed, however tenuous it might be. They unchained Ikenga from the wooden beam, the metal links clinking as they fell away from his bruised wrists.

"Time to go," the first soldier ordered. The men grabbed Ikenga by the arms, their grips tight and unyielding, and dragged him toward the tent's entrance.

As they moved, the strange sensation returned, the fullness in Ikenga's blood vessels intensifying with each passing second. It was as if his body was expanding to break free from the confines of his skin.

They had barely exited the tent when the first soldier let out a blood-curdling scream. "He is burning me!"

Ikenga's head whipped around, his eyes widening at the white flames engulfing the soldier's body. The fire emanated from Ikenga's hands, a realization that sent a jolt of terror through his veins.

In an instant, the flames surrounded Ikenga, their intense heat searing the surrounding air. The second guard, caught in the inferno, screamed in *agony as the fire consumed him, his desperate attempts to extinguish the flames proving futile.*

Ikenga watched in horror as the soldiers' skin charred, their cries of pain echoing through the tent. The acrid smell of burning flesh filled his nostrils, making him gag. He wanted to help them, to stop the flames, but he was powerless against the fire that now engulfed them all.

∼

IKENGA STOOD STEADFAST, his eyes fixed on the towering gates of Nago Sango's castle in the heart of Orisha. The bustling crowd of civilians and traders flowed through the open gates, a ceaseless stream of life and commerce.

"Are you sure about this?" Daeva asked.

"I possess a clarity I have never experienced," Ikenga declared, meeting her gaze. For the first time in an eternity, an overwhelming sense of purpose replaced the weight of fear sitting on his shoulders.

A guard stationed at the checkpoint caught sight of the pair. His eyes widened in recognition, and a scream tore from his throat as he scrambled into the depths of the castle. The scene was set. The moment of reckoning had arrived.

Countless stares bore down on Ikenga and Daeva as recognition dawned on the faces of the curious onlookers. Whispers and gossip rippled through the crowd like wildfire, their hushed voices carrying the name of the man whose image had been plastered across every corner of Orisha for years. How long it took for the people to notice him standing there, accompanied by the striking presence of a red-haired demon, surprised him.

A score of guards burst from the gates, gripping spears and swords. The clatter of their armor and the pounding of their feet against the ground filled the air.

"This is your last chance, son of Umoren," she warned, her eyes searching his face for any hesitation.

He ignored her.

The guards closed in. "On your knees! Hands up!" they commanded.

Ikenga complied. Daeva followed. They lowered themselves to their knees, raising their hands in surrender. Once eager to glimpse the spectacle, the onlookers maintained a cautious distance.

The guards wasted no time in securing the pair, cold metal chains biting into their skin as they were bound. They urged them to their feet with a rough shove, marching them through the looming castle gates. Utaka was in a dungeon somewhere inside the walls. *I am coming for you, cousin. You will not endure another day here.*

~

KING NAGO SANGO'S face contorted into a mixture of surprise and rage as Daeva and Ikenga kneeled before him in the opulent receiving room. "Not only are you weak, but you must also be incredibly foolish," Nago Sango seethed. "And now you have the gall to bring a demon into my court?"

Behind the king, his sons stood tall and imposing, their eyes ablaze with barely contained fury and a hunger for revenge.

"Father, allow me the honor of striking down this insolent creature," the eldest son demanded, his hand reaching for his weapon.

Nago Sango raised his hand to shut him up.

"We have come for Utaka. His imprisonment violates the Niri–Orisha peace treaty, and we will not stand for this injustice," Ikenga said.

"Every extra breath Utaka takes is illegal," Nago Sango retorted. "Every extra breath you take is unlawful."

Ikenga rose. The guards surrounding him drew their swords, the sound of metal scraping against scabbards filling the room. "Back on your knees!" one of them shouted.

But Ikenga paid no heed to their demands. Instead, he met Nago Sango's gaze. "You blame me for Moremi's death, but have you ever considered your responsibility in the matter?"

At the mention of his daughter's name, Nago Sango rose from his throne, black sparks emanating from his eyes. His sons' faces lit up in excitement, eager to witness their father unleash his wrath.

"Do not dare speak my daughter's name again," Nago Sango warned.

"I will mention the name of the one I loved!" Ikenga declared. "You must take responsibility for her death, just as I have. She ventured to Fourth Purgatory in secret because of you. The depth of my love for her drove my actions. They may have been reckless, but they were also a result of your unyielding stance against our union. Your inflexibility played a role in this tragedy. While my doing summoned the spirit, your lack of empathy and love pushed her to such desperate measures."

"How dare you!" Nago Sango roared. Electricity crackled and surged from his eyes, bolts of raw power hurtling toward Ikenga with terrifying speed.

Ikenga clenched his fists, the searing heat from his hands weakening the shackles enough for him to break free. He willed Formless, a ring on his finger, to transform into a shield. The crackling electricity collided with the shield, protecting them. The impact's sound resembled a wire on the verge of catching fire.

"Daeva! Now!" he screamed.

Her wings erupted from her back, forming a protective cocoon as she crouched low, bracing herself.

Ikenga squeezed his other hand, channeling a black fire pulse from his palm. He slammed his fist onto the floor with a powerful strike, creating a small crater. The shockwave of flames spread across the room like a tidal wave, knocking everyone off their feet. Nago Sango, caught off guard, was blasted from his feet, his massive body hitting the floor with a resounding thud. As the dust cleared, Daeva unfurled her wings and stood.

Ikenga focused his mind, willing Formless to transform into armor. Although he had never attempted it, the shield retracted, forming a protective suit around his body. The glowing silver encased him from neck to toe, flames still flickering in his eyes.

"I do not know if I am stronger than you," Ikenga said to Nago

Sango, still reeling from the shock as he struggled to his feet. "But you will give me my cousin, or many in your court will die."

Nago Sango let out a short, dismissive laugh, which his sons, though confused, echoed. "The man who tried to marry my daughter was not even half the one who stands before me now," Nago Sango said, a hint of respect in his voice.

"I must right the wrong I have caused." The fire in Ikenga's eyes dissipated, replaced by determination.

"You can take his place in the cell if you want," Nago Sango offered, a cruel smile playing on his lips.

"I cannot agree to your terms," Ikenga countered. "Demons are invading Kirina as we speak. I have more wrongs I must right."

Nago Sango appeared to contemplate Ikenga's request. "I have heard the news," he admitted.

"Father! We cannot give in to his terms! Look what he did to our sister, and he comes here and disrespects us!" Nago Sango's oldest son interjected.

Nago Sango turned to his son, a mocking look on his face. "Perhaps you should teach him a lesson, then?"

The son glanced at Ikenga, assessing the situation, but the sight of Ikenga, clad in armor, must have made him hesitate.

"I must do what I can to stop the demons. After that, we can settle our dispute. If there's one thing you know about me, it's that I am a man of my word," Ikenga said.

Nago Sango looked at him for a moment too long before speaking. "Bring in Utaka!" he shouted to a guard.

∼

When Utaka was brought into the room, a deep pain stabbed Ikenga's heart. His cousin's once muscular form, now emaciated and even skinnier than Legba, was too much to bear. The guards unchained him. Ikenga rushed to his side, overwhelmed with emotion.

"Cousin," he said between sobs.

Despite his weakened state, Utaka smiled at Ikenga. "You are alive," he said, revealing a broken tooth. "The Vodun man found you."

Ikenga nodded, tears streaming down his face. "He did," he confirmed, crouching low to embrace his cousin. "I am sorry," he whispered.

Utaka looked at him, noticing his silver armor for the first time. "Son of Umoren, you are finally ready to walk in your father's steps," he said.

37

INVASION PART 2

*D*amballa leaned against the stone wall. The white linen bandage covering the stump of his hand was a constant reminder of their encounter with the Bondye. If he were lucky, it would grow back after a few months. "Grand Bois Loa has sent another request to parle," he said.

Amadioha's hands clenched. "Parle, parle, parle! How many more Loas must we defeat before there are no more?"

Nestled on a time-worn bench next to Damballa, Amadioha was like a brooding storm amid the serenity. They were in an ancient courtyard, one of the many within the sprawling expanse of the Kal Mysters. The massive tree dominating a significant part of the courtyard seemed as old as the Mysters. Its gnarled roots broke through the ground in places, while overhead, its branches wove a thick canopy that filtered sunlight into dappled patterns. The whisper of leaves and the occasional chirp of a hidden bird were the only sounds that dared disrupt the weighty silence of the age-old enclave.

"If they are so eager to talk, it means they are cornered and desperate," Amadioha observed with bitterness.

Damballa clicked his tongue. "We are a few hundred men in a

Mysters full of thousands of unfriendly civilians and two armies outside our walls."

Amadioha flung a rock at the tree. "Kush, Ikora, Aksum... our triumph should have fueled them. They should be launching offensives against Vodun. What are Ojukwu and the other Ezes in Niri doing?"

Damballa sighed, "Kush has been mobilizing to the border at Dan, but they have stopped short of an invasion. If not for that, we could have had an army three times bigger at our doorsteps."

Amadioha's gaze settled low, lost in thought for a moment. "I am the king of Vodun. A parle does us no good," he mused. He hurled another rock skyward. It struck a tree branch, dislodging a flurry of leaves.

Damballa's face was pained, and his voice wavered. "Beyond these walls, everything we cherish, every soul we love, is at risk. Our home is still in Canis. Let us talk to them. Let us hear them out."

"Very well," Amadioha conceded, struggling to wrestle with his anger and pride. "We will parle here, inside the Mysters, but Grand Bois must come himself."

Damballa nodded in acknowledgment. "The message will be delivered."

∼

Amadioha sprawled on the massive throne, its golden inlays catching the sun and throwing dazzling spots of light across the courtyard. The ornate seat looked absurdly out of place among the weathered stones and gnarled trees. He could still hear the echoes of his men's grunts and curses as they'd hauled it through narrow corridors and doorways.

A smirk tugged at his lips as he remembered their efforts. Putting the throne here served two purposes: to impress and to hide. The wreckage in the actual throne room would have raised too many questions.

Damballa and Omoro sat on either side, their faces blank. Behind the throne stood Ijele, with three guards nearby, their hands resting on their sword hilts.

Grand Bois Loa sat on an extended bench across them, flanked by five men. The man to his right spoke. "We seek audience with the Bondye."

Amadioha raised an eyebrow and gestured at Grand Bois. "Can he not speak for himself?"

Grand Bois scoffed. "We see the Bondye, or we leave and handle this differently."

"I am the king of Vodun," Amadioha said. "Only I make demands."

"King of Vodun," Grand Bois laughed. "You are not even king of Canis."

'Maybe provoking them is not the best plan right now,' Damballa thought.

'Who is doing the provoking?' Amadioha fumed, 'them or me?' He glanced at Damballa but received only a noncommittal shrug in return.

Ijele spoke up. "Amadioha Kamanu, War Eze of Canis, has held this throne for thirty days. By Vodun law, his rule is indisputable. He is king of Vodun. Your king."

Grand Bois laughed. "I bend you over and fuck your arse with the law."

Amadioha slammed his hand against the armrest and stood. "You dare disrespect your queen?" His guards swiftly drew their swords, the rasp of metal filling the air.

Grand Bois rose, his eyes turning a soulless black and his skin darkening. Rage contorted his features as he extended his hand, a sword materializing in his grip. The blade gleamed menacingly, a mysterious white liquid dripping from its tip. "We settle this now," he said.

Damballa lunged between the two adversaries with one arm outstretched toward Amadioha and his stump toward Grand Bois. "Enough!" he bellowed. "Koca ci! Fout Tonne! Everyone, stand down!"

Amadioha and Grand Bois remained locked in a tense stare. After several heartbeats, they sank back into their respective seats. When Grand Bois settled, his transformation receded and his sword shimmered out of existence as quickly as it had appeared. He thrust an accusing finger toward Amadioha. "Withdraw from Kal Mysters at once," he demanded

"I will occupy this seat as long as Vodun has occupied my lands," Amadioha retorted.

"Demons are invading Kirina as we speak," Grand Bois said. "Your actions have left us exposed."

Amadioha laughed, the rest of the Niri joining in. "Demons? I would rather bed my men than ally with Vodun."

"I see it now," Grand Bois said.

"See what?" Amadioha wanted to resist his question, but his curiosity got the better of him.

"I see blind ambition and hate. I see a warrior lucky enough to have capable advisors and fortune." He glanced at Damballa as he spoke.

Amadioha scoffed. "You are as blind as a bat flying through the darkest night."

Grand Bois continued, "Rada Mysters, the poison in the water. The tip was from Ghede Ghadou's man."

Amadioha let out an uncomfortable laugh. "You are full of stories."

"Nnabu Valley, the tip of troop movements through the forest. Also, Ghede Ghadou's man."

'What is he talking about?' Amadioha thought to Damballa.

'The tip came from one of our scouts. I never met the man he got the information from.'

A chill crept down Amadioha's spine. Had Ghede Ghadou been the one feeding them intelligence all along? The notion was silly. Why would he provide information that led to a raid against his forces? Of course, he was lying. That is what the Vodunese did. "My patience wears thin," he said.

Grand Bois pressed, "You sit upon that throne by chance, a pawn manipulated by demons who preyed upon your unchecked ambition and festering hatred. They used you to further their machinations. And when they have finished with Vodun, they will turn their sights on Niri, and you will yearn for the days when Vodun's armies guided and shaped your land with honor."

Grand Bois's words cut deep, and while Amadioha wanted to deny them, he couldn't. "Any member of your army that nears my castle will face the consequences," he said

Grand Bois let out a frustrated huff. "How did a man like you orchestrate a rebellion and unite Niri? Attempting to reason with you is akin to arguing with an infant," he said. "Where is the Bondye?"

"The Bondye is no longer your concern."

The eyes of the man next to Grand Bois's turned black and then white. "The Bondye is not here," the man said, his voice eerily calm.

Grand Bois looked perplexed. "You didn't even capture the Bondye? What victory do you think you've achieved here?"

Damballa's thoughts filtered into Amadioha's mind again. *'He isn't lying.'*

'Lying about what? Demons? Or that Niri's might alone did not win the war?'

'Canis stands great, yet what we have achieved may be beyond what one would expect,' Damballa thought. *'There may be some truth to what he says.'*

'So what do I do now? Give in to his demands? If we let him into the castle, we could all die.'

'I have no interest in killing you. Only in defending Vodun,' Grand Bois's thoughts invaded Amadioha's mind.

Amadioha and Damballa both had surprised looks on their faces. "How did you do that?" Amadioha looked at Grand Bois in shock.

"You don't even begin to know what I can do," Grand Bois said aloud. "Stop wasting precious time."

"The Niri will never fight alongside Vodun."

"I have no need for your men to join my forces. I just need them to get out of my way."

A brief stalemate was broken by a man running into the courtyard. "My king! Demons. All over the Mysters. They came from nowhere."

"You fool!" Grand Bois said. He jumped from his seat and glanced around the courtyard. "Order your men to stand down from the towers now! We can make their best defense inside the Mysters."

"The Vodun Armies have already surrendered," the man said.

"What?" Grand Bois exclaimed.

The air grew charged, pulsating with an unseen force. In the courtyard's center, the forms of two dozen men coalesced from the ether. They solidified and rose to their full stature from a crouched, misty form. While all stood taller than most men, the figure in the middle towered above the rest. Adorned with a crown featuring two horns jutting out to each side, he exuded an aura of commanding presence. His armor shimmered like polished obsidian, its dark sheen reflecting light in a mesmerizing dance. His face, pale as moonlit chalk, contrasted the unfathomable darkness of his eyes. And his raven-black hair cascaded down, nearly brushing the ground, resembling a dark river flowing endlessly from his head.

Demons. The Vodunese Loa was right.

With a chilling synchronicity, the demons unsheathed their swords. They settled into menacing stances, their malevolent intent filling the air.

The towering figure drew his sword last. The blade erupted in an otherworldly black fire, casting an eerie glow that nearly blinded all present. One demon, stepping forward with a reverent bow toward the figure, proclaimed in a voice that echoed in the silence, "All hail Lucifer Morningstar: the King of Kings, Ruler of Hell, the Usurped King of Heaven, Father of all in Kirina, and the rightful Sovereign of all Realms. Bow before his majesty."

~

LILITH AND SENET lay prone on the ground. From their vantage atop the southwest tower of the Kal Mysters, the courtyard sprawled out before them. Senet handed Lilith a bullet crafted from a pure crystalline diamond. Its edges were so razor-sharp a mere tap drew a bead of blood from her finger.

The bullet was heavy in her hand, not just from its dense form but the weight of the action it symbolized. With a deep breath, she loaded the bullet into her rifle, nestling her eye against the scope. With deliberate focus, she adjusted the crosshairs, centering them atop Lucifer's crown.

"We don't even know if this will kill Lucifer," Senet said.

Lilith met her gaze. "Everything that lives can die."

Senet squinted, adjusting her binoculars to focus on their shared target. She evaluated the conditions—the distance, the wind speed, the delicate dance of the environment. "Distance confirmed at 0.1 miles," Senet whispered, her voice steady. "Wind coming from the northwest, around 0.4 miles per hour. Adjust your aim accordingly."

Lilith's world narrowed to that moment, everything else fading to black. She breathed out, long and slow, as she made a minute adjustment to her aim. Her finger curled around the trigger, steady despite the adrenaline thrumming through her veins. Their voices overlapped, soft but fierce. "For Masina."

The rifle bucked against Lilith's shoulder, the bullet cracking through the still air like a whip. Smokey gunpowder filled her nose as she watched with anticipation. Lucifer spun and pulled his blade from its sheath, moving faster than she had ever seen a demon move. He sliced through the bullet with a blinding flash. An echo rang. Two glittering halves pinwheeled past him. One sunk deep into the wall at the far end, leaving a charred, gaping hole. The other sheared through the neck of the nearest demon.

Before the body could crumple, Lucifer snatched the demon's sword with his other hand and hurled it like a spear straight at the tower where Lilith and Senet perched. Lilith abandoned the rifle and rolled over to Senet before hugging her—no words needed to be spoken. The top of the tower blurred as they Navigated to safety. There was a flash, an explosion, just as they vanished.

The Eden Ruse

THE TEMPORARY DISTRACTION gave **Amadioha** the perfect opportunity to attack.

'Amadioha, no! Hold!' Grand Bois's voice entered his mind.

'Think this through!' Damballa's words echoed the warning.

Amadioha registered their warning, but the prospect of having another enemy rule his lands blurred all caution. He grabbed his axe, his fingers closing around the worn grip, and charged.

Amadioha hungered to bury his axe in the self-proclaimed demon king's skull, to watch the light die in his inhuman eyes. But there were other demons he had to get through first. The Niri soldiers surged forward in Amadioha's wake, weapons flashing. Grand Bois attacked with them, cursing at his forced action.

The demons moved with speed and agility Amadioha had not seen before. His axe swung at the empty air as his target twisted aside with boneless grace. The demon swiped its blade of black burning fire at Amadioha. Damballa jumped on him and pulled him to the ground as the blade swiped down where he had stood a moment before.

Amadioha rolled to his feet, rage galvanizing him. His eyes sparkled, and he sent a surge of electricity at the demon. Wings tore from its back and covered its body, absorbing the power. Amadioha took his chance. When the demon unfurled his wings, Amadioha swung his axe. A spray of blood blinded him as the blade cleaved skin and bone. The demon's death scream skirled through his skull. He toppled like a felled tree.

Around him, the Niri and Vodunese paid a steeper price. Mangled bodies littered the ground, limbs jutting at unnatural angles in spreading pools of blood.

Amadioha locked eyes with Lucifer across the melee. He leveled his axe and charged again, electricity sparking in his eyes. A bolt of electricity shot from them, but Lucifer's sword absorbed the magic like a vortex sucking in air. The demon flowed forward and responded in kind. Amadioha parried, staggered by the sheer force of Lucifer's blows. His return stroke carved only air. Lucifer's backhand caught him in the sternum, folding him nearly in half. A knee snapped his head back, followed by an uppercut that launched him skyward in an arc of blood and spittle.

Lucifer loomed over Amadioha's crumpled form, sword poised for the killing blow. But he froze. Across the courtyard, Ijele stood with arms outstretched, face contorted in concentration. Blue light emanated from her hands, pulsing and holding Lucifer in place. The demon snarled. With a contemptuous flick, he kicked a nearby rock. It flew, slamming into Ijele, sending her tumbling backward on the ground.

Lucifer rounded on Amadioha, death in his eyes. He brought his sword down again to finish him.

Clang!

Lucifer recoiled as his sword rebounded off a double-bladed weapon that had materialized in the space between them.

The Bondye!

The Bondye, with his stout frame, stood with his weapon braced overhead, the parry reverberating up his arms. He slammed into Lucifer like a compact battering ram, driving him back with blows. His double-bladed sword whirled and slashed. Lucifer fell back, parrying frantically. The Bondye leaped, twisting in midair, and kicked Lucifer's chest. The demon flew backward, fetching up against the wall. Raising his free hand, the Bondye made a fist. Howling winds hit Lucifer and sent him to the ground. The Bondye moved to finish him, his blade slicing at Lucifer's throat.

Lucifer rolled to his feet. His sword hammered up in a rising arc, catching the Bondye's weapon at the crosspiece. The weapon exploded into a thousand razored shards, sending the Bondye flying back and landing in a heap next to Amadioha.

Amadioha stared at him, groggy, uncomprehending. The Bondye gritted his teeth and squeezed his fist before closing his eyes in concentration. The shattered fragments of his weapon trembled, then rose into the air. Whirling like silver dust, they spiraled together, reforming the double blade.

The Bondye stood and extended a hand to Amadioha. After hesitating, he clasped it and allowed himself to be hauled upright. The two stared at each other wordlessly, mutual enmity warring with necessity.

The enemy of my enemy must be my friend. At least for now.

∼

LILITH AND SENET materialized next to the men fighting Lucifer and his demons. They pulled out their pistols as they looked on, anger and vengeance in their minds. Eight demons left, and Lucifer himself.

"Who are you?" Surprisingly, the short, stocky man spoke in a language they could understand.

"We want the same thing as you," she responded.

He looked at her with his head high and grunted. "Let us finish this."

Lilith's breath caught in her chest. For Bez. For Masina. For every life ruined. Together, they charged.

∼

AMADIOHA PUSHED HIMSELF UPRIGHT; teeth bared in a feral snarl. He didn't know who the two demons were, but from the look in Bondye's eyes, they were on his side. Together, they charged toward their common enemy.

GOODBYE FOR NOW, DEAR READER

Well, well, well! Look who made it to the end! Congratulations, you magnificent bookworm!

Now, if you're sitting there thinking, "That was a good read," why not spread the love? Imagine you're a book fairy sprinkling magical star ratings and reviews across the internet. Even a tiny sprinkle can make this author's heart soar.

So, if you've got a moment to spare between your next Netflix binge and your breakfast coffee, consider leaving a review on Amazon, Goodreads or wherever else you hang out in the virtual book club universe.

Remember: Every review you write puts you one step closer to becoming the literary influencer you were born to be.

ABOUT THE AUTHOR

Dez Udezue's story isn't your typical D.C. transplant tale. After growing up in Nigeria, he now calls Washington home. But don't go looking for him on Capitol Hill. He is the guy you'll spot zipping past the Lincoln Memorial on his bike, the one he swears is "vintage" but his friends just call "old."

Printed in Great Britain
by Amazon